ERICA MANWARING

Notes from a Physicist Lost in Time and Space

For H and for my village

Chapter One

Through dust motes dancing in the overhead lights, she looked out over row upon row of eager faces. Circles of brightness against the dark varnished wood and tiered leather benches. Six centuries of students had come here to Edinburgh University's oldest lecture theatre to hear Hume, Higgs and Ross explain the very secrets of the universe. Now they were here to see her. It was pretty full.

Give it time.

"Good morning, everyone. My name is Dr Alison Howden. I'm a research fellow in applied theoretical physics. This class is about bubble universe theory. In other words: alternate realities. Do they exist and can we see them?"

She had said these words every year for almost a decade. The first time, she had picked them with great care and attention, writing draft after draft, memorising every word. Now they emerged with no conscious effort at all, allowing her brain to wander.

A girl near the front, her brand-new laptop open and two, no three, crisp notebooks next to it, was surreptitiously checking out the people in the other front rows. Probably a first year. She liked the girl's eager expression. She had been like her once. But everyone makes sacrifices for the ones they love. She caught herself spinning her wedding ring on her finger and clamped her hands together.

The first years hadn't yet realised that taking a class on the physics of alternate realities was going to be really hard. Half of them were there because they had to choose an extra course to make up their quota for the year. They wanted proof of other worlds, or at least make their resumes look less humanities heavy and to help them get a job. With any luck they would be gone within two weeks and others would drift off in dribs and drabs over the term, their enthusiasm draining, class after class. Eventually she would be left with a smaller class, but they would be the real students. The ones willing to put in the hard work.

She had reached the part about tutorial schedules. Cosy groups in King's Buildings on the other side of town, surrounded by scientists, closeted with her students, talking about the underbelly of the universe.

There were bound to be, as always, a couple of hangers on. Students who weren't even taking the course but wanted to know a bit more about the world. Randoms from off the street who wanted something to do on a Tuesday morning at 10.30am. She was supposed to take a register to weed out these non-paying walk-ins, but she never did until week 5. If they stayed beyond the lecture on the equation to calculate the red shift of a wormhole, she would let them stay, maybe even invite them along to the tutorials.

She was reaching the crux of her introduction. They still looked keen. She clicked to the next slide. *Here we go.*

"Theoretical physics sounds cool. There's always a physicist in a film who plots the route through a black hole, deciphers messages from another planet, or proves once and for all that the earth can be saved by numbers.

"That's not what this course is about. You're going to be learning about proper theoretical physics. We are talking tiny numbers over vast distances and measuring the slightest changes which can mean something, nothing or everything and it can take years to work out which one it is. My last piece of research was to decipher two years' worth of background radiation to look for a slight discrepancy between two telescopes to identify a possible touch point which might indicate another universe pushing onto ours or might be the shadow from a passing meteor." Who was looking interested? "It was the meteor."

There was a titter from the room. Someone always thought she was joking. She kept her face neutral until they stopped.

"You don't have to stay. I won't be offended if this isn't for you. If you do stay, and if you like hard work, it will be worth it. If you can make it through the first four years you can be involved in unpicking how the universe works. At its core."

Unusually there was a hand up. It was a boy near the back. She nodded at him.

"Didn't one of the lecturers here go to Hollywood? Didn't he win an Oscar?"

Her stomach twisted but she kept her face calm. "Yes, that's right."

"So, it's possible to make a proper career out of this then?"

A proper career. She didn't bother answering.

Another hand. It was the enthusiastic girl at the front. "Dr Howden, I heard that you were supposed to go and then you didn't. Didn't you want to go?"

What a strange question. What could she possibly say to that? That it wasn't that easy. That when you became a grown up, you couldn't just follow shooting stars. You had to consider other people's needs.

"Dr Dickenson is an excellent physicist and I'm very happy for him. Shall we continue?

"This is a year one class, so I'll be taking you through the basics." Her voice sounded flat to her own ears, but she couldn't be bothered injecting the requisite enthusiasm. "This class is about maths. We are going to be looking at readouts from radio telescope. You will not see a supernova or a black hole. You will see pages and pages of numbers and we will be discussing whether they are all the same or not. That's applied theoretical physics. And if you stick around for the rest of your university career, I might let you run some numbers yourself."

The room had gone totally silent. The real students were busily taking notes, planning their schedules. They'd be here next week, ready to get on with it. The others, near the back, were already packing their bags. She'd receive apologetic emails from them tomorrow morning.

The girl in the front row was sitting back in her seat, looking at the board, the desk, anything but her. She wasn't going to be one of the ones who stayed after all. That was fine. Better to know now.

She clicked her computer for the next slide and ploughed on with the term outline.

There was one face in the fifth row whose enthusiasm hadn't dimmed. All the faces around him were turned away but he kept eye contact. He was leaning back in his chair, completely relaxed. It was hard to see past the strong lights, but it looked like he was smirking. Maybe a mature student? But he didn't have the serious, hungry look of a mature student. In fact, he looked tickled. When scraping noises from the back indicated the bravest students slinking out of the lecture theatre doors without waiting for the class to end, he raised his paper coffee cup in a silent salute.

She frowned at him and turned her back to sketch out her starting points on the white board.

At the end of the hour, she packed up her bag and wiped down the board methodically to give the worried students a chance to make their escape. Tomorrow the "I'm sorry, but" emails would come drifting in. They tended not to want to do it to her face. She didn't mind.

She turned her phone back on and it pinged. A text from Jess. *Hey sis, I can't write these vows! I've officially failed at being romantic. Send me the ones you wrote - they were so beautiful. Promise not to plagiarise... too much. Thx. Love you.*

She couldn't help but smile. She was probably going to end up writing them for her.

As she put her phone back in her bag her hands brushed the two ominous brown envelopes printed in red ink that had been on the mat this morning. She tried to ignore them, but she already knew they were going to ruin her day. Why couldn't she have been allowed to wait until she got home to deal with this crap?

The walk back to the office would take her across the Meadows, a beautiful field of green criss-crossed with cherry trees and filled with joggers, laughing children, and leaping dogs. But it took her too close for comfort to her beautiful flat.

Her tiny, shabby, mortgage-free flat. Small rooms with huge windows, the flooding light. It was the right choice selling it to start Chris' dream business. It wasn't his fault there was a downturn in the economy. It could have happened to anyone.

Being angry wasn't achieving anything. She had to forgive and forget. They could fix this. She could fix this. The alternative was unacceptable. Within a lifetime, three years of hell is a small price to pay for a marriage. Right?

From the windows she could see the Meadows were awash with bright sunshine. She liked it better when it was raining.

It dawned on her that it had got quiet, so she allowed herself to turn around. The smirking man was still sitting in his seat.

"I liked the class," he said. "Very off-putting."

She snapped her laptop shut without bothering to reply and made for the door. He stood up and matched her pace to the end of the row.

Now that he was standing, and she was out of the glare of the lecture hall lights, she saw he was dressed in a very expensive suit. He wasn't much taller than her, but he stood straight, like he was daring gravity to challenge him. He was smiling at her in a knowing fashion.

"Can I help you with something?" she said.

"I want to know everything you know about alternate universes." That was supposed to sound charming, she thought.

She kept walking. "That would take a while."

He fell into step beside her. "I have time."

As they emerged onto the Quad a beam of sunlight lit up his face and danced on his burnished hair. His eyes were the most incredible mix of green and blue. In the sunlight they flashed like a peacock's wing. "I was interested in what you were saying about the battle between string theory and super gravity. How many dimensions do you think they need to make it work? I was wondering if you could expand on it for me. Buy you a coffee?" His tone implied that it was unimaginable that she might say no.

"No."

But her stomach twisted with guilt. It wasn't his fault she was angry. It wasn't his fault he looked entirely relaxed and at home on this beautiful day. She tried to inject some professionalism into her tone. "My office hours are posted on my door. I'm afraid I can't help outside of those times."

"I'm not a student, Professor."

"And I'm not a Professor, Mr?"

"I'm Jack Shepherd. Jack."

"Mr Shepherd, Dr Howden is fine. If you are not a student, then who are you?"

"A writer."

"Of what?"

"Parables. Fables. Truths that the world is not yet ready for." He waved his hands theatrically. But his eyes were twinkling. He was taking the piss out of himself.

He was clearly used to getting his way. Charming and probably rich from the look of the clothes. This self-deprecating manner, suggesting humility about his own brilliance, probably helped him schmooze his way into anything and anywhere.

"I'm sorry but I don't have the time," she said.

"I'll pay you. Handsomely."

Her heart thumped. "Excuse me?"

"A consultancy fee. To help me with research for my next book. Name your price."

She stared at his winning smile and cocky stance. She so wanted to tell him to go to hell. That she couldn't be bought. But she didn't have that luxury. She stalled. "Are you published? Have I heard of you?"

"Would it make a difference if I was?"

"It might."

"Alright." He inclined his head graciously. "I'll see you in another time and space." He turned to go.

"Where are you going?" He was already ten steps away. "Wait, what do you mean by handsomely?" A trio of passing students turned to look at her and she died a little inside.

He had already stopped, with his back to her, completely still.

She walked up behind him. "Mr Shepherd?"

"Shame I can't get famous in an afternoon."

She laughed. He didn't. She stopped.

Should she say something? The charm was easier to deal with. Then he looked back around, and his eyes were smiling again, as if that moment of stillness had never happened. "Trans-dimensional portals."

"Sorry, what did you say?"

"Trans-dimensional portals. I understand the theory, but I need to understand how that would work in practice. I've spoken to your colleagues and they all say that you are the only one who can help me. I'm running out of time and I can pay you whatever you want."

"Whatever I want?"

"Whatever you want."

She pushed her uncomfortable feelings aside. The only defence here was a good offence.

"Ok." She reached into her bag. "My standard consultancy

fee is by the hour. No haggling over the time I'm taking. Send me your questions and I'll take a look at them this week. Come to my office next Thursday at three. We can go through them and come up with a strategy."

He grinned a sudden mega-watt smile. "Dr Howden, I will see you next Thursday."

He turned and walked away with a jaunty step, like he didn't have a care in the world. She watched him go. Maybe a coffee wouldn't have been so awful.

No, back to the real world.

To get to her office she had to go past Simon's.

"Ali," he shouted as she went past.

"Yes?" She stuck her head around the door, only her shoulders showing to him. Surely a sign that she had to get on.

"Good lecture?"

"Fine, thanks. Good crowd for a Friday. You? Many takers for the wonderful world of string theory?"

"I'm going to need a bigger lecture hall. Thanks to the wonderful world of financial modelling, I'm very popular."

"And still wrong," she said. His grin was undaunted as usual. "You can have mine."

"Really? What about you?"

"I'm happy to swap. You've got all the fancy sponsors. May as well show them off properly."

"Speaking of which, Morgan Stanley are doing a weekend away in Jersey. Partners welcome. Sue is already booking the flights. There's loads of space. Want to come?"

Her heart sank. They could never afford the flights, but she couldn't say that because she earned the same as Simon. How on earth to explain? Simon was watching her expectantly. She should be looking excited. She'd come up with some lame excuse later. Again. She smiled brightly, pushing an excited sparkle into her eyes. "What a wonderful idea! When?"

"May 15th."

"May. Ok. Well, let's say provisionally yes and I'll check with Chris."

"Great."

"Bye, Simon. Say hi to Sue for me."

"Say hi yourself. She's still chasing you about that girls' night tonight."

She swallowed back the shame. "I'll get back to her right now."

She walked back down the corridor, ears burning from another lie.

Chapter Two

That evening Alison opened her front door to a dark and silent house. She listened for a moment then let out a held breath. There was no one in.

Her ritual was always the same. Coat on the hook, shoes in the rack, every door open, every light on. Brushing through every room transforming it from dark and cold to warm and welcoming. Chasing out the shadows.

She ended up in the huge kitchen. There was no warming up this room. Stainless steel. Gadgets. Black fridge. Cold stone floor. He cooked, she didn't.

Her thing was baking. Muffins, scones, giant fluffy cup-cakes with mountains of icing sugar on top. But she'd stopped after they moved in. The cakes tasted metallic here.

There was a post-it note on the kitchen table. She ignored it.

Once upon a time it would have been a love note. Now Chris only left notes when he was late and angry. They pointed out little flaws in her housekeeping and had phrases like "please remember…" underlined twice.

These notes must make him even later. She had hidden the post-its once to see if that would stop him, but he had hunted them down for a full ten minutes before leaving in a fury, the

11

hastily scribbled post-it note firmly in place.

She took her cup of tea and headed for her sitting room. The kitchen was his, but this room was hers. Almost worth losing her flat for. Warm red walls, throws, rugs, cushions on every surface. She had already closed the curtains and it was a cocoon of warmth and light.

Ah, this was what he was annoyed about. The empty teacup from last night, still on the coffee table. She couldn't remember the last time he had come in here to actually use the room; he must have specifically come in here to look for something to be annoyed about.

She sat down on the sofa, leaving the teacup where it was. The cup wasn't on a coaster - it had probably left a ring. She should have tidied it away. But even so...

She plumped her cushions to create a little nest and settled in with her tea.

Jess's text popped into her mind. She went over to the bookcase and pulled out the white leather-bound bible that had her vows inside.

She told him she had finally figured out what love was, finally understood the songs and films. For five years he had made her world brighter. She had felt, for the first time, that someone in this world had her, and only her, as the centre of their concerns. She was cherished.

She had cried when she had read it out. Sometimes she still cried when she remembered.

Where there's smoke there's fire, they say. Well, now they existed as wisps of smoke, coiling around each other, never touching. Her sigh sending him dancing away out of reach. His puff of irritation pushing her off balance, sending her twisting away past him.

There must be an ember there somewhere.

Stop it, Ali. This is stupid thinking.

She'd trained herself out of this way of thinking. Focus on the neutrino problem instead. She pulled one of her notebooks out of her bag. Computers were for modelling but her best ideas came in her notebooks. This one was nearly full of attempts to bring dark energy into the cosmic inflation model using some of Simon's string theory equations around neutrino clusters. Mostly it wasn't working but, like Edison, ten thousand failed attempts were all that was needed to find something that worked.

But her mind drifted. Neutrino clusters, to her unpublished paper, to her pile of admin, to her to do list, to the final notices cramming her bag. This was not what she wanted to think about either.

The kitchen door bumped off its stopper.

Chris.

He put his head around the door. "Sorry, didn't meant to startle you."

"No, it's fine."

"Badminton was cancelled. Didn't realise you were home."

"Honestly, not a problem."

She tried to smile at him. He didn't smile back, just continued to stare at her with that hangdog expression. He was clearly waiting for her to say something.

"Did you have a good day?" She felt like wincing at how bland it sounded.

"It was pretty tough one. We had a total disaster this morning and it just got worse from there."

She knew he was hoping for a follow up question. His look said as much. And she knew if she didn't ask one he would bring it up at the next counselling session. 'She never expresses an interest in me anymore.' But she also knew that if she did ask she would get an answer. A long one. Reasons why his life was awful. His disappointment about having to do a boring 9-5 job. Cursing his fate to be adrift in a world of timetables and appointments when he should be free to be his own man. A shower of angry thoughts, battering her head with familiar complaints, dampening her warm cosy space, soaking into everything they touched. A wave of sadness rising in front of her, enough to drown in. The roar was deafening. Her ears rang.

"Oh." She said and looked down at her mug, cutting him off dead. "Sorry to hear that." The roar subsided.

When she looked up again he was looking at the floor. He sighed briefly, tapped his fingers twice against the wood and nodded. "Better get back to it then."

"'K."

"'K."

He was gone. She let out her breath and settled back slowly. The cup of tea tasted of sweet relief mixed with a salty, guilty tang. She put the cup of the table. She didn't want to drink it anymore.

How did it ever come to this?

The evening passed them by. He closed himself in his study until dinner was ready. She knocked politely on the door. He came downstairs to collect his plate and then was gone again. Like yesterday and the day before.

She slid under the duvet and gathered a book, a clock, anything to fill her attention.

Why were they doing this to each other? She knew why

she was here. She would find a way to make this work. What kept him in this endless cycle?

It was cold. She stared at the pages of her book. They were blurry again.

A knock on the door. Chris came in.

She sat up. Tried a smile. "Are you coming to bed?"

He picked up his book from his bedside table. "Yes, in a bit." He walked back to the door.

She nodded. "I see you," she said. Their signature phrase. The one that meant I love you, I know you, you are important to me.

"Night night," he said, turning to go. "I see you too."

As the door closed behind him she had never felt so invisible.

Chapter Three

When she arrived at Mum's house, Jess was sitting at the kitchen counter crying. Their mum was cutting bread. She had let herself in with her key, so a moment passed before either looked up.

It was a familiar tableau. Mum had the bearing of a sergeant major. Always in heels, always immaculate. She held the breadknife like a surgeon, each cut deftly delivered, severing the slice from its loaf.

Jess, in contrast, always seemed like she was made of mist. The kitchen bar stool was barely high enough to support her tiny frame as her shoulders slumped onto the newspapers on the counter. Her cloud of curly hair wafted around her face, untameable. It needed lots of looking after. So did Jess.

Her mother was focused on the bread. When Jess let out a little whimper she didn't turn around.

Alison stepped into the picture.

"Oh Ali!" Jess cried. "Thank god you're here!"

"Darling," said her mother's back. "So glad you made it." As if she was unlikely to be reliable. As if she had regularly missed an appointment. As if once meant always.

Alison focused on Jess's tear-stained face. "Jess, what's wrong?"

"The wedding's off," Mum's back informed her. "Again."

Oh no.

Jess sniffed and hid behind her hands. "You're late."

"Sorry. Want to talk?"

Jess's blotched face appeared just long enough to glance at their mother. Alison nodded and inclined her head at the kitchen door. Jess gave a relieved smile but when Alison opened her mouth to speak her mother suddenly swung around.

"She decided they have nothing in common anymore. Even though yesterday he was the perfect man." She plonked the breadboard down in front of them a little too hard. The baguette looked untouched; each slice perfectly aligned. Alison was tempted to take a photo and use it as her screen saver.

Jess sighed. "We had a fight."

Their mother turned back to the soup.

"We'll set the table!" Alison trilled, grabbing the breadboard. She shoved it into Jess's hands then dragged them both into the sitting room and to the dining table in the window.

"Quickly tell me," she said.

Jess garbled her story out as quickly as she could. She had read an article in Brides magazine – questions you should ask each other before you get married.

"They asked where you see yourself in five years and he picked living abroad. He knows I hate to travel. Why would he choose that? It's a sign. Maybe this is all a terrible mistake!" Ah, one of those disasters. Alison sagged in relief. The last time she had found Jess crying into their mother's newspapers

17

had been because Pete hadn't wanted to go see Mamma Mia with her. That had been a sign too.

"Jess, Pete, is the kindest, gentlest, most patient person I've ever met. He would live in Timbuktu if you asked him to. Or live forever in leafy East Lothian and never raise an objection." How was it that the same childhood experience had moulded her and Jess so differently?

"Jess, you love him, yes?"

"Yes, of course."

"And he's good to you?"

"Of course he is!"

"So what did he say when you asked him?"

"Asked him what?"

"What he meant by choosing that answer. Where he wanted to live. Whether he saw you there too."

"I didn't ask him. I just waited to speak to you."

"So you just left him sitting there? Did you even explain why you ran off?" Poor Peter.

"I needed to talk to you. Tell me you think it's ok and then I won't have to worry."

Alison tried not to roll her eyes. Why was it her responsibility? "It's not up to me. What do you think?"

"I don't know. That's the problem. Mum and Dad were perfect for each other. Perfect. And look what happened to them. I can't handle a divorce. I cried for days when a girl at work got divorced and I barely know her. It would kill me."

She rearranged the breadboard on the table and went to the sideboard for placemats.

"You don't mean that. You'd get through it," she said.

"No," said Jess, taking the placemats and flinging them around the table. "I wouldn't. I swear to God, Ali, it would

18

be the death of me. One divorce in my life was more than enough to handle."

She went back for coasters. *It was more than enough for all of us.* Jess plonked herself down at the table. Just like she had at 5 years old. Asking where Daddy had gone, and why Mummy was always crying, and when were they going to be a family again.

She had made up trays of food for Jess and for her mother, cooking all afternoon so she would have her favourite foods, decorating it with sprigs of fake flowers from the display on the sideboard. Hoping this would tempt her to come down and be their Mum again. She would bring the still-full tray back down hours later. Place the flowers back in their vase on the sideboard for another night. If only he had had the courage to stay.

When she turned back Jess was looking up at her hopefully. "It doesn't matter though, right? Isn't that what you always say? Love is enough. Even if other things aren't quite lined up. I mean Pete won't make me live abroad? Or leave me if I won't?"

She pictured Pete with his gentle smile and moleskin trousers. He absorbed Jess's fears like they were drops of water shed by a passing rainbow. "I'm pretty sure Pete would move in here if he thought it would make you happy." They both looked around at the minimalist furniture. She tried to imagine cuddly Pete curled up on the upright chairs and her mouth twitched. Jess let out a snort and gasp and then they were both laughing.

Their mother chose that moment to come in through the door holding the tureen in front of her like a shield.

"All sorted?" she asked.

Jess hopped up and flung her arms around Alison's waist. "Yup," she said, snuggling into Alison's shoulder. "I was just being silly. Ali made me see that we don't have to be the same as each other to be perfect together." Alison hugged her hard. She just had to get Jess through the wedding. Pete was going to make Jess happy; she was sure of that.

They settled around the table. Jess and her mum went quickly back to easy chat. Maybe it was safe to share her worries. If she could tell Jess and her Mum what she was feeling then Chris would be a doddle.

She took a breath to speak.

"So wedding back on then?" said her mum into the brief silence.

Jess gave Alison a watery smile. "Yes, even if it scares me."

Their Mum smiled indulgently. "Don't be scared. Just be sure. Marriage is something you must do right. And when you're in you're in. Can you see yourself with Pete forever?"

"Of course I can."

"Exactly. So do it, and then work through it, no matter what. It's never easy. But then nothing worth having is easy. Just ask Alison."

She looked away. The words on her tongue had crawled back down her throat. What could she say to that? She found herself focusing on the photos on the sideboard. Her mum was glamorous even then as a young woman just starting out. She already had that steely glint. And the mythical father, the perfect man, stood beside her. If only he had had the courage of his convictions they could have been the perfect happy family.

"Alison?"

"Hmm?" Jess and her mum were both looking at her. What

had she missed?

"Follow through," said Jess.

The family motto.

There was nothing else to say.

She was sipping her glass of wine in the bath when she heard the door go and footsteps on the stairs.

"In here," she called.

Chris bundled through the door like a Labrador making her jump. The wine sloshed in the glass. His face was flushed with excitement - she hadn't seen that expression in years.

"Good day?"

"The best. A company called me; they're looking for a consultant on a project in Qatar. They approached me on the recommendation of an old colleague."

The world froze.

"It's a fantastic opportunity. I can start the business back up, proper consulting like I always wanted. It's a top-level position, Ali and they're not looking at anyone else. This is everything I wanted. It's perfect. They'll pay all the expenses, relocation. It's six months to start but I know I can get an extension."

He wouldn't stop talking. He wasn't even asking a question. Was he seriously not even going to phrase this as a question?

"What did you tell them?"

"I said yes, of course. Ali, you're going to love Qatar. I looked it up, they have a great ex-pat community, the weather is amazing. You can relax by the pool all day. We'll finally be able to pay stuff off. We could even just give this place back to the bank and move out there full time. There's loads of work there for me."

Chris still had his coat on. She had a strange feeling that instead of just arriving he was just about to leave. Her head was pounding. Relax by the pool, had he even met her before?

"No."

"What?" he said.

"No. Chris I'm not giving up my life and moving to Qatar."

"Why not?"

She grappled for words that might get through to someone who needed that sentence explained. "I don't want to."

"But this is the chance of a lifetime. It solves all of our problems."

"It doesn't solve all of mine. I have a career. I have friends. And what about this house? Where would we live? I'm not just going to hand the house back to the bloody bank!"

He was looking at her like she was insane. "Why not? We could start again. The money is too good to turn down and I can't go on my own. They're paying for everything, Ali. This is the perfect solution."

She was suddenly very aware of how naked she was. She climbed out of the bath. The towel felt hard and scratchy as she wrapped herself up in it.

He followed her through to the bedroom.

"I don't get this," he said. "You're angry because I don't earn enough, now you're angry because I have the chance to earn a fortune and make everything right. I can put back the money I owe you, I can pay you back for the flat."

He was trying to do the right thing. "I'm not angry."

"Then what are you, Ali? You're not happy. I really thought you would be happy."

She took a deep breath. What should she do? Keep her mouth shut until she could think it through in private.

Pretend to be happy until she could work it out later. Agree to it and just go? But her career was here. Her life was here. He was asking her to choose between it and him. She needed time and space to process this. She had to put this on hold.

"It is such a good opportunity, Chris. And a great compliment that they only want you."

He was looking a little less defeated. "It is a compliment isn't it."

"Absolutely. You must have made quite an impression on your old colleague for him to do that."

"He did really like my work."

"Exactly." Ok, this was working. "Look, I'm not saying no, Chris. I'm just saying that *I* can't go to Qatar. Let's just enjoy the fact that you got offered the job of your dreams. Let's bask in that glory for 24 hours and then we'll figure out some way to make this work."

"I just wish you would be a bit more supportive of my dreams," he said and left the room.

The unfairness of that hit her like a punch.

The silence in the room crept up her legs and made her feet cold. She could climb back into the bath, but the thought made her even colder. She fetched her wine glass, swallowed it in one and facetimed Sue.

"You ok, chick?" Sue asked. "Everything alright?"

"Of course," she said. "I just fancied a chat." She'd tell her. Probably.

"Excellent," said Sue. She would be shoeing Simon out of the room and asking him for a glass of wine.

She went downstairs, ignoring Chris' closed office door. The wine bottle was half full. She took it with her into the sitting room. It wasn't long before the bottle was empty, and

Sue was making her laugh again.

Sue was moaning about how much time her husband spent cycling. "It's like he forgets that the rest of the world even exists. He was an hour late home tonight because he thought of a new route. Total tunnel vision."

Alison snorted with laughter. Because everyone argued, everyone fell out with their spouses sometimes. She felt the drink slosh uncomfortably in her stomach.

"He's moving to Qatar," she blurted.

"What?"

"He got a job offer in Qatar and he's going to take it." There was silence on the end of the phone.

"What does this mean? Are you going with him?"

She felt tears prickling in her eyes. She knew what she had to say, that it was fine, that she was happy for him and it was great idea. She had to be loyal and supportive.

But it would be so easy just to give up, drop the heavy backpack halfway through this hike. But that wasn't the way. She had to keep going and get the hot tub at the other end. But the hot tub had never seemed so far away. Have faith, Alison. "We haven't worked it out yet."

"You're not seriously considering this are you? Don't go!"

"I still might not, but it's a great opportunity for him." She forced herself to sound cheerful. "It pays so well. How could he do anything else?"

"He could stay." Sue's face looked weird on the screen. "Why would he want to leave you to go live in Qatar?"

"It's his dream."

"I know, but this isn't what you signed up for."

"That's not how marriage works. And besides, I'm an independent woman. I don't depend on anyone. If he wants

24

to follow his dream I'm happy for him."

"Did he pay you back?" asked Sue.

It took a moment to adjust to the shift in direction then she cursed herself for having shared her dismay when the sale of her beloved flat went through. This was why she should keep her complaints to herself.

"Listen, this is meant to be a fun chat. Come on, let's talk about something else."

"Ali - "

"Sue." She glared at her friend. Her best "don't" look. Honed over years of glossing over the bad bits it could have stopped a raging rhino. Sue deflated. They went back to talking about movies and the night was fine.

As they said their goodbyes Sue said, "Are you really ok with this?"

"It's really ok. I'm fine, Sue."

"Oh, Ali. I don't know how you do it. Or why."

What a strange thing to say. She was married to him. That's what marriage was, for better or for worse. Damned if she was going to turn out like her father. You stick with things, no matter what.

Chapter Four

It was only eight thirty on Thursday morning when she rounded the corner and found that man standing outside her office. No, not standing; lounging. He smiled when he saw her and offered her the coffee cup he was holding in his hand.

"I brought coffee: latte, no foam."

It smelled amazing. Her mouth watered. "No, thank you."

He shrugged, drank from it himself.

"I thought we agreed on three o'clock."

"I know but I can't wait to get started. May I come in?"

She braced herself against the door jamb. "I'm actually quite busy today."

He held up his hands in apology and gave her a mea culpa smile. "I'm sorry. I'm excited. I've been looking for a solution for so long. Just half an hour. We can call it double, for the inconvenience. I'll leave whenever you tell me to."

She scowled at him. With this Qatar thing, did she even really need to do this? In two weeks she was going to be sunning herself on the beaches of Qatar. The university had been kind about her sudden sabbatical, Simon had offered to take over her classes - it's not like there were that many students to cover. It was the right thing to do. It would like an extended research break. She would get so much done.

As evidence, Chris was already a new person. For three nights in a row Ali made dinner and he had come out of his room to eat it. They talked over spaghetti Bolognese or chicken salads about where they would live, what sights they would see. All the dreams they used to have together were re-emerging from the darkness.

On Wednesday he had taken her out for lunch. A picnic of her favourite foods on a tartan blanket in the park. He even came in and chatted to Simon. He clapped him on the shoulder and invited Simon and Sue to dinner before they moved. "I love dinner parties," he said. "I'll cook something special. We can play Pictionary. Ali and I will make you weep."

They had plans. There were no post-it notes. Maybe they were coming out of the end of whatever that had been.

But with Chris having already quit his job there was a gap to fill. She still had to pay for the house even if there wasn't going to be anyone living in it. His flights had been expensive, and it was a long six weeks until they were reimbursed. Temporary pain for long term gain.

At double her inflated consultancy fee, even half an hour would help. She stood aside and let him in.

She sat down behind her desk. He looked around the cluttered space, examined her Rothko print. She looked around too. Her office was too small, too magnolia, and didn't have nearly enough shelves. But every book, every piece of paper pinned to the ancient walls contained something important, something that delved into the deepest parts of the universe and asked "why". When she looked back, he had

NOTES FROM A PHYSICIST LOST IN TIME AND SPACE

sat down opposite her and gone very still, staring at his hands.

"Trans dimensional portals, you said?" she prompted.

"Yes," he said. "I'm stuck. I need you to help me take the next step."

"Ok."

He leaned in. His eyes were a deep blue with flecks of green, like the wings of a kingfisher, and his stare was intense. "Tell me how I get to an alternate universe."

"Well." She paused to give him a moment to get over himself. "Traditionally there's a number of devices that have been used in sci-fi. Wormholes are a good one. They're trendy. Of you can call them Einstein-Rosen Bridges if you want to sound clever. Or there's spaceships or teleportation devices. Michael Crichton probably got closest to an actually scientific plot device in Timeline, but the quantum foam scenario was a bit overly complicated to follow. If you've sent me across your story, I'll be able to come up with something suitably believable."

"Story, right." She'd unsettled him. Good, he was too cocky by far. "I can send you a few extracts."

"Do you have a synopsis?"

"Not yet. I can talk you through it, though." He pulled out a notebook. No surprise he hadn't sent the email, but it was still annoying that he hadn't followed through her simple request. But it was his half hour. With a quick check of the clock, she nodded for him to go on.

"The main character is called Bill," he said. "He travels between universes."

"Right."

"He's on a mission. From his home universe. They have experienced a catastrophe and he is looking for a solution."

"What kind of catastrophe?"

"It's a plague. Well, lots of plagues. The antibiotics have failed. Even the smallest thing is causing people to die. It's horrible." He shuddered. For a moment he looked so sad. "He's been sent to find other medicines, from other worlds, travelling between universes to find something that hasn't lost its effectiveness."

"Makes sense," she said.

"Except now he is trapped in this world. The portals aren't working, and he doesn't know why." He leaned forward intently. "He has got to get them open again. Everyone is relying on him."

"Ok. How does he travel between worlds?"

"There are doors. Door-sized spaces. You can't see them but if you walk through one you end up in another universe. For instance, have you ever looked at a shop front that you pass every day and thought, 'didn't that used to be blue?' But the paint is still worn and flaky and it hasn't been touched in years. Then you've probably walked through a door. People don't tend to notice.

"But he can find them. Use them. It's second nature. Like breathing." The sadness was gone, his eyes were aglow. "Any problem, any crisis, he can solve it in a heartbeat. It's the best feeling in the world." He sighed. "And now it's gone. He's trapped."

I can sympathise. "Right. Let's see what we can do for Bill. What kind of alternate universe theory are you using? Bubble? Daughter? Pre-determined or intercorrelated?" He was looking blank. "Ok, let's start with: are they infinite or created by each decision and/or chance event that occurs?"

Now he looked panicked. That told her everything she

needed to know - he hadn't thought the science through.

"Ok," she continued, projecting unruffled professionalism. "You can't just say "alternate universe" and leave it at that. There's lots of different kinds based on the causal relation between fractures. If you pick the wrong theory then that will drive your story and you'll find yourself stuck in a narrative cul-de-sac, like you have. How far into the story are you?"

"A long way."

"Ok, then we need to fit the theory to the narrative instead of the other way around. I'll come up with the theory that fits, or maybe even concoct a new one for you."

He nodded. "Thank you."

"Why don't you tell me about Bill's travels, and we can see what fits."

While she made them cups of tea, he told her about Bill's journey. He told her about fantastic worlds - worlds of pink skies and blue sunsets, a world where London was a tiny backwater and Cambridge was the capital of a giant global empire, a world where tribal communities had never been overcome by the march of progress and everything still worked by barter, and about worlds almost exactly like this one where a tiny fraction of things weren't the same.

"So, you send Bill to a world exactly like this one except that the shops don't close early on Sundays."

"Yes."

"Why?"

"Because you can get a macchiato at any time of the day and night. Who wouldn't want to go there?"

"The waitress?"

He grinned at her. "That's the great thing about other worlds. The endless possibilities."

She felt the corners of her mouth lift. Her alternate universes were mathematical. Every conversation she had with her students was about numbers, about physical properties of the universe, ones and zeros, <0.05s, cause and effect. She had never thought about what they might be like if they were real. Jack had imagined all the missing detail.

She checked the clock on her computer and realised with a jolt over an hour had been and gone. She nearly choked on her tea. Her computer bleeped at her, overjoyed that she had finally looked its way, looking forward to her full attention.

He was looking at her, head to one side. "Do you need me to go?"

"No, it's just you've been here over an hour. I don't want the cost to get away from you."

He looked at her with his head on one side. "How much do I owe you?"

Should she charge him the full amount they agreed? Surely that was too much. "£300."

"That's fine. Shall we keep going? If you have the time?"

She felt awkward charging him. They were only chatting now. But she still had half a cup of tea and she couldn't bill for an hour and ten minutes. And they were only part of the way into his story. And she hadn't solved his problem yet. Just twenty minutes longer, then.

"And miss out on all this fascinating inventiveness?" Her sarcasm was rewarded with his infectious grin.

She cleared her throat. "Let's get on with it. I think your best bet is the bubble universe theory."

"Excellent." He was teasing her, echoing her formality.

She ignored him. "If the bubble universe theory is correct then alternate universes are floating all around us, unseen

31

and undetectable, pressed close together like bubbles in a bubble bath."

He raised an eyebrow but thankfully didn't pursue that one. "What do they look like?" He said, instead.

"You probably wouldn't be able to tell the difference," she said. "You got that spot on. The ones nearest to us would be almost identical. Except for tiny changes. As you go further away the variables get more dispersed and they start to look really different. I think you 're writing from the theory already without realising it. I'd never thought about what it would be like to actually go to one, though."

"Freeing," he said.

"In what way?"

"Think about this philosophically. What we're saying is that there's a thousand thousand versions of you out there living every possible version of your life. Nothing is impossible because everything happened somewhere. So why not here? Basically, if you don't like something in your life, you have the power to change it." He was leaning back in his chair now, balancing on two legs, completely at home. He had her spare mug, the one with all the quarks on it, on his ankle which was crossed over his knee.

She laughed. "If only real life were that simple."

"It is. Just choose a different outcome."

"You can't *choose* an outcome. You can only control what you do. Simple cause and effect. I do x: insult my boss. The result is y: he fires me. So, I better not insult my boss."

"Oh, so simplistic. You're thinking about this all wrong. All backwards. It's cute that you think you have so much of an effect on the world."

She raised an eyebrow at him. He seemed to think he was

being charming.

"You didn't make him do it," he continued. "His childhood, his relationship, whether he spilled his coffee that morning. That's what made him fire you."

"Plus me."

"Nope." He landed his chair with a thud and put the cup down on her desk. "The point that your massive brain is missing is that you have the cause and effect concept right but the order wrong. You are very rarely the cause. The causes that matter are not you, your actions or your behaviours."

She felt her eyebrow arch at the mansplaining. Lucky for him he was paying.

"You are simply a person in the wrong place at the wrong time. Or in the right place at the right time. The causes were set in action long ago. If you want a different outcome you have to change those causes, not you."

For all his hubris and charm, he was wrong. The only thing you could control was yourself. No amount of fantasising could get away from that fact.

He lowered his voice, about to impart something. "Theoretically - according to your own theories - you could walk from world to world, looking for the one where conditions were exactly right."

"You mean adjust the variables until you've got it the way you want it. Like setting up a simulation. Get all the variables right and you can have any outcome that you like."

"Exactly," he said.

"How would that work, in practice?"

"Imagine, you're in a bar. Across the room a beautiful man is smiling at you. He comes over, takes your hand. Says, 'Ciao.'" He was fixing her with what she assumed were his come-to-bed eyes.

She stared back, cooly. "Not my type."

He laughed. "Ok. He says, 'Wanna exchange fermions?'"

She rolled her eyes but there was no stopping him.

"Anyway, the point is he's hot. You get chatting but it turns out his ex was called Alison. It didn't end well. Now he doesn't date Alisons."

"What a shame."

"If you happened to be in a universe where his ex was called Gloria - love connection."

"You can't just adjust history to suit your purposes," she said.

"*You* can't."

"You can?"

He laughed then lifted the cup to his mouth. His next words were spoken into the bottom of it. "That would be insane. Bill can." He looked up. "But if I could? Wouldn't that be fun?"

"No. Not really."

His grin dimmed slightly. "It would be great fun, trust me."

"Look," she said, leaning forward over the desk. "It's a lovely theory but there are a number of problems. Firstly, variables don't all act in predictable ways. It's more like a spider's web than the trousers of time because time and causation are far too complex. How would you know which way to go? How many variables would you change each time? What kind of impact would these changes have on the other people in that reality? Maybe I would talk to that guy in that bar but then he'd get hit by a bus on the way home. Without me delaying him he would have had a long and happy life. There are consequences."

He leaned in. Now they both had their elbows on the desk. He seemed closer than the space allowed. "Or maybe not talking with him is what got him killed. Trust me, you are not the cause of everything in this universe." She felt a little stab, piqued by his words, but he carried on. "You cannot control how things turn out. If you think of yourself as the central pivot of the whole world then you'll get nothing but crushed."

She felt a wave of heat. "And your way is better is it? Divesting yourself of any responsibility at all?"

"Yes. Much better. More fun, at least."

She put down her cup and braced herself. "Fun isn't the point though, is it?" The sudden rush of emotion was unsettling. Clearly she still wasn't back to normal. Time to bring this to a close.

He got to his feet first. "Can I use your bathroom?"

She was unbalanced, but politeness won. "Of course. It's just down the hall."

When he was gone, she logged into her computer and started checking her emails. There were fifteen "I'm sorry but…" from students. A lump in her throat caught her unawares. Ridiculous, this happened every year. It was better to clear out the chaff early. Her small classes of dedicated learners were the point.

Maybe in one of her alternate universes out there was an Alison whose classes were full. Many Alisons living different lives. Were they all married to Chris, she wondered? Clearly hundreds of them would be. Maybe thousands. One of the definitions of chance was just the number of universes that something did or didn't happen in. Chances were….

Then chances were, in another world, she had plucked up the courage to ask out that cute boy, Nick, who worked with her at her summer job handing out canapés at posh people's birthday parties. He wore corduroy jackets and wrote screenplays in his spare time. He told her how he had spent the summer building a log cabin for his friends. In that world they had fallen madly in love and got married on the cliff tops on Capri.

Her phone pinged. A text message from Chris. As the words sank into her brain everything else faded away and all she was left with was a single thought that faded to black. *Now I have nothing.*

Chapter Five

There was a stain on her desk. It was an inch to the left of where her phone sat winking at her, the text notification still front and centre: "No go on the contract changes, contract definitely void. Qatar off. Sorry, Chris"

The stain was a blemish on the beautiful surface of the wood. That wood had sat there for a hundred years in the university, unblemished. Now the brown wood grain stood out in little peaks and ridges against the darker valleys filled with inky colour. The spill was the shape of a seahorse. No, a dragon. A baby dragon, all spiky wings and pointy snout. Maybe the dragon was the cause of all this fog. Maybe the dragon was to blame.

She blinked and the dragon disappeared. How odd.

In its place was a mug of coffee. The heat was going to bake the stain in place. She should move the cup. She didn't move the cup.

The room was oddly quiet. Her hands rested in her lap. They looked like someone else's hands. Maybe that's why they didn't seem to want to move.

The coffee looked good, but she couldn't smell it. Perhaps the sense of smell was the first to go when you're in shock.

Or maybe colour is the first to go. Colours didn't seem to be working right. The coffee was kind of grey-ish. Maybe it wasn't coffee. Maybe it was dishwater. Maybe it was poison.

Her hands reached out and took the cup. The first swallow burned her throat, so she took another and another. The empty cup felt light and fragile in her hand. Like the finest porcelain. As if it might shatter in her hand.

She squeezed.

Nothing happened.

The phone vibrated again. She hadn't cancelled the notification, so it was going to buzz until the end of the world. So, for another ten minutes. When was the next house payment due? How long before they foreclosed completely? Something shifted in her throat.

The cup should fucking break when she told it to. How dare it stay whole? How dare it be strong? Break damn you, smash into a zillion fucking pieces.

She stared at the shattered remains of the cup on the floor. *That's better.*

Hands gripped her shoulders and pushed her gently into her chair. When had she stood up?

She looked up into a tanned unsmiling face. It had dark hair and sparkling eyes. Jack. What was Jack doing there?

He was speaking. Or at least his mouth was moving. She squinted. Where was the sound?

Jack nodded at her, so she nodded back. That seemed to please him, so she nodded again.

God, she was tired. Maybe if she just had a little sleep. She let her head drop onto the desk. That was better.

She was done.

No more.

After some time a pain climbed inside her neck and settled in to build a home there. She shifted. A sharp dart of pain across her forehand suggested she had been resting her head on the edge of something. A roaring in her ears resolved itself into the busy hum of her computer fan.

Her tongue felt raw. Everything felt raw.

She used her hands to push herself back into sitting position. Something creaked and groaned. Probably the chair.

Jack was sitting in her armchair on the other side of her office. His body position and closed eyes suggested he was sleeping. His expression was neutral.

She rubbed some life back into her shoulders. She could trace the line of soreness across her forehead. It was probably red and swollen from the feel of it.

Her lungs ached as she took a deep breath.

She had smashed her cup.

There were no pieces on the floor but in the bin was a jumble of ceramic lining the bottom. Shame, that had been her favourite mug, bought from the Kunsthalle in Hamburg. It had a modern art picture printed on it, the picture she had stood in front of for what felt like a day. A mother, dressed in a yellow shawl, holding her baby in her arms and gazing down at the upturned face. Chris had bought her that mug on their last good holiday together.

Oh well, she tried. But her trademark stoicism didn't have the effect she expected. The empty feeling was too big, too all consuming.

She looked back at Jack. Had he picked up the pieces? When

had he arrived? Or had he been here already? She couldn't remember. His hands were clasped in his lap, resting on his notebook. Oh right, they'd had an appointment.

She glanced back at his face. His eyes were open. She yelped.

"You scared me," she said.

"You scared me," he said, his eyes flicking to the bin and back.

"Sorry."

"What's in Qatar?"

Her stomach lurched but she took a deep breath and answered anyway. "Nothing is in Qatar. My husband quit his job to take a contract there. And the contract isn't valid in European law. It's been withdrawn." Why was she telling him this?

"He quit his job?"

"Yes." Her eyes stung so she got up and went to the cupboard and got out two mugs. "Tea?"

He shook his head. "What the hell was he thinking?"

She tried not to shout at him. It wasn't his fault. He couldn't understand - him with his free flow lifestyle, tons of money and world-ending charm - what it was like. So she finished making a cup of tea.

Well, she tried telling herself again, it wasn't the first time something like this had happened. Of course, it felt like they were slowly losing every part of their lives into a black hole of debt. But life was like that and it only took one thing to go well for them to climb back out of it.

Some milk slopped onto the counter. She steadied her hand.

The tea was ready. She had to put her head back together.

As she walked back across her cluttered study to her enormous Victorian desk she allowed the soothing dark wood panelling to work its magic on her. How had she ever found this room gloomy with its tiny window looking over the delivery yard. The mahogany shelves were filled to bursting with papers and books, a hangover from the days when looking something up meant pages and printouts rather than search engines.

As she placed the cup of tea on her desk she took a deep steadying breath. Right now, he was the only way she could save the house. She had some recovery to do.

"So, Mr Shepherd, I think I have enough to start with. I'll do some researching and come back to you with some suggestions. I'll let you know when I'm ready."

He looked like he was going to say something else but thankfully just reached out and shook her hand firmly. "Thanks. And send me an interim bill. I've taken up enough of your time. Just don't forget, you have a lot more influence on the course of your life than you seem to think you do."

What an odd thing to say.

When he was gone she sipped her tea and thought about his parting words. According to Jack there was a version of herself out there that had everything she ever wanted. In his book she could swap with any of these lucky women. Let them take her burden for a little while. They were probably fresh to the fight and would do a better job that she ever could.

It was a magical solution. A wonderful dream. Like winning the lottery, and just as impossible. You couldn't go jumping from world to world, taking people's places. Even if they were sitting in a world next door, just as tired, wishing the exact same thing. Even if that felt almost like permission.

Chapter Six

She was meeting Jack for coffee in a cafe in town. She shuffled the notes in front of her on the desk. She had scoured everything she had ever known or read to find a solution for him. He was going to be so pleased. She was going to get paid.

He was buying. He was late.

Out of the windows the Meadows were teaming with people. This used to be a little Italian place. It wasn't far from her old flat. She skipped over that thought. She tapped her fingers on the table.

Jack's cleared throat made her jump. He was standing next to the table as if he had arrived from nowhere. She was taken again with the colour of his eyes.

She looked back at her notes as he sat down opposite. It was nice here. The central bar, covered in flowers, was framed by chalkboards covered in barely legible writing. French onion soup was the special of the day. The waitress came straight over even though the cafe was busy. How did he have that affect on people? He flirted his way through ordering a simple latte and a pastry and the waitress left with a little bounce in her walk.

She waited until she had his full attention again. "So, I have had an idea that might solve your story problem."

He sat forward, probably in response to her professional tone. "Oh yes?"

"It's an old idea I had when I was a postgraduate, to solve the problem of the Cold Spot. It went nowhere but it might help us here." It had come to her in the bath last night as she thought about Jack and his problem. All those days of calculations as a post grad, building a theory she could never prove. And now it was useful for something after all.

"What's the cold spot?" he said, accepting the latte and the huge raisin Danish from the waitress with a wink.

When the waitress left he pushed the pastry across the table to her. She felt her face form into a smile, for the first time all week. It felt false, but he didn't seem to notice.

She carried on. "It's a location in space where all kinds of strange things happen. It should be filled with light and heat, but it isn't, hence Cold Spot. A colleague of mine theorised that it could be a place where another bubble universe is pushing into ours. Proof of alternate universes."

Jack put his cup of coffee on the table. "That's so cool," he said, leaning forward. "So we have proof of alternate realities? Why doesn't anyone talk about this?"

"There's no proof. I spent a whole year trying to figure it out. But the measurements, or rather lack of measurements, are from several million years ago. That Cold Spot could have come and gone during the time of the dinosaurs and we'd only be finding out about it now. And there's nothing to detect. The point is it's a lack of anything. Not a black hole, not stars or planets. Literally nothing at all."

44

He nodded. His gaze was so intense, like there was nothing more interesting in the universe than her theory. It didn't happen very often. It was nice. She took a bite of the Danish. It was soft and buttery and good, making her mouth water.

She swallowed. "So, back in the day, my theory was that, if it were a pressure point from another universe, then the Cold Spot would emit ionised particles as it's happening. It links up with several other theories about how bubble universes would maintain their integrity while crowded into the omniverse. But the problem is that ionised particles are susceptible to things like radiation, to heat and cold. The effect of them is diminished over time and space. So by the time they reached us they would all have dispersed, and we would never see them.

"In other words if we were standing right next to the Cold Spot we'd be able to measure it easily. But we're not. We're millions of light years away. The only reason we see this one is due to its size and therefore the effect it is having on the space around it."

The waitress came back over to the table with a napkin nobody had asked for. She said thank you, but Jack didn't even look up at the poor girl. He just motioned for her to go on.

"There could be billions of these cold spots all over the universe. Billions of little pressure points where the universes all crowd together. But you'd have to be right there, when they bump together, to detect them. And be using the right equipment. Otherwise you'd never know."

He was looking thoughtful. "My doors," he said.

"Exactly. I put that research aside years ago because it'd be impossible to prove. The Cold Spot is the size of a galaxy. If it were sitting over our planet it'd just register like normal background radiation.

"But if we assumed that these pressure spots were the size of doorways then not only do we have a valid theoretical basis for your doors, but we also have a valid theory for seeing them and using them."

There. He was paying her to make his novel plausible, more appealing for the film producers in Hollywood or whoever. And now she had done it. She took another bite of the pastry and let the sugar soothe her thoughts.

Imagine if all these little normal-sized doorways were real and what this would mean for the theory. You would be able to detect them, use them, just like he'd written. You could build a detector easily. A basic photon detector, using the principles of the double-slit experiment, and voila. He could take liberties with how to filter out all the other photons in the vicinity. You could use radioactive tagging, of course, but you'd need a flat surface behind the door to bounce off.

But, being so small, the wave forms would be too unstable to actually exist. Shame. What a fantastic discovery it would be.

"So basically, what you are saying is the doors could emit ionic particles. And that's how Bill can detect and use them?"

She nodded with a full mouth.

"How would that stop them working, though?" he asked.

She swallowed. "For starters, if you introduce matter through an ionically charged anti-matter portal it would discharge the ions which would explain your doors being one trip only. They'd take time to recharge."

"Huh. Makes sense." He reached across and broke off a piece of the pastry. She nudged the plate towards him.

"And secondly a really big ionic disturbance could disrupt everything."

His hand paused halfway to his mouth. "An ionic disturbance."

"Yes."

"Like what?"

"You can relate that back to anything: EMP, solar flares, a meteor storm. Any of those would work for the story. Changes in the magnetic poles would do it. Like, just now there is a major shift in the magnetic poles. They've moved about ten degrees. That would change the ionic pattern of the doors, completely throw off the balance, make them undetectable. Something that like would be ideal. Voila, plot solved."

The pastry was finished. Maybe she'd get another one. He was paying. Or maybe she'd buy her own pastry because she was about to get paid, double time.

He was frowning. "You've actually solved it."

"Well, yes." Cue flowers and champagne?

He had gone completely still. She had been expecting joy, or gratitude, or something. Still this was nice. Maybe he'd get her a bottle of something later.

Clearly this was a good solution. Her job here was done.

She was about to get paid. Handsomely, if she remembered rightly. She would be safe for another month. Maybe Chris would have a job by then. Maybe she'd be talking to him. Both were doubtful.

Jack still hadn't moved.

"You ok?" she asked.

He unfroze, looking startled. "Um, yes. Fine. You fixed it."

"I did."

"Which ions?" he said

"I don't know. Any one you like. Pick one."

"I can't just pick one. It has to be the right one." He was getting louder as he spoke. She spoke more quietly to compensate.

"You can take some poetic license you know. You know, any old ion." She was pleased with the joke, but he didn't even notice.

"No, I can't. It has to be right." She glanced around at the other cafe patrons who were now looking at them.

"I know this means a lot to you, but your readers aren't going to know the difference."

"I'm sorry." He sat back. The intensity faded. "It's just... I thought I was stuck, forever. And now you have solved it for me. I feel like I've been set free."

Was that tears in his eyes? From one extreme to the other. "It's just a silly theory," she said, embarrassed.

"No, it's not. You have no idea what this means to me." He reached across and squeezed her hand.

"It's fine."

They sat in silence for a little longer. It wasn't a pregnant silence like she was used to. There was no expectation in it. No requirement. It was companionable, it was nice. He finished his coffee.

They smiled at each other again when he got up to pay the bill.

He walked with her to the door.

"Thank you for the pastry," she said.

Thank you for being a bright spot in an otherwise dreary month. Thank you for looking after me when I fell apart in front of you. Thank you for bringing your story to me and not to someone else.

He walked with her to the door. It was time to say goodbye. They shook hands.

"Well, I guess this is it then," she said.

He didn't let go. "Come and celebrate with me," he said. She nodded.

They went to the Caledonian. He guided her through the bar like he owned it. She sat down in a plush tartan armchair and he sat on the velvet bench beside her.

"We need a drink," he said and gestured to the waiter. "Whisky, please. Something expensive. We're celebrating."

She rolled her eyes at the extravagance, but he was right, they were. The waiter brought over two glasses and a leather covered folder with the bill. She couldn't help but see it as he signed it to his room. The number almost made her choke. Once the waiter was safely on the other side of the bar he leaned across the gap between them. "To you."

She held up her glass and touched it gently to his. "To us." She took a slug and the burning liquid flowed into her veins and hummed.

Jack emptied his glass and put it down with a little clink of ice.

She sat back, feeling the whisky burn in her stomach. A lovely warm glowing feeling.

"Another round?" she said.

Jack looked delighted. "Sure."

She called over the waiter and went for round two. Jack raised the second glass like he was making a toast.

"You've given me my life back, Ali. Thank you."

"Oh, lord. Let's not overstate things."

"You have no idea how hard the last weeks have been."

She looked around the luxury bar. "Oh, yes. Terrible."

"I mean it. Thank you, Alison Howden." They clinked glasses again and took a drink.

She smiled at his sincerity. It wasn't there all that often and sometimes it was hard to see but if you caught him at the right moment he really meant what he said.

As the evening went on she felt herself finally relax. Her life was in ruins, but right there, in that bar, it didn't seem so bad. It was almost funny. She found herself telling him all about it.

"The worst part about it," she laughed, "is Qatar isn't even the first time he's done this. Last year he started a consultancy business. He quit his job, rented out a huge office, hired a secretary, spent thousands on a website and it turned out that he didn't have a single bit of work lined up. I had to sell my flat to bail him out and now he complains every time we can't get a takeaway that it's not fair. I mean, what did he think would happen? It's like he missed the memo on how the world works, you know." She giggled into her champagne - he had finally bought her champagne. Why wasn't Jack? It had gone weirdly silent.

She felt the drink slosh uncomfortably in her stomach. Maybe she shouldn't have shared that one. I mean it was ancient history now.

Jack finally spoke. "Why are you still married to him? Why don't you just leave?"

She sighed. "That's not how marriage works. And besides, it's not his fault."

"What do you mean?"

"The economy hit a downturn. It might have worked in another economy. He did it his way and it didn't work; I can't punish him for that. It wouldn't help. Besides he's punishing himself enough for the both of us."

"I could punish him for you if you like," said Jack, laughing. She hadn't even told him about losing her lovely flat. What would he say then?

"No," she said. "That's not how relationships work. A person is who they are. Nothing I can do will change him. And he shouldn't have to change. He's a person with his own way of looking at the world. Just because it's not how I would have done it doesn't mean he's wrong." Smooth words that flowed familiarly. "I can't change him, so I just have to live with it. People have to compromise to live together."

"When's the last time Chris compromised?" said Jack quietly.

But Alison was on a roll. She waved her drink around to punctuate her point. "There are things he likes and wants, and I am willing to listen. Because then he's happier and is free to look after me." Was that right?

"And how exactly does he do that?" said Jack.

Alison squinted at his face. It was blurry in the darkness, but he looked pissed off. Why was he frowning?

"Dunno." This wine was going to her head faster than she planned. She had better get some water. She stood up and went to the bar, colliding with it slightly. She straightened her top with dignity and stared at the barman until he came over. Armed with the water she went back to the table. She sipped it in the silence that had fallen.

Then Jack put his drink down with a clink. "He's a shit husband," he said.

She stared at him for a moment. No one had ever said that to her before. Not so bluntly and she found there were no words left in her arsenal to protest. "I know," she said.

"He's manipulating you. And doing a really poor job of it. It's insulting the crap he expects you to swallow."

The slam made him jump. Her hand stung where it had impacted on the table.

"You don't think I know that?" The pressure in her skull forced tears into her eyes. She was horrified to hear her voice catch. "You don't think I haven't watched my savings, my friends, my career, dwindle and die, and wondered when I was going to draw the line. When was I going to walk away? But he's my husband. I promised, until death us do part." Her throat was full of stuffing. "A marriage isn't something you just give up on when it gets tricky. It's not a short-term deal. In a relationship of 50 years this is a blip. It's a small problem that we can get past if we work together. And then there's 30 years of happiness to make it worthwhile. That's what marriage is." It sounded hollow, even to her.

"No, it's not. A marriage is two people working in partnership to solve their problems. What you have is a feudal overlordship. I bet he complains about not getting a regular rota of sex either."

She ignored that one.

"A marriage is a promise," she said. "Whether it's a fair promise is not the point. It's a promise that you will be together, for better or worse."

"But Ali, it's all worse."

"It isn't! Not all of it. I mean, it didn't used to be." She wiped the tears away with an angry hand.

Jack's face was scrunched into a new emotion. He looked so sad.

"Don't pity me, Jack. Don't you dare. This is my choice. I did this. I knew what I was getting myself into. It's not like he

52

turned up with pots of cash and a resume of excellent works. He was a mess when I met him. I chose this and now I have to live with it."

"Ali, I'm not pitying you. This is just… and I know I'm the last person to comment because I don't stick anything out… but this doesn't seem right."

"I know. It's not right." She looked down at her hands. Her fingers were automatically twisting the rings around and around. The red sore skin a testament to the frequency of the habit.

He reached across the table and took her hand.

"Come with me."

"What? Where?"

He laughed a gentle chuckle that felt far more familiar than it should. "Come with me through the doors. I'm not supposed to tell anyone. I'm supposed to just arrive and depart with minimal impact. But you've been so good to me. And life has been so unfair to you. So I wanted to say thank you and offer you a way out."

She stared at him. Ha, ha, very funny. Surely he would start laughing now. But his face was still, his eyes were intensely serious.

"You're joking," she said. He shook his head once.

She stared at his unblinking gaze. Everything she had ever dreamed of. An entire multiverse. No, it wasn't possible. But he was just staring at her.

He was Bill? He was a man from another universe. It made a sort of sense. He was so different, so confident. The things he must have seen, the things he must have done. It would be so good to feel that way, for once. So assured. Like you could handle anything or save anyone.

"Then you're the one looking for... It's your world that's...."

He nodded again. What an incredible thing he was doing, saving an endangered world. As simple as a trip to the pharmacist. No wonder he was distressed about being here. No wonder their conversations had been so intense.

She didn't know what to say. He was offering her something unbelievable and incredible. Surely the only thing to do would be to take the offer with both hands and walk away from your painful, miserable life. Walk away from your family without a backward glance. What kind of person would turn their back on an opportunity like that?

She looked into his peacock eyes which seemed to be glowing in the candlelight of the bar.

"Let me show you what it's like," he said. "Travelling through multiple universes. This is your life's study – you could help me. I could help you. Everything you ever dreamed of. Let me show it to you." It was intoxicating.

But even so.

"I can't." She looked down at her hands to avoid his reaction. An ugly feeling, that tasted like regret, burrowed into her chest. Her hands in her lap had started to shake, she saw. She was holding on to her wedding ring like a lifebuoy. "I made a promise." Follow though.

There was no response, so she steeled herself to look back up into his accusing eyes. But when she did there was no coldness there. No rebuke.

He nodded calmly with no hint of censure at all. "Ok."

The taxi pulled up to her house. Alison stumbled on her way in, tripping over her tipsy feet. It was pitch black and completely silent. Was Chris out? Asleep?

She kicked off her shoes at the bottom of the stairs, dropped her handbag strap over the banister and crept upwards.

Five steps, or six, and her eyes were level with the first landing. She knew it before she saw it - the light was on in his study. A faint sound of gunfire emerged. Working hard, then.

Her words from earlier that evening echoed in her mind. "No, really, he tries really hard... It's not his fault... We are in it together..." Standing on this cold stair staring at the closed study door like she did every night, the echo rang false. The booze had dulled her control of the narrative. He wasn't trying. It was his fault. They were not in this together.

Each little pock, pock, pock landed like flies on her skin. They itched.

She felt a wave of tears rise. She made it into the bedroom and stuffed her mouth full of cushion to stifle the sound. Huge heaving sobs invaded her body, as they always did these days whenever she drank too much. She let them roll through her, wetting the pillow with her tears.

Why was she living this way? How could she have allowed this to happen? This wasn't right.

Eventually the sobs slowed.

She turned over on the bed, leaving the wet cushion to one side and stared at the ceiling. The windows in the room were dark. It was still and quiet. The tears took the fog with them and a kind of hollow calm remained behind. She felt something brighter stir in her mind. She had to get out of this ridiculous situation. Living day to day terrified of bailiffs, living with an angry bear of a man who had withdrawn from her completely, and all after something *he* had done to them.

Because this was his doing. She had to end this pointless

torment. No one would be harmed by her leaving. Not really.

In all those other worlds that Jack had spoken about, somewhere she had left Chris years ago. Somewhere she had never married him. This wasn't fixed and immutable.

She pulled the cushions around her in an impromptu nest. Her mind fumbled through the mush and options began to emerge. As the windows lightened she made a plan. She could do this. There was nothing stopping her. Just walk away.

A rosy glow rose up the wall. It was morning now. The bed was unslept in. She was still fully dressed in the outfit from the evening before. The sequins on her black top sparkled slightly in the dawn light. Chris had clearly slept in his study again.

The night had passed with no rest, but the tiredness was gone. She felt lifted. Out of the window the clouds shifted from pink to white and the sky lightened to a pleasant grey-blue.

She was going to do it.

She shrugged out of her old clothes, leaving them in a pile on the floor. The shower was warm. It caressed her shoulders and she found herself humming a little ditty.

Looking into her wardrobe she picked out clothes for comfort today. Cosy leggings, a voluminous blouse, perky boots. Things she hadn't worn in a while. The front door went as she chose a scarf. Perfect timing. She pulled a small rucksack from the back of the cupboard and within minutes she was packed. She trotted down the stairs to an empty house.

Her shoes had been tidied away. Her handbag was placed on the hall table. A post-it note sat on top. "Please in future remember to…" was all she read before she scrunched it in her fist and dropped it in the bin.

Chapter Seven

The car park was nearly empty. Jack was staring at his arm then looking at the blank brick wall in front of him.

"Jack!"

He turned as she ran towards him.

His face was a picture. "What are you doing here?"

"I'm coming with you," she gasped.

He looked troubled. "But you said -"

"I know what I said. But I am doing all the right things and my life is going down the toilet. Because of Chris I'm going to lose the house. What do I have to stay for?"

"But, how did you find me?"

"I went to the Caledonian."

"They gave you my note."

"They gave me your note. Thank you for leaving a note."

His eyes were shining as he put his hand on her shoulder. "Are you sure?"

"I'm sure. I'll help you with your mission, I'll do everything I can to get you where you need to go then you can help me find somewhere better. One or two tiny changes and then everything will be fine."

"I could change everything."

"No. It goes against what I believe in. Everything. I need you to take me to the same life but one where Chris hasn't stopped trying. I hate myself for thinking like this. But I'm drowning and I refuse to be beaten."

Jack nodded. He appeared to be having an internal conversation. His eyes were flicking back and forth, and his mouth was twitching - classic signs of internal conflict. Well, at least he was conflicted. Maybe there was some hope for him after all.

"Ok, I'll take you with me." Her heart leapt. "But Ali, your theory is wrong. It's like saying 'I just need a tiny win on the lottery'. Why not make it a big one?"

"Because that would be walking away from every decision I ever made without a backwards glance. You might as well say, just step into a world where I never married him, or one where we never met. Everything would be different. You could take me somewhere where I'm a millionaire or a playboy bunny -"

"There's limits to what is possible even in these alternate worlds, you know." His eyes twinkled.

She smiled. "But then I'd be set adrift from my entire past. All the choices I've made. And I wouldn't know what to do with myself. Besides, I'd never give you the pleasure of being right."

He grinned at that. "Well, I think you're mad, but I see your point."

"Hallelujah. Perhaps I have made an impact after all."

He opened his mouth to say something but clearly changed his mind.

"Thank you," she said. "You're saving me. And I promise I won't be any trouble. I'll do whatever you say, I'll help you. I'll be useful."

"You don't need to. You've already helped me, more than you can possibly know."

He squeezed her shoulder then went back to staring at the wall in front of him and then looked down at his arm.

She tried not to cry. This was it then, the end of her life in this world.

"Hey," he said. "It's ok. I know this is a big deal. Let me get us some coffees?"

She hadn't realised he was still looking out for her, or that she was being so obvious. He was being so kind. She put her bag down while he went over to the coffee truck on the edge of the car park and tried to pull herself together. There had been a minute there where she couldn't see him over in the corner. She had thought he was gone already, that she had missed him. The feeling was still circulating her body, making her feel jittery. After finally making up her mind to go, the thought of being left here was too much to bear.

He brought the coffees over and she sipped hers gratefully while he went back to work. He got a piece of equipment out of his bag. It looked like a portable hairdryer. It was a portable hairdryer.

"What is that for?"

He looked over, sheepishly. "You gave me the idea with your ions theory. The magnetic poles are off so that's why the doors aren't working. This seemed like the simplest way of repolarising the doors." He pointed at the blue button on the side. It was an ionising hairdryer. Surely not.

He shrugged. "It's working, look."

She stared at the brick wall where he was aiming the hairdryer. This was laughable, surely. But as she watched, the air about a foot in front of the bricks began to take on a slight haze, like it was moving around but also trapped. It was just a small patch but as Jack moved his hand around the patch started to grow.

Was that a door? He nodded when she looked over at him.

"There's still a lot to recharge but I think it might work," he said.

It took an age. As she waited for the door to be ready she scuffed her foot in the gravel, forcing the stones into little mounds and leaving behind a streak of brown dirt. On the other side of the car park people were hurrying to work, chatter and traffic blaring, but it all seemed very far away, muted. They had no idea what she was about to do. The wind was blowing slightly, ruffling her hair and manipulating a discarded sweet wrapper, purple and blue, trapping it in an eddy against a lamppost in the half empty car park. She found herself noting the colours of the parked cars, committing them to memory, the last things she would see in this world.

She'd spent her whole life theorising about whether this was possible, whether alternate worlds even existed, and this was her about to walk into one. She had brought notebooks, her laptop stuffed with software. Jack was saving the world, but she was going to be the first scientist to actually measure alternate worlds from inside them. Her butterflies had butterflies.

She wondered what it was going to feel like. Jack described a feeling of passing through yourself. Her only possible point of reference was a time when, diving in the Med, she and Chris had swum into a little cave in the rocky shoreline

61

that was fed by a freshwater river. Ten feet from the mouth of the cave the water switched from sea to freshwater and everything went all wobbly, like a bad 60s TV show special effect. Her eyes had felt like they were twisting in her head trying to keep up. It was disorientating and unnerving but when she closed her eyes it felt like nothing at all. Maybe it was like that.

It wasn't like that at all.

Afterwards she was staring at the ground where she had just thrown up her breakfast. Grey, jagged gravel stared back. Through the ringing in her ears she could hear traffic, people talking, the beep of a pedestrian crossing. The red and blue sweetie wrapper she had noticed before skipped its little dance in the lee of the lamppost.

She looked around from her crouched position as her breathing normalised. The gravel was still scuffed at her feet, the pattern was the same. The cars in the car park were the same, the shops across the street were the same. Had they left at all?

There was pressure on her back, moving around. The wind blew her hair away from her face, shifting the smell of vomit and replacing it with Jack's aftershave. He was standing behind her, hand on her back moving in slow circles. The pressure was reassuring. As the wind subsided she could hear him murmuring gentle sounds.

Were they here? Had they done it? The wobble in her legs and the hollow pit in her stomach were the only clues. But they were big ones. She felt tears prickle her eyes.

She had left. Gone forever. She wanted to go back. No she didn't. She wanted her legs to stop wobbling. She wanted the panic to go away. She wanted to stop feeling so weak. So she started shouting.

"What the hell, Jack? You said it was a slight wobble!"

"Well, it is, normally. What happened?"

"I don't know. I felt like my skin went in two different directions at once. Bloody hell."

"Are you hurt?"

"No." The air felt good in her lungs. Her throat was still raw, and her mouth tasted horrible. "It didn't hurt at all; it was just really weird." More breathing. She was starting to feel better. "I just wasn't expecting it."

"I'm sorry. That's not what it's like for me. That's not what it's like for anyone."

"What do you mean?"

"I've seen people walk through these doors before. Stumble into them really. They don't even notice it's happening."

"Great. Perhaps I'm allergic."

"Ali, I can take you back."

"Just give me a minute."

"Seriously. This is not good."

"Just give me a minute, Jack."

She walked away and leaned on the red car she had seen before. This world was the same as far as she could see. It felt the same, tasted the same. They were in the car park still and the cars were the exact same that they had just left. There was nothing to distinguish this car park from the other one. It was all a bit of an anticlimax. Where was the big soaring musical score? You'd never believe you had stepped into a different universe if you felt nothing from the transition.

Maybe Michael Crichton had it right with the quantum foam after all. At least that was a visual marker of change. The only difference here was just her being sick.

Jack was a few steps away, leaning against the blue car, fussing over the small satchel he brought. She'd not seen him anxious before. He looked smaller, like a little boy.

The deep breaths were helping. The panic was settling, bringing back the solid certainty she had felt before. She was doing the right thing. This was the right thing.

She looked around for the coffee she had left balanced on the bollard. It would take the taste out of her mouth. It was gone.

Then she saw another difference. The coffee van was still in its position at the edge of the car park, and it was still Harry inside the van. But the van was now a blue Citroen, vintage and cutesy. It had a daisy on the front windscreen. Her Harry wouldn't be seen dead in that.

This was a new world.

She was in an entirely different universe. She was travelling dimensions.

What the hell had she done?

She threw up again.

Jack was over in a flash. He stroked her hair and muttered comforting platitudes to her.

"Sorry," she mumbled.

He just tutted and wiped the tears off her face. "It's a big thing. You're fine."

Jack led her over to Harry's van and ordered teas for them both. She knew that van so well but that was the one in her home universe. Harry greeted them both with a smile. He asked Jack how he liked it but started her order without asking.

Harry looked the same. She studied his face while he poured the milk. Was it the same man? He had the same blonde dreads, the same nose ring. His t-shirt looked familiar. But the van… She had never met this man until today. He turned back from the hot water tap and put two sugars in her tea without asking.

"There you go, Al," said Harry, handing it over.

She took the paper cup. "Harry? When did you get this van?"

He squinted at her. "I got Ellie last year. But you know that. You feeling ok?"

"Yeah, I just… it's like I've never seen her before."

"What, like deja vu?"

"No - I…" Where to begin with that? "Not exactly."

"Happens to the best of us," he grinned and turned back to his fridge to put the milk away.

Jack pulled on her arm. "Careful. Stop pointing stuff out." He led her away. "They don't like it."

"'They'…"

This was utter madness. A whole new world where Harry had a classic van and she took tea with two sugars. However, the sweet tea was helping. Her stomach had slunk back down her throat. Jack was staring intently at her again, so she waved him away with a request for napkins. When he and Harry were chatting serenely she allowed herself to slump onto a bollard.

They should go back.

But what the hell was she going to go back to? All the same problems were waiting there. In fact, all the same problems were waiting here. Maybe there's one fewer final demand. One more chocolate bar in the fridge. She knew the theory. One or tiny events in this place were different. This place was the worst of both worlds. Enough the same to still scare her, but enough different that it already didn't feel like home. She felt like she'd lost something fundamental to herself in that moment of tearing skin. Did she just leave something of herself behind? Was that what happened when you left your home universe, did you split in two and never become whole again?

Jack came back over with the napkins and led her to a bench. She sat down gratefully and plastered on a smile.

There was going to be lots of these jumps, maybe even hundreds, before they got to a world where it was different enough. Could she do that a hundred times?

Yes, if it meant getting to her perfect world.

"Well, you've freaked Harry out," said Jack, not unkindly.

"Sorry."

"It's alright. I told him you had a hard night. He's sympathetic."

She nodded. "What else is different here, then?" she said, to distract herself.

"Not much. Just that I never came to see you in this world. A few other tweaks in other people's lives but basically that's it."

"So you and I never met here?"

"Nope. Just think of all the fun you never had." He smiled. Clearly some things didn't change.

She felt herself smiling back. "Just think of all the monologuing I was spared."

He clutched at his heart dramatically.

"Right," she said, pushing herself to her feet. "Where's the second door?"

His smile faded. "Not tonight. I think you've had enough for one day."

"Do you want to stop mollycoddling me, please?"

"Let's just find somewhere to stay and then we can get going after a full night's sleep."

He was right of course. She was tired and shaky, for all her bravado.

Before she had left she had wandered around the house looking at everything for the last time. Last cup of tea in her kitchen. Last time sitting on her sofa. She had wanted to touch everything before she left it behind forever. She wanted to imprint every detail of this version of her life into her brain. Then if she didn't recognise her life in the new world she could recreate this version within it. *A perfect version of the real me even in my ideal world.*

And she had stared at her wedding photo for perhaps a bit too long. He would not be the same in the new place. That was the whole point. And maybe this room would be filled with joy again, with laugher, with love. Maybe he and she would be together again, real husband and wife, full of hope.

Jack was looking at her intently. How long had she been sitting there, silently? She nodded. Maybe some sleep would help sort through all her crazy thoughts.

Chapter Eight

"The Balmoral, are you bloody joking?" The huge Georgian hotel loomed above them. Standing by itself at the end of Princes Street, towering over Waverley station, it had been Edinburgh's luxury hotel of choice since the golden age of railways. It was also the most expensive hotel in Edinburgh.

"What?"

"I'm not staying here."

"Why not? It's a big deal what you just did."

"Well, for starters you have no intention of paying them."

"What? What do you mean?" The door men were looking at them intently. They were used to tourists clustering around for photographs, drunk students stumbling past. If they found her hysterics of interest she must have been making a proper scene. But there was absolutely no way. He pulled her over to one side. The balustrade was taller than her head.

"Here." She rooted in her bag. "The Caledonian gave me this to give to you. The bill that's outstanding. You never paid them."

"The other Jack will pay them. The one who took my place."

"You don't know that."

"Of course I do. You have to trust me. This is how it's done. You just travelled inter-dimensionally. Your life's work has been justified. Have a night off, live a little. The next Jack is offering to treat you." He shook her arms gently. "Ali, you're in another universe!"

She smiled at his exuberance. "Yeah, that's actually pretty cool."

"So...?" He flung his arms out, encompassing the sandstone splendour.

"No." She flourished her phone. "I took out all the cash I could before we left. And my phone and my online banking is still working, I checked. I'll pay my own way and I'm not paying for here."

Jack looked deflated but he nodded.

She led the way into the Registers of Scotland across the road. They had a cafe, nestled deep in the building. You had to walk past the Records Room to get there. In that huge domed room were stacks filled with records of all the births, deaths and marriages in Scotland going back to the 16th Century, colour coded in blue, red and black.

Somewhere in that room was her marriage certificate, printed and bound in leather. A record forever of the promise she had made. If she ever got tempted to give up it was the perfect way to gain a little perspective.

A cup of coffee, some free wifi and one of her favourite booking sites later and they were in a taxi to Newington, to a little B&B on one of the main roads out of town. There was an advantage to being the solely responsible person in a marriage. She was amazing at logistics.

Jack was less thrilled. As the taxi swept past charity shops and greasy spoon cafes he was keeping his face blank, with some effort, she could see. *Oh ye of little faith.*

The B&B was plain on the outside. It was a fair way down the hill, half way to Cameron Toll shopping centre, and surrounded by almost identical B&Bs. Years ago these would have been grand Victorian houses, lining the main route into Edinburgh from the Borders, displaying their owner's status. Most had fallen into a poor state, with greying net curtains at the window. Hence Jack's expression.

But she had interrogated the site while Jack had fidgeted next to her. This particular one was newly opened. The owners were part of a gentrification renaissance, having created the first boutique hotel in the area. The front entrance way was freshly decorated. The brass shone. Everything was quietly elegant, freshly painted and bang up to date.

Jack's expression shifted as they walked through the door. She allowed herself to feel a little smug. When the woman at the front desk asked her to sign in on an iPad he looked impressed.

The receptionist downloaded the room key to her iPhone. Meanwhile Jack had wandered off to the door of the bar and peered in. Alison could almost hear him thinking, *perhaps this isn't so bad after all.* She wanted to laugh.

The receptionist was looking across at Jack expectantly, waiting for him to bring over his phone. Alison waved to get his attention.

"Jack."

"What?"

"Your phone."

"Huh?"

"Your phone. The woman needs your phone to upload the

key."

"My phone? Um, no. No, thanks. We'll just do the one key."

"Are you sure? It just takes a second." The woman had her polite voice on. Alison shifted awkwardly.

Jack's megawatt smile sprung back to his face. "Yes. I'm sure." He came up next to her and slipped his hand around her waist. "It's not like we'll be leaving the room."

The woman smiled at them. "Ok, that's all sorted for you. I won't keep you any longer. Room 5, just up the stairs."

"What the hell was that all about?"

Jack was standing in the middle of the beautiful bedroom, nodding in approval at the muted colours, the mix of fabrics. Her outburst got his attention though. He held his hands up in apology.

"My phone doesn't work here. Your SIM card is close enough to still register but mine's from a few worlds ago, it gave out when we arrived. I need to get a new one."

"You could have just said."

"In front of the receptionist, how was I going to phrase that one? I'm not used to travelling with someone else and you keep making decisions without me. I panicked." He shrugged.

That was fair enough. She was probably overreacting. Her hands were still shaking when she looked down at them. Whether it was fear or excitement she couldn't tell. She went into the bathroom to give herself time to calm down.

Everything felt strange and familiar, all at the same time. She was in another universe with a man she barely knew. She felt adrift and untethered and like it was nothing at all. Maybe that's why she was being so snappy. She had to remember this was new for him too. He was used to doing things his own way and she had, on the very first trip, taken over.

A few splashes of cold water later and she went back into the room. Jack was sitting in the armchair in the window looking out at Arthur's Seat looming green and grey against a beautiful blue sky. She took his apology, partly out of embarrassment and partly because he had made them both a cup of tea. There were two armchairs, so she joined him. The view was breathtaking.

"Good choice, Ali."

"Thank you. You thought I had booked us into some old lady hell hole, didn't you?"

He gave an apologetic shrug.

"If there's one thing I'm good at it's finding aesthetically pleasing hotels on a tiny budget. It's what you do when your husband has champagne tastes and lemonade pockets."

He didn't reply but bowed his head in acknowledgement of her strange skillset. She smiled at him. Awkwardness gone. A line of tourists was climbing the summit, looking like little ants.

"It's a really weird feeling knowing that all of those people are from another universe. Not a single one of them was born in the same universe as me. How do you handle that? How are you not shouting for joy? Or crying in a corner?"

"How are you not? This is old hat for me."

"I honestly don't know. It just all seems so familiar. So normal. Nothing is different here. My phone works. My bank accounts. If it wasn't for the memory of that feeling when I stepped through I'd think nothing had happened at all. That this was all some elaborate con."

He frowned. "I'm not conning you, Ali."

"No, I know. I don't mean you. I just mean, it all feels the same."

"It does here. This is just a single step away. And remember, at the end of all this your perfect world is not that dissimilar to this one. The people are going to be the same people. The technology, the culture. The only thing that's going to change is him. Unless, of course, you want your life to be different too." He looked away from the window and sat forward.

She knew what was coming. Why did he keep pushing this?

"You have literally saved my home universe by unlocking the doors for me. I want to do something in return. I can make you rich and famous. I could give you everything you ever wanted, if you'd just let me."

"I know. Thank you. But I don't want to be rich or famous. I don't even want everything I ever wanted."

"You'd still get your perfect husband."

"It's not that. I know you think I'm mad, but the impact is too big, the stress of living in a life I don't know would be too big. I want it to be as close to my real life as possible."

"Just so long as it makes you happy." His knee was jiggling now. He went back to staring out of the window.

"Thank you." He looked around and she was surprised by how sad he looked. But it was just a flash and it was gone. He took her hand in his and leaned right up close to her, his eyes dancing again.

"Do you want to order porn?"

Her shout of laughter broke the tension and she swatted his hand away. "No!" He was pleased with himself. She didn't tell him she knew it was coming, that he'd try to distract them both with some outrageous statement. After all, it worked every time.

The sun was setting on the hillside. The tourists were

starting to come back down. You didn't want to be descending Arthur's Seat in the darkness. Even on a sunny day there were treacherous winds and the path could suddenly shift under your feet. No matter how well you knew the route, one step off the pathway and you could be totally lost.

"Tell me about your mission," she said as she got up to make another cup of tea. It was suddenly darker; he had closed the curtains. The room felt cosier, closer. He turned on the desk light and she thought of her sitting room at home. It felt cosy like this.

"You know the story, already."

"Yes, but I didn't know you had actually lived it."

He sighed heavily. "It was horrible. It is horrible. But I feel better knowing I'm doing something about it. If I can find the right medicines I can prevent a catastrophe. I just have to focus on that."

"Were you personally affected?"

"No. Just saw it on the news. They briefed me before I left, told me what to look for."

"Why you?"

"I entered a competition."

"You're joking!"

He laughed. "Seriously. I think they chose me because I'm single, no family. If I don't come back then it minimises the damage."

He was treating it so lightly, but he had left everything he knew behind for this mission, with no idea he could definitely get back. But she was here now. She could help with more than just unlocking the doors. He had a physicist on his side now.

It was pitch-black outside, and the tea was cold. She turned on the bedside light and picked up her rucksack. There was no point unpacking, but she needed her washbag and pyjamas, so she arranged them neatly on the pillow. Jack was doing the same, or rather dumping his out in an untidy pile. As she turned back from putting her suitcase out of the way she saw the two pyjamas lying there together. The way his had fallen they had an arm over hers. The bed suddenly looked really small.

He caught her look. "I'll sleep on the floor."

"No, seriously, its fine. I'm just being stupid. I slept next to my husband without any hanky-panky for two years. I can handle myself around you."

He laughed, as she intended, and pushed his pyjamas closer so the blue and grey flannel leg flopped over the front of her floral M&S monstrosities. "That's what you think." She threw a pillow at him.

She thought she would sleep like a log after the day she'd had. Her eyes were as heavy as rocks by the time she'd slipped under the duvet. But the enormity of what she was doing was making it difficult.

He was big in the bed. Not in a sexy way, but in the way of a man who is used to not being considerate of other people's space. Back home, ten years of marriage and her sharp elbow had trained her husband into sleeping compactly. And two years of estrangement meant that, as the space between them grew, their sleeping envelopes got smaller and smaller. But even perched on the edge of the mattress, with her back to the middle, arms tucked under her body, she still had Jack's knee digging into her back.

And he snored.

When she woke up the sun was shining through the crack in the curtains, right across her face. Her nose felt hot. She rolled onto her back, but the room was empty.

Her head was mercifully clearer and sharper than yesterday.

As she got showered and dressed she kept chanting over and over in her head: *this shower is in an alternative universe, this towel is in an alternative universe.* Maybe if she said it enough it would stick.

She heard the door go as she brushed her teeth. *This toothbrush is in an alternative universe.*

"Hello?"

"I'm in here."

"I brought breakfast."

Good, she was starving.

They sat in the chairs and watched a new ant line forming on the hillside.

"Better?" he asked.

"Better," she said. "I just have one question. Followed by about a hundred more."

"Shoot."

"How are you doing this? How do you know where to go?"

He pushed back his sleeve. She started to see the dark lines of his tattoo spreading up from his inner elbow. There were small shapes and lines scattered across his upper arm. Dark blue, black and purple. No curlicue tribal lines or snarling tigers here. This was organic, delicate, like stamens of baby's breath.

Her breath caught. He stepped forward and presented his forearm for examination.

Up close the little shapes were tiny fireworks, threads and flares of colour. It felt like each one was made of smaller versions of itself, like you could dive inside and reach an infinity of connections.

"That's a node map." She had seen things like this before. Maps of interference patterns. Interaction registers.

"That's my map. These are the doors," he said, pointing at a cluster of the circular nodes, all of them inked in black.

"Wait there." She walked over to her bag. After a short rummage she came back with a magnetometer. His arm was still extended so she plugged it in next to the desk and switched it to reverse polarity. She put the wand next to his arm.

Some of the black nodes turned blue.

"But that's incredible." She couldn't help herself, she leaned forward and grabbed his arm, pulling him closer so she could stare into the shapes. They were beautiful. Mesmerising. He ran a hand over his bicep, almost affectionately.

"That device, what did you do?" he asked. He rolled his sleeve back down and the beautiful tattoo was lost from view.

"It just measures polarity. I didn't do anything; it was just picking up on the magnetic fluctuations in the ink."

"When they turn blue they are active. That's how I know where to go."

"How many worlds have you been to?" she asked.

"Twenty-five so far, not counting the travelling. I had to do a lot of jumps to get far enough away from home to find new types of medicine then lots of jumps between each world to create enough difference."

"How will you find your way back home?"

"I've been tracking it. I'll have to retrace my steps although I did a fair bit of doubling back in the beginning until I got the hang of it. It was nerve-wracking at first, heading out into unknown worlds so I followed a pattern. Then I got stuck in your universe. I genuinely thought that was it for me."

He shuddered. Her home world had been a prison for him. She looked around the room imagining being stuck in this place forever. Like her home but not her home.

"You must have been terrified."

He shrugged it off. "Well, it had some compensations. Without that solar flare I would never have met you."

He was joking again, deflecting. He didn't like admitting how scared he had been. Same old Jack. He changed the subject and she let him. She was just along for the ride, after all.

When they finished breakfast he returned to the matter at hand.

"We'll start again later today," he said. "A burst of jumps to get us somewhere new."

She felt her stomach lurch a little - in anticipation, she hoped. "Ok. Maybe I'll react better this time."

"It's ok. We can take it slow. I owe you. We can go whatever pace you need."

She nodded but she really didn't want to slow him down.

Chapter Nine

J ack had showed her their route on the node map but her befuddled brain couldn't make sense of it. They were on, what, jump four or five of the day's allocation.

She slumped back in the scratchy train seat, resting her elbow on the window to cradle her head. Her stomach lurched as they left another station. The fog was invading every corner of her brain.

Jack was talking but the words sounded like gibberish. She caught the word dimensional - that was something she knew about. Or she used to. It hurt to try and remember.

Why was she reacting like this to the jumps? Jack was bright-eyed, chattering away opposite her, like nothing had happened. His smile was too bright.

She turned to stare out of the window. Jack's voice continued but she stopped trying to catch the words and just let them wash over her like mist.

The passing gardens blurred and merged. A swing stood out. A shed. Nothing important. The blur was restful, but she could feel her thoughts, somewhere in there, fighting to come out. Like half-heard voices. They merged with Jack's until the murmur shifted, became a drone, then melted into a dream.

A hand shook her awake.

"Come on, sleepyhead. We're almost there."

She peered out of the window. More gardens and stone-built houses. Had they even left Edinburgh?

"Where?" she managed past her sticky and swollen tongue.

"Newcastle." He nodded out of the window at an old mill building sliding by.

She pushed herself up to sitting, trying to bring some saliva back into her mouth. Jack slid a coffee cup across the mottled plastic table. She gratefully gulped it down, not caring that it was bitter and slightly too cold for comfort.

"You snored," said Jack, mischievously. "The whole carriage was agog. They'd never heard a sound like it."

Right enough two of the other passengers were looking across at them. She couldn't read their expressions. She sank further back into her seat under their stares.

Jack leaned forward and said, loudly, "Don't mind them, they just don't appreciate beautiful music."

"Jack!" she hissed, half horrified, her stomach curling into a tight ball. More people turned to look at them.

Jack burst out laughing and in return she felt the ball in her stomach unclench. She was suddenly immune to their judgement in his company. She laughed with him.

Jack hauled their bags down from the rack, grinning in delight at her reaction. He made space for her to stand and pass him and she walked the length of the carriage, her head held high. When she looked back he was holding their rucksacks aloft. He waited for her attention and then announced, "the maestro has left the building!" Irritated faces turned away, but she laughed at them.

The train slowed to a stop and they climbed down to the platform. A couple of people were still staring from behind the windows, so she waved at them, emboldened by Jack's presence. They turned away.

As they strode up the length of platform 3 and crossed over the bridge she felt all bubbly and warm. It wasn't until they stepped out into the dusky air that she stopped to wonder why they were in Newcastle.

"We're getting on a plane," said Jack.

"Why?"

"I need to go to Venice."

Her heart leapt. Venice!

He pulled up his sleeve in answer to her questioning look. "I read about a new drug trial. There're two sites. One is in Glasgow - I could probably sweet-talk someone into giving me a sample. Or we could go to the other one in Venice. I can sweet-talk just as well in Italian. So I figured, why not?"

Venice. Could she? Could they?

They were supposed to be in a hurry. Detours were not part of the plan. Shouldn't they be going the most direct route? There were people relying on them.

"But won't there be fewer doors there. Fewer instances where Alison and Jack go to Venice? Aren't we going into a dead end?"

"It's Venice, not Outer Mongolia. It's a two-hour flight, tops."

"But there's one in Glasgow too."

"Yes," he said with a look that spoke of anticipation. "But then we wouldn't get to go to Venice. Gondolas. Canals. Gelato!"

Venice.

"And," he continued. "We'd have to get the train back to Edinburgh and on to Glasgow anyway which is about the same time as a flight to Venice. It's quicker to go than to go back."

It wasn't her place to tell him where to go or how to get his samples. She was just a passenger at this point. But the uneasy feeling wouldn't shift. Wouldn't it be disrespectful? To Chris? They'd always said they would go together.

"I don't have my passport," she tried.

"You only need a picture ID; you have your driving license. And you look the same no matter what world we're in."

"We don't have the right clothes."

"We'll buy some."

Still, she hesitated.

"Alison, what's wrong with you? It's Venice! Haven't you always wanted to go?"

"Yes, of course." How did he know that? "It just feels a bit frivolous."

"Of course its frivolous. It's Venice!" He took both her shoulders in his hands and pulled her face close. Her heart thumped. "The reason you were so unhappy in your last life is that you always did the right thing. Experiment with this time you have. Do the wrong thing for a moment, while we're on this journey, before we get to where you are going, and you have to do the right thing for the rest of your life."

He had a point.

"I'm getting cold," he said into her indecisive silence. "Let's just get on the airport bus while you decide. If you decide against it then at least we can eat airport sushi before our bus ride back to the station."

Chapter Ten

I t was the morning after another day of multiple jumps. They were back in another Edinburgh, just as Jack had promised, and her brain was just starting to come back together. The buses in this Edinburgh were blue instead of burgundy. They set off the red sandstone of the buildings and the yellow post-boxes, the colours switched like they were seen through a filter. She had to keep blinking to stop herself feeling dizzy.

The memories of gondolas and gelati swirled around them, protecting them from the cold Scottish wind. Enough to be eating ice-cream in the park. It was everything she had ever dreamed it would be. The sunrise over the Lido was something she would never forget until the day she died. She should have felt guilty she had gone there with Jack instead of Chris but then she would have missed out on eating pizza in the shadow of the Bridge of Sighs. Or the tiny trattoria he knew of that made perfect spaghetti. He took her to Murano and bought her a rucksack beautifully crafted out of recycled leather.

He was the perfect travel companion and presented her, on

the second day, with a map of the perfect tour of churches and museums while he went to find the doctor for the antibiotics. He was even thoughtful about that.

How long had they been travelling now? A fortnight? Or was it a month? Every day or two was a new world, a new universe, sometimes three or four. She was getting used to the jumps now. She no longer felt like her skin was peeling off. But the strangeness always left her disorientated for a while. They limited it to five jumps a day.

Bacon rolls and carrot cake were the best at quashing the queasiness that followed. No coffee or fizzy drinks. And she would be bloated for hours afterwards no matter how much lemon water she drank. It wasn't the easy hop skip and a jump that she had been expecting.

But each stop over had something fascinating about it. The first few were fascinating because they just weren't that different. The next few started to get noticeable. Silly little things like post-boxes being a different colour. Adverts for British Caledonian, a long defunct airline she barely remembered having existed in her world. A different Prime Minister in the news. But everything else continued as normal. The people were the same. Seemed to be living the same kinds of lives, even if they sometimes preferred pet pigs to pet dogs.

The days when they jumped she was just a mess. By the end of the day she could barely stand. Jack would leave her slumped in some hotel while he went off to get drug samples. She would gulp back water like a fish but always felt parched. And then at the end of the next day they would be off again.

But somethings never seemed to change. Apparently, in every world they had travelled to, in everything they had seen,

Alisons always seemed to live in Edinburgh.

She shifted her new rucksack on her back. It was lighter than the old rucksack with her laptop, her notebooks, her trinkets. She'd lost it a while ago. But the photo album, her PhD certificate and her Hamburg mug had just weighed her down anyway. It was more sensible to travel light.

It was strange. When she had travelled around Eastern Europe with her friends there were three things she must not lose. Her wallet, her passport and her rail pass. Everything else was replaceable, literally disposable. You could attend a German rave in a crochet hat and sundress, walk miles down a beach in strappy sandals (even if you did get blisters the size of golf balls), meet your friend's dad in his posh business hotel in sweat stained combats, carrying an army surplus bag with badges sewn onto it, so long as your travellers cheques were tucked into your bra. Carrying a sensible wallet was just what you did.

But her wallet has turned out to contain useless pieces of plastic, their magnetic stripes containing information that just didn't fit. Perhaps at her final destination some of the things in it would come back into relevance. But here and now they held no sway at all.

Her phone however was the most useful thing she had ever owned. She could restore it from backup in each new world and pay for anything she liked with the new details and clever new payment technology. Had this been five years ago she would have had to beg borrow and steal like Jack used to. Thankfully for her morals that was no longer necessary. And now she had nudged him along the way Jack didn't have to either.

Jack was talking about his favourite topic, why on earth she was still married to Chris.

"There must be something you always wanted to say to him but never did."

She was amused. He seemed baffled that anyone would stick to their marriage vows through thick and thin. The single, unattached, carefree adventurer. Of course he didn't understand. "Why must there?"

"I get that you are all 'power-through, the-end-justifies-the-in-between suffering, I'll take one for the team'. But sometimes you must want to punch him."

"Of course."

Jack checked his watch. They had hours yet before yet another doctor's appointment. More antibiotics to add to the stash.

"So what would you say to him?"

"Nothing."

He turned her to face him. "Seriously. Imagine I'm him and just tell me what you'd tell him. You need to get it all out of your system before you get to your perfect world or you are still going to be holding on to it. How can your world be perfect then?"

He had a point. She scrunched he face in annoyance. Why was it he always made such good points? Her lack of response made him nod.

"So what would you say to him?"

"I'd tell him that I'm disappointed in him. That it's a shame that he couldn't follow through with his promises."

"That's it?"

She shifted uncomfortably. "What else is there to say?"

"Come on, close your eyes. Now take two long slow breaths. Imagine his face. He is standing right in front of you. What would you say?"

The park was empty. This was stupid. But there was no one to see her stupidity. She looked askance at Jack who nodded encouragement. So she closed her eyes and took a long deep breath. Chris' face swam in front of her eyes. The hangdog expression. What was there to say? Nothing. Because it's always better to say nothing.

But Jack was right. She had to get it out of her system. So she imagined him saying his favourite phrase, "I just don't understand what you want from me?" She felt her lips purse. Remembered that text message saying there was no Qatar contract. The sinking feeling, grasping at the flotsam and jetsam of her sinking life, and how his only response was that he needed her to help him feel better about it. Her hands started to tremble. She gripped them into fists.

"Chris," she started. Her voice was quiet and a little bit hoarse. She cleared her throat. "I feel like you let me down. You promised to fight just as hard as I did for our future and you didn't."

She paused. This was hard. She wasn't used to saying things like this outside of her own head.

"Go on." Jack's voice was gentle.

"I worked so hard to give you what you wanted. I gave up so much. And you just sat there. Or did stupid things. Or just complained.

"I wanted a future with you. I thought we would be together forever." She felt a dull ache in her chest begin to shift up her throat. "You chipped away at us until there was nothing left. You let it all go like it was nothing." Her throat was full and there were tears coming.

"All you had to do was get off your backside and try.

Anything. Sell something. Phone someone. Send an email. You didn't do anything. For what? For pride? Inertia? Some ridiculous sense of entitlement?

"You think you deserve everything. That you're due something. But you're not! No one is. You're not special." She was struggling to talk over the tears, but the words kept coming.

"You just carry on doing stupid things and expecting everything to fall into place for you. And when it doesn't I have to make it work. Do you know what I have had to do to make it work? I sold my flat for you and you never even said thank you.

"If you were single then fine, fuck your own life up if you want. But it's my life you are fucking up too. I end up holding back a dam of disaster and you keep shooting holes in it! What the fuck is wrong with you. I'm right in front of you, drowning. Don't you even care?

"Fuck you, Chris."

She took a deep breath and opened her eyes. Chris's face was still in front of her. Her blood ran cold. Chris was in front of her. No! She took a step back.

Yes, she was still in the park. Yes, it was still a cold clear day. She could still taste the ice-cream on her tongue.

He was crying.

"I'm so sorry. I never realised how much I was hurting you," he said.

How was he here? She looked around for Jack. Where was Jack?

"I didn't know you felt this way. I wish I had known. I would have done things differently. I think I finally understand why you are so angry."

"How are you here?" she managed. The wind dried the tears onto her face, leaving it sticky.

"Jack asked me to come." He pointed behind her to a tree some distance away. Jack was standing next to the trunk. He waved.

"Why?"

"He's trying to help. Don't be angry with him. He's a good friend." She snorted but he carried on. "I know things are hard. But we can get through this. The business will pick up. It's only been six months. I'll try harder. I love you, Ali. It's you and me against the world!"

Her brain unfroze. He didn't have a beard. His hair was longer. He was wearing plaid. Chris hated plaid.

This wasn't her Chris.

He had tears in his eyes. "I understand now that this is how you see things. No wonder you are angry, I wouldn't want to be with someone who behaves like that." He stepped forward and put his arms around her.

Something went click in her head. "Chris." She pushed him off.

"Yes?"

"Am I right in thinking your business still exists?"

He gave her a curious look. "Yes."

"So it's not bankrupt yet?"

He shifted his gaze away. "Um, no, it's -"

"Do you have offices on Dundas Street?"

"Yes." His gaze came back.

"And a PA?"

"Yes. What's going on?"

"How many contracts do you have?"

"There's a few I think might really…"

"Chris. You don't get an office and a secretary when you have no work. You don't go for lunches and pay for endless client entertainments while your panicked wife is sitting at home pawning her engagement ring to make ends meet."

His eyes filled with tears. He looked so shocked that she was talking to him this way. How could she be so cruel? How could she misunderstand him so badly? The love of his life, the woman he would do anything for. She remembered the thousand times he had said all of that to her and more.

This was the point where she always backed down, felt bad about hurting him, did something else for him to try and ease his suffering. This is the point where his pain was too much for her to take so she would do anything, everything to make it stop.

But this wasn't her world. This wasn't her Chris. She could say whatever she wanted to him. For his Alison's sake. "Go the fuck home, fire the secretary and do you own goddamn paperwork. Get off your lazy entitled arse and do something. You are capable of doing this properly, I know you are. So do it. Or I swear to god I'm going stick your stupid head up your stupid arse. And then I'm going to divorce you."

He had stopped crying and was gaping at her.

"Well, go on then."

Why was he just standing there?

"Do it!" she bellowed. He jumped, turned tail and ran. She watched him trot out of the park, plaid shirt-tails flapping. She felt full of fire and fury. Tingly. It felt good.

"Nice!"

She jumped. Jack.

"What the hell, Jack?" she barked.

"What, you needed to say it."

"Jack!"

He shrugged and looked irritated. Maybe he was expecting a medal. "You gave him the fright of his life. He's going to go home and pull himself together. Probably. Maybe he'll make a go of it. Maybe they'll be happy. You are only saying what you already know she is thinking."

"No, that's no excuse." But her fingers were still tingling, and she was just preventing herself from giving him a high five. She glared at him, instead. "Not good, Jack. This is interfering in other people's lives. From now on there is a ban on interfering. I want you to get us as far away from Edinburgh as you can."

"That's going to be harder. We're going to have to go the long way around."

"Fine. Do it. We're supposed to be just passing through, not leaving a trail of changes that might do who knows what."

"Ok. Fine. Jeez, I thought you'd be happy. I thought it would be good for you."

He turned and walked off across the park. She followed him but as her irritation subsided she noticed the trees were looking exceptionally beautiful here. Maybe the air quality was better. The colours were vibrant and lush, and the gentle breeze ruffled them in a playful fashion. She felt buzzy and a bit like skipping. He was right. It had helped. But Jack couldn't just keep doing things without discussing it with her, so she kept her face neutral.

Chapter Eleven

They were sitting on a beach watching the sun go down. The sunset was green and pink: it reminded her of pictures of the northern lights. It was all wrong, yet it was completely beautiful. The breeze was warm on her skin. The long yellow sand was empty, no sound except birds and the crashing of the waves.

"How far away are we from home?" she asked.

He was wearing a short-sleeved shirt, so his tattoo was clearly visible, but he pulled up the sleeve anyway and squinted at the top of his arm. "Long way," he said.

"I keep expecting to see a dragon or something."

"A dragon? What kind of physicist are you?"

She gave him a friendly shove with her elbow. "The kind that's sitting in an alternate universe many miles from home." The waves were getting nearer but from where they sat on top of a dune the beach was still vast and untouched. The tip of a piece of dune grass tickled her knee when the wind blew. As the dusk fell the temperature was starting to drop but the breeze was still warm. "Maybe aliens then," she said eventually.

He snorted. "I can't count the places I've been, and I've never yet met an alien."

"Any dragons?"

"Only the human female kind."

She raised an eyebrow at him, but he was already laughing at her reaction. "You're so easy to read, Dr Howden."

"I'm easy? Mate, I know everything there is to know about you."

He laughed again at that. "I don't think so."

"Oh, you think you are so inscrutable. The mysterious traveller from another place." He shrugged in acknowledgement and turned back to the view. The sun was on the horizon. The greens were shading into blue. The colours of his eyes. She studied them. Yup, the colour was exactly right.

The sun dipped below the horizon. It was getting colder and she shivered. He shrugged out of his coat and put it around her shoulders. He didn't mention it and neither did she. She just pulled it around her and let the smell of him seep into her pores.

"Ok, if you know me so well." He shifted in the sand until he was facing her and put a finger to each temple, staring her down. "What am I thinking about now?"

"Sex."

"Obviously."

"But that's just a distraction because you're also surprised how calm you feel sitting here with me." He dropped his fingers and looked at her curiously. "You travel all over the universes to save lives and you enjoy every second of it. You can make people fall at your feet purely by employing that ballistic charm. But I think you are bored." His smile was fading. Not so inscrutable now Mr Jack Shepherd. "You're lonely. I think you step into these worlds and see people in relationships, and you wonder why you've never had one. Deep down, I think, you wonder what is wrong with you."

He turned away and looked at the darkening horizon. "Psychology 101." He said and laughed lightly.

His face was in shadow now and she couldn't read the expression, but the sense of calm was gone. She thought about apologising. But she knew she was right.

She pulled her coat further around her to shut out the cold. They sat there until the stars came out. He was completely still.

"When I was young we moved around a lot," his voice came out of the darkness. She could barely see him now. "Every year a new school. Every summer we travelled. New friends. New experiences. Nothing ever stayed the same. It was amazing. I loved every second of it. Then we came 'home.'" The word was drenched in emotion but not the emotion she would normally associate with it. "Everything became the same. Every day, every month, every year. My parents couldn't handle it. They divorced. So I left. Carried on the journey. Like I said, Psychology 101. But I'm not lonely."

"Yes, you are."

He didn't reply to that. After a moment he reached out and took her hand. "Time to go, before we freeze to death."

He stood up and hauled her to her feet. They walked back to the boardwalk together in silence. The boardwalk lights fell on his face. He looked shell shocked.

"Hey," she said, catching his arm. "You Ok?"

By the time he came to face her his smile was back in place. "Of course I'm Ok. You can't get to me that easily Dr Howden."

"I wasn't trying to 'get to you', Jack."

His face softened. "I know." He looked at her for a long moment. "I've never in my whole life met anyone like you Dr Howden."

"Me too," she slipped her arm around his as they walked along the wooden path and laid her head against his shoulder. She wanted to make up for unsettling him. It was almost surprising how easy he was to read, for someone so adept at throwing people off the scent. The feeling of knowing someone better than they seemed to know themselves was a new one. A close one. It felt warm and cosy.

It was tempting to just keep on walking, but she felt him shiver slightly and realised how cold it had actually got. When she looked up his breath was condensing in the cold air. "Come on," she said. "Let's go inside."

Chapter Twelve

T his world was the nicest so far. An eco-friendly nirvana that they found at the end of a tiring seven jump day. The sky was a beautiful blue from morning to night. They had been there for two days and she hadn't seen a single cloud. And this was Norfolk. Or Northampton, she couldn't remember which. They ate bacon rolls from a diner overlooking the beach. There was no plastic cutlery or bottles. Everything was on draft. The sea was a beautiful blue and the beach pebbles gleamed. Maybe it was Newhaven they were in.

Jack was sleeping on the towel next to her, his breath a gentle swell in the warmth of the day. The beach was pretty empty, it was a Tuesday afternoon, but there were children playing somewhere over the tide barriers and an ice-cream van (electric of course) tinkled its way around the road behind her.

The extra time here was having a healing effect. Something about sitting on the beach watching the waves going in and out and listening to the lovely sucking noise the pebbles made her brain work again. The book she had in her lap had been chosen specifically for its lack of heavy thinking. Convalescent literature. At the familiar feel of her brain kicking into gear she put it aside and got out the half empty notebook and pen. She started with a comprehensive formula for everything she had understood so far.

But her calculations didn't seem to be working. Every time she tried to model this fractal pathway it just didn't match up. There was something missing. But then this wasn't entirely unfamiliar. If a theory of everything were easy it wouldn't take great minds like Einstein and Hawking to come up with it. She would start, like she always did, with the known knowns.

To travel to worlds they need to find a door where the other Alison and Jack were waiting on the other side, ready to swap. If one of them were dead or missing they couldn't swap. The universe wouldn't let either of the worlds end up unbalanced, she could understand that, even if she couldn't model it yet. How many worlds did they know each other in? Very few. And how many worlds could there be where she and a Jack were standing side by side near a door. Even fewer. Maybe they had to find a place where they happened to be in the same coffee shop, side by side, with no clue who the other was. So the pathway by necessity had to be zig zag.

A quick sketch of the route through the first few doors was easy. Each jump would create a slight but significant change in the world they ended up in. It seemed like a lot of worlds weren't accessible.

She looked across at the tattoo. The edge of it was just visible on the swell of Jack's arm. Not for the first time she was amazed how much it looked like a standard tribal sleeve that the average guy would get for no reason other than to look cool. Even looking closely it was hard to see the node and nodules, they were so small. And Jack was the only one who could read them. She would have to study it more closely in future. She was always so anxious about the jump and afraid of where they were going to end up that she forgot to examine it before and afterwards to see the minute changes that he charted. And by the end of a jump day there was no hope at all.

She picked up her phone and took a photo of it on a whim. After all she had to study the whole process if she was going to understand it. Jack wouldn't mind.

The newspaper lying next to him fluttered in the breeze. The headline was a scandal about a politician who had flown to Madrid for a meeting. The sky was blue because nobody flew. The outrage at someone squandering the earth's resources emanated from every line of the article. Here, everything tasted clean and healthy. The water from the tap was crystal clear and fresh as a daisy. The people looked healthy and tanned. It was impossibly perfect. She was glad to see a toddler throwing a tantrum down the beach to dispel the Stepford feeling.

When they had arrived here Jack convinced her to take a longer time out to recover. They stayed in a little guest house near the beach. Jack was getting used to her eclectic tastes, so it was cluttered and cosy. The bathroom had a little basket containing a doily swamped in mini shampoo bottles, sewing kits and mints. There were even tweezers and a shoe-shine brush. It was called the Shangri-something. This place was perfect. She had agreed to stay an extra couple of days, just to build up her strength.

That morning, day three, for the first time, her head had started to clear. She started being able to think again.

She started asking Jack more questions. *How do we know we are heading in the right direction? When we jump what happens to the mess we left behind? Why do we have to go such a long way around?*

That last one was the only one she really understood the answer to. The variables they were looking to manipulate were specific, he said. They could easily reach a place where those variables were one way if you didn't care if everything else was all to hell. The bees had vanished, for instance, or everyone still drank small beer. Or children had to start work at aged ten. Because everything was interconnected like a spider's web and each change changed everything else. To get to a place where everything was exactly the same except for one variable they had to go through the web to a point nearby but along a different strand. And getting to that strand required the long way around.

For not the first time she wished she had had the presence of mind to take better notes as they had gone on their jumps. She had started well, tracking each jump, each door, each world. It was the scientist in her, wanting to chart the route, note the variables. And a part of her probably wanted a way back, just in case. But then her notebook had gone missing. Maybe at the hotel when her head was spinning from lack of sleep because of the air raid. She had got another book and jotted down everything she could remember. But every time she started writing there seemed to be something else to do.

Her career had taught her many things, but the most valuable right now was, if you look at the whole universe all at once you will go hide under a table and never come out. The problem is too vast and intractable, but if you look at a single variable, data point or theory you can start to unpick the finer details.

Jack stirred. She went back to her models. The basic trip calculations were fine. And she could work out the differentials between the worlds themselves. That was a simple matter to chart as well. What she couldn't figure out was the interaction between the two. Why this direction, why these doors? Was there a shorter way? Jack couldn't help her with the maths. She wished she had her laptop here. A quick simulation or two and she'd have it, no bother. It really wasn't that hard. What was she doing wrong?

Now, to think of it, why didn't they just go and get the laptop? Their journey seemed to be taking them further and further south. In fact any further south and they'd be in the Channel. Yes, definitely Newhaven, then. The other Alison was here when they had swapped with her. Maybe she lived here. Maybe she was visiting. Either way she would have a laptop. Perhaps they could map a simpler path. She'd bring it up over dinner. A few more days in this pleasant little world wouldn't do them any harm and they could shave weeks off the journey.

They were sitting in their bedroom at the B&B when she brought it up. Jack, fresh from a shower was doing up his shirt. He looked relaxed so it felt like the right time.

"I was thinking, we should see if we can find out where this Alison lives."

He glanced up. "Why?"

"If she's anything like me there's a programme on her laptop I'd like to use."

"What for?"

"I think I can help us chart a route."

His hands went still on the buttons. She tapped the lipstick on the tabletop but stopped under the weight of his stare.

"What's wrong with the route that we're taking?"

"Nothing. It's great. This place is especially great. I'm glad you brought me here. I just want to get involved. You know, scientist." She shrugged and laughed. His smile was unreadable. He went back to buttoning up his shirt.

"I just want to have a go at mapping all this," she went on into the silence. "My whole career was based on hypothesising this was possible and now it is. My scientist brain wants to get it all down on paper. Pin it to the table with maths." She tapped the lipstick again for emphasis. "No one has ever mapped this all out. It's the opportunity of a lifetime."

The back of his head nodded. "I get that. But what happened to not getting involved with the lives of these Alisons? What happened to treading softly?"

He was right. She had said that.

"Alison I don't want you to do something we can't undo. Or something that goes against your morals." He sat down next to her on the bed. "Your whole philosophy around all this was to stay away."

"Yes, I know. But I can't do that entirely can I? I'm already using her money, using her phone account. I've been here three days, she's somewhere else, that's already messing with her life. What harm could we do, poking about a bit?"

"It's a slippery slope."

She stood up suddenly. "I'm travelling the length of the multiverse and I haven't got a single piece of usable data from it at all. I'm basically luggage."

"Why don't we move on, get going. Do this in another world?"

101

She thought of the photo in her phone of his tattoo. In the next world it would be gone. But she was reluctant to mention it. She hadn't asked permission after all. "No. I need to do this Jack. Otherwise this is all just a selfish little girl running away from home. I've lost my notebooks, I've barely paid attention at all. In the next jump my brain will be mush again. I just need five minutes with the laptop and your tattoo and then we can go wherever you say."

He sighed, rolling his sleeves down and buttoning them.

"Ok, how are we going to find her?"

"I'll reinstall Facebook, or whatever they use here. See where she was last checked in."

Jack pulled on his coat. "Let's do it over dinner. I'm starving."

There was no Facebook but there was something called IseeU. According to the description in the Store it was roughly the same idea. The name felt a little creepy, but she opened it up anyway. She logged in with her fingerprint and watched it load.

Jack was sitting across the table, eating a chicken salad. There were no hamburgers in this world, too environmentally unfriendly she supposed, and everywhere was very whole foods so he was eating healthily yet again. He didn't look pleased which made her smile. He was like a toddler some-times.

When the app loaded there were tabs called IseeU lately, IseeU later and IseeU now. She clicked on lately and looked down the list. Last log on three days ago, Newhaven, a place called the Home from Home Hotel. Success. She grabbed another fork of tabbouleh and opened the maps. It was about

3 miles away. Perfect.

She filled Jack in on the plan. She would say she had forgotten her room key, had been staying out a few nights, brought the fellow back, nudge nudge, what a party, she'd pay for the replacement obviously.

As it turned out they didn't need to explain. The hotel receptionist handed over another key without a second thought. Jack was still being quiet, but she could bring him round later. Right now her fingers were tingling in anticipation of all that potential data.

The laptop was charging on top of a fancy leather-topped desk. If this place was a home from home then Alison was clearly doing well for herself. She flicked up the lid and switched it on. At the password screen she hedged her bets and went for the one she used at home.

Bingo.

When she got to her perfect world the first thing she was going to do was change every password she had. She was embarrassed how easy it was to break into her most private spaces.

Jack was stalking around the room opening drawers. He held up a hairbrush. "Oh look," he said. "A vital clue to your doppelgänger. Do you want to use it?"

She rolled her eyes. He was being tiresome. "Why don't you make yourself useful and go and get us some coffees. I saw a Costa machine in reception."

"Fine." He glanced at the laptop as he walked to the door. "How long do you think you'll be?"

She thought back to that day in the car park. Then she had been the grumpy passenger being sent to get coffee. She smiled at him fondly. "It won't be long," she promised.

The laptop had finally loaded as the door clicked shut behind him. She scanned the programmes and saw the same SDS software that she used at home.

The algorithm in her notebook was quick to put in and she started to calculate the parameters. She got out the photograph of Jack's tattoo and started entering the relative points of the nodules. It was a painfully slow process. There must be a better way.

Ten minutes later she had built a model. She bluetoothed the photo to the laptop and uploaded it to the programme. Instantly it started mapping all the nodules for her. It was only a partial model, the photograph didn't have every part of the tattoo in it, but hundreds of points were being loaded in one by one. Enough to build a basic testable model.

She sat back and watched the numbers run. This was familiar too. Restful. Meditative.

Her phone bleeped. She looked down. She had logged out of the IseeU app, hadn't she? No, it was uploading something. She picked it up to hit airplane mode when it rang. Her eyes registered Chris' name and picture but her panicked brain didn't have time to react. Her finger had already landed on the screen where the airplane mode button had been and where it now said "answer." His image popped up on the screen.

Fuck.

"Alison! Oh my god!"

Fuck. "Chris, hi!" She went for nonchalant.

"Where the hell have you been? I've been worried sick. Are you ok?"

"I'm fine!"

He looked pale. His brow was furrowed. She felt a familiar wave of guilt at seeing Chris needy and panicked. But this was not the real Chris. She had to get off the line.

"You don't look fine, Ali. I mean what the hell. You said you needed space but vanishing off the face of the planet is a bit extreme. Everyone's been worried sick."

There was a strange moment where the world swam and she had a sudden, crazy, thought that this had all been a dream. "I'm...sorry?"

"Sorry isn't going to cut it, Ali. I'm coming to see you."

"What? No! Wait, where are you?"

"I'm in Newhaven. I came to find you."

Fuck.

"I'm coming to the hotel right now."

"Wait! No, don't!"

The door opened behind her. She dropped the phone and swung around in horror, expecting Chris to be in the doorway. But it was Jack holding two coffees and a newspaper. She held up a frantic hand to shush him and dove for the phone, kicking it under the table in the process. Jack strode into the room, placed the coffees on the table and waved the crossword section of the paper at her. "I thought we could pass the time with something a little more entertaining."

Oh god.

"Who the hell is that?" said Chris' voice from the floor.

Fuck

"Who are you there with, Alison?"

Jack's expression said it all. She scrabbled for the phone which had thankfully ended up face down.

"Nobody!" she yelled at it.

"Who is he? I'm going to fucking kill him!"

She swallowed her nervous giggle. "It's no one! It's the TV." That worked in films.

105

"I'm going to be there in two minutes and I'm going to fucking kill you, pal."

Alison's hand finally found the phone. She gestured at Jack who instantly dropped to the floor behind the bed.

"Look!" she practically shouted at Chris. "There's no one there. Don't come to the hotel. I'll come and find you."

"I can see the coffee cups, Ali."

Fuck.

"Right, fine, gotta go, bye!" She stabbed the red button.

Jack's head appeared over the bedding. "Time to go?"

"Yup. Where?"

He held out a hand to her. "Not far."

They sprinted down the street giggling like children, still holding hands. As they reached the second corner she pulled him to a stop, gasping for breath. The street was clear of angry doppelgängers. It looked peaceful and strange with the lack of cars but the people passing by were smiling. Was it always glorious here?

"We need to head back and get our stuff," he said. Jack's face was lit up from the exertion, or the game of it all, who knew? And her own ragged breathing was tinged with a smile too. She couldn't remember the last time she had laughed that hard. "It's just one jump and then we're safe. We don't need to go any further than that. Then we should celebrate your scientific progress."

Then she remembered she had left the notebook. Next to her laptop. The laptop still running her simulation.

Chapter Thirteen

"Are you sure about this?" he said.

Jack was facing her through sleeting rain. They were standing in a field, the tall soggy grass clinging to her boots like glitter. Her coat was already starting to soak through.

"Come on, it'll be fun," she said. It was a doctor's appointment. How hard could it be? He'd been reticent at first but backed down when she insisted, when she made him understand how tired she was of being just a passenger.

Jack was still looking pensive. His satchel was slung over his shoulder as usual but this time his hand was resting on it protectively.

They walked together to a point near the middle of the field. She could see the slight haze of the door as they approached. You had to know what you were looking for. You had to dismiss your mind telling you it was spots on your contact lenses or a trick of the light.

As they stepped through the door her world lurched. Her skin seared and her stomach turned over in a huge lump. Her vision swam. She took a long slow breath, as quietly as she was able. Jack was looking at her, gauging her reaction, probably. She smiled at him through the echoes of the flash of pain. The nausea rose in her throat as usual. He didn't look reassured.

She set her jaw and strode forward. It wasn't raining here. The air smelled of mown grass and honey. This field was mown short and her strides moved her quickly towards the hedgerow edging, leaving little clumps of damp grass from the old world behind. Walking helped her stomach settle. By the time she reached the edge and turned back to find Jack just behind her she was feeling just fine.

"Ok?" he asked.

Her nod was genuine this time.

"Ok, then," he said. She felt a glow of pride, she was getting better at this. "But it's that way." He pointed to the other side of the field where a gate was sitting open. She glared at him, but he just laughed. "Come on."

They took the tractor tracks around the edge of the field to save Jack's shoes. His oxford brogues hadn't enjoyed the damp of the last world or the walk across the soft earth of this one. It was going to be a fair walk into the small market town where they were catching a bus into Glasgow.

She was going to play his wife accompanying him into his appointment at the GP. They were a couple on holiday from the USA which would explain their lack of medical records. He had fake insurance paperwork already prepared just in case. Apparently he rarely needed it as the doctors were either happy enough to prescribe whatever he needed or would just refuse point blank.

She felt like a spy heading behind enemy lines. But a small lie would potentially save the lives of millions of people back at Jack's home. She hoped her US accent would pass.

The town loomed in the distance. It was cold but bright. The fluffy clouds chased each other across the sky. Jack was walking next to her on the tarmac road, looking relaxed. Clearly this was just another day and another mission to him, just another trip.

What strange twist of fate had brought him to her universe, to her life. A solar flare the only thing which made the difference between her staying in her old life and this adventure. In her other life she would be opening brown overdue envelopes and trying not to scream. Instead, they had gone to Venice, eaten ice-cream bundled in blankets on a gondola ride, like something from a travel brochure. She could still feel the wind from their vaporetti rides from the Lido to St Mark's Square every day, waving at the water buses as they sped by.

The bus stop came into view. The country rode ended abruptly at a modern housing estate, the rambling wildness of the verge cut short by manicured lawns and privet-edged pathways. One even had an American style letter box on the lawn. If she stood at the bus stop with her back to the road she wasn't in Scotland at all. She turned back to face the tumbled hedgerows.

Jack was checking the bus times on the board. "Ten minutes," he said.

She nodded. Now that they had stopped walking the wind felt brisker. It whipped around her ankles and pulled the warmth from her damp coat. She stamped her feet and rubbed her arms. Jack immediately started taking off his coat.

"No, I'm fine. Thank you," she said, and started pulling it back up his arm. "I'm just adjusting." He was so sweet.

He looked dubious but shrugged his coat back onto his

shoulders.

"Are you ok with the plan?" he asked.

"I'm fine. Just need to get a good American accent going."

"You surely do, ma'am," he drawled in the worst Texan accent she had ever heard. Oh dear god.

"Yes, ma'am," he said, tucking his thumbs into the loops of his jeans and notching a hip. "This surely is the purtiest little slice of the world I ever did see." He started a shambling cowboy walk around in a circle, nodding to imaginary townsfolk.

She burst out laughing.

He mimed tipping his hat and she fluttered an imaginary fan in return. "I do declare," she trilled. Then she couldn't think of what came next.

He had moseyed the full circle and leaned in, his voice suddenly high. "After all, tomorrow is another day." He batted his eyelashes at her. She couldn't breathe for laughing.

A rumbling sound made them both look around. The bus was rounding the corner. They both straightened up.

"I guess this is us," he said, in a perfect New York twang. It was flawless. Maybe she'd just be monosyllabic at the surgery instead.

The bus pulled up and he bought them both tickets with exact change. Prepared as always.

They settled into the blue and red patterned seats as the bus drew away. The modern housing estate soon dropped away, giving up space to sandstone houses and rows of shops. The speed of the change was in sharp contrast to their long walk.

Jack was still smiling faintly, probably at her terrible Scarlett O'Hara impression. It was cosy, pressed together on the slightly too small seats, feeling flashes of sunlight on the side of her face.

The bus trundled on out of the small town and it was impossibly soon that the industrial ring around Glasgow hove into view. Thirty years she had lived in Edinburgh and Glasgow, only forty miles away, was still a mystery to her. An industrial city of factories, imposing red sandstone tenements and huge neoclassical office buildings, making the city centre look like a congregation of banks. The bus trundled on through the grid system. They could have been in Liverpool, or New York. She had been less than a dozen times and she always got lost.

The bus station was busy and noisy. Jack had the map of Glasgow in his hand as they made their way out to the exit, held aloft like a prize - like an American tourist would. As he led her out of the station his gait changed. His shoulders went back, his stride increased. He radiated confidence, assurance.

She scurried along beside him. Was she supposed to be playing her role too? How did an American walk? She tried adjusting her feet.

Jack's voice made her look up. "Hey, careful, keep up." His accent was spot on.

"Sorry," she murmured.

"That reminds me. If we get separated, meet back at the bus station, ok?"

She nodded and tried to match his broad, American strides. When they were ensconced in the waiting room of the doctor's surgery, empty except for them, he relaxed back into himself. His arrogant expression softened, and he reached across and squeezed her hand. She squeezed it back, enjoying it's familiar, reassuring strength. She didn't speak as they waited, worried in case her terrible attempt at an accent might give them away.

All these weeks and she had never seen him do this. She would just sit in a hotel room waiting for him to come back. He was literally saving the world one visit at a time and, before now, she had done nothing to help. He was probably going to be smooth and unruffled throughout the whole thing. A practiced charmer at work. Like James Bond.

The receptionist came in and ushered them into the corridor. Jack was immediately taller and brash again. He nodded imperiously as the receptionist told them to use the third door on the right.

Jack led the way, opening the door onto a small, grey room containing a desk and three chairs. And a harassed-looking GP.

"Come in," the doctor said, and waved her hand at the two empty chairs. "How can I help you today?"

They settled into the padded wooden chairs and Jack began.

"We're here on vacation and I've fallen ill," he said in a beautifully cultured New York accent, two notches up from what the receptionist had got. She nodded helpfully.

"What seems to be the problem?" asked the GP.

"I have stomach flu. Both ends, if you catch my drift."

Alison went rigid. In all their planning they had never discussed what the fake illness was going to be. The doctor was nodding, and Jack was still as relaxed as before. What was he doing?

"How long has this been going on?" asked the GP, sitting forward in a professionally interested way.

"Since yesterday," Jack said. Alison wondered if she should kick him. No doctor was going to prescribe antibiotics for what was clearly viral gastro-enteritis.

Should she interrupt? Nudge him? But he had done this hundreds of times before. Surely he knew what he was doing. She had to trust him.

The doctor asked a few more questions then sat back. Her expression spoke volumes.

"Well, Mr Peters, I'm afraid there is not a lot I can do for you. It sounds like a nasty bout of gastroenteritis. A couple of days of rest is all it needs. Keep drinking plenty of water and something to keep your electrolytes up. Chicken soup is good."

"No," said Jack. "I am here for some antibiotics."

"I'm afraid antibiotics won't help. This is a viral illness and will get better in a few days. You're welcome to come back again in 7-10 days if things haven't improved."

"No," said Jack. He was looking flustered. His accent was sounding strained. "I am here for you to give me antibiotics. I have insurance. My doctor would give it to me."

"I'm afraid we don't do things that way here, Mr Peters." The doctor's polite tones were sounding more strained. "Taking antibiotics when they are unnecessary is unwise and leads to antibiotic resistance in the population. We're very careful about how we prescribe them these days."

Thankfully, Jack didn't reply. He was looking furious but defeated. What were they going to do now? Why had he chosen that illness? They had to change direction, or the antibiotics would be lost.

The GP had made a note on her computer and turned back to them. Her expression was cold. "Is there anything else?"

Alison had a sudden idea. She leaned forward, praying her accent would come out ok. "I'm sorry doctor," she said. Ok, it was coming out mildly southern but not a pastiche. "I need to apologise for this situation." Jack turned to look at her, his frustrated expression turning into one of surprise. She plunged on. "My husband is very kindly covering for me."

The GP was looking interested now. She pointedly turned on her chair away from Jack and leaned in, perhaps because of Alison's low tone. She didn't dare speak any louder in case her accent slipped. Besides it suited what she was about to say. "I have a woman's problem and my husband was trying to save my blushes." Jack looked astounded. She ignored him.

The GP nodded as if this was entirely normal and she plunged on "I have what I think is a urinary tract infection. It is burning and sore when I go. I've had one before. I recognise the feeling."

The GP nodded and went back to her computer. She typed out a prescription and printed it out with no further discussion.

As she handed it over, with a list of instructions, Alison nodded gratefully, keeping her hand in Jack's the whole time. She thanked the doctor and they stood up to go. The GP seemed warmer but just in case she said, "I'm sorry again for the deception. I just get so embarrassed to talk about such things. And my husband was kind enough to cover for me." She slipped her arm around Jack's waist and gave him her most grateful, sunniest smile. In return, his expression was warm. He put his arm around her shoulders and pulled her close. They ended up standing there, in front of the doctor, grinning at each other like teenagers.

They left the room arm in arm. It wasn't until they were on the street and down the road that Jack let her go and spun her around.

114

"You were amazing!" he said.

She beamed at him. Should she ask about what on earth he had been trying?

"You totally saved the day." He wrapped her up in a bear hug and swung her around on her feet. When he set her back down again he kissed her on the cheek. She felt herself blush.

"Come on," he said. "Let's find a pharmacy and get out of here."

They went down the street hand in hand all the way to the nearest Boots, looking in the windows they passed like the perfect married couple. It had been fun. Being his wife. The pharmacy counter was at the back and they were soon waiting in line for the prescription to be filled, triumphant.

A simple signature and they'd be done. Back to Edinburgh, through another door, one step closer. Such a simple thing to save a world, all those people, from destruction. She felt like Indiana Jones.

"Alison?" The voice made her spin around. Simon. Standing ten feet away in the deodorant aisle.

"Simon!" She dropped Jack's hand and took a smart step forward. "What are you doing here?"

"Shopping with Sue. Who's that?"

Without looking back, her heart thumping, she walked straight towards him and looped her arm into his drawing him away down the aisle. "No one. A friend from back home. Where's Sue? Do you have time for lunch?"

Simon was looking back over her shoulder towards Jack but her determined step kept him off balance and he was drawn along with her.

"I… I don't know. I'd have to check with Sue."

"Great! Let's go find her!" She kept pulling. They were

nearly at the front door.

"But your friend —"said poor Simon.

She looked back. Jack was shaking his head, coming after them, gesturing for her to come back. What was he doing? She pulled Simon faster onwards.

"It's fine," she said. "I'll come back and get him in a minute."

They were nearly out of the shop. And then she saw, straight in front of her, a shimmer in the air, like spots on her contact lenses. *No*.

But she was going too fast to stop.

She only just had time to look over her shoulder and see Jack's horrified expression. He was too far away. There was nothing he could do. She was already in the doorway and was pulled almost off her feet by the lurch as she left that universe and was flung into a new one - away from Jack and with no way back.

Chapter Fourteen

She stumbled as they emerged through the door, her stomach twisting and lurching. Simon's arm was the only thing holding her upright. She fought against the pain and nausea.

They were out in the cold street; the door must have lined up exactly with the exit of the shop. She turned to look back. Inside the shop there were three customers. None of them were Jack. Her knees buckled and she sagged forward. Simon caught her. He was looking at her strangely. How was he still upright? In fact, he looked fine. How was he fine?

"Hey," Simon said. "What's wrong?"

This couldn't be happening. She shook him off and pressed her hands against the plate glass of the shop window. It bit like ice. She let her head drop against it, willing the scene inside to be different. Willing Jack's mop of black hair to be at the counter.

Simon was behind her, plucking at her shoulder.

"Alison?" Sue appeared next to her. Thankfully, Simon stopped fussing at her. The two of them went off and muttered to each other. If they would just shut up she could think. She closed her eyes and fought the urge to just curl into a ball.

The bus station. Of course, they were supposed to meet at the bus station if one of them got lost.

"Simon," she said. He looked around. "Where is the bus station?"

Sue stepped forward and tried to say something. But it wasn't directions to the bus station, so she interrupted quickly. "Do you know? Where is it?"

They were both staring at her. Useless. She set off down the hill. Not caring if Sue and Simon were still following her.

At the bottom of the hill was a junction. The bus station had been at the top of a hill. She stared at each road in turn. They all looked the same. Every single one was a hill, going up. How was that physically possible?

Simon pulled at her elbow. She rounded on him. "Where is it?" Her voice came out shrill.

"If we take you there, will you calm down?"

"Yes!"

He led the way, finally. It took forever to get there. When the station finally appeared she couldn't wait. She ran.

The concourse was still busy, still noisy. She scanned the crowd, but he wasn't there. Maybe he was looking for her. She climbed onto the bench behind her. Good, now he could see her.

But he didn't appear. She waited for his shout, for him to come running in. A driver appeared next to her and told her to get down. Then Simon and Sue made her get off the bench. They tried to make her sit, tried to talk to her, but she stayed standing up so he could see her. When he came for her.

Minutes passed. Then other minutes. Buses left. Other

ones arrived. He didn't come. Why didn't he come?

A coldness settled over her where there had been heat. She found herself sitting on the bench. Sue was next to her.

"He's not here," she said to Sue.

"Who? Chris?"

Simon pulled Sue up and muttered something else she didn't hear. Sue sat down again but didn't put her arm back around her. Fair enough.

Where was Jack now? Why hadn't he come?

But then it hit her. He could be in this very bus station. He could be on this bench. But he was unreachable.

Why hadn't he bought an Alison with him to the bus station so they could swap? Why couldn't he find a door? What was going on that he wasn't there?

"Alison, can we take you home?" said Sue gently. She was looking at her like she was mad.

"I can't go home," she said, but Sue didn't understand.

Then they were in a car, heading back to Edinburgh. She sat in the back, in the darkness, trying to think of what to do. She thought back to her statistical model back in the hotel. Plotting backwards had been so simple. Now instead she had to consider every possible permutation. Every possible connection between every possible world and every other one.

She lived in Scotland, in Edinburgh. So going back there opened an infinity of possible doors - every time she got near one of those other selves. How to find a door in that multitude when each door could be to anywhere?

How did Jack do it? How did he know which way to go? And even if he knew, for all she knew this was a world which he couldn't get to. What if the Jack in this place lived in Dubai?

119

Or was dead? He might not ever be able to travel here.

Should she look for a way back? But with no map and no guide she'd be blundering around. Every jump might send her further and further away.

Should she stay still? But even staying still carried a risk of blundering through another door. Did the doors move or just wait to be walked through? Hurtling along at 80mph was probably worse.

She needed to get away from any place she might normally go. When you're lost you stay still and let the person in charge find you, right? She was getting further and further away from where she had last seen him and straight into danger.

She stared out at the darkness. Maybe she'd get the bus back again tonight after Sue and Simon left her.

A flash of colour in the dark made her jump. She recognised the sign for Harthill Services.

"Simon, I need the loo," she said abruptly.

"Uh, now?"

"Yes. Now."

Sue turned around to look at her, her head a dark shape in the light of the oncoming traffic. She tried to smile at Sue reassuringly. Tried to look sane.

Simon thankfully started pulling over into the slow lane as they neared the services. She kept a calm and neutral expression as they pulled up. She would go out the back door. Go cross country to Bathgate and get the bus from there. It was, what, ten miles? She had never done the walk before. At night, in the cold, no other Alison would be mad enough to be out there - surely that would be safe enough.

They pulled up and she got out. Sue, to her annoyance, got out with her. She couldn't think of a reason to make he get back in the car so just smiled and set off, Sue close on her heels.

As they walked to the back of the services she clocked the back door, out into the lorry park. It was next to the door of the ladies. Easy access.

The bathroom was small, only two cubicles. One was taken. She went into the free one. Sue leaned against the wall.

She sat on the loo, ready to go as soon as the other cubicle became empty. The terrain between the services and Bathgate was scrubland, fells with sheep and wind turbines. It was cold but if she kept moving she would be fine.

The other cubicle door clicked, and someone left. She tensed, waiting for the lock to click again. She heard the taps go and the rumble of hand towels from the holder. But no click of the lock.

"You alright, Sue?"

"Fine, just waiting for you."

Shit.

"I'm fine. I'll see you in the car."

"I'm fine. I'll wait."

Shit. "Sue, honestly. Are you honestly just going to hover out there?"

There was silence. "Fine."

The door closed and the lock clicked. Finally. She waited until she could hear a trickle of pee and then opened her own door.

"See you at the car," she said loudly and headed for the exit.

"No. Wait for me!" cried Sue.

She ran out of the back door out into the lorry park. A few strides took her across the tarmac, onto the verge and into the brush.

The lights of the services were bright behind her as she pushed through the undergrowth into the deeper trees. The ground sank under her feet and a wash of cold flooded into her shoes. Whips of pine slashed her face with icy drops of water.

She marched, determined, into the darkness. Pricks of shrubby pain peppered her unseen hands as she stumbled.

Step after step and then she was out of the trees onto a hillside. Behind her the services had disappeared into the wood. She could hear the roar of the motorway traffic, but it was dulled, like an aeroplane flying high above. The noise swelled around her, from all directions at once.

The stars were bright. If she could navigate by them she could make for Bathgate across the hills. Shame she had no idea how to navigate using stars.

She picked a direction at random, one that was away from the wood, and started off. Her feet were cold and squished as she walked. It felt like heather underfoot, springy and tough. The darkness was starting to ease but the ground was just blackness.

The stars were brightening. Little pin pricks of light piercing the endless sky. They stretched from horizon to horizon. The sky seemed to grow as she looked at it. A balloon of emptiness. She became small as she took in the vastness. A tiny morsel of life in all that space. Unimportant. Lost. Alone.

What the hell was she doing? If she died out here no one would find her. She had wanted to get lost, to be free, and now she was. She was free of everything. Untethered to anyone in this entire universe. A piece of film flapping loose. Not even Jack could find her here. This was madness.

She had to go back to the services. Just go home to Edinburgh. At least she could be warm and dry.

She turned and headed back down the hill. Gorse tore at her trousers. Had there been gorse before?

The roar of the motorway grew louder, but the lights were gone. She stumbled on, heading for the sound.

It was just a trick of her senses. She was just a few hundred metres from the services. Not a significant distance in the big scheme of things. But the hill seemed to stretch on endlessly.

This was the way. It had to be.

She got out her phone to use the torch. It had no signal. Of course there was no signal. This was the middle of nowhere. Simultaneously inches from civilisation and completely in the wild. Jack would never have been able to find her even if he were in this universe. She was sending herself out into the wilderness because she was stupid and not thinking straight.

Statistically there was no hope at all of Jack finding the right world. It was impossible. She was going to be stuck here forever and she didn't even know what kind of world it was.

She wrapped her arms around herself to try and slow the chatter of her teeth. Her feet weren't cold anymore because they were completely numb. Her breath puffed in front of her face, leeching warmth from her body.

Where were the services? At least they had been warm. At least Sue and Simon had been kind even if she didn't know them from Adam. And now she had lost that too. She had no one to blame but herself. Why hadn't she listened to Jack and stayed put in the cosy hotel instead of making him bring her. She'd ruined everything.

Eventually he would have to stop looking. Go on with his

mission. She was just some idiot along for the ride. It served her right. Now she was going to die on some cold and lonely hillside.

What was that? A faint cry over the rumble of the road. Sue?

A burst of energy drove her forward, but she stumbled and fell, her knees and hands landing in a shock of ice-cold sticky something. The light went out. The darkness was even darker than before.

Her phone. Her phone had been plunged into the ice-cold water. She hauled it out and shook it, jabbed at the buttons, but the screen didn't respond.

Not her phone. The only thing she had kept for every jump, every world. The death of her phone felt like the end.

There. The noise again. She pushed herself up on her knees, up to her ankles in mud. She stumbled up another hill and as she crested it, bright lights stung her eyes. A shape a hundred yards away, standing in front of a glow of lights, backlit like an alien spacecraft. Sue. She stumbled towards her. She was saved.

A sudden noise off in the darkness to her right made her flinch and then hands were grasping her.

She cried out, struggled.

"Alison, stop."

She knew the voice instantly. "Jack?"

"Come with me." His strong hands pulled her after him. Away from Sue and the lights of the service station.

"Jack?"

"Yes, it's me. There's a door right over here. Come on."

He hitched an arm around her waist and practically carried her. There was a lurch and the familiar feel of a door, leaving her retching and shivering with tension on the other side.

"Come on," he urged her forwards and she let him guide her. He was here. Somehow, magically he was here. She clung to his arm. As they came nearer to the station the glow of the forecourt lights fell across his face. His hands were warm.

They emerged onto the tarmac. She felt solid ground under her feet again. He led her to a car and propped her up against it. She wondered briefly whose car it was.

How had he managed it? An infinite number of worlds and he had found her.

He pulled a blanket out from the back of the car and wrapped her in it. It was scratchy and wonderful. She allowed herself to be sat in the car and watched him pull her muddy, ruined shoes off her feet. His hands burned with heat as he rubbed some warmth back into them.

Only when they started to lose their waxy sheen did he put new warm socks on her and the finally look up into her face.

"Are you ok?" was the first thing he said. She didn't deserve such kindness.

"I'm sorry," she tried to say but it came out in a garbled whisper. Her throat was rapidly closing, and hot tears warmed her face.

"It's ok. You're ok," he said kindly.

All she could do was nod.

He strapped her into the seat and gently closed the door on her, walking around to the other side. When he climbed in he put the heater on full and angled all the blowers at her. He looked cold too, but she couldn't protest. The hot air felt so good.

He started up the car and set off. In between changing gears he put his hand on her knees, over the blanket even that little tether brought tears of gratitude to her eyes.

She was safe. She was ok. But her stupidity and carelessness had nearly ruined everything. From now on she would always do exactly what he said.

Chapter Fifteen

They were strolling along another beach. Seagulls swooped overhead, looking for the chance to steal chips off the people on the beach. A wind kept the strength of the sun playful and light. The air smelled of sea-salt and the faint tang of sewage outflow pipe.

Jack had bought them an ice-cream. Hers had melted. The sugar cone was squashy in her hand. She knew she ought to eat it, but it didn't tempt her anymore. She was being ungrateful. For the ice-cream, for everything. So she carried it along with her. Any moment now the bottom would soak through and ice-cream would end up on her shoes.

She glanced across at Jack. His eyes were half closed. He was basking in the sunshine.

But she just had to ask. "How long do you think we will be here?"

Jack stopped walking and looked at her.

He eyed the ice-cream. "Not in the mood for Mr Whippy? There's a cafe a bit further down."

She stared at her ice-cream. She cast about for a bin but there was nothing nearby.

Jack was grinning at her. He took the cone gently out of her hand and tipped it wholesale into his mouth, squashy cone and all.

"Better?" He mumbled through the sludge. She smiled and slapped him on the arm. He was such a loon. They started walking again along the almost empty promenade. Not many people out on this unseasonably hot day but then it was a weekday and normal people had jobs to go to.

Jack was still licking at his ice-cream which somehow had stayed immaculately frozen. A cloud passed over the sun and the wind made its bite felt.

She tried again. "How long are we here for?"

Jack indicated the cafe with his waffle cone, but she shook her head.

"No, I mean here in this universe."

He turned to look at her. "What do you mean?"

She shifted her feet. She was such a heel for even asking. After everything he had done for her and everything he was doing for her.

"It's just we've been here for over a week."

He nodded and then cocked his head on one side, like a dog getting unknown commands from its master.

"And, I just wondered when we were moving on?"

"You said you wanted to stay for a while."

"Did I?"

He nodded. "When we arrived."

She thought back to the fog. "It's been great. I love it here. I just wondered what the plan was."

"I figured we'd stay for another couple of weeks and then work out a plan."

"A couple of weeks!"

"You said you needed a break."

"Ok, maybe. But I feel great now. Really rested. I kind of feel like it's time to move on."

"Why didn't you say?"

"It's been fine. I just want to move on now."

"Now? Are you sure? It's just..." he waved his hands abut in a non-specific gesture.

"Please."

"Ok." His expression didn't change but he shifted gear. "We'll go today." He dropped his ice-cream into the mouth of a waiting bin and turned back up the path. She had to trot to keep up. She studied his face as he strode up the promenade. Was he annoyed at her? But his face wore the same open, easy smile as always.

Back at the hotel she started packing her belongings, such as they were. Jack popped down to reception to square things away. It was still long before noon so it surely wouldn't be a problem.

Once her bag was packed she sat at the window watching the seagulls. They swooped and soared in the blue sky, laughing insults at each other. The game seemed to go on forever.

Finally the door snapped open and Jack came back into the room.

"All ok?" she said.

"Of course."

He pulled his jacket out of the wardrobe and slipped his phone into its inside pocket. That and his man bag filled with samples was all he carried. How he got away with so few clothes or belongings was beyond her.

As they went down the hotel stairs she considered asking

where the next door was. But, after their last disaster, he was always so careful to keep her next to him. So it wasn't necessary. She wondered where they would be going next, how many jumps there were still to go.

He turned a confident left and she trotted along beside him. The sun was hot on the back of her head as they strode along the pavement. No cooling breeze this far from the front.

No, something was clearly bothering him. If this were Chris he would refuse to tell her, would sulk for days, give her the silent treatment, act out. Arse. But this was Jack.

"Everything ok?"

"Of course. All fine." He turned his smile on her. "You?"

"Fine," she said through a sweaty top lip.

"Oh, sorry, you should have said." He slid the backpack strap off her shoulder and heaved it onto his. They were walking up a gentle hill and she could feel prickles of sweat between her shoulder blades. It was much easier without the weight of the bag.

The shimmery haze of a door hove into view with all the subtlety of a mirage. She could taste a tang of something in the air. Ozone maybe? Regret? It was so nice and sunny here, they had had such a nice time, and now she felt bad for frogmarching him out of town.

The pavement had started to give way to grass verge when he stopped and handed her back the bag. He checked his arm and nodded. Then he turned to her in what felt like the first time in an hour. "Ready?"

"Yes. Is everything ok?"

"Me? No, not at all." He put the rucksack down and stepped closer. "I just wanted you to have a good long rest after what happened but you're right, it's time to go. You weren't worried were you?"

"Ok, great." The volume of relief was a surprise.

"I'm glad you said something, though. I'm not Chris, you know. You can tell me when you're worried about something."

"I know. I'm sorry." She pushed her sweaty hair out of her face and beamed at Jack to reassure him. He beamed back. He took her hand as they stepped through the door.

There was a cold wind here, on this identical hillside. The sky was covered in scudding clouds and a drizzle hung in the air. The sweat on her top lip and in her hair chilled instantly, leaving her fumbling in her bag for her sweater. Even that wasn't enough for the biting wind and she shrugged on her coat too.

Jack stood waiting for her; his coat collar turned up against the breeze. Once she had herself put back together in every sense of the word, they set off back into town. There was an ugly petrol station within a few hundred yards, garish yellow against the gentle gold of the wheat fields.

Jack's hand was still in hers, steadying her.

"So where are we going now?" she said.

"I have no idea. The last plan is out of the window and I haven't had a chance to adjust."

"Right."

But he squeezed her hand in a reassuring way.

They were coming into town now. The hotel they had just stayed in was closed, a *no vacancies* sign winking in the window. Jack led her on down the front towards the cafe she had rejected earlier. The windows were fogged up against the cold air. They shuffled thankfully inside, and Jack left her at a table and went to the counter for tea.

She wiped a drip off the end of her nose and shrugged

NOTES FROM A PHYSICIST LOST IN TIME AND SPACE

out of her damp coat. Jack brought two Styrofoam cups of lukewarm beige liquid to the table. She sipped hers gratefully. As she did her brain fog started to clear.

"What was the other plan?"

"Hmm?"

"The other plan. You said you had a plan at the last place but not here. What was the other plan?"

"It doesn't matter now."

"Ok. But what was it anyway?"

"I had invited Megan to come visit."

"Megan?" Actual Megan. Best friend Megan? Who had moved to South Africa when she was 14? The person who had got her through her parent's divorce, Megan?

She was gaping at him. She shut her mouth with a click. "Why didn't you say something?"

"I would have but you were so insistent on leaving."

She stared into her cup of tea. Now the door was closed and the Alison from this world got to spend a sunny afternoon with lovely Megan. She could cry.

"Alison, I'm so sorry. You were so adamant."

"I was. I know. It's not your fault. It's mine. You tried to tell me. You did such a nice thing." He looked sad. The spike of loss got drowned in the sludge of shame.

"It's ok," he said, kindly. "We've still got a long way to go."

She'd spoiled everything. Again.

Chapter Sixteen

Every world seemed to blur together now. The one where she had three cats and lived in an attic. The one where she still had her beloved flat and was a single, successful Hollywood superstar, thanks very much Dr Dickenson. The one where Sue had a pink hair, and everyone was in horrible 80s clothing. The one where everyone was speaking German; they hadn't stayed there long. The one where Jess was married to a horror show called Darren who tried to feel her leg up under the table.

Every possible permutation of her life. She had met so many versions of her sister, her Mum, her friends that she felt like she couldn't quite remember where her old life used to fit into it all. And, somehow, that made her think about it even more.

Jack took her to the park for lunch. He directed her to a bench near the pond and then went back to the car for blankets. She sat herself on the icy bench. Even through her jeans the cold creeped into her skin. She pushed her hands deeper into her pockets and stared out across the water through the clouds of her breath.

The pond was long and thin with one side overhung by a tsunami of shrubs and hedges and reeds. The opposite edge was a manicured lawn with carefully placed flowerbeds. The pond in between looked like a portal from wilderness to civilisation. The short edge, nearest to her, was paved and had a small railing which seemed to say, this pond is not for here for the people, this pond belongs to the ducks. There were no ducks.

The park felt deserted. There was only a single someone, off in the distance, a burgundy puffer jacket with legs who slowly disappeared behind a tree.

She hunched her shoulders. Whatever surprise Jack had planned she hoped it included a thermos of hot tea.

A family came around the bend. A mother pushing a buggy containing a child that was too big for it and a girl almost entirely wrapped in wool. They were heading towards the pond. The girl had half a bag of bread in one gloved hand. They were going to be out of luck.

The smaller child, in the buggy, was wrapped in a pink blanket and topped with a pink hat with cat ears on it. Woollen whiskers spanned her forehead. Between the two were a pair of cobalt blue eyes. They were the exact same shade as Jess's. The little girl looked her way and she felt herself trapped by that frank stare. Something about the steady, unashamed look made her unable to look away.

In the background the mother was chatting to the older girl. She could hear their easy love through the crisp air. The older girl laughed at something and the mother joined in.

She swallowed around the lump that formed in her throat and forced herself to look away. If this were her family, if Jess were in that buggy, she would be the one pushing it. Her mother would be at work, or on the phone, or perhaps present in body only, gazing at the trees, the sky, anything except the daughters who had their father's eyes.

The family were nearly level with her now. The older girl was swinging the bag of bread. The little one was looking at the pond. They had a brief conversation about the lack of ducks and the mother decided they would carry on home. On cue the youngest dissolved into wails. It was a proper meltdown, from zero to a hundred in the space of five seconds.

Her breath puffed in front of her face; her heart was hammering. The mother was kneeling in front of the child, but it wasn't going to work.

The sound went right through her like little heat seeking missiles, straight into her heart. She knew it well. The wails were echoes of Jess's; the pain was still raw.

The child was too upset. The screams would last for forever while everyone stared and tutted that the child should be better behaved, that her family should be able to contain it. And the shame as the world dissolved into nothing but wails of pain and rage and the agony would never end. And she couldn't breathe now because she couldn't breathe back then. Her mind filled up with fog and her chest was tight and she didn't know what to do and Mum wasn't helping, and Jess was so unhappy, and she had failed them all.

Except that the noise was quietening. Through the clouds of her breath, she saw the mother was kneeling beside the buggy and looking deep into her daughter's eyes, not saying anything but just radiating a kind of open strength.

The toddler's wails had already reduced. She was staring back at her mother and then suddenly she put her arms out for a hug. The mum leaned in and the little girl sobbed into her mother's shoulder. And then it was done.

So simple. She could breathe again.

The other little girl was nearby, hopping on and off a low brick wall. Not involved in the slightest, not responsible. It was like magic.

A hand landed on her shoulder making her jump.

"Sorry," said Jack. "That took a lot longer than I thought. Are you frozen? I brought extra blankets for warmth."

She couldn't reply. He bundled the largest around her shoulders and then another around her knees, tucking it in to lock out the cold.

The family moved on.

Jack sat down and pulled another blanket over his knees. He was holding a bag.

"Ok," he said. "Let's see what we have here."

Her hands felt frozen into her pockets, her mouth wouldn't move.

"What is it?" asked Jack.

She tore her eyes from the pond. His peacock coloured eyes were filled with concern.

"Sorry," She said. "Bad moment."

"What happened?"

What had happened? She had watched a child have a tantrum. The most normal thing in the world.

"Memories." She turned back to the pond.

A plastic cup emerged in her eyeline. The top of a thermos.

"Here," said Jack. "This might help."

She pulled her hands, finally, out of her pockets and took the cup. The first sip burned like fire. It flowed into her chest. "Whisky," she gasped.

He looked amused. "I brought it for warmth, but it might help."

He was right. The cup gifted heat to her fingers and the second sip sent warmth down into her frozen legs. She took another. "Thank you."

He lifted the thermos to his lips and took a swig. He topped up her cup. She took another swallow. The world was already a little softer.

"Want to talk about it?"

She shrugged. "Maybe."

"Family stuff?"

She nodded. He nodded back then the silence flowed back in. That special silence that was simply an open space. A bit like that mother with her child. A silence that seemed to draw the words out of her.

"My dad left when I was 9. He just didn't come home from work one day. Jess was 4. She was destroyed, terrified, like the laws of physics had been torn apart."

She could still see the moment when her Mum had just stopped, like a toy when the batteries ran out. They had been in the kitchen eating breakfast and her Mum was reading something on the table - the note her dad left, she found out later.

Then Jess spilled her drink and started crying that she wanted another. And she had looked at Mum, waiting for her to get up and find the spills cloth and make it all fine again. But even though Jess was wailing, and it was turning into a tantrum, her Mum did nothing. So she had got up and got the cloth, and a clean cup and more milk. And she calmed Jess down and helped her finish her breakfast. And when the clock turned 8 and Mum was still sitting there she cleared all the breakfast things away and took Jess upstairs to get dressed. And when Mum hadn't moved from the table she walked Jess to nursery and dropped her off on her way to school. Because once school was over everything would be fine again.

After school she had come out of the building and her Mum wasn't in the playground. That was when she realised it was different now. Someone was going to have to look after Jess. And that became the new normal. Walking her sister to nursery and back again before and after school. Getting her dressed and undressed. Finding food for them both and never telling anyone what was happening because that's how children got taken away.

"So what happened?" said Jack. She had forgotten he was there. He was wearing a rainbow bobble hat. How had she not noticed that before? She took another swig and he topped up her cup again. She sighed. It felt pointless rehashing this, but he wanted to know.

"They were both in bits, so I looked after them. Mum didn't come downstairs most days. I'd try to keep Jess out of the way, but she used to get so upset. At the smallest things, all the time. I had no idea how to make it better for her. For either of them. It went on for months. And then one day Mum came out of her room. And then a while later she started looking at us again. And a while after that she went back to work. And then we carried on like nothing had happened at all."

"That must have been tough."

She shrugged. "It just was what it was."

The blankets and toddy were working. She felt warm and her cheeks were burning. A lone duck emerged from the tangle of reeds on the wild side and drifted slowly out into the middle of the pond. Below the surface little flashes of orange were the only sign it was even alive.

"Did you ever talk to her about it?" Jack asked.

"No. What would be the point? She was ill. She got better."

"And what about you?"

What about her? She had stayed quiet and careful and kept Jess out of the way; Mum could get ill again at any moment. Jess came to her now when she was upset. Mum got a second job so they could stay in the house and they thrived, all working together to make it a happy home. And the pictures of Dad got moved into a cupboard. That's what happened to people who didn't keep their promises.

"I was fine. I am fine."

He let that statement go. She was grateful to him for that. She watched him sip from the thermos again.

"Thank you for listening to me," she said. "And taking care of me."

He chuckled and looked a little embarrassed. "You don't need taking care of. You're the strongest person I know."

"Thank you, anyway."

She put her head on his shoulder. He put his arm around her, and she felt him kiss her lightly on the head.

They had run out of coffee and the cold was starting to creep back in again. The wintery sun had done a poor job of shining and had now slunk off behind a building, exhausted from trying to climb into the sky.

As they walked back to the park entrance, two blankets wrapped around her shoulders, she wondered whether he believed her protests about being fine. She barely believed them anymore.

Chapter Seventeen

L ondon, winter, late afternoon. Jack's arm around her waist was essential as they stumbled down the street. It looked almost entirely normal. There were dark clouds in the sky, cars on the road, people scowled at them as they walked down the street.

She pulled him to a stop on a street corner, fighting against the nausea crawling up her throat. He put one hand on her shoulder, steadying her, while she fumbled in her bag and stuffed ginger biscuits into her mouth, pushing down the queasiness.It took a few moments but the feeling subsided and she felt ready to go on again. She shivered in the cold night air. Her coat was not sufficient.

They took the tube with crowds of scarf-bundled faces, deep-set woolly hats, hands plunged in pockets. The trains were delayed. Nobody spoke over the rush and clatter of rails and tunnels.

She and Jack sat side by side. The warmth of his hand was the only guard against the chill - so unexpected and all consuming after the brightness of the last world. She didn't want to look at him or read his expression in case he was also troubled by this world like she was.

They had such a long way to go, had already travelled so far. Getting to the perfect world was a long drawn out business. Detours on beaches with blue green sunsets she could handle but this place was so normal, so depressing, so like home.

He squeezed her hand as they drew into a station. She followed him out onto the deserted station platform and up the howling wind tunnel of the escalators. The rush of air rattled her fuzzy brain again.

Out on the street it had started to rain, stinging drops of sleet, and the few people out and about hurried by, collars up, hats down.

They ran a short distance up the street to a blue front door. Alison's stomach lurched and she took some deep breaths to steady herself. She needed a cup of tea and something else solid in her stomach. Jack buzzed flat 1 and asked for Mrs Patrick. Alison hopped from one foot to another. The cold seemed to be creeping up her legs from the soles of her feet. She just wanted to be warm again.

There was a brief conversation and the door buzzed. Jack pulled her inside the cold hallway. He took in her bleak expression and gave her a hug.

"Nearly there. Go up to the top floor. Red front door. I'll be right there."

She nodded miserably and set off up the stairs. Looking back she saw him tap on someone's front door. As she rounded the first landing she caught sight of a little old lady opening the door with a smile. They clearly knew each other. The conversation echoed unintelligibly up the stairs as she climbed. She caught her name and a laugh.

She was at the second landing now and waited, stamping

her feet to try and restore some circulation. The voices spiralled up to her.

"Again?" For how long?" The woman was saying.

"Oh, you know. Maybe a day, maybe forever," he said and chuckled.

"Oh I hope so, dear," said the old woman, buying it entirely.

Hurry up, Jack. She missed his warm hand. She could still see her breath. It felt bleaker up here waiting on her own than out in the sleet with Jack.

Down below the door closed and Jack appeared a few moments later on the stairs. She watched him round the landing, the sleet sparkling in his hair. Where they were and why was so unimportant. It only mattered that they stayed together. Jack knew the way and she knew Jack and that was all.

He smiled as he joined her on the landing and squeezed her elbow reassuringly. He had a key in his hand.

"This world's a nice one," he said. She gave a forced smile back, willing him to open the door and end the cold.

The door swung open easily and a warm red glow wafted out. She stepped onto the doormat and closed her eyes to better feel her cheeks melting. Jack followed her in and closed the door on the cold grey world outside.

As she came back to her senses she opened her eyes and looked around. Jack already had his shoes off and was bustling about the hallway hanging up his coat.

Her eyes widened as she took it in. The hall was filled with light and colour. Mirrors, painting, coat hooks, hanging plant pots, sconces, chandeliers and a feather boa clustered on the deep-red walls. The pale carpet looked to be a mile deep, the hall to be a hundred years long. All the colour and happy chaos nudged inside her coat, seeping into her fingers and toes and melting her from the inside out.

Jack's chuckle drew her attention. He was watching her with a wonky smile and warm eyes.

"Like it?"

"I love it," she breathed. "Whoever decorated this is a genius."

"She is a genius indeed," smiled Jack.

There was bookcase halfway down the hall overflowing with books. She saw book after book that she loved. They were well thumbed, spines broken, like books should be.

"Who lives here?"

"You do." He stepped forward and handed her a picture that he had plucked from the wall. It was her, leaning against a balustrade in front of a statue of a giant dog-faced dragon-mermaid - it could only be Sentosa Island, the national theme park of Singapore. Her hair was a pale pale blonde that she could only have ever dreamed of being brave enough to go for. She was smiling broadly at the camera.

She had always wanted to go to Singapore. Now she had. If only she could step into that Alison's memories the way she stepped into this flat.

Jack came forward and helped her out of her coat. He bent down and took off her damp boots. He indicated towards the door at the end of the hallway.

"Make yourself comfortable," he said.

She took a step forward onto the deep pile, clutching the picture to her chest. The carpet accepted her frozen feet graciously, enveloping them in warmth and softness. The chandelier sparkled over her head, its light reflecting in the mirrors.

She hung the picture back in its rightful place. Surrounding it were more pictures. Her and Jess in what looked like Central Park. Her mum and Jess at the dining table, smiling next to a birthday cake. Sue and her friend Kathleen holding glasses of wine. Simon and Sue in a park or garden she didn't recognise. She ran her fingers lightly over the glass of each. Everyone she loved was here.

Jack was down the end of the hall. He was standing next to a white panelled door.

"Come on," he said. "Let's explore."

She went to him, letting her feet sink into the carpet with each step. He opened the door and the hall was flooded with light. She gasped.

The space was huge. Someone had cleverly taken down walls so that what had clearly been a poky Victorian attic flat was now a large open plan space. The light wood kitchen flowed into a perfectly positioned sitting room, into a welcoming dining space and around the corner into a cubbyhole bedroom. And above all of it, running the length of the ceiling, was a glass lantern skylight, like you'd find in the roof of a factory.

All the lights in the space were on, reflecting off deep coloured walls, and a dark polished floor. The big dormer window that dominated one end wall was shuttered. Facing it sat her little red sofa that she had let go with her flat. The same sofa she had bought in that thrift shop all those years ago and lovingly nursed though broken legs, torn cushions and red wine stains. She hadn't seen it in years. She fell into its familiar embrace and buried her face in the cushions.

She felt like she was home.

Once she had refilled herself she looked around for Jack.

He was sitting, tactfully out of the way, on the edge of the double bed in the bed nook.

"Wow," She said walking over and sitting down next to him. The bed was of course incredibly soft.

He nodded. "You have good taste."

"It's perfect. Everything I ever imagined."

He grinned at her then, delighted.

"Coffee?" he said.

"Mmm."

He made her coffee while she lay back on the bed and closed her eyes. Even the smell of this place was right. Roses and cotton and coffee and, faintly, the smell of Jack.

She felt her shoulders release their tension and she sighed in contentment. The peace was rattled by her stomach rumbling.

"Takeaway?" said Jack from the kitchen. She got out her phone, rebooting it in a practiced process. When it started up she found a delivery app already installed. In recent favourites was a Thai restaurant and half of the dishes from the last order were things she would have chosen. She read the rest of the past order out to Jack.

"That's spot on," he said.

She grinned. This world couldn't have been designed to be better. Two clicks later it was on the way.

When the kettle started to whistle she moved back to her sofa. She accepted a mug of steaming coffee from Jack with a smile. He put his mug on the table and went to open the shutters so they could watch for the delivery driver coming up the road. Beyond the window was a vista of rooftops and tower blocks. The windows pointed directly down a side street giving a long light-speckled view. It was beautiful, especially through the raindrops cascading down the window.

She drew her feet up onto the sofa and took another sip of hot coffee, listening to the gentle patter of rain on the skylight, the whoosh of a bus going past. Jack sat down next to her and she slipped her feet onto his knees. He rubbed the last of the cold out of her feet. Thank god for delivery drivers. They could stay holed up in this flat forever.

They sat in silence, watching the rain. She had no idea whereabouts in London they were, couldn't even remember the name of the tube station through the fog of the jump. She had lost track of how long they had been gone and without her notebooks she couldn't track it back. The mission was done, his world was safe. Now it was her turn. She had no idea how much further they had to go. She was adrift. And, for now, that was fine.

The Thai food was delicious. The wine Jack opened was sweet and fragrant. The music on the radio was cheery, the songs blurring into one. The pyjamas from under her pillow were soft and cosy, the toothpaste on the brush was sharp and minty, the pillow for her head was voluminous and dreamy and the sleep she slept was as deep as a well.

She awoke before dawn. The flat was cushioned in silence. The rain had stopped. The bed was comfortable but colder than she had expected. She cast about for a reason why.

From the living room came a gentle snore. Jack was sleeping on the sofa. Why on earth, it's not like they hadn't shared a bed before. She wandered over, padding across the cool floor in bare feet.

Jack was lying on his back, one knee up against the back cushions, the other foot trailing down to the floor. His mouth was hung open. She stood and watched him for a while.

How had she ever thought he was cocky and sleazy, like a salesman. Under all that shiny, surface, defensive charm, was a kind, reliable, lonely man. Sort of like an anti-Chris.

The flat was dark, but the moon was shining through the lantern and it drew chalky highlights across his face. In this light his face was narrower, more defined. He looked younger. Vulnerable.

She leaned down and gently woke him. He sat up bleary eyed and stretched out his back.

"What are you doing on the sofa?" she asked.

He rubbed his bleary eyes. "It didn't feel right. Like taking a liberty. You passed out before I could discuss it with you."

She was touched.

Against his protestations she insisted he come back with her to the bed. She felt his gaze on her back as she led him sleepily across the flat.

She wasn't feeling sleepy anymore. She could feel the cloth of her pyjamas grazing her back with every step. The whisper of cotton seemed suddenly rough against her breasts. His hand in hers was sending a tingle up her arm. She let go.

She climbed under the covers and watched through half-closed eyes as he walked to the other side of the bed and leaned down to arrange the pillows next to hers.

The bed springs compressed as he sat down, rolling her towards him. His back was to her, easily within reach.

Then he swung his legs up onto the bed and lay back, closing his eyes. His profile was inches away, a shadow picture against the paler wall. His face was unmoving, his breathing even.

She felt exhilaration lying here watching him sleep. He never went to sleep before her, and it was rare to see his face unguarded. Usually it was his eyes on her, when he thought she wasn't looking. But tonight it was a struggle to look away.

She made her eyes close and searched for sleep.

Somewhere in the flat a clock ticked. The fridge hummed. She was aware of every noise, every movement, but nothing so much as his body next to hers. Separated by no more than a couple of hands' breadths.

She felt him shift slightly, settling more comfortably on the bed. She forced herself not to react with anything other than a swallow. Another shift and she felt his hand settle against hers, palm up, little finger to little finger. Was he awake? His face was in darkness. He didn't move again so she tried for sleep.

With her eyes closed her awareness became concentrated on the side of his hand resting against hers. The hairs tickled her skin. Each prickle sent pulses through her arm, up through her body and down into her core. The heat of his skin, a slight twitch in his finger - the sensations filled the room.

Her heart was beating loudly now. Did he know the effect he was having on her? Was he sleeping soundly while she was dying next to him?

She should move away. Roll over. Forget this feeling. This was so profoundly not allowed.

But this heat throbbing through her body was long missed and so warming. Each breath left her a little more alive. She had forgotten she could feel so good. She could feel every inch of her body glow.

She wanted more than anything to take his hand. Maybe draw it closer to her. In their everyday lives she took his hand a thousand times a day, like it was nothing. But here and now it was a bridge to somewhere new. Somewhere she was not supposed to go. Which made her want to visit it even more.

He was probably asleep. He probably hadn't even noticed. There was no one to observe what she would do next.

She felt her fingers twitch. There was no response. So she allowed her fingers to curl up and reach over until they were resting across his fingers. Her cheeks filled with heat and her breath was uneven. Her thumb traced a line along his fingers.

In a smooth movement that made her gasp his fingers bent up and laced with hers. Her eyes flew open. Unthinking, the pads of her fingers pressed into his palm. His face was still in shadow profile. It was inscrutable like a statue, belying the soft touch of his thumb tracing along hers.

She lay next to him in that comfortable bed, not allowing herself to do any more than absorb the touch of his fingertips. She watched his face for any sign he would turn to her, willing him to, wanting it with every fibre. But he lay silently, his ragged breathing the only sign. Clearly he wanted to, but he was holding back for her. And she knew she couldn't trust herself to make a clear-headed decision right now. There was nothing to do but lie there until the sky started to lighten.

She must have fallen asleep because she awoke to sunshine and the smell of frying bacon.

She sat up in bed. Watched him cooking. Tried to make sense of the night before. He was in his t-shirt and pyjama combo. It emphasised his broad shoulders and narrow waist. She could see the muscles moving under the thin fabric. His hair was tousled. It was getting long, curling against his collar. She could cut it for him again. The thought of running her hands though his hair made her feel too hot.

"Hungry?" he said, turning around and catching her staring.

The table was already laid. She padded over and slipped a piece of crispy bacon into her mouth. She watched Jack's expression as he dished out the eggs. There was nothing knowing in his eyes, and nothing triumphant either. He offered her toast, looking her directly in the eye as he did so. No avoidance at all. He smiled and joked as usual. She felt herself drawn to him by invisible threads, spun by his hand on hers last night. His normalcy left her fidgety.

Her feelings last night had overwhelmed her. Today the memory was strong in her mind.

But now they were eating scrambled eggs and commenting on the decor. She wanted to reach across the table and shake him. She wanted his hand to rise off the table and entwine with hers. She wanted to see a spark of recognition, light in his eyes, see them turn molten. Wanted his grip to tighten, his pulse to quicken. Wanted to feel his hand slide up her arm.

Which she couldn't do. Which she mustn't do. But the perfect world that she had imagined so clearly, with the perfect Chis, felt like nothing but a fairytale. A dream that she had woken up from to find Jack standing in front of her, eating toast.

"Another coffee?" he asked. Was he entirely oblivious? She nodded past the lump in her throat. Had his reaction been a dream? It had seemed so real.

She abruptly stood up from the table and walked off to the bathroom. The water was mercifully cleansing. The feeling of his hand in hers sloughed off down the drain. She plunged her face into the stream, emerging clearer and fully awake. By the time she got back to the living room she was back to herself.

Jack was standing by the window looking out into the street.

No, no feelings there. Nothing to worry about. And when he smiled his winning smile and went for his own shower she, honestly, had no urge to go with him at all.

Chapter Eighteen

J ack was gone.

He had sat her down the previous night, over a glass of wine and an omelette. He had come to the end of things. For a horrible moment she had thought he meant his journey with her. Had he got bored or fed up? Was he going to leave her here? Had she been slowing him down after all?

"No, you silly idiot. I'm finished with my mission."

"You are?"

"I'm done. After the appointment today I have all the medicines I needed to get."

"Jack that's amazing!"

They clinked glasses. He grinned. She called him a hero. He took a bow.

"I've just got one more trip to make. To deliver what I promised."

"You're leaving me here?"

"Why not? It's a nice place. You're comfortable and it's a lot of jumps back to my world. I'm…"

"Not sure I could handle it?"

He shrugged. "Sorry. It's just, you're still getting sick and it's such a long way. If I go on my own I could be there and back in a day, two tops."

She nodded. She was slowing him down.

But this was good news. His world was going to get what they needed to save themselves. He was going to literally save the world. How many people ever had a chance to do something that amazing?

Did they know? His world. That he was coming back? Had he sent on ahead, somehow? Was he going to be received with a ticker tape parade and a knighthood?

"What's wrong?" he asked, perceptive as always.

"I...I was just thinking that maybe they will need you to stay. To share what you've learned. If I had my mitts on you I'd want a full debrief, maybe a ceremony, maybe a medal."

"I'll tell them no."

"You can't do that."

"Why not? I'll just tell them I made a promise, and the person I made it to is very unforgiving about unkept promises."

She felt herself blushing and couldn't hold his eye. "It's your big moment."

"I'm not going to abandon you, Ali. I'll be two days. I'm not going to promise it won't be more because you can't promise that, you never know what might delay me. But I promise you I won't stay there a second longer than it takes to drop them off and file a report – which I have already written, by the way. And I will come straight back here to you."

"You don't have to."

"I want to."

She looked up then. His eyes were glowing in the candle-light, the peacock's colours bright. She didn't want to tell him how frightened she was that he might not come back. There was nothing more terrifying than the thought of being lost in the wrong world. She needed him to come back. He was her only point of safety in this whole multiverse.

The day had been bleak and colourless without him. She kept herself busy, going out to the cinema, shopping in town.

She decided to unpack so she had a lighter bag to carry around. Besides she finally had somewhere to put her things that wasn't a hotel room. The battered leather rucksack disgorged its contents onto the bed. Three notebooks now filled with her notes and scribbles. They represented hours of calculations, and hours of waiting around for Jack to come back from his missions and from scoping ahead. She looked around the flat. It didn't seem right to put them on the bookshelf, but a bit of a hunt discovered a small drawer in the Victorian pine blanket box, probably for candles. She stashed them for safekeeping. Damned if she was going to lose another batch.

The second day she spent at an art gallery. Something she rarely did back in her world, something she used to do all the time. She was pleased that she had felt so comfortable to go on her own, even for a few hours. This world was becoming less alien. It was the first one, in a long time, that reminded her of home.

Walking back towards the flat, she ran her hand along the rough brick wall. This part of London was filled with rows of red brick houses. Every one alike with patches of garden at the front and high blank end walls on every corner, only adorned with the street sign placed right up high. This wall had a single yellow brick in the middle. A repair maybe. Or an interloper into the batch. It tickled her fingers, a patch of bright colour in the otherwise monotone wall.

How had she ever walked down this street cold and confused? How had she ever seen hostility and darkness in this pretty corner of London. Admittedly no one returned her smile or allowed more than a second of eye contact, this was London, but they felt indifferently friendly. She quite liked being invisible. It reminded her of a time before Chris, before Jack.

She trotted up the step to the front door of the flats and slid her key in the lock. As she walked into the hallway she heard a scuffle on the landing above. When she looked up she saw the toes of a pair of men's shoes vanish and the door went click.

What was going on?

She climbed the stairs a number of scenarios played through her head. Impromptu parental visit? Jess? Mum? Friends from this universe? What would she say to them? What would they be like?

Her heart started to clatter in her chest.

She was in front of the red door now. It was utterly silent. No voices. She would hear them, even from out here. She would certainly hear her mum.

She put her key into the door and watched her hand turn and the door fall open. The hallway was deserted. She stepped lightly onto the mat and shrugged off her coat. The silence was loud in her ears.

"Hello?"

No reply.

She clicked the door shut quietly and slipped off her shoes. The door at the end of the hall was ajar. She tentatively pushed it.

Something yanked on it from the other side and she stumbled into the room.

"Surprise!"

The room was full of people all cheering and waving streamers. She gasped at the blur of faces.

Then Jack was standing in front of her. "Happy birthday," he beamed and kissed her on the cheek.

Her birthday? Was it?

Had he organised this? Why? What was he thinking inviting all these people here? Oh god, there were so many people.

Over his shoulder was a flash of yellow fuzz and then Jess was all over her, hugging and kissing. Her hair tickled her nose. The skinny arms, so familiar. Beautiful Jess. She smelled right, felt right. Alison wrapped her arms around her and hugged her back, hard. She buried her face in her sister's hair to hide her tears. She could have stayed in that hug forever.

But Jess shrugged her off, as she tended to do, and grabbed her hand, dragging her into the room. She looked back at Jack for help as she was hauled away but Jack just grinned at her.

Her mum was suddenly there. She gave her a little peck on the cheek and a squeeze of the arm. And Kathleen and Sue, who proffered gifts. Someone she didn't recognise handed her a drink. Gin and tonic, so they either knew her well or she was too predictable.

Taking a second to scan the room she took a healthy gulp of gin. There was an old friend from university, Nick, who raised a glass from the other side of the room and grinned. There was Alan, from Edinburgh, the one who always peer reviewed her papers with a red pen. He was talking to someone she thought she remembered from school.

Then her heart stopped.

Chris.

The room went cold. The glass slipped in her hand and she grabbed it with her other hand down to steady it.

When she looked back up he was still there. And now he was looking at her and smiling. He was walking over. Oh god.

She cast around for Jack. Should they run? Which Chris was this?

She found Jack but he was walking over to her too.

She watched the two men bearing down on her and braced herself.

Chris arrived first. "Surprise," he said, softly smiling down at her.

She stared back, unable to respond.

"Happy birthday," he said. Then he leaned down towards her. He was going to kiss her. *Stop him*, her brain shouted but she was frozen into place. Why couldn't she move?

At what seemed like the last moment he weaved, and the kiss landed on her cheek. She flinched. When he stood back his eyes looked sad.

"I'm sorry," he said, just as Jack arrived next to them. "I did say to Jack this might not be a welcome surprise."

"No...I...um." She looked helplessly at Jack. He had his reassuring face on and slipped his arm around her waist.

"Sorry, Chris," said Jack, cheerfully. "I probably should have warned her. But..." he indicated around the room full of smiling people. "You know."

"Not your fault, Jack. It was a good idea. She'll be fine in a minute."

Why weren't they fighting?

"I want you to meet someone," said Chris. He held out his hand and a woman appeared at his elbow bringing with her the most glorious smell, roses in a field of bougainvillea. She was older than Alison. Her hair was peppered with grey. She looked like someone's Mum. Someone's glamorous, wealthy Mum.

"This is Nicole," said Chris. "I don't think you two have met."

Nicole slipped her arm through Chris'. Two beautiful people making an elegant tableau. Chris was beaming with pride.

"Hi," said Nicole and without hesitation stepped forward and kissed her and Jack on the cheek. "It's so nice to finally meet you."

"Yes, isn't it," she managed.

"And 'happy anniversary' is in order, I understand," said Jack. He slipped his arm through hers. She was grateful for the support but didn't like that it meant they were exactly mirroring Chris and Nicole.

She looked down and saw a diamond and a wedding ring glinting on Nicole's finger where it rested on Chris' arm. Right.

Her heart thudded. She was still wearing her wedding and engagement ring. From her wedding to Chris. She clasped her hands together and wriggled it off, slipping it into her pocket before anyone saw. Jack caught her eye.

"Nicole," said Jack. "Let's get a drink." He reached out and shook Chris' hand. "Chris." Chris shook it back, firmly. Nicole separated them and drew Jack away.

Right.

"I'm sorry, Ali." Chris looked awkward. "Jack thought you'd be pleased to see me. And I figured, given how much time has passed…"

"Right. How much time has it been again? I lose track."

"Three years next March." He gave her a sympathetic look. She remembered the tone. *Not having that.*

"That's right. I honestly stopped paying attention after a while." She smiled cheerfully.

"Of course." He took a sip of his drink.

"So," she said, forcing upbeat and cheerful. "You and Nicole. I didn't realise you were actually married."

"Yes. Nearly a year, now." He looked across at where she and Jack were pouring drinks. His face softened. She hadn't seen that look in years. It used to be her look.

Was she jealous? She rummaged through her feelings and found a little green throbbing ball. It was smaller than she expected.

"How is married life treating you?" she asked, sipped at her drink again. God, the gin was good.

"Good. She's as a rich as Croesus so even I can't fuck this up."

Her bellowed laugh startled the guests nearby. Chris grinned at her.

"Well," she grinned back. "I'm very happy for you." And she was. The little green ball could be easily ignored. She felt ok with it.

"Jess tells me you are doing so much better now," said Chris. He nodded at the drinks table. "And I see you found someone too."

She caught his meaning and shifted uncomfortably. Chris

giving his approval for her and Jack made her feel weird.

"I like him," Chris continued. "He's clever. And you like clever. And he hasn't stopped staring at you since you walked in, so it's safe to say he's smitten."

She looked over at the drinks table. Jack was indeed looking at her. He twitched an enquiring eyebrow. What could she possibly say that wouldn't give away her complete lack of knowledge? She smiled nervously at Jack and he smiled back. He was clearly enjoying himself. His face was glowing.

He said something to Nicole, who nodded, and they started making their way back. She felt her face start to go red. When they arrived back Nicole slipped her arm around Chris. Jack did the same to her. Nicole leaned up and kissed Chris full on the mouth. She didn't know where to look so turned her head and found herself looking into Jack's eyes. The chaos in her mind went silent. Then Jack leaned down to kiss her - in front of Chris, in front of Jess, in front of her Mum. And she was too surprised to stop him.

When his mouth met hers a jolt went through her. Where the room had been cold it went warm, where it had been noisy it went silent.

Then the world snapped back, and Jack was standing next to her chatting to Chris like nothing had happened.

Jess appeared at her side and dragged her away. Her head was still spinning. Both Jack and Chris raised their glasses to her as she stumbled after her sister.

Jess pulled her into the bedroom nook, pulled the empty glass out of her hand and replaced it with a full one.

"Sorry, sorry, that was all my fault. I gave Jack Chris' number. Are you ok?"

"I'm..."

"I know, I know. Awkward! But it's done now, and Nicole is lovely. Everyone has found their other half and all's well that ends well."

"Other half…"

God, was her brain ever going to re-engage? She took another swallow of G&T.

"And Jack is so perfect," Jess was saying. "I mean, so perfect. I can't believe it's already been six whole months!"

She stared at her sister chattering away excitedly. Alison and Jack were a couple. And had been for six months? No wonder no one reacted to the kiss. She slugged back the rest of the G&T.

"That's right," she said blindly. "Perfect. Entirely perfect. Drink?"

Jess nodded happily, clearly thrilled that she was forgiven.

Alison had the opportunity to make a beeline for Jack. He was chatting to someone in the middle of the room. It was Katie, her weird second cousin, who probably didn't know a soul here. She brushed back the feeling of gratitude.

"Jack, darling. A word?"

He stopped laughing at her expression and nodded.

But as they were heading for the living room door they were intercepted by her mother, who neatly looped her arm through Alison's and drew her away towards the kitchen. Jack shrugged as she was hauled away, returning her glare with a grin. But there was nothing she could do about her mother. Another G&T arrived in her hand. She glared at it and thumped it down on the kitchen island.

"Now, now," her mother said. "Don't be cross with Jack. This is my fault. We haven't seen you in months, so I got him to set this up. And it was Jess's idea to invite Chris. Bygones, and all that."

She nodded weakly. She recognised the constriction around her throat, her reluctance to engage. She could fight back against her mother's assumptions. She was getting good at fighting back. But there were too many unknown variables. And it seemed here she was already his.

"Come on, buck up," her mother ordered. "It's your party. It's meant to be fun!"

The people all around them were laughing noisily. A crowd of faces all there for her. It wasn't their fault that the situation wasn't what they thought it was. She was being unfair to them.

Just get through the party. One last hurrah before the end of her long journey. So she picked up her G&T and went off to mingle, to her mother's delight.

She met Alan. A friend from work, who filled her in on the office gossip while she was off on her sabbatical. She was off on sabbatical?

She met Dauphine, her neighbour from down the street, who clearly knew her well, given the beautiful patterned, red pashmina that was her gift.

She met Anna, who she vaguely remembered from school but who she hadn't seen in over ten years. Mostly because her Anna was working for GCHQ. This Anna was a journalist and regaled her with terrifying stories from the Afghani frontline. Apparently they were still close friends here.

She liked these people. Their quick wit, fabulous stories, lack of self-consciousness. Anna and Nick had a stand-up row about the state of the NHS and then poured each other a drink. Kathleen turned out to be a whizz at choosing party music. Jess and Jack played tag team with her, bringing new people over to talk to her every time the conversation dipped. Drinks and nibbles and brightly wrapped presents were in endless supply.

How was she this popular here? She had never had a party like it in her life. It was overwhelming.

Eventually she made her escape and found a quiet spot on her ottoman laundry basket. Right in the far corner of her bedroom where she could watch the room from a distance.

Jess and Anna were laughing over something on Jess's phone, like sisters. After all they had known each other for almost their entire lives. Nicole and her mother were sitting on the old red sofa, deep in conversation. Kathleen was scrolling through her phone for music and Chris, of all people, was dancing.

"Hi."

She looked up at Jack hovering nervously. "Want to talk now?" he said.

She shook her head. She was tired and her head was muddy. He looked relieved and sat down next to her. She sipped from another drink. The room was hazy with a tipsy glow.

"I figured you deserved a last hurrah, after all the hard work you have put in. Look how well you handle yourself now."

"Let's not discuss it tonight. You're in trouble tomorrow, though," she said.

He tipped his drink to her, exactly as he had done with his coffee, all those weeks ago in her lecture theatre. He nudged her playfully with his elbow. She let her head fall onto his shoulder.

The party went on late, even after Kathleen departed with her music. Sometime after the food ran out she found herself sitting on the sofa with Chris. Jack, Jess and Nicole were opposite them, playing I Have Never. She was trying not to listen. She had a feeling Jack was going to lose.

"Having fun?" asked Chris.

She grinned at him. "This is nice."

"It is. I'm glad we can do this. It's always bothered me that we left things on bad terms."

She twisted in her seat and looked him squarely in the eye. "Was that my fault? Did I handle it badly?"

"I think we were both at fault," he said magnanimously. "I was a spoiled child. I guess that's why you became like a parent instead of a wife. But that's behind us. Now I have Nicole. She is so perfect. Breaking up was the best thing that could have happened to me."

She squirmed, the green ball flaring up again. After everything she had done for him. Everything she had put up with. And now he was swanning about living the good life.

She forced a smile onto her face. "Yeah, the best thing."

Jack was watching her expression from his place across the coffee table. She gave a minor shake of the head to convey she was fine. He smiled encouragement and let his gaze the sweep the room. The beautiful flat, the London lifestyle, the dregs of a damn good party. She got the point. She was living the good life too.

Maybe she should have dumped Chris' arse years ago. Clearly they were all much happier.

Chris was still watching her. "You should come out to our house in Provence sometime," he said. "Or maybe the boat. Friends?"

Chris's beautiful face beamed down at her. He looked the happiest she had seen him in more than five years. "We can be friends," she said. *Twat*.

Jess caught a lift in Chris and Nicole's taxi at about 3. Alison saw them off at the door, wiping down her cheeks from Jess's multiple kisses. There were promises of lunch on Sunday and dinner at Chris and Nicole's next time they were in Edinburgh. Nicole hugged her in a cloud of floral perfume and said she was so glad to have met her.

The door closed and the footsteps faded down the stairwell. She leaned her forehead against the solid wood, letting its strength flow into her.

She heard Jack approaching, caught his scent. She didn't move a muscle. Waited to see what he would do.

The answer was nothing. The silence stretched out until she couldn't help herself. She turned and looked at him.

He was standing in the hallway, feet half buried in the carpet. As always his expression was open and guileless. He simply stood and waited for her to react.

This man who had thrown her a surprise party and kissed her in front of her family and friends.

He walked towards her down the hallway. "Have fun?" he said, gruffly.

She felt herself engulfed in his shadow. She inhaled his aroma of gin, aftershave and salt. She nodded, lost in his eyes.

Jess adored him. Her mother approved. Kathleen clearly fancied him, and even Chris said he was good for her. Here, in this world, Jack was the love of her life.

What did anything else matter anymore? She felt her chin tilt upwards, her lips part.

He took the invitation and lowered his mouth to hers.

She felt the same jolt course through her. Felt his mouth open and his hot breath enter hers. She let her control slip.

She wanted to let her control slip. Her hands snaked around his waist, feeling the hardness of his body beneath his clothes.

Her mouth moulded to his and when his tongue touched hers she crackled with electricity. His shirt chose that moment to bunch up and aside and her hands blundered onto his skin. They sang as they absorbed the heat from his back.

He let out a groan. She wanted him naked, but instead she moved her hands up inside his shirt, pulling him closer, pressing herself against him.

His arms finally ventured around her, his hands exploring the waist of her jeans. Her skin tingled and she felt a core of desire work its way down her spine. She gasped as he gripped her back and, abandoning any remaining control, started pulling at his shirt, his jeans, her top. He fumbled with her belt.

For a moment she caught herself and pulled back. She could still stop if she wanted to.

His eyes were like pools of petrol.

Maintaining eye contact she slipped her shirt over her head and let it drop to the floor. She took his hands and moved them up her waist and under her bra. His breath caught and he bent down to kiss her. She closed her eyes to feel his touch and leaned back. A sudden movement caused her eyes to fly open and she saw him drop her bra to the floor. She arched her back to his greedy mouth, allowing her hands to explore the contours of his shoulders.

He raised his head and said, "bedroom now?" Punch drunk and reeling, she took his hand and led him through, naked to the waist.

She lay back on the bed, feeling the cool sheets press against her hot skin. He stared at her for a moment. She basked in his gaze. He helped her shrug out of her jeans. She pulled him down on top of her and wrapped her legs around him. His breathing was ragged as she kissed him again, guiding his hands back to her breasts. He leaned into her neck and his breath was hot on her collar bone.

When the sensations had tied themselves into a tight little ball she pulled his hand aside and drew him down instead.

As his body moved with hers she felt moulded to him, a private experience that only the two of them could share. He knew where to kiss her, how to touch her and she surrendered to the waves of pleasure coursing through her. It felt like a slice of forever but in no time at all she was collapsing on top of him, gasping, laughing. He shuddered when she ran a hand across his chest.

She kissed him on the nose. He returned the kiss.

"I love this mouth," she said, running her fingertips across it.

"All the better to eat you with," he grinned.

Days passed after that. Failing to get out of bed. Getting out of bed and then getting back in. He was carefree and excitable, his mission finished, he said he felt freer than he had ever felt before. It felt like a dream. A wonderful impossible dream.

They went to a show at the West End. He made her breakfast every morning. He walked with her to the shops to buy bread.

He was always smiling, always putting his arms around her and always kissing the back of her neck. This impossible, charming, wild man seemed to want nothing more than to be with her every hour of every day. A perfect little oasis in the middle of the desert. A holiday from reason.

So when she found her wedding rings in the pocket of her skirt she'd been wearing at the party, she slipped them into the change pocket of her bag for safe keeping. Out of sight.

Everyone deserves a holiday.

Chapter Nineteen

I t was a Saturday. The second week of her holiday.
Something had jolted her out of her sleep, and she found
herself too wide awake to lie in. She got up and dressed
but Jack was still fast asleep. Only downside of open plan
living, no watching TV or listening to music early on the
morning.

Instead she found herself staring out of the window into
the cold dawn. It was, what, February now? Christmas and
New Years was gone with nothing else to look forward to
but rain and shivery mists until Spring. The thought made
her itchy and cold, so she went into the kitchen and made tea
quietly by boiling a pot on the hob.

The dishwasher was full but dirty - another problem with
the trendy layout, everything had to wait until morning. She
rooted quietly in the back of the cupboard and came out with
a yellow, faded mug. It had a modern art picture printed on
it, the picture she had stood in front of for what felt like a day.
A mother, dressed in a yellow shawl, holding her baby in her
arms and gazing down at the upturned face.

A memory came back to her with the force of an explosion.

"Alison, can I come in?"

Chris, standing in the doorway of the sitting room, his blond hair was backlit in the light from the hall, giving him a golden halo that smelled like summer.

The smell of Darjeeling drifted into the room ahead of him. He was holding two cups in his hands. One of them was her favourite mug, bought from the Kunsthalle in Hamburg. It was faded and blurred from so many trips through the dishwasher, but she kept it anyway.

This was not long after the business had failed. They had fought. She had been distraught.

He stood in the doorway, a silhouette that was so familiar that she could spot it from a hilltop, in a crowd, from behind, at night. Her Adonis, the beautiful man who she would never have believed could have noticed her but who somehow did. The lines she had traced with wondering hands. The mortar that had flowed into the spaces in her soul and moulded around the building blocks of her life, strengthening them, forging a steely core.

"Of course, come in."

He came over and sat next to her on the other end of the sofa. He didn't say anything, just sat staring at his cup. Maybe if she turned out the light they could sit like this for a while, feel their way back into comfort, rediscover companionship.

"We need to talk," said Chris.

Or not.

He refused to meet her eye. The side of his face looked distracted. Sad. Did he know she was thinking of leaving? Or had he had enough?

What would she do? Where would she live? She didn't have enough money for a flat. Her mother was going to be so unhappy. But at least now maybe she could tell someone, share some of her pain before it spilled out and hurt someone. And thank god there were no children - maybe that had been for the best after all. She should move on and find someone better suited and have millions of children and live in a tiny cluttered house with a tiny cluttered garden and grow cucumbers and write her papers in a tumbledown summerhouse with azaleas growing around the door.

"Ok," was all she said.

His fingers drummed on the cushions. The little pom-poms on the edge danced in response.

"I miss you," he said. "I want us to be us again." She was confused. Surely he had already given up. That was the point wasn't it?

But here she was thinking of azaleas and *he* was trying to make things better.

He went on, "I'm sorry. I don't know how to make it up to you. And I'm lonely, Ali." He looked up at her then. His eyes were filled with sadness.

She heard the counsellor's dulcet tone: *try not to bombard him with your feelings. Think about how he likes to communicate. What might be happening for him? What do you really need to say?*

The silence encouraged him to keep going. "I feel like I can't talk to you anymore. I just feel like you don't want me."

How to respond to that? How could she explain the complex interwoven feelings that crowded into her mind? Her feelings of betrayal, the loneliness, the suffocating coating of bile on her tongue. There were a million ways to start but every one was a short slippery slope to anger. But she wanted to find a way through. She had to keep her temper, keep her

171

mouth shut. She had to think clearly.

"Ok," she said.

"Ok you do or ok you don't?"

Her head was throbbing, her brain felt thick with emotion. Fog was rolling into her mind. It was getting harder to think. The back of her skull prickled, and she reached up to scratch it. It felt like thorns digging into her scalp. Her neck was burning.

What was the question?

"Do you even like me anymore?" he was saying.

She looked down at the mug of tea in her hand, the faded yellow print. The mother's expression of unconditional love. There was a reason it wasn't a father in the picture. Mother's love would hold up against any disappointment, any trial. Love that was infinite. Love that was constant and true. The way love was meant to be. Had to be.

She considered his question from a distance. When had they last had fun together? When they'd bought this house? They'd been so excited. They had finally arrived at the life they wanted. He got his big house. She got her family home. They'd chosen colours together. Painted wall after wall. He'd lifted her onto his shoulders to reach the high spots. They'd got paint in their hair, their clothes. He'd 'missed a spot' on her nose. She'd slapped his arse with a paint covered hand. He'd outlined her breast with his brush, leaving a red smear, and teased the nipple with the bristles. Making love on the dust sheets with no regard for the mess.

The tea had formed a skin on top. The mug had been the prized possession from their trip to Hamburg for their fifth anniversary. They'd walked everywhere, stopped for pastries every mile or so, drunk beer in huge steins carved with gruesome trolls. She'd told him about why the steins had clear bases (so enemy warlords couldn't stab you while your cup was raised and your guard was down) and he'd stolen kisses on her arms and hands every time she took a sip. She could barely drink for laughing so hard.

They'd had no money, so he picked her flowers from the park and saved wrappers from the sugar packets to build into little origami swans. He called her "Liebchen" and she called him "grosser". She made goblets from the foil from the pillow mints and they drank to each other's health and their long and happy marriage.

"I like you," she said, her mind full of origami swans.

"Then why do you never show me anymore?"

"Because I'm sad."

"I'm sorry that you're sad."

"Me too."

The yellow of the mother's shawl blurred and swam. Every cell in her body ached for the peace she had felt when she had first found him. This great big man with a single-track mind and thoughts that moved like glaciers over a deep dark ocean. When he had spoken she heard her ideas and wishes reflected back to her. He cut through her analysis and doubt and gave her clarity. A calm place to rest her fevered mind.

The warmth of his hand was gentle. She allowed her head to guide the way to his shoulder even though he was a mile away.

She landed awkwardly, bent in half, but he slipped an arm around her and shuffled closer until her head was resting in the crook of his shoulder.

The cup got placed next to his on the coffee table, the cushions were cast aside, and the tears dropped from the end of her nose.

"Let me make this better," he said, his large hands rubbing warmth back into her frozen arms. She nodded into his shoulder. "I just want you Ali-bee. Nothing else matters. Nothing else makes me happy. I'll pay you back for your flat, I swear I will. Let's just spend our time together like we used to. You and me against the world."

It had always been the two of them together. If they stuck together they could take on anything, everything. They could do that again. She sat back and looked up into his big blue eyes, blue like the sea. A window into the shuttered depths of his soul where his feelings swam like whales in the deep. Unfathomable. She had lost herself in those depths before, where the whales were a song that she often heard but had never seen. Once again she followed them into the deep.

He had never given up on them. Never walked away. Never abandoned her.

The alarm blared on the bedside table and Jack coughed and sat up. She struggled to place herself back in the room.

"Morning," he said and came over to where she was sitting. He leaned in and gave her a kiss on the cheek. She couldn't move, her thoughts lost in a haze of the past and the present.

All day she struggled to adjust. Jack didn't notice her mood, or if he did he was too kind to show it. They had a busy day already planned with Jess and Pete, thank god, so she didn't have to think about it at all.

It wasn't until that night, when she was bathed, brushed and pyjamased, staring at their empty bed covered in scatter cushions, that the feeling returned. She picked them up one by one. Like petals off a daisy. Placed them gently them on the floor. She loves me, she loves me not.

Jack was still awake, playing a game on his phone. She kissed him on the cheek before climbing into bed.

Her eyes were drawn to the cushions lying on the floor. They knew the truth.

Chapter Twenty

She felt like a fraud. Sitting here at a perfect lunch at a perfect restaurant in a perfect world. Anna and her girlfriend Caitlin we're doing a double-act about their time in Japan, teaching English, Jack laughing uproariously in return. She was starting to feel itchy. And there was no reason to. Everything was entirely perfect. Maybe that was the problem.

She looked across the table. Caitlin was gently chiding Anna about her haphazard approach to life. Anna was smiling back at her and shrugged good-naturedly.

"I wouldn't have it any other way," said Caitlin and leaned across to kiss Anna on the cheek. She loved to see how much they loved each other.

Jack suddenly placed his hand over hers and interlaced his fingers with hers. She fought a sudden, mad urge to pull her hand away.

Jack leaned in. "You ok?"

"Of course!" She smiled at him and freed her hand to cut up her meat.

"You sure?"

"Mmm-hmm."

Caitlin was looking across at them. She looked puzzled. She shook off Jack's attention and leaned forward. "You were saying about the bullet train."

Anna launched enthusiastically into another story and she relaxed as the conversation started to flow again. What was that look in Caitlin's eyes?

After the dessert menu had been rejected, she excused herself to go to the bathroom. Not long until this cosy quartet would break up.

She sat in the cubicle feeling strangely like she wanted to cry. She had been so looking forward to seeing Anna, hearing about her life, meeting Caitlin. Of course from Anna and Caitlin's perspective they were all already friends. That must be why she felt unsettled, left out, discombobulated.

She hoped she hadn't asked questions she should have already known the answers to. Maybe that explained Caitlin's look.

She allowed herself a little gasping sob, muffled in loo paper, before opening the cubicle door.

Caitlin was waiting by the sink. Her heart thudded in her chest. Caitlin's expression suggested she had heard the sob.

"You ok?" asked Caitlin. She was leaning against the sink, her arms crossed.

"Yeah fine. Just a touch of indigestion." She moved to the sink, head down and quietly washed her hands. Caitlin didn't move so they were practically hip to hip. The rushing water sounded loud. She rewashed her hands. Cleanliness was next to godliness, after all.

She shut off the tap and stood back up, avoiding the mirror. Caitlin hadn't moved. She was still gazing at the cubicle doors, as if they were the most important thing she had ever seen. For a brief, mad moment she looked like Sue. The same fixed expression. Which was madness because Sue, with her mid-blonde hair, pale, pale skin and angelic smile, looked nothing like Caitlin with her mad black curls.

She dried her hands on the roller towel. As the seconds stretched into minutes she felt uncomfortable just standing there, and it felt rude to just leave, so she went and mirrored Caitlin's pose.

"What happened?" Caitlin's voice made her jump.

She didn't reply. She had no idea what the question meant. What if she tried to reply and accidentally said something revealing about her journey?

But the other woman was waiting for a response. Jack was back at the table, waiting for them. She had to say something.

"I don't know."

"Do you need help?"

Help? "Uh, no, I don't think so."

"Do you have a plan in place?"

"Yes?"

"Ok, so what's stopping you? Why haven't you gone already?"

Her stomach twisted. How did Caitlin know? Her face was passive when she risked a glance. But what else could the question mean?

"Are you scared to?" said Caitlin.

There was a long gap before she could bring herself to answer.

"Yes."

Caitlin nodded. "I know the unknown is terrifying. And while this is comfortable right now, I know you know that this is not the life you want."

Her heart pounded in her chest. When had she told Caitlin? Wasn't that breaking some kind of code?

"You do?"

Caitlin didn't budge an inch even when she turned to look at her. Her face was neutral and calm. "You can leave any time you like."

Her brain answered without her permission. "How?"

"You just tell him. Just say the words. I promise you that nothing bad will happen. He's a reasonable person. He'll let you go. It's not fair to him to let him believe that you love him."

She couldn't breathe. Her darkest, innermost thoughts were being spoken to her face, like a horrible, horrible echo.

Caitlin carried on talking, firm but calm, neutral. Almost like she was trying not to spook a frightened child. "This is your life. Yours. Don't sell yourself short. If you want to leave, find a different life, just say so. Do you?"

She opened her mouth to say something but then couldn't think of what to say. A dripping tap, suddenly loud on the silence, brought back to mind where they were. Caitlin couldn't understand. It was only Jack that could take her where she needed to go. But how could she ask him to now?

Caitlin suddenly stood forward and turned and gripped her shoulders, looking her deep into her eyes. "We're all here for you. You can do this." Then folded her arms around her and gave her a fierce bear hug.

Caitlin took her arm and they walked through the door back out in the restaurant. At the moment they emerged from the corridor Caitlin's expression changed, a huge smile lighting her face. "That's what I said!" Caitlin brayed heartily and laughed a huge belly laugh. She felt her face form a smile automatically in return, so when they neared the table they were the picture of jollity.

Jack and Anna were deep in conversation and barely noticed. Anna was enjoying being the centre of his attention, the most important person in the world. She studied the side of Jack's face as she got closer.

Wasn't this supposed to be the perfect world? Weren't she and Jack supposed to be the perfect couple here?

Then Jack turned to face her, and she pushed her thoughts to the back of her mind where they wouldn't show.

On the way home in the car she brought them back out again. Jack was driving and had his music up loud, nodding away in the seat next to her. She turned her face to the side window so he couldn't read her thoughts. She stared out at the passing streets and bright lights.

Did she really want to leave?

Guilt squirmed in her chest. After everything he had done for her she shouldn't be feeling this, thinking this. She was so ungrateful.

But that wasn't what her brain was arguing for. A jolt in the road made her bag knock against her ankles and she thought about the wedding and engagement ring in the inside pocket. She wanted to see Chris again. The life she had chosen. Her husband.

The leaden feeling hadn't gone away. It settled a little deeper when she smelled the rich warmth of coffee wafting through the flat. Jack had got up and prepared everything, as usual. The clinks of cups and the gentle bang of a cupboard door paced him, so she kept her head still and just stared at the ceiling. Her neck ached from the forced immobility. She just wanted to stretch.

When was the last time she had woken up alone, or spent any time alone?

She had been alone in the fields near Bathgate. But the familiar feeling of panic didn't arrive with the memory. It had been terrifying but now she couldn't quite capture that same feeling. Instead she felt a little silly for being so afraid, so desperate for Jack to find her.

In years gone by she had been so independent. Travelling to Russia for the summer at Novosibirsk State University without knowing a soul. How had she been so confident?

Or all those days and nights living in her little flat with no flat mates, content in her own company. But now she wondered if she had been content, or just stoic.

Was it Chris who had made her so clingy? No, he was always out with friends, had all his hobbies. If anything he had left her even more alone. He had left her lonely. She had always wanted someone who could really know her. Not just the one she tried to be, but the one deep inside.

In the early days it had been nice coming home to a companion, someone to talk to, or just sit and read with, knowing that you could get up and do your own thing with no guilt. Until, of course, things changed, and guilt was all they made you feel.

Jack was different. When she eventually moved he would be over like a shot. He wanted to know her every thought and feeling, his perceptiveness like a microscope into her inner world.

Which meant he would understand.

She opened her eyes then and rolled over noisily. Jack, with a cup of coffee, appeared in seconds.

"Morning sleepyhead," he said. "How's the hangover?"

She tested her head, but it was fine. "No, no hangover."

"That's surprising. You had a good bottle to yourself last night."

"I did?"

He nodded and put his hand on her forehead dramatically. "It must be worse than we think!"

She shook him off. She wasn't in the mood for humour. She sat up in bed and hugged her knees.

"Jack."

He looked up from rearranging a pillow, perhaps sensing her tone. "What's up?"

He looked so handsome, in his t-shirt and pyjama trousers, hair all spiky and tousled. He had been so kind to her. He had shown her an entirely different way of being. It had been fun. She hoped he wasn't too disappointed.

"I need to go home. I need to carry on, to find the right world." There. She had said it. How would be react?

He looked at her for a full ten seconds, his face unreadable. She started to get nervous.

"Ok," he said.

"Ok?" she said. "Really?"

"Of course. I promised I would take you there whenever you were ready."

"Ok. Thank you." She breathed a sigh of relief. He got up and went back into the kitchen, started doing the washing up. Like nothing had happened. But what had she expected? A sudden declaration of love? Begging her to stay? A part of her kind of wanted that but this was the right thing to do.

Was he so unaffected?

The cup he was holding slipped form his hand and fell into the sink with a clatter. He didn't move to retrieve it, just put his hands on the edge of the sink and went completely still.

Oh no.

She walked up behind him and slipped her hands around his waist, resting her forehand against his back. She could feel his heartbeat thumping hard inside his chest.

A wave of guilt swept over her. She could take it back. Take her words back.

Except that she couldn't. They had been said and they were the right words.

He was allowed to be upset. She wasn't going to ask him not to, just to assuage her guilt.

They stopped there for a while, a little tableau. Then he straightened his back a little and patted her hands with one of his, leaving a bubbly blob. She knew what he meant and dropped her arms. She went over to the table and sat down.

They didn't speak about it again for the rest of the morning. At lunchtime he said, "I'll book us some flights to Edinburgh." Then he changed the subject. She took her lead from him. They were both going to pretend it was ok.

Jack was still upset. She'd asked him twice if anything was wrong. He kept saying everything was fine. She wished she believed him.

She walked alongside him trying to fight her discomfort. He had his rucksack slung over his shoulder, his hand gripping the strap, effectively raising his shoulder against her. His coat was flapping in the wind. The street was busy, but she could only see him. The guilt squirmed in her chest.

Chris often lapsed into long silences. Silences that meant

he was upset or brooding over something. That's why this silence made her nervous. But Jack had said he understood. He had never been passive aggressive to her. He was open and honest. Always. She just needed to give him space to be upset.

She walked next to him as they continued down the road. His stride was long, and she tried to match it, but the wind kept blowing her hair into her face and she kept thinking she was going to bump into someone. As usual, she had no idea where they were going.

Normally he was chatty and charming, passing comment on the people that they passed. Today he was silent. She felt how much she had hurt him. He was trying to be stoic, but his jaw was tense. He had brought her all this way and was fulfilling his promise, taking her to her dream. She wished there was something she could do so they didn't leave on bad terms.

"Shall we stop for coffee?" she asked brightly. Maybe she could find words for her gratitude over lunch? He didn't respond.

She looked across at his face as he strode up the Royal Mile. It was set in stone.

"Or lunch maybe?" as they passed a sandwich bar. Her mouth watered at the display of cheesy scones and paninis in the window. When had she last eaten? Last night.

He stopped abruptly and she had to dance on the balls of her feet not to crash into him. He was looking around, frowning. She opened her mouth to ask what was happening, but his expression was unreachable. She had lost the right to pester him. So she waited.

Now that they weren't moving with the flow the Mile

turned out to be swarming with tourists, all chatting and laughing. Maybe she should just go and get something to eat while he stood there, looking purposeful. Unless this was leading up to something important.

"She touched his hand lightly. "Jack?"

He glared at her.

"I'm sorry. I know I've hurt you."

"It's nothing, I'm fine."

"Jack," she whispered.

His glare didn't waver. She pulled him sideways out of the flow of people until they were closeted in the gated entrance to a close. The flow became distant. It was quiet in the archway. Behind them the cobbled street slipped and slithered it way down the hill between towering stone walls. A single wrong step and you'd end up crashing into the station.

He was looking down the hill. "I'm sorry," he said.

"For what?"

"I'm trying to be fine about this, but I'm not."

Her heart gave a painful little thump. "Jack - "

Her turned to look at her. "I know, it was just meant to be a bit of fun," he said. "A holiday from reality. I thought I could do it, make love to you without - "

"Don't," she said. She ached for his pain.

He nodded miserably. She pressed his hands in hers. What the hell could you say to that?

"Now I have nowhere left to go." His words came out bitter and sad.

"You go home. You saved your world. You're a hero."

"None of that means anything anymore."

Words queued on her tongue. I'll stay. I changed my mind. I want you too.

But she couldn't say them. She didn't have the right. She was a terrible wife, a terrible person. Jack was standing there, heart broken. Because she had let go of her principles for a brief, amazing moment. Now he was paying the price and there was nothing she could do to fix it.

She had to finish her journey. Make both of their sacrifices meaningful. Follow through.

She put her arms around Jack and held on tight.

He pulled back sharply. "There's only one more doorway to go."

"Only one?"

"Whenever you give me the word."

"Show me."

He pulled up his sleeve. The tattoo was swarming with blue dots. "This one," he said.

She stared at it. That was it. Her doorway. The last one she would ever take. The dot was nearby. She could go now. Her perfect world. She looked up at Jack, but his eyes were averted.

Again she nearly crumbled. But again she didn't quite.

Something appeared in her hand. It was a book. She looked up at Jack who was holding it out to her.

"What's this?"

"A goodbye present. Something to remember me by."

She opened her mouth to protest but he interrupted her. "I've not put my name in it or any messages that might get you in trouble. It's just a keepsake."

She turned it over in her hands. It was a book of Shakespeare's sonnets. Traditional, at least. And generic enough to be something she could take with her. Her stomach twisted. Should she take something like this into her new life - like a gift from an old boyfriend - was that ok?

But he was looking at her imploringly, so she closed her hand around it and took his hand in hers. "I'll treasure it," she said.

He nodded then. And seemed to brighten.

They started walking towards Arthur's Seat. The final jump.

"And if you ever change your mind," he said. "If you do. There a couple of notes in the back to help you find your way back to me. Just in case." He pushed back her protest with a firm hand, taking the book and putting it in her backpack and closing the flap. "Just in case."

She let it go. It seemed churlish to protest. And there was something comforting about it. If she wanted to, if it all went wrong, she could find her way to somewhere else where she was wanted and waited for.

Arthur's Seat was suddenly before them. They turned and walked down the hill towards it.

Chapter Twenty-One

She stepped through the doorway. This time there was no feeling of tearing in half. If anything she felt something come together.

The field was incredibly green, the sky a cobalt blue. Of course today was a beautiful day. This world was as familiar as her home. No flying cars, no strange creatures. A bee flew past. It was yellow and black. Just like it should be.

This was her new home.

Jack was standing next to her, in reach, but his expression was far away. She wanted to take his hand, to feel his arms slip around her. But that would be inappropriate.

She spun her wedding rings on her fingers. They itched. Today was the first day of the rest of her marriage. And everything would be perfect. She sighed.

Jack looked around and tried to smile. She matched him.

"So. Home," he said.

"Yes."

The wind blew softly, bringing the smell of the sea. She looked out over the city. It was all how it should be. Everything in its place.

They could stay here for a bit. Sit on the hillside and just enjoy the weather. But the rest of her life lay down that hillside.

Better get on with it then.

They walked down the grassy slope to the car park in the shadow of Holyrood Palace, around the Parliament and up to the Royal Mile. A taxi passed. Neither one of them flagged it. They continued walking, without a word, up the Royal Mile, past the Castle, down Lothian Road, up Bruntsfield Avenue. It was a long walk but neither suggested anything different.

Eventually they were standing at the top of her road where her giant house was.

They both stopped, as if on cue. She looked at him.

"Thank you, Jack."

"My pleasure. And I mean that." His eyes were warm peacock feathers. His hand was cold in hers, but she felt a glow from it anyway. She felt strength in her fingers, passing between them.

"It's been quite an experience, hasn't it? I - well, I just wanted to say that I think I'm a better person for having known you, Jack, and that's all anyone can ever ask of someone else. My life is better for having had you in it. And I don't mean this new reality, but I mean who I am is better for having met you. So thank you, and I will always miss you. Goodbye."

She turned and marched off down the road. Her eyes were blurry with tears. Focus on the end point, Ali. This is the right thing to do.

She felt a hand on her arm, and she was swung around into a bear hug. Jack's arms laced around her back and she felt enveloped. The smell of warm grass filled her head as she

189

buried her wet face in his collar bone.

"No, you don't," he mumbled into her hair. "You don't get the last word on this one." Her arms slipped around his waist and she felt her shoulders heave in a tiny sob. She hoped he hadn't heard it, but he planted a fierce kiss in her hair. She closed her eyes, and just for a moment, relaxed into his arms, breathed him into her, felt her body mould into his until the two of them were standing in a single spot together.

He was talking "- never met anyone like you. You've shown me things about myself that I didn't want to know, and it hurt like hell but I'm so glad I met you. I'm so glad you showed me.

"I hope you find what you want here Ali. I absolutely respect your resolve and commitment. It's something I'm going to aspire to. So, I'm not going to ask you. And I'm not going to tell you. But I do, and I would, more than anything."

She kept her eyes closed, her arms fully clasped around him, her breath neutral. She didn't dare move a muscle. Not one. Everything else was pushed away and she lived a lifetime in a glorious second. No promises, no restrictions, no consequences. Just moments of pure joy. A single sentence could open a hole in the fabric of the universe and allow a blinding lightness to flow in, swamping every doubt and fear and leaving behind nothing but a pair of peacock eyes.

Every Ali before and since stood behind her, beside her, and inside her and their stares told a single truth. And the light faded. And the world flooded back in.

His arms loosened and she opened her eyes to greyness.

"It's Ok. I know. It couldn't be any other way," he said. She couldn't speak. Her mouth was numb. Her throat frozen. "Have a nice life, Ali Howden. I'll never forget you." He leaned

190

down and kissed her on the nose. And then he turned and walked away.

She turned and started to walk down the hill. Into her new life.

The house seemed so far away. Every step took her away from one world and into a new one.

What would Chris be like here? What would he say when he saw her? Would he be able to tell the difference? Would he smile at her, kiss her? What would kissing him feel like? Like kissing Jack?

No.

She put the thought out of her head. That was then. Literally another world. She had to focus on this world now. On this life.

Chapter Twenty-Two

When a hero gets to the end of a quest like this, a tale of bravery and derring do, they feel sure and fiery and just and good. The world should feel aligned, right, fixed.

She couldn't tell if that were the case because everything looked exactly the same. The light was the same. The coats hanging in the hall were the same. The key tray, same, the photographs on the wall were the same. Monica's wedding, Mum's 60th, Chris. Her and Chris smiling and holding hands, arms around each other, shoulders pressed together.

The albums in the bookcase in the hall outside the kitchen.

At first they looked the same. Her pictures hadn't changed a jot. A five-year-old smiling by a pool, a teenager standing awkwardly in her velvet dress wearing the wrong shade of lipstick.

But then she picked up a book of Chris'. Chris as a young boy, curled up in the lap of someone who could only be his father. Chris in a school uniform. Birthday parties, his dad at every single one. As a teenager standing by a small aeroplane. Getting some kind of diploma.

He was here. They were together. So was this the perfect world she craved? In the next book there was her and Chris together at a party. He's smiling and looked relaxed. She remembered that party, and he hadn't been there. He'd declined to attend at the last minute. Too stressed. Too tired. Too bored of people. And yet there he was with a drink in his hand and a smile on his face. And a lot more hair than she remembered.

Another picture. A holiday she didn't remember taking. Somewhere warm, somewhere breezy. Her hair was in her face. She was looking svelte and tanned and relaxed and Chris was standing taller.

Something is changed, she thought. Something good. Something is better.

There were other differences too. There were books on the bookshelf that she didn't recognise. Car books and plane books, of course, but also books that she had never seen before. On design concepts and aerodynamics. They looked expensive. In fact everything in the hall looked a little more expensive. As she looked closer she could see the white bookshelf that the albums were on was not the rickety Ikea monster that had been resurrected after every house move. Instead this one was solidly built, real wood from the feel of it. A finer, better version. And the junk shop armchair under the stairs, which was the exact same chair she had, was in fact recovered in what felt like leather. It was buttery soft under her fingers. Clearly their tastes were the same, but there was more money.

She ventured into her living room. It too was the same but different. She remembered Chris couldn't sit in this room without rearranging things. Twitching cushions in a way which meant he really wanted to rip them open and burn their fluffy hearts. She had bought more whenever she could. The sofas here had two cushions each. When she tested the seat it didn't groan in protest. Someone had fixed it.

The pictures on the walls were subtly different. Every second or third one looked like something Chris would pick. There were less cushions. Less lamps. It was sleeker, tidier. It looked good. Still homely, just not quite so crowded with intent.

A noise made her jump. It sounded like a car crash, but she realised it was just a key in the lock, amplified by the intense silence.

He was home.

"Chris?" She took a step towards the door. Nervous but excited.

"Alison?" he was mocking her formal tone in a friendly way. There was warmth there. "Who else would it be?"

He came into the room and she couldn't see anything anymore except him. He was so tall and handsome. Shoulders back, toned muscles outlined against the neck of his polo shirt. He was wearing gym kit of some kind. The warm musky smell of him filled her nose. His brown eyes were warm and clear. His tanned skin was glowing. He pushed his big strong paw of a hand through, surprise!, a thick shock of blonde hair on his head. His mouth was smiling. Then he tilted his head slightly, quizzically. He must be wondering why she was staring at him like this.

There was such warmth there. Warmth she hadn't seen in years. He was looking at her like she was best thing that had ever happened to him. She felt transported back in time to when they had just met. When everything was joyful and fresh, when the world hadn't eroded their fascination for each other. This Chris had clearly never weathered that storm.

She was home.

He leaned down and kissed her gently on the mouth. It was like a drink of water. Cool, refreshing, leaving her wanting more. He pulled back from the kiss, then pecked her lightly on the nose.

"Let me go change. I stink."

"Ok," she said and followed it with their signature greeting. "I see you."

"Of course you see me. I'm standing right here. What a funny thing to say."

As she watched him climb the stairs she swallowed back an uneasy feeling, but this was the right thing to do.

She heard the shower start upstairs. She went back into the sitting room, trying to recapture that same feeling from before. But the room felt darker somehow. It was just her nerves. This was a new world, a new life, things would be different here. Then she would get used to it and it would be the heaven she had been dreaming about.

The shower shut off. She went up the stairs and into their bedroom. It was the same as back home, even down to the scatter cushions. The familiar smell of vanilla candles made her nose itch.

Chris came out of the bathroom, clad only in a towel. He was still damp, and a single drop of water ran down across his chest. He had always been the most handsome man she had ever seen. He caught her eye and came closer. He was smiling and his eyes were burning into hers. He was going to kiss her again.

The kiss was familiar but this time there was no coolness

to it. It was hot and urgent. She wanted to feel that way too. She pushed past her doubts and kissed him back. She slipped her hands into his hair and drew him closer.

Then his hand was on her waist, moving up to her breasts and she went cold.

The last time he had touched her that way was back in her world. Was she right back where she started? Which Chris was this?

She pushed him off her. Her hands were shaking.

"Are you ok? What's wrong?" said Chris.

She sat down on the edge of their bed. The same bed. Words hung in the air. Every argument, every name they'd called each other.

I wish I'd never met you.

You are such a disappointment to me.

Can you do anything right?

I wish I had never married you.

Selfish prick.

Stupid cunt.

Here he was standing in front of her. Her husband. And she was his wife. This was the right choice.

Not only that but for the first time in years he was looking at her like he used to. The absence of judgement in his eyes. The heat of his hands. The lust in his eyes. How long had she wanted this? How long had she dreamed of it? Everything she had given up to be here.

She had to look away. She felt tears plop onto her hands as they wrung in her lap.

"Sweetheart, what's wrong?" He came over then, never one to leave a woman crying. He covered her hands in his, stilling the twisting of her rings.

196

His care was genuine. Every fibre of his being was focused on her, she could sense it like a plant raised in darkness senses the sun. There was no selfishness there. No resistance. No judgement.

The tears fell. It had been such a long journey, such a long time, since she had felt safe and cared for in this house. And now she was finally here. The end of everything. She let herself cry in his arms for a while. It was nice there.

"I'm sorry," she said when her tears had abated a bit. "I'm just emotional today."

"It's Ok. We're all allowed to have bad days."

She nodded and tried a smile.

"I'm just tired. Can we go to bed?"

"It's only 7 o'clock," he chuckled. "But why don't you have a lie down. I'll make you some tea."

"No! Please don't go. Just stay while I sleep."

"Of course, whatever you need."

He pulled back the covers and gently manoeuvred her in. She curled up in a little ball pushing away the uneasy feeling.

She was home. This was her home.

When she woke up Chris was still there as promised. He was curled up next to her on the bed, scrolling through his phone. It was dark outside.

"Hey sleepyhead. Feel better?"

She nodded. Did she?

He leaned in. She forced herself to lie completely still. Her breath was held. He kissed her gently on the mouth. The softness startled her.

"Hungry?"

"Yes."

"I ordered some takeaway. It'll be here in a minute."

"Ok, thank you. What're we having?"

"Indian. Chicken tikka masala for you, of course."

She smiled up at him. His face was so young, so unworn. His smile lines were lighter, softer. "Thank you."

"Come on, up you get."

He held her hand as they made their way downstairs. He led her into the kitchen and perched her on a stool as he got plates.

She looked around the kitchen, interested to see what differences there were here. Her tea station was now on the counter right in front of her as she walked in. The spoons had a bigger pot.

A tea towel hung on the steely oven, softening the industrial lines. The taps were rounder, a rose gold colour, instead of the German boiler tap affair. She wondered if she had chosen them.

There was a rug in the middle of the cold tile floor. It had coloured stripes. As did the runner on the table. There were spice pots and oil pourers on the counter. A pot plant. Magnets.

This room was jointly lived in. It was shared.

The doorbell went. Chris put the plates on the table and went to answer it. She didn't realise she had tensed until she heard friendly voices, it was the delivery man. She made her shoulders relax.

She stared out of the window into the dark of the garden. She wondered whether this Chris had let her get a bench swing.

"Drink?"

She jumped. Nodded.

Chris set about dishing up and poured her a glass of lassi.

She had to adjust. Had to live this life in front of her. Jack was gone. She had what she wanted. She had to let go of her natural reactions around Chris. That other Chris was gone. She didn't have to be on her guard now.

"Ali?"

She looked up. He was watching her curiously. "Eat something, baby."

Baby? "Sorry."

He smiled warmly at her. She smiled back. "How was your day?" God, was that all she could ever think of to say?

"Good. Looks like we're going to have to take on some more people again. Paul and Kath have got the hang of the Diageo account and they're asking us to take on another project."

"That's amazing!"

He frowned in confusion at her enthusiasm.

"Isn't it?"

"Well, it's hardly unexpected."

Damn. "Right, yeah."

"So anyway, the point is, we can take that trip once we've signed the contract. That's me officially management only from now on."

She tried for genuine enthusiasm. "Great! The trip. Fantastic." Clearly things were going well here. She wondered what his business was. Was it the same one he had tried and failed with in her world? How did he start it? How was she going to ask these questions, find out what their life was like here without seeming completely mad?

"So can you find out when your hiatus is, and I'll book it all?"

"My hiatus?" At least her university job and the lack of investment in her field of study meant she knew the answer to this one. "Um, whenever suits you, I guess."

He looked up from his curry, surprised. "I thought you had to negotiate the dates with the PhD students."

Damn. She had to be more careful. But she had PhD students, plural?

"Right, of course. I meant just tell me when's best and I'll try and negotiate that."

"Ok."

"Where are we going?"

"Oh, have you changed your mind?"

"No, I just… want you to remind me."

"The Cayman's, of course. Butler service. Infinity pool. Remember?"

"Of course. Sorry. Of course I do. I can't wait."

Caymans? Infinity pool? Luckily for her the conversation lasted only a few minutes more and was more easily navigable. They cleaned up the dinner and settled down in front of the TV to watch the news. Chris was calm and relaxed throughout. As each new report began she watched his expressions but nothing beyond a wry smile was forthcoming. At the end of the news she realised she hadn't even paid attention to the content, only to his reactions, and mentally noted the need to get up to speed on the news of this world.

After that she excused herself to go to bed. He smiled a goodnight, gave her a gentle kiss and squeezed her hand, and that was it. A guilt free bedtime. The novelty.

As she climbed the stairs her brain felt heavy and over full. There was so much to take in. Even a nap wasn't enough to keep her going on such a momentous day. Her eyesight felt blurry and it was all she could do to follow her normal routine and slide into bed. She'd deal with it all tomorrow.

Chapter Twenty-Three

He woke her the next morning with a kiss. She had been warm and comfortable in the bed. The kiss matched that warmth, reaching through her sleepiness, drawing her awake. By the time she had opened her eyes he was halfway out of the door with one hand raised in a friendly goodbye.

"Bye," she mumbled. There was thudding on the stairs and the front door clicked. How had she slept through his morning routine? The bangs, the swearing? There hadn't been a morning in years that she hadn't buried under the pillows to escape the drama. Maybe here his morning routine was different. She propped herself up on her elbows.

The room was tidy. No half open drawers, no discarded ties or shoes.

She flopped down on the pillows with a happy sigh. The ceiling was mottled with sun. A scent of flowers was traced back to the duvet. She pulled it up to her nose and inhaled deeply.

Today was Tuesday. That meant she ought to be at work. The clock said 7.17. Wow, Chris was out early.

She allowed herself five minutes lolling time then swung out of bed. The first day of the rest of her life.

The shower was hot, the shower gel expensive. It smelled of seaweed. She could almost hear the seagulls. Who was she kidding? This was Edinburgh, they were seagulls nesting on every rooftop. Atmospheric though. Maybe that's why the Alison from this world had chosen that shower gel. It was definitely hers. Mine. Chris had a black bottle with a lion's head in silhouette. It probably smelled of diesel oil.

She stopped herself from sniggering. Laughing at one's own jokes wasn't cool, even in the perfect world.

Her wardrobe was the same piece of furniture but the clothes inside it were new. Nicer. And colour co-ordinated. Yikes. Hopefully this Alison wasn't a Stepford Wives type. There was still so much to figure out. But at least here there were nice clothes to do it in.

She chose a lovely Hobbs trouser and blouse combo and slipped her toes, clad in the softest cotton, into comfortable and clearly pricey black leather loafers.

This was the life.

She skipped down the familiar stairs, then paused to take a moment over the photos lining the walls. Somewhere sunny she didn't recognise, skiing (damn, shame she'd missed that trip, she hadn't been skiing in years). Another one of somewhere warm.

Was that George Clooney? She felt her jaw drop. Did they know George Clooney? Oh my god!

This was amazing. Her new life was clearly a lot more fun that her old one.

The living room was pristine. The kitchen was neat as a pin. Clearly Chris was still a clean freak.

She made herself a cup of tea in the front and centre tea station and then hesitated a moment.

Normally she would go straight into the sitting room, closing the door behind her. But here all the doors stood open. Even the double doors between the kitchen and sitting room. She had forgotten those even existed.

The kitchen table had mats, a vase of flowers and a newspaper on it. She sat down and looked back and forth down the length of the open, sunny house. In one window she could see the opposite neighbour picking up milk bottles. In the other a bird was plucking nuts from the squirrel feeder in the generous, lawn clad garden.

This was so much nicer. Why had they ever closed off these doors. In her world she had a bookcase in front of them, hiding the way through.

But never mind that old world. What about the news here in the new one? She took a sip of her tea and picked up the newspaper. As she did so a flash of yellow caught her eye. Underneath the newspaper was a little yellow post-it note. It said "Morning" and had a little heart drawn on it.

It felt like an age before she could move again. Her throat was closed tight, and her eyes prickled. She carefully put down the newspaper and picked up the note.

It was actually real.

She breathed in the inky papery smell and then her throat was clear, and she was taking huge gasping breaths. She didn't seem to be able to take in enough air. Tears plopped onto the post-it, smudging the ink but she realised she was laughing so hard she couldn't catch her breath.

More than anything else in this perfect house, that post-it signified she had really arrived. She was here. 3 years of hellish marriage, walking away from her life, leaving behind her family and friends, betraying all of her principles, walking away from Jack, all of it worth it for this tiny slip of paper with a heart drawn on it.

She drew a deep breath. She had to keep this post-it forever as a reminder. She went to get her bag, pulled out her wallet and slipped the note snugly inside.

Also in her bag was her phone. She plugged it in and chose reinstall.

The familiar message popped up that said "all existing data will be deleted. You cannot undo this. Are you sure you want to proceed?"

She had done this a hundred times; in every world they had gone to. Any contact numbers would be replaced by ones that worked in this reality. The music was expendable. The only thing was the photos. Photos of her life with Jack. In every one of a hundred worlds she had backed up those photos to the thumb drive in her bag before choosing "yes."

She cancelled the reboot and instead plugged in the thumb drive, calling up a picture of him standing on that pebbly beach. Laughing. Tanned. His peacock eyes flashing in the sun.

Should she keep them? They were a record of the fact she had travelled to the far-flung edges of the universe. Not that you could really tell; most looked entirely normal except for the fact they had Jack in them.

He had been the most aggravating, exciting, beautiful, infuriating, mesmerising, lust-inducing man she had ever met in her life. He had pushed her to try new things, step out of her comfort zone, abandon her assumptions and convictions and caused her to take an entirely new relativistic view on life. She had thrown caution to the wind and travelled to entirely new universes. Had seen things that otherwise she would never have seen.

But now she had a yellow post-it note with a heart on it and all that was behind her.

She hit "delete."

Chapter Twenty-Four

Chris was taking her out to dinner. She wondered if either of them cooked here. It was a shame. One of the things she had missed the most was watching him chop and slice and combine food, all off the top of his head, no recipe required. But it appeared that, with money, Chris was more of a consumer than a creator.

She looked through her wardrobe, uncertain of what to wear. Chris had assured her it was just a little mid-week dinner so nothing special. But her clothes all seemed to want to be dressy and very special indeed. Well, better lean into her new life. She chose an elegant and flowy little black number and dressed it down with simple flats and a scarf. She popped a sparkly necklace in her tote bag. If she got it wrong she could whip off the scarf and embellish with the necklace.

As she came out of her dressing room she came upon Chris looking dashing in chinos and a jacket. He turned and dazzled her with a hundred-watt smile. She felt shy and frumpy in response. Maybe she should change into something more glamorous. But he came over and slipped his arms around her waist and she forced herself to try and relax.

"Ready?" he pecked her on the nose while she tried not to blush.

He was so close and smelled so good. Her stomach did a little flip when she felt her breath on his cheek as he leaned down to kiss her.

"You look hungry," he said. "Let's go."

She nodded and picked up her bag.

She watched Chris' back as he descended the stairs. When he reached the bottom he opened the door and let it swing back, forcing her to dart forward and catch it. So that hadn't changed then. Didn't people hold doors anymore? He said it was a commitment to equality, that he was complimenting her by not assuming she couldn't hold her own door. Dick.

He turned and smiled at her on the path. "Taxi's here."

She forced a smile in return.

On the journey to the restaurant she fought to relax. She had come too far and done too much. She just needed to let that all go.

Chris was chatting about plans for the Caymans. He was planning where to stay, had researched a dozen options and was describing them to her, the pros and cons of each. All she had to do was listen to the thread counts, as the taxi rattled through the streets. The benefits of infinity pools over plunge pools over private beaches. It all sounded like something out of another world and she hadn't had to lift a finger.

They had never been on a holiday like that. The last time they had tried to go away Chris had taken an instant dislike to the apartment she had booked and threatened to fly home.

Dammit, focus Ali.

"Which do you think we would like more?" Chris was saying.

"I don't know, it's hard to visualise them."

"Here. Let me show you." He pulled out his phone and flipped through picture after picture of holiday homes of the rich and famous. The villas were huge. All modern, all spectacular. Her jaw dropped. Surely they couldn't afford this, even if his business was doing well?

They had arrived at the restaurant, so she was saved from giving an opinion. He hopped out of the taxi and strode into the restaurant. *Really?* She pulled out her handbag to pay the driver, annoyed all over again. But the driver just nodded at the machine which showed the words "on account". She thanked him hastily and left. Chris was waiting for her.

"Ok?"

"Of course," she said avoiding his eye, embarrassed for judging him again so quickly. Was she ever going to get the hang of it here? But it had only been a day. She had to give it time.

She looked up at the building as Chris strode on ahead. She knew this place. On their first anniversary they had wandered past it, eating fish suppers from their greasy paper with chip forks. They had looked in through the huge, multi-paned windows at the diners beyond. A hundred years ago it had been a gentleman's club and it still retained the dark panelled walls and lavish decor of the time. He had stated grandly that when he made it, he would treat them both to dinner.

As she went walked inside she took the opportunity to look around. The tables were small and widely spaced. The vaulted, corniced ceiling supported multiple giant pendant lamps, each suspended over a table at just above head height, making each table a personal little pool of light.

The immaculate host guided them to their table in the

window. As she passed the other diners she sussed out their style. All of the women were impeccably and tastefully dressed, to a person wearing subtle jewellery and 3" slingbacks. Neither of which she had. She wondered whether she could excuse herself to go to the ladies and upgrade to her necklace.

"I should have worn heels" she muttered to herself. But Chris heard her and slipped his arm around her waist.

"No. You made the right choice. You look spectacular. All these women wish they could look as good as you do in these loafers." He squeezed her lightly and popped a kiss on top of her head. They weren't loafers but she squeezed him back and smiled up at him, her self-consciousness erased by his touch.

She held onto him tightly until they got right next to the table. As they sat down the waiter buzzed over with menus. But when he tried to hand Chris the wine list he waved it away. She watched it go with dismay. Chris was smiling warmly at her again, like he had just done something important. She gave him a smile back. Maybe they were both on a diet?

"So," he said after they had ordered the tasting menu. "Which villa do you think?"

"Um. Can I see them again?" he handed her his phone and she scrolled through the pages. She struggled to tell them apart.

A price caught her eye. How much? *Bloody hell.*

She scrolled through again. Each price was worse than the last. This was insane. She couldn't spend that! But he was looking at her expectantly. What to do? She deployed the same tactic she used when took her to restaurants they couldn't afford back in her world. She found the second cheapest and handed it back to Chris. "This one." It was just as luxurious as all the rest but half the price of the most expensive.

"Really? This one means flying Business, not First."

She nodded enthusiastically. He looked disappointed. She cast about for a reason that wasn't *I've never spent that much on a car, let alone a holiday.* Her brain fumbled and came up with, "It reminds me of the place we stayed on our honeymoon."

"Really?" His eyebrows went up; she wasn't surprised. They had stayed in a modest, traditional cottage in the Italian countryside. No pool. No air-con. Tiny room. She had loved it. Sitting under the cypress trees, drinking local Chianti and gorging herself on cheeses. He was staring at the photos on the phone, probably trying to figure out what it was about the achingly modern villa perched on top of a cliff that she was seeing that could possibly look like a rustic cottage. Every space vast and empty, every wall glass. All mod cons. A view over the ocean as far as the eye could see.

Her stomach squirmed. "Um, metaphorically."

"Oh…kay." He shrugged at the phone. "You can have whichever one you want. This is our last holiday for a good long while. Don't forget, money is no object."

She hid the wince and just nodded. Business class and 5 stars. She would make do.

The food arrived then, and she buried her discomfort by trying tiny morsels of lamb, fish, five kinds of potatoes, mini tomatoes and petite dollops of parsnip puree. Everything was beautiful.

In eating she felt herself fall into a familiar flow: without thinking she started taking bits off his plate, watched him do the same. She pushed to one side the things she knew he didn't like and saw he was saving bits of her favourites to share. They could forget the stresses, focus on the joy of flavour and texture, compare sensations, compete half-heartedly over who had ordered the most delicious dishes.

How handsome he was, sitting in the half-light, the darkness of the window behind his head. How charming when he laughed at her expression after he gave her a piece of fish that looked like chicken. How easily the conversation flowed. How safe she felt in the centre of his attention, the reason for his happiness, the only place he wanted to be.

This was what she had done this for. With all the stresses and strains stripped away they were perfect for each other.

Chris was telling her about a meeting at work. "The Head of bloody Marketing came out and said that the strap line should be 'Literally the best thing since sliced bread'. 'Literally'. I mean what exact evidence does he want me to show the advertising standards authority on that one?"

They laughed together. "Maybe they could survey 100 bakers," she giggled.

"That might work. What a nonsense."

She sipped her tonic water. "Although, technically you could get away with it."

"How?"

"Well, given that a word means what the majority of the speakers think it means, technically if you surveyed the public and they understood literally to mean figuratively then the ASA wouldn't really have a leg to stand on."

He stared at her. "That's an argument?"

"Yeah. It holds up. Technically."

"You genius. You might have just solved my problem." He raised his glass to her. "Literally."

She bowed her head in acknowledgement. "Touché."

The evening flowed on like the wine they had never ordered. She wasn't missing it now. When she looked up from her cheese board the restaurant was almost empty and the door to the kitchen was still.

She looked at her watch and was shocked to see it was gone 11 o'clock. She shifted in her chair, suddenly uneasy. According to her diary she had an early meeting in the morning. Chris always hated it when she suggested they leave something because of a schedule. He felt slighted and somehow rejected because she would rather honour the clock than time with him. Maybe she had better stay and just be tired tomorrow instead. But when she glanced up from her watch his face was serene.

"Shall I get the bill?"

She leaned over and took his hand. "Thank you." He really was not the man she had left behind. She had never meant a thank you so much in her life.

All the way home they sat in silence. She stole glances at his beautiful profile, overcome by him. It felt like their first date all over again. As they climbed the front steps he held her hand lightly in his. He kept her hand as they walked through the door and as it closed behind them he swung her around into his arms.

His face was inches from hers. She studied him closely. Would he want her? This her, not the other woman who he was used to. As he gazed down at her she felt enveloped in warmth and light. Long-buried feelings erupted under her skin. Before her brain could even engage he had leaned down and was kissing her.

His lips were so familiar but at the same time it felt like a lifetime ago. She felt dizzy from a sudden rush of memories. Their first kiss on a street corner that had gone on long enough for a man walking his dog to go past them twice. The first two weeks of their relationship when they had barely left the bedroom. The feel of his hands imprinted on her body forever.

They were somehow now in the bedroom. The memories merged and flowed with the sight of his naked torso, the feel of his buttocks under her hands, the gasp in her ear as he shuddered under her. She couldn't tell where the past ended, and present began. All the forgotten joy, ecstasy and release tied up in a single explosion that blew her totally away.

As the ringing slowly faded from her ears she pushed herself up on his sweaty shoulders and marvelled at the look on his face. Surely hers told the same story.

"Wow!" he said, squeezing her waist again.

"Yeah." She laughed. What a feeling. He was gazing at her like she was only woman in the world. Her heart swelled.

All those long years of loneliness, of feeling unwanted, and undesirable, the long nights sitting alone, the months and months of counselling, the searching of her mind, body and soul for some way to make her marriage right. All the worlds she had travelled through, the dangers, all the things she had left behind, she had done it to find this moment of connection, of happiness. She was finally here. She was finally whole.

"Hey, what's wrong?" A tear had plopped onto his chest. He pushed up on his elbows, tipping her gently onto her back. Leaning over her his face was softened with concern. "You ok?"

He wiped away a tear with his forefinger, the gentlest sensation she had felt in over five long years, and then she was sobbing, tears pouring down her cheeks in a wave of relief.

Chris simply held her and let her cry. As the tears slowed she pushed them aside and looked up into his kind eyes.

"Hormonal?" she suggested and laughed self-consciously. He nodded and kissed her lightly on the forehead, gently on the nose, and softly on her lips.

She sighed with pleasure and wrapped her arms around his neck. She drew him down to drink the sweetness of his breath as his mouth opened to hers. Screw the early meeting. She could do this all night.

When she woke the next morning Chris was already gone. The early hour of meeting was nothing compared to his. On the pillow next to her was a yellow post-it note. It said "wow!" and had a picture of a firework going off. She grinned and added it to her stack.

She sang in the shower, happy bouncy music sung with gusto into the showerhead. She chose something bright to wear to match her mood.

Before she left the house she pulled out the pad of post-its from the hall table and drew a single heart. She stuck it on the mirror where he would be sure to find it and danced out of the house.

Chapter Twenty-Five

Her office phone rang about noon the next day. "Hello?"

"Dr Alison Howden?" She felt a jolt of recognition. He sounded the same as four years ago when he had introduced himself as Andrew Jankowitz, Hollywood producer. Four years in which she had watched Dr Dickenson's career go from strength to strength. Not that it mattered now. "Mr Jankowitz, what a pleasure hearing from you again."

There was a pause on the line. "I'm sorry Dr Howden, but you have me at a disadvantage. Have we met?"

Wow, he'd forgotten her already. That was harsh.

"Only briefly Mr Jankowitz, and a few years ago. We spoke about a project."

"I'm sorry, I don't remember. Well it must have been a very small project."

Small? Only the biggest Hollywood hit of the decade. Unless…. She snatched up her phone and quickly googled. Oh my god. No Interception. It had never been made. Which meant… oh my god!

"It doesn't matter." She tried to keep her voice level and calm. "I also know of you from your documentary on null space."

He laughed. "You'll be the only one. Where on earth did you see it? It's basically unknown."

"I've a feeling it's going to get more popular over time. After all, all it takes is a single commercial success for the more niche projects to become famous. I think people are going to love it. I'm a fan."

"Well, it's nice to meet a fan. It's nice to have a fan. It's actually exactly what I wanted to speak to you about."

"A commercial venture."

"I'm looking for a consultant on a new project."

"A film."

"Yes." He was sounding alarmed.

She needed to back off a little bit. "I assumed."

He paused but continued anyway. "We're shooting in Scotland next summer and your name came up as an expert on the approach we are taking. It's heavily based in multiple node theories. It's got a lot of potential to it. We have a studio lined up and a few major names are interested. It's script work at first, trying to make it sound reasonably realistic."

She found that she was standing up. "I'd very much like to work with you, Mr Jankowitz."

"You would? Already?"

She chose her words carefully. "I've got a good feeling about it. I've seen your work and I think you are an excellent storyteller. I'd be excited to work on any project of yours."

"Well that's very flattering. I'd need you to come with me to California to work with the scriptwriter. He's a bit creative with the science. And then probably a few months on set here in Scotland. It's a big commitment. If you need time to think about it, talk to the university, family, friends, of course I understand."

"Thank you, but an offer like this is once in a lifetime."

She put the phone down and did a little dance of joy. This life literally could not get any better.

She had lunch at her Mum's house the next day. It had popped up in her calendar. She was looking forward to it. This family were her family now. Chris came with her.

They knocked on the door a good fifteen minutes late with a bag full of cheese and crackers in hand. Jess opened the door. She was enormous, a huge pregnant bump out in front of her. Alison fought her feeling of surprise, so her face stayed neutral. Chris gave Jess a kiss on the cheek.

"Come on in," she said and led the way inside.

Pete was waiting in the kitchen, sitting on a stool and chopping carrots.

Everyone gave everyone a hug and kiss. It felt normal, natural and fine. Even with the change in Jess there was no awkwardness.

"Where's Mum?" she asked when everyone had a glass of non-alcoholic Pimm's, for Jess's sake.

"Upstairs getting dressed. Dad is getting more bread - apparently there is only enough for one army, not two."

"Dad... is getting..."

Dad. She didn't have a dad. Obviously she had a father. But he gave up being Dad 30 years ago. He was a biological entity, not a person. Apparently in this world he was Dad.

The door went and he walked through it into the hall. "Hello all," he said.

She felt her heart start to hammer in her chest. Her dad was here? Really here?

She watched him walk in and start kissing cheeks and shaking hands. He was taller than she remembered, his face was creased like an old apple and his balding head was ringed in silver. He was wearing a cardigan with a collar that looked new and uncomfortable. Perhaps one of his sons-in-law had picked it out for him. Because he had sons-in-law, and that's what they do.

He came towards her. Luckily she was rooted to the spot so the kiss on the cheek landed without her flinching away.

Then Mum arrived into the room and the noise level went up by several decibels.

They ate on the lawn. All she could do was watch as her mum and dad teased each other, picked off each other's plates, poured each other a drink without asking. Her Mum looked relaxed. None of the icy calm that usually followed her around. She laughed. Twice.

And Dad, because she had a dad, now, apparently, was really funny. He played the fool and became the butt of the jokes and she was finding it harder and harder to hate him. Because what did she have to hate him for. He had stayed. And everyone was happy.

It got late and Chris left to go to a friend's birthday party, because he had lots of good friends now, and Jess and Pete got tired and left too. So she stayed back with her Mum and Dad and helped tidy up the lunch things like it was normal Saturday, and she was normal.

Which she was.

Chapter Twenty-Six

As she left Mum's house she was still in a daze. This was everything she had ever wanted but now she felt like she didn't deserve it. How was it possible that everything was so perfect?

There was a shout off to her right and the sound of running feet. Before she could turn her head a huge weight slammed into her right shoulder, making her stumble and flail for balance. She lost her footing and fell. As she did so the scene went fuzzy for a moment, like saltwater mixing with fresh.

"No!"

She landed heavily and the weight landed on top of her. It was a person. She pushed them off and scrambled free. The back of his head was eerily familiar.

"Jack?" he was still crumpled on the ground, clutching at his arm. It looked like he had hurt something. "What the hell do you think you are doing?" She looked desperately around. Everything looked the same. Maybe she had imagined it. But the hollow feeling in her stomach told her everything.

"What the hell, Jack? Take me back."

He still hadn't looked up. He was still lying there, clutching one arm, face pressed into the ground.

"Jack, are you hurt?"

"Yes." It was muffled by the grass.

"Your arm?"

He finally moved, pushing himself up with his good arm. He tucked his legs underneath him and pushed himself to his knees. "Everything. Everything hurts." He stood then, holding his arm gently with his other hand. And there they were. His peacock eyes, but this time crowded with pain.

"You pushed me through a doorway. What the hell?"

"I had to."

From beyond the numbness she found anger. "You can't just come along and push me through a doorway. Normal people just use the phone! Take me back to my world, Jack. That's my life you just shoved me out of." Jack was staring at the ground. He looked like a little boy up in front of the headmistress. But her rage was growing. "You have no right to come along and literally push me out of my life without even asking first. I told you, I'm committed to that life. To staying there forever. You can't just come along and change that without asking. Take me back. Right now. How dare you."

"I had to. I had no choice, Ali. You were in danger."

"Danger, what danger?"

"A bus. There was a bus, coming right at you. You were going to die. I saw it. I couldn't leave you there to die. No matter what promise you made. You're too important to me."

"What bus, Jack? There was no bus."

"You didn't hear the shouting?"

There had been shouting and running feet. But no engine noise.

"The engine had died; you couldn't hear it coming. I had no choice."

"You have to take me back."

"I can't do that, Ali."

"You can't just take me out of my life."

"Ali, the bus was heading straight for you. We went through a doorway. You know what that means."

Her stomach dropped. "Oh my god. The other Alison went the other way."

"You can't go back there."

"No, we have to go back, help her."

"There's nothing you can do. There's no way she survived that."

"She's dead? The other Alison is dead?" She sat down heavily on the pavement. The traffic moved cheerfully down the street. Birds tweeted. The sun shone. A bus went by. Her ears buzzed. She was going to be sick.

"I had no choice, Ali. I had no choice. It was her or you." His voice was soothing. He was crouched by her, hand stroking her hair. "I couldn't let you die. I'm so sorry." But the thump of words in her head drowned him out: *she was dead, she was dead, she was dead.*

"Come on, let's get you somewhere warm." He was pulling at her arms, hustling her to her feet. She couldn't find the words or the strength to resist.

She was dead.

They were in a taxi. Jack was counting out change.

She was dead.

Climbing out of a taxi at a hotel. She stared blankly at the sign: Caledonian Hotel. Her stomach lurched again. He took her arm and led her inside.

She was dead.

A porter led them to the lift and then out into a lushly carpeted corridor. The hotel guy opened their room door, smiled sweetly and turned to go. She could stop him, call him back. But the words stuck in her throat.

The man closed the door behind him with a click.

Jack sat her down in a chair and busied himself making tea. From the window she could see Arthur's Seat. A different angle than their stay at Minto Street but the memory caught her unaware anyway. The same people, probably, tramping up and down like little ants. The view made her eyes hurt.

She stared down at her hands. They were wringing each other, twisting her wedding band until her knuckles were raw.

What was Chris doing right now? Back in the world where his wife had just died. Her stomach heaved and she grabbed for the wastepaper basket just in time to catch the vomit.

What the hell was she going to do? Jack was right. She couldn't go back. That door was closed forever. Alison Howden was dead. She was dead. She just died. And yet here she was sitting in her favourite hotel being handed a cup of tea. This couldn't be happening. She sipped the tea. It helped.

"Thank you." She meant the tea, but he seemed to read more into it and smiled warmly at her.

"Thank god you're Ok," he said. "I nearly lost you." He was suddenly kneeling next to her with his head in her lap. She held he cup of tea up, trying to avoid spilling it all over him. He was grasping her knees. The back of his head was quivering. He was shaking.

She put the tea down carefully on the table and stroked the

back of his head, shushing him. What else was she supposed to do. "I'm fine."

"I'm so sorry, Ali. I didn't know what else to do."

"No, it's Ok, Jack." *It's not Ok.* "I'm fine." *I'm not fine.*

He looked up. His eyes were wet. "I'm so sorry."

"I just… I just need a minute."

"Of course. Oh god, how stupid of me. I'm sorry. Let me go and get you something. What do you want? Chocolate? I'll get chocolate. Just -." He snatched a blanket off the bed and tucked it around her. "Just stay warm. And drink your tea." He pushed the cup back into her hands.

She nodded and gave a smile of encouragement.

"I'll be back soon," he said. "Well, not too soon. In a little while. Try to sleep. I'll be back soon." The door gently clicked behind him as he left.

She sipped her tea. She felt oddly calm.

She sipped more tea. Outside her window the sun was still high, the people still climbing the hill. In this world nothing had happened. Everything was entirely normal. Alison Howden, mediocre theoretical physicist, was sitting, hale and almost hearty, in a lovely hotel room booked and paid for under an assumed name by a man who wasn't her husband. A man who, two hours ago, had thrown her in front of a bus.

Her hands were shaking again.

But he was right about one thing. It's not like she wasn't complicit in this. That wasn't her life, it wasn't her world. The Chris she had just left behind, the perfect Chris of her dreams? The person he thought was his wife was dead. And that poor innocent Alison from this world was dead. And it was all her fault.

She found she was lying on the bed. She didn't remember moving. Her face was wet. The pillow was wet. How long had she been here? The sun had moved on the hillside.

She had to get out of here. She couldn't stay in this room a moment longer. The betrayal, the awfulness of what she'd done was pressing on the back of her head. She had to go and apologise to Chris.

She scrambled off the bed with a sudden burst of energy. Coat, phone, wallet. Jack's coat was sitting on the edge of the bed. She looked at it for a long moment.

Time to go.

It was three strides to the door. She had no idea where she was going to go. Or what she was going to do. She just knew she couldn't stay here anymore.

She hauled the door open and came face to face with Jack.

"Where are you going?"

"I…" he was looking at her hand. The one holding the phone and her wallet. And coat. His eyes went cold.

"Where are you going?"

"I wanted some fresh air."

His expression warmed again. "Ok. Let's go."

She started to protest but he was inside grabbing his coat and back by her side before she could say a word.

They walked together back down the stair and out of the hotel. She picked a direction and set off. He took her hand. She didn't protest. They walked in silence for a while. Thoughts crowded her mind. When she stole a glance at him his face was troubled. Well at least he was bothered by it too.

Their walk took them to the bottom of Arthur's seat. She could see the spot where she had arrived into her perfect world. The hill was emptying. It was getting colder. She shivered.

"Cold?" It was the first thing he had said in almost an hour. She shook her head.

"I know it's hard, but it'll pass I promise. It was you or her. Someone was going to get hit. It was going to happen regardless."

She wished he would shut up. She nodded.

"It's not your fault, Ali," he said. She nodded again. "I know you're hurting now. But you're alive. That's what matters. What? Don't cry. I'm sorry."

His hand felt dead in hers. Or was that her hand? She felt a moment of relief as he let it go. Then he was hugging her. Pressing her face into his neck, making her want to scream.

She stood completely still, as the sun set, and the shade of the hillside slid over them. A tiny part of her brain spoke up finally, so she patted him reassuringly on the back until he let her go.

"You blame me, don't you?" He had that eagle look about him again. His eyes were colourless in the lengthening shadows. "I didn't do this lightly, Ali. You know that, right?"

She nodded.

"Ali, please talk to me."

She opened her mouth, but nothing came out. He grasped her hands in his and tried to rub some warmth back into them. She tried again.

"I'm just in shock, I think."

"I know. It's such a shock. One minute you're enjoying your new life and then I change it all again. I'm truly sorry. I had no choice."

"OK."

"OK." He leaned in to kiss her and she felt herself lean back.

225

He retreated, chastened.

"Sorry. You thought you were going to be there forever. You had committed to that, to him. And I'm a poor substitute. But we can adapt. We can move on. I'll help you. I hate to see you hurting."

She nodded and squeezed his hand. She just wanted to be alone. His attention was strangling her.

That night she feigned sleep as soon as they lay down. He put his arms around her and buried her head in his chest. She couldn't breathe.

He didn't move for a long time. His breathing was regular and measured. She counted 100 breaths then shifted her hand slightly. No reaction. So she moved her arm. Nothing. His breathing stayed the same.

She waited for another 100 breaths then rolled quickly onto her back, her eyes closed, her breathing smooth. He grunted but let her go. Settling back into his position. She didn't dare open her eyes for another 100 count. No movement. Deep breaths.

Now's the time. She stole a glance.

His eyes were wide open. She stifled a little squeak. He was staring right at her. He smiled warmly.

"OK?"

"Yes, fine. You?"

"Yes. Go back to sleep."

She nodded. Closed her eyes. Her heartbeat was loud in her ears. She lay quietly for as long as she could. Forcing her limbs to relax, breathing to slow. She had to keep her mind blank. She focused on her breathing.

The next time she risked a glance it was light. It was morning. Shit.

"Morning sleepy head." Shit.

It was only a couple of jumps back to their perfect world together. Their flat in London was waiting for them. She was going to be so happy there. Apparently.

She felt like she was in a dream. There was nowhere for her to go. She couldn't go back. There was no back to go to. All she had to do was say the word and he would book a flight and they could start their new life together.

She walked around their hotel bedroom. It was pure luxury, but it felt like a prison. She sat down on the sofa. Jack ordered coffee from room service. She wanted tea.

The coffee arrived along with biscuits and cakes and strawberries dipped in chocolate. Jack offered her one, but she couldn't.

It was ok to grieve. Her life. Alison. She felt herself starting to cry again.

"Are you ok?" Jack said.

She shrugged. "I just keep thinking about Alison."

"I know. It's such a tragedy. Here, some food will help." He came across and put the plate into her hands, but she put it back down on the shiny coffee table.

"Jack, what about Chris?" Chris thought she was dead. In his world she was dead. Alison was dead. What was wrong with her that she kept missing that fact. He was going to be heartbroken.

All those versions of herself out there. One less today. An entire life changed, and entire world changed. Jack fussed around her some more, but she couldn't move from the spot.

When the light faded from the sky she allowed him to lead her to the bed and take off her shoes.

227

The light from the chandelier cast wispy shadows across the ceiling. A tangle of dark and light reaching into the furthest corners of the room.

In one of the patches of light the ceiling was cracked. A jagged line that ran into the fuzzy softness of the shadows. An irreparable dart of destruction. The ceiling could be repaired but it would never be whole again. That crack would undermine and destroy any sheen of smooth plaster.

Better to pull the whole ceiling down.

She woke to find another cup of coffee next to her. The smell turned her stomach. She rolled away from it, squeezing her eyes tightly shut. Jack was somewhere in the room. She could hear him moving about. She squeezed her eyes tighter.

She woke again and it was later. The bedclothes were rumpled like she had been thrashing about. The coffee cup was gone. That was probably for the best.

Sleep was the answer.

When she opened her eyes for the third time she found Jack sitting on the side of the bed. Had he woken her?

She didn't want to look at him. It wasn't his fault. He had chosen to save her. Save this her.

She wished he hadn't. She wished she had died back in her perfect world, surrounded by what she had always wanted. Happy. Now what did she have?

"Hey," he said. He reached out a hand a hand to smooth her hair away from her brow. She didn't move away but it didn't feel reassuring like he probably meant it to. "How are you doing?"

She shook her head. A tear plopped onto the pillow. She allowed a few more to fall. But any more felt like selfishness. She wasn't even sure which bit she was crying about.

228

"I had no choice, Ali," he said. "At least you are still alive."

"I wish you'd left me there," she told him.

He started at that. "What do you mean?"

"We killed her."

"To save you."

"I wish you hadn't."

He grabbed her hands and pulled her up to sitting. "Don't say that. Don't ever say that. You're alive and that's all that matters."

A sudden surge of energy propelled her across the room. "That's not all that matters," she said, rounding on him. "A woman died. That matters."

"That's not what I meant. You're upset. But can't you see that I had to save you?"

"No, you didn't." She cast her arms around, taking in the room. "Why did you bring me here? Why were you even there? That was my home, *my* world. We said goodbye. Why didn't you go away?"

"Why? You told me you loved me."

"I *never* said that."

"But you did." He stepped forward and she still felt the closeness, the thrill she had felt when he had leaned down and kissed her. "Maybe not with words." She hadn't stopped him.

She closed her eyes to block out the shame. But an image was waiting, of him naked up against her, the sound of him groaning as he came. Her stomach flipped like an echo of that lust. But it was embers where it had been flames.

What had she done?

"I'm sorry," she whispered. "I'm so sorry. I didn't mean to."

"That's why I saved you." He came towards her, hands

outstretched, eyes lit up like fire. "And soon we'll be home."

She recoiled. "What is wrong with you? A woman died and all you care about is setting up a cosy home. Is this what you wanted?"

"No, of course not. But we can make the best of it."

"Make the best of it? She died!"

"And if I had to choose again I would still choose you over her." He went back to the sofa and sat down with a thud. "You think she is the only Alison who has ever died? A thousand Alisons a second are dying out there right now. Maybe a million. And a million Jacks too. So what? Are you mourning all of them? Were you mourning them while we were on the gondola in Venice, on the beach in Spain? Were you? Because if not then what you are feeling right now isn't about that, it's about you."

He was wrong. It sounded right but he was wrong. "She died because of me. Because of you. Because of our choices. That matters."

"You are so obsessed with doing the right thing." He ran his hand through his hair. "Making yourself responsible for all the sins of the world. Is this because of your dad? You can't keep compensating for his failures forever."

"What are you talking about? This isn't about my father. This is about Alison and Chris."

He glared at her. "Oh, I see. This isn't about morality or mourning a poor dead woman. This is about your beloved Chris." He came towards her across the furry rug. "Chris is gone. That life is gone. You can't go back to it. So just let it go."

He was in her face breathing hard. She stood her ground and stared back at him hard. "No, I won't let it go. I will never let this go. This will be the thing that is the only thing I think about for the rest of my life."

He flung his hands in the air. "God, you are so unreasonable. Do you have any idea what kind of work it takes to make things the way you want them to be? To fit your ideal of how the world should work?"

"What do you mean 'fit my ideal'?"

But he was turned away and talking to himself. "I mean it's my fault. I forgot about your stupid morality. I should have thought of something else. Obviously a dead Alison was never going to work."

"What are you talking about?" Then it hit her. "Is she not dead? Jack, is she not dead?"

He rounded on her and cast his arms out. "Nope. The precious life is yet unsnuffed."

She was on her feet. "Is this some kind of sick joke?"

He laughed. An ugly sound. "The joke's on me. Because apparently even this is not good enough to make you let go of him."

"Oh my god!"

"What? I had to do something. You were throwing your life away for your stupid morals."

He was still across the other side of the room. He looked wild and agitated, he started pacing like a cat. There was not a hint of apology in his eyes.

Who would do something like that?

"You drive me insane," he said. "You're all over me and then you walk away without a backwards glance. I'm never good enough for you."

"I always told you what I was going to do. I never lied to you."

He stepped forward and took her hands before she could stop him. "Not with your words you didn't." Then his face crumpled, and he started to cry. His voice was hoarse. "I know you wanted me then. I know you want me now." He tried to kiss her, but she stepped hurriedly back, hands up. His fists clenched but he stopped.

"I can't," she said. "That was a mistake. I gave into temptation, but I was wrong. I'm married."

"Not here. Not in this universe." He turned away and she thought for a minute he was leaving. But he went to his bag and brought back a white leather album which he thrust into her hands. "Here, you are my wife."

"What is this?"

He opened the book. There was a photo of them, standing side by side, just married. They looked so happy. She looked so happy. She turned a page. They were signing the register. She could almost feel confetti swirling in the air, hear a cello playing. It was a warm summer's day and they squinted into the camera, trying for natural smiles. She turned another page and they were standing under a tree, wrapped up in a kiss. She slammed the book shut.

"This isn't me. That isn't you."

He snatched the book and held it in front of her face. "*Here*, it is."

"Jack, stop it."

"I'm not the only one playing around with people's lives." He threw the book, hard, onto the floor. She darted to catch it, but it landed with a thump and the cover tore. She picked it back up, cradling the pages. This was someone's most treasured possession. How could he treat it so badly?

"I'm leaving." She wrapped the book in her arms and started

for the door. He appeared, barring her way.

"Move," she demanded.

"Not until you hear me out."

She took another step forward. "Get out of my way."

He squared his shoulders. "No. Explain to me. Why him?"

She glared at him, but he was too big to push. His breath was hot on her face. She looked from one eye to another. His pupils were huge. Seconds passed, her breathing the only sound. She focused her energy and felt her expression harden. "Take me home."

Then his face crumpled, and he started to cry. "Please, Alison. Don't let it end like this. I'll take you anywhere you want to go. But, after everything, please give me something to help me understand." She was taken aback at the change. She flinched back but he dropped his head onto her shoulder. She was unable to think of what to do. His tears dampened her shirt.

She had to do something. She raised a hand and patted his arm. He stood back, his face wet and pale. He walked over to a pile of boxes, towing her with him. She eyed the door, but he kept her hand in his when he sat down. She gently pulled it back and braced herself to leave. But then he dropped his head into his hands and started to cry. He seemed so helpless, so small. The anger of a moment ago was gone.

The guilt returned in a big, cold wave.

Their travels together had felt like an adventure. Like following breadcrumbs through an endless, green forest, pointing out the birds and the pretty pink flowers. But all the time Jack had held all the breadcrumbs. What had been a path was now a thicket as far as the eye could see. The forest was no longer so inviting.

"Why won't you stay?" he whispered.

Because you are acting unhinged, said a voice in her head. But to him she said, "Because I'm married to Chris. Maybe not here." She waved her arms around the room. Then she placed her hand on her heart. "But here."

He was looking at her now with a grim smile. "This is all a sham you know. He's the same person that he was in your world. He's no different. He'll do the same thing to you that he did last time. He always does and you always go back to him. Why do you do that?"

"What?" Every time? Which times?

"Alison, stay with me, please. Do this for me."

"I'm leaving Jack. I want you to take me home but if you don't I will leave anyway. There is no version of this where we are together."

Jack sprang up and the fury in his eyes had her stumbling backwards. Then her feet bumped against the back wall. There was nowhere else to go.

"What is it about you? Why do you always do this to me? After everything I do for you. I've turned the universe upside down to please you and it's never good enough. You're just the same as all the others."

"The others?"

He didn't reply to that. He just stood in front of her. His face was hard.

Then he stepped slowly forward until his chest was pressed against hers. She faltered and looked away from his furious stare. The pressure on her chest increased. She felt like a rabbit in the sight of a fox. She tried to breathe slowly and quietly as her heart hammered in her chest. She didn't know this man at all. She felt his hot breath on her face, felt herself pressed into the wall, saw his fists open and close.

She heard her mother's voice in her head. *What are doing? Are you waiting to be rescued? Get on with it.* She steeled herself and raised her head. She met his gaze and held it, trembling. For a long moment nothing else happened.

Then he blinked, his face changed, and he looked away.

She put her hands on his chest then and pushed him backwards into the room. He moved limply, no resistance and he ended up standing in the middle of the floor with his head hung low. She resisted the urge to shove him. She stepped around him, closer to the door.

"Can you please take me home," she said as calmly as she could.

"Why won't you love me?" he whispered. She couldn't see his face, but his voice was tortured, broken.

She kept her voice steady. "Nothing. There's nothing you can do. Please take me home."

His head snapped up. "That's not your home." She felt a wave of real fear and backed away from him. "You want to go home; I'll take you home." He came at her and grabbed for her arm.

She ducked out of his grip and pushed him hard. He fell over backwards, and she used the moment to snatch open the door and run down the corridor.

As she turned the corner she saw him coming after her.

She leapt down the stairs two at a time. The next level down the stairs ended abruptly and she ran down another corridor, ending up in an empty restaurant area. She saw another exit and sprinted for it. She heard the door crash open behind her. Thankfully up ahead was the lobby and she was quickly out into the street, turning blindly right and sprinting down

Lothian Road.

The street ahead was busy with traffic and she looked madly around for which way to turn. She was alone, in a universe that was not her own. Again.

Chapter Twenty-Seven

She turned left at the next traffic lights and ran down the empty street. There was a building in front of her, a 60s community-centre thing, looking out of place in the shadow of the castle. It was squat and brutal. The doorway was like a maw, but she mounted the steps two at a time and let it swallow her.

Inside a cavernous hallway led inexorably onward. Her footsteps echoed on the tile floor. The echo was a single retort, her own steps reflected back at her. How long before she heard others, before he found her?

She pounded around two corners, fluttering the posters on various pinboards. Open doorways on every side, faces staring. They couldn't help her. She needed somewhere to hide. A sign on a door flashed into her vision. *No entry. Private.*

She slammed open the door and tumbled into the room.

It was empty. Lifeless.

Her lungs gasped for air. She scanned the room, listening for footsteps past the pounding in her ears. No cupboards. No other doors. Not such a good choice after all. The room was big and square, high set windows showing only clouds. No, she needed a different hiding place.

She turned back to the door. Jack was standing in the doorway.

She felt, rather than saw, him start to chase her. There was nowhere to go but she ran anyway.

A pull on her arm signalled the end. But as she turned back to scratch and bite a familiar feeling overtook her. Jack was still ten steps away. The tug intensified into the familiar wrench of a doorway. She had found a doorway. She let it swallow her into safety.

She arrived in a circle of people, all staring at her in alarm. They all looked frightened. She scanned the room but no Jack.

She looked for the way out. There.

Someone appeared in her eyeline, was blocking her way to the door.

"No," she gasped. She had to leave. She tried to push past. She glared at the figure. It was woman, tall and skinny with a mop of silver hair like a bottle brush. She appeared to be saying her name.

"Alison, it's ok." The woman was staring at Alison's nose. That just irritated her more. She tried to push past again.

"It's alright," the woman said. "You're having a panic attack."

She tried to snort but her pounding heartbeat and rasping breath wouldn't let her. She looked around the room. The people were all sat in a circle on plastic chairs. Their expressions showed compassion, pity.

She pushed her sweaty hair off her forehead. The tall woman nodded understandingly. The expressions around the circle softened.

Realisation dawned. This was a support group. Then she really was laughing, big sucking gulps of laughter. They thought she was in the middle of a panic attack. That this whole thing was all in her mind.

She couldn't breathe. She sank to her knees. The woman was there again, putting her arms around her.

"It's ok," said the woman. "You're safe. You're safe here."

But that just made her laugh harder. Her sides ached. Only her hands on the floor were holding her up. Her breaths kept catching and sticking and then she was crying. Huge bodily sobs. The woman's arms tightened across her back, lifting her up into a hug. Alison clung to her; a shipwrecked sailor unexpectedly washed up on a beach.

The tight feeling dissolved and the waves receded, leaving her feet on the ground.

She pulled back, embarrassed, expecting to see pity or disgust. But instead the woman smiled reassuringly. No one was pointing or whispering. In fact they looked proud of her.

The woman helped her to her feet and led her to a chair.

She didn't sit down. "No. Thank you, but I have to go."

"No, Alison." The woman's resolve was an anvil. "That was an extreme release. You need to recover. Remember, Jack is in jail. You are safe here."

"No, he's right behind me."

"He is. I checked for you this morning."

Her brain struggled to catch up. "You did?" That's right, she was in another world. And if this Jack was in jail then he couldn't follow her here. She was safe here.

The woman squeezed her arm and walked away to the other side of the circle where an empty chair waited.

239

"Sit here and just breathe for a moment," she said. "Let yourself come back to this place."

Alison nodded and wiped her face self-consciously. Her fingers and toes were tingling, and the back of her head felt weirdly hot.

A hand on her knee made her turn groggily to her side. A wizened young woman was holding out a tissue. Her mouth was lined, and gap teeth made Alison internally recoil but she immediately felt bad. The woman's eyes were kind. And young. And bruised.

"Don't worry, hen. He's banged up. Can't hurt ye." The woman pushed the tissue into her limp hand and patted her knee.

Her return smile was probably nowhere near what that kindness deserved but her whole body still felt numb. Washed out. She wiped her face of sweat and tears and balled the tissue in her fist. She should say thank you. But the wizened woman was already listening intently to something the bushy haired lady was saying.

She got her phone out and let it reboot. It took an age while the woman murmured on in the background. Finally it was loaded. One of the young men looked across at her and she smiled and shrugged. He raised an eyebrow, not unkindly, and went back to watching the group leader.

She googled Jack's name. It took a moment to find an article in the Edinburgh Court News but yes, Jack Shepherd was imprisoned for ten years. Ten years! The date of the article was almost a year ago. She allowed herself to slump back in her chair. She really was safe here. She allowed herself some deep, steadying breaths.

As she relaxed she started to pay attention. Around the

circle were women, old and young. They were all listening intently. No, two young men as well. Every one of them was shrunken somehow, pulled into their seats by invisible straps. They looked trapped.

"...profile of a victim," the woman was saying. "The main difference is how people present themselves. And I don't mean clothes or flashy cars. It's the signals that they send about themselves. We're going to do a little experiment. I want you to pair up."

None of this was relevant. How far was it to the door?

"You too, Alison. It'll help you refocus. You can work with Helen. Come on."

All the people in the group were turning their chairs to face each other. There was grumbling and nervous laughter. She caught the eye of the woman next to her, Helen apparently, who had the same *oh no* expression she probably had. But the brush haired woman was bearing down on them, so they exchanged a look and then obediently shuffled their chairs around to face each other.

"Let's get it over wi' or Pam'll have us," said her partner with a wink.

"Right," said brush-haired Pam, from back in her seat. "Everyone close their eyes. Good. Now, we're going to start with a moment to centre ourselves, just like we've practiced. Just to clear out the energy in the room."

She opened her eyes for clues as to what on Earth that meant. Everyone around the room was breathing deeply, their eyes tightly closed. A large black woman on the other side of the circle had her hands upturned on her knees, finger and thumb pressed together. Om. She suppressed a nervous giggle.

Her gaze was caught by Pam's raised eyebrows, so she hastily shut her eyes and tried to breathe. Centred. Right.

Huffy breathing from all corners of the room invaded her ears. But the sound was reassuring and calming, like white noise. She focused on her breathing. Four breaths in, four breaths out. She found her shoulders dropping back another notch. She was safe here for as long as she needed to be. The tension from the last day gently dissolved from her lungs as they cleansing air was drawn in, and all the poison was expelled.

"OK, well done. Now, keep your eyes closed, and I want you to try and find your partner with just your remaining senses. Smell, heat, noise, anything you like."

All the breathing suddenly went quiet as everyone in the room tried to hear everyone else. With her eyes closed the room suddenly felt empty.

Helen was right in front of her. Where else would she be? Helen could probably place her easily enough. She must stink by now, all the running about she had been doing the last few hours. All that fear and panic must be pungent. A presence all by itself. She expected to feel an echo of that fear, but it already seemed to have happened to another person, a long time ago.

"Anyone?" Pam's voice invaded her thoughts.

There were a few murmurs but not the kind that said, totally got this. More the murmur of a group of people who really didn't know what it was they were trying to achieve.

"Ok, open up."

She opened her eyes to look at Helen but to her surprise she was a good foot to the left of where she thought she was. The look on Helen's face said that she had misplaced Alison too.

Pam said, "There's a theory that says that people who've undergone trauma react by pulling in their sense of self. The bit of them we call personal space."

Trauma. Was this a PTSD group then? Why was she there? What had Jack done in this world.

"It's the bit that stops people bumping into you," said Pam. "The bit that makes a bar-tender see you in a crowd of waving hands. Some people are brought up to suppress theirs, be a little bit more invisible. Others have it taken away by events."

Then was a grunt from the young man to her right. "This smacks a bit of victim-blaming, Pam," he said in a surprisingly gruff voice. Pam nodded for him to continue. "You're basically saying we all asked for this by being too shy, or whatever."

There was an angry noise from a couple of people around the group. Pam seemed unmoved.

"No. Not blaming. Just letting you know why things may have happened and giving you something you can do about it. Being shy isn't the point. You can be shy and have a great deal of personal space. I'm not blaming anyone. I'm giving you a tool you can use to stop it happening again.

"We've discussed before that recognising when your boundaries are being crossed is the best way to identify someone who doesn't respect boundaries. This is just an extension of this."

The young man didn't look convinced. No wonder. It sounded like nonsense. Was Pam saying it was her fault that Jack turned nasty?

"You're talking about trauma," said a voice. It was her own voice. She hadn't even meant to speak. "About being taken advantage of."

Pam nodded. "I'm taking about domestic abuse."

"Oh ok. That's not what's going on here." She sat back. This group was for the other Alison, not for her.

"Alison this is a safe space to discuss what he did to you."

"He didn't manipulate me. He just…" What did he just? He lost his temper. He was heartbroken. He chased her down the street. He stole her from her life.

Her head swam. No, this was just a misunderstanding. She wasn't a victim of abuse. That was other people. Sad, lonely people. Weak people. She looked around the room. Maybe those people were. But not her.

"We are finding ways to prevent this from happening to you again by understanding how you were targeted. Close your eyes again," said Pam, calmly. "Try finding me now."

She noted Pam's position and closed her eyes. Yes, she could tell where Pam was, but that was because she was prepared now.

The heavy breathing of her erstwhile partner nearly drowned out the shuffle of feet from the other side of the circle and the sniffing from a runny nose. Her attention was drawn briefly to the left. A quiet scrape. A cough. The air was very hot and still and smelled faintly of perfume, floor polish and dust.

The silence extended out but still she felt her attention getting pulled to the left. Like the feeling of being watched, of there being another person in the room.

Her eyes snapped open, but it was Pam. She had moved silently across the circle of chairs and was now standing on exactly the spot that Alison's attention had been drawn to.

Other people in the circle were opening their eyes, looking

at each other.

"I used to have no personal space. Just like you do. I had drawn it back to take up as little space as I could. And I fell from one abusive relationship into another.

"But I learned how to spread out again. I found myself again, as corny as that sounds. And you will too. Homework this week: look at how much space the people around you fill. And think about what it means to take up more, or less, of your fair share of personal space."

Pam gave a little closed hand bow, like a geisha. People started getting up and making their way to the corner of the room. There was a tea urn and biscuits laid out.

Pam soon came over, maybe noticing she hadn't moved. She braced herself for Pam to say something, but Pam simply sat down next to her.

The room was huge now that everybody was across the other side. A shadow from the window darted across the sunbeam on the wooden floor. Pam's perfume was large in the space. She fought against the urge to move her chair just that bit further away. Or that bit closer. To escape from it, or just to surrender to it.

Maybe that's what Pam had been on about. She felt small in comparison. Invisible. And ashamed for being so weak.

She had to say something, or they would be sat here forever. "I'm sorry about scaring everyone earlier," she said, into the sucking silence.

"It's not your fault." The practiced ease with which Pam said it spoke of a thousand repetitions - and yet it sounded entirely sincere.

She nodded. "I'm sorry anyway."

"Do you have a sense of what happened?"

Jack's angry face in the doorway swam into her mind. She followed the memory through, watching his face fuzz and fade. She forced her shoulders to unclench again.

Pam was watching her kindly. She wouldn't understand. How to explain she wasn't some basket case having a panic attack like they all thought she was. That the danger had been actual and real. She shrugged.

Pam smiled acknowledgement. "It's been a while since you felt like that, I think."

How would I know? she thought. Pam was being kind, but she hadn't been there.

Pam nodded. "I know it felt really real. That's how flashbacks work. Does it still feel real?"

She nodded.

"Well. Try those grounding techniques we talked about. Find five things you can see. Four things you can touch. Three things you can hear. Two things you can smell and one you can taste. Bring yourself back to the present. The present where Jack is in jail and cannot hurt you anymore. Where you are safe."

"Safe." She took a deep breath and let it go.

The sunlight had reached her foot and was infusing it with a pleasant warmth.

"Alison?"

She jumped. "Yes?"

"Is there something else you need to talk about?" Pam's voice held not a trace of reproach.

"Oh. No, sorry." She jumped to her feet. "Sorry."

Pam stood and reached out to squeeze her arm gently. Alison resisted the sudden urge to fold forward into a full hug and just let Pam take over her life.

246

"Remember what we talked about," said Pam. "You're very folded in right now. Try to spread yourself out a little bit."

Alison nodded guiltily. Had Pam heard her thoughts?

She put on her coat and eyed the door. There was no Jack waiting for her. But it was still an alien universe and she was still trapped. She started for the door. Her breathing was speeding up again. Deep breaths. Five things she could see. The door was one. She squared her shoulders and headed for it, ticking the rest off one by one.

Four things she could touch. Door handle.

There was nobody in the corridor. Her footsteps echoed on the tiles as she followed the route she had run before. The echoes of her previous panic ricocheted off the walls. Three things she could hear. Each footstep counted as one, right?

When she edged around the front door she saw the street was busy. It was crisp and cold. A gentle wind was blowing dropped leaves across the pavement. No sign of Jack. Or of any danger at all. She inhaled the smell of autumn. Crispy leaves and a faint hint of a log fire.

She picked a random direction and walked down the busy streets to the first cafe she found. She ordered a decaf tea and took a great big sip.

She put the class behind her. It didn't matter what Jack was like, what he had been doing. She was in a world he couldn't get to. She had to solve the problem of how to get back home.

She looked herself up on social media. It wasn't good news. Divorced, from Jack, of course. Working as a teaching assistant in a dodgy part of town. Her Facebook had hardly any friends. Her bank account had £174.36 and it was only the 19th March. She scrolled back to her last paycheck and winced.

So her choices were this. She could stay here where she was safe - and friendless, alone and poor. Or she could blunder about looking for another universe, praying she would stumble upon the right one, but in which Jack could surprise her at any minute.

No wonder she was still having panic attacks in this world.

An hour later her tea was cold. She pushed it way in disgust. A laugh from the table next door grated across her ears and she pushed up from the table and out into the cold street. The sunshine irritated her eyes.

She had looked up her address on the emergency contact page. It was in a part of town she didn't know well. She had no inclination to go there. She followed her heavy feet. Maybe she'd stumble through another door.

At least it wasn't raining.

Her wandering took her to the centre of town. It was familiar path she had trod in the old days when she went shopping or to see friends. Old, happy days, when all of this was just a dream she hadn't dreamed yet. Had she ever felt so light, so free of burdens? Her feet now shuffled long the ground, barely able to raise step. Each breath was a sigh, each thought moved sluggishly through her head. There were people everywhere but not a single face she recognised. How was this tiny little city so empty of familiar faces?

She came out onto the North Bridge, squinting in the sunlight. It was too hard to walk anymore, so she leaned against the parapet. The bridge hovered over the city centre, the old No'or Loch that had been a cesspool and drain for the entire city until the clever Victorian's had filled it in and built a train station and beautiful art galleries there. In front of her the glass roof of the train station shimmered, a glittery carpet reaching out to the National Gallery, framed by the majestic castle. Behind her left shoulder she could feel Arthur's Seat's benevolent gaze. To the million-year-old volcano this town was barely a minute old. What must a being like that think of all the ingenuity and industry to forge a city of stone and steel out of a little hollow in its shadow? Impressed? Amused? It was a sight to lift even the dullest of hearts.

Perhaps this world would be home for a time. She could regroup, come up with a plan.

Someone jostled her from behind. She jostled back in irritation, applying a firm elbow, but the hulking man had already veered away. Bloody tourists.

By the time she reached the other side of the bridge she had started to feel hopeful. She was safe, employed. Clearly the Alison who lived here was browbeaten and exhausted, but she still had some drive yet. The last few weeks had been a lie, but they had at least been restful, and cathartic, and now she had space enough in her head to consider fixing things. And with no useless Chris or scary Jack around who knew what she could do.

She passed the expensive shops on George Street. Who cared if buying a single item would wipe out her life's savings? Instead of wallowing in despair she would go back to whatever grotty hovel she lived in, take stock and make the best of it.

She felt in her pocket for her phone. It was gone.

Chapter Twenty-Eight

I t was Tuesday. Again.

The alarm that blared next to her head was like the trumpets of Jericho. Today was the day it would all come tumbling down. But then she felt like that every single day. How many Tuesdays had she made it through now? Four. This was her fifth. And how many to come?

3,120 weeks left, based on average life expectancy.

3,120 weeks of drudge, teaching a class she hated to a class she hated. Living in this godawful bedsit. With a criminal record to her name, she had found out in an excruciating incident at a job interview. And no driving license.

She checked her email on her shitty laptop as she did every morning for a response from Jess. She had begged to be forgiven but then Jess had asked her what she was apologising for and of course she didn't know.

Her mum wasn't returning her calls.

No one was.

This world was hell. Her punishment for her hubris and cavalier disregard for the fortunate life she had lived.

Jack had blown through this world like a hurricane, scattering her family, picking up friends and career and slamming them into walls and right out to sea.

So today she went to work again.

She sat on the bus staring out of the window. It was an hour to get home from her job. She couldn't afford to live closer. On the plus side there was nothing to do where she lived and with no one to visit or to come and visit her she lived like a sparrow off her meagre wages. Last months she had saved £124. Another 3,120 weeks to go and she'd be loaded. And dead.

The world of greater suburbia drifted past her window. People with set expressions going about their day. It was April. People were emerging from their winter hibernation; one girl was even in shorts. As far as she knew she had no shorts.

Only another 40 minutes to go on this stupid bus.

She had visited the Jack from this world who was now in prison. His easy manner had been replaced by a nuclear kind of hate. His eyes were pools of petrol. She'd ruined his life and taken everything from him, he said.

So she visited his other victims instead. She had thought maybe she could help them. They were open and kind to her, but she felt like a fraud. All he had done to her was scare her. To them he had done much worse. She had given them Pam's number and, to everyone's relief, left them to their privacy and their recovery.

She spent her weekends walking around her old haunts. This world was so different from any other world she had been in. Her life was so different here. And just because she had met Jack at the wrong time, just before she should have met Chris.

The irony of that wasn't lost on her. It was something she had been wishing for since almost the moment she had met Jack with his easy charm and wild promises. She had wondered a million times what her life would have been like. Well this was it. This is what it now was.

She let herself into her bedsit and dropped her bag on the bed. It was only just big enough, besides the bed, for a single armchair, stuffed into a corner, and a dining table for one. There was no message more impossible to ignore than these daily reminders of how alone she was out here. No one in this universe knew her. Even her family had no idea who she was. She could feel herself, day by day, sinking into the shape left behind by the damaged, broken person that they knew.

The door rattled, like it did when someone knocked.

It was Pam. "You've missed the last four classes," she said, with no hello.

She stood back and let her in. Pam settled on the armchair, so she made them both tea from the scaly kettle in chipped mugs and perched on the dining chair next to her. She would have offered biscuits, but she didn't have any.

She opened her mouth to do the requisite small talk when Pam said, "What's going on?"

"I'm sorry. I should have called. I just don't feel the classes are for me."

Pam nodded and took a sip from her cup. There was a smudge of dirt on the side. Alison couldn't take her eyes of it. There was a long silence. It was like that day in the park with the Mum waiting for the toddler to cry itself out. It wasn't going to work on her.

The dripping tap in the bathroom became the only noise

in the room. Eventually she could swear she could hear her watch ticking.

"Pam, thanks for coming over to check on me but I really don't need anything right now."

"You've gone back to deflecting then?" said Pam.

"Sorry?"

"You once told me that the reason you pretend to everyone that you are fine is because you hear your mother's voice in your head. That you are waiting for her to expel you from the family if you are shown to be in any way weak."

She shifted uncomfortably on the creaky wooden chair. "I told you that?"

"And you told me that Jack was the only person you had ever been really vulnerable with, so you were frightened to be vulnerable again."

She stood up abruptly and went over to the window. "Sorry, I'm not sure what you're getting at."

"You had a big flashback in group the other day and you have shut yourself down entirely to cope. I understand. But you can't go back to being that person from before."

"Why not? It's my life."

"Because that's what got you here in the first place."

She put the cup down with a thump. "No, Jack is who got me here in the first place. If it wasn't for him I'd be safe and warm and happy."

"Would you?"

"Yes! I don't need you coming in here and telling me it's my fault I ended up like this. You don't know what happened to me so don't judge me."

"I'm not judging you. I'm worried about you."

"You have no idea what has happened. I'm lost and helpless

and completely alone. I don't know you. The person you thought you knew is gone and there's just me. And I'm fine being on my own. I'm living with the consequences of what I've done and that's the end of it."

"You did this last time too."

"What are you talking about?"

"When you first came to the group you shut everyone out and tried to do it all on your own. Do you remember what I said to you then?"

"No!" she yelled. "I do not, because I was not there."

"You said that this was where follow through had got you and you were done with it."

The air rushed out of her and she sat on the bed with a thump. "I said that?"

"You did. And you were making so much progress. Let's not go backwards, hmm?"

"Progress? I was making progress? Living in this shit hole, doing a crappy job, my family not speaking to me."

"Yes. You are strong. A fighter. You refused to be beaten and you work so hard to do it right."

She looked around incredulously. At the tiny space and her torn coat.

Pam stood up to go. "Read your journal. Read what you wrote. This last month I have seen an Alison I barely recognise. Defeated. Hopeless. Why not get back in touch with the version who was doing so well. Was rebuilding her life. Was owning her mistakes and making amends for them. I miss her."

Pam handed back the mug she was drinking from. It was very worn and faded but there was a flash of yellow.

She said her goodbyes and saw Pam to the door by standing

very still.

A small hunt later brought out a plastic covered journal that she had overlooked as an old notebook before. She started reading.

It was dark when she finished. She had switched on a small lamp, but the room still felt crowded in shadow. This Alison, whose world was awful and sad, was the most determined person she had ever read. She was proud of her flat. Proud of her job. Proud of what she had done by getting Jack arrested. She had a life that Alison couldn't imagine having lived but she was fighting every day to make herself better, her life better.

And here she was lying around complaining how difficult it was to be here for a month. Alison had lived it her whole life.

She was spoiled, entitled and a scaredy-cat. If this Alison could make something out of herself then she could too. She was a trained physicist. She knew how to travel between worlds.

Chapter Twenty-Nine

She was standing in the middle of the Meadows, underneath the cherry trees. In a million universes she must be a Physicist. In a million universes she would walk this way to work every day. Who knew better than herself what her boring old habits were?

She had taken every spare day of holiday she had and spent ten days walking up and down Middle Meadow Walk. Any day now. Any time now she would feel herself lurch through a door and be somewhere new. And then she had a plan.

Everything around her was familiar. The paths were empty, as expected this early on a Wednesday morning. She had walked this pathway a hundred times, a thousand. Every day on her way to lectures, every time she wanted to go into town. In front of her was the old hospital building, now trendy flats. Behind her was her home, her neighbourhood.

She turned to look at it. All the other Alisons. Where were they now? What versions of her life were they living? Were they as brave as the Alison she had "met" here?

It was boring walking up and down and she got some strange looks. Back in her world she would see colleagues, students, locals, all the time. A stream of good mornings and good afternoons. Here she didn't belong, and no one even smiled at her. But she was determined, and it felt good to be doing something.

She had been back to the group twice. She was learning. If it took her a few weeks, or a few months, she could do it. She carried on up the path towards the whalebone arch which gave this walkway its name. The plinths were still there with the whalebone proudly standing. Definitely not her own world. In her world the whalebones were in a museum and the plinths were just empty carved stones. When she got to the bottom she would turn around again and head back the way she had come. And maybe top up her water bottle. She wished she could afford coffee.

She reached the bottom and turned. As she did she felt a lurch and her stomach heaved. Her skin felt like it split in two.

A door. She had gone through a door.

She staggered to the edge of the path and then whooped, loudly, frightening a squirrel.

She'd done it. She was out of that world. She was free.

Then back of her neck started to itch. Jack was probably not in jail in this world. He was free and could be anywhere. She felt completely exposed. She stepped behind a cherry tree, for the little disguise it gave her. Standing in the middle of a field, in the middle of a city, visible on all sides. No, she needed to get moving.

She set off at a jog down the hill towards

As she neared the arch she slowed down. It was more sheltered here. There were buildings, sheds of some sort and she stopped in the lee of one to think.

She had a chance now, to get back to her world. Not the shambolic one she'd started in. But the perfect one he had stolen her out of. This couldn't all be for nothing.

One thing at a time.

There was a taxi with a light on heading her way. She flagged it down and asked to be taken to the University campus at the King's Buildings. Her lab.

It was risky. Jack would surely predict she would go there. But he couldn't know what door she had gone through. She needed equipment. There was nowhere else to get it from today, and for free.

Still, she kept an eye on the street when she arrived and hurried inside. The security guard just nodded as she trotted past his desk. Clearly she was a workaholic in this universe too.

The corridor to her office was empty but the door to her room was locked. She rattled it a few times helplessly. She never locked her door.

She cursed this Alison for being a stickler. The door didn't budge, even when she shoved it hard. When she peered in the gap the mortice was clearly locked.

Shit.

Now what?

A noise down the corridor. She flattened herself against the wall. Was it Jack?

A creak, a scraping noise and then a slam. A door.

Her skin prickled. Any minute now he would walk around that corner and she was doomed. She couldn't talk her way out of this. What would he do? Would he push her under a bus? Start again with a new Alison?

The corridor remained empty. No Jack.

Come on, you silly woman, she told herself. *Standing around here isn't going to help.*

Simon's office was on this floor. Maybe Simon was in today. After a few more nervous seconds where nothing happened she set off towards Simon's office. Maybe he would magically have a key.

She peered around the corner. There was a light on in Simon's room. The floor squeaked as she tiptoed along it. There was someone in there. She knocked tentatively.

"Yes?" That wasn't Simon. She took a step back to run but stopped. Where was she going to go? This was her only play. The plaque next to the door said *Dr Andrew Cochrane, BS CE PhD*. Not Simon.

The door opened. A tall black man was standing in the doorway. He was wearing corduroy trousers and a polo shirt from GAP. His hair was peppered with grey. She had never seen him before in her life, but his expression was friendly. "Dr Howden?"

"Dr Cochrane." A last-minute effort to keep the question out of her voice.

"Do you need something?"

"I... no... sorry. I just locked myself out of my room."

"Again?" His tone was admonishing but also amused. She shrugged helplessly. "Hang on, I'll get your key."

"Oh. Thank you."

She hopped from foot to foot while he went back into his office. Clearly they knew each other.

Come on, what was taking so long.

The man reappeared with a keyring in his hand.

"Here you go." She took the key and the book that he followed it up with. "Sorry it took me so long to get it to you. Interesting read, I thought."

She glanced at the cover. *Nonionic surfactants and the mutation effect.* Never seen that before in her life either. She made a non-committal noise.

"It would be interesting to apply that to your ionic bridge problem." He continued. Her heart stopped. How the hell did he know about that?

"I thought your rewrite of our paper was excellent. But I still think we should be careful about peer reviewing it too soon."

What the hell? She was aware that she was standing and staring it him like a fool, but her brain didn't seem to be working. Who was this guy? Why was she sharing her findings with him?

"I... of course. That's why I'm here. Just going over the data again."

"Really?" His eyebrows almost lifted the top of his head off. "I thought this was all finalised." He didn't look so friendly now. But then neither would she if she had been reviewing his paper and then he announced uncertainly about his calculations.

"Just a final re-run. Honestly, nothing to worry about." She cursed her stupidity. She was thinking like a fugitive, not a physicist..

"Dr Howden, this is most worrying. My name is on this paper too." That did it. She pulled herself back up to her full height. She was world renowned. Probably. This pompous man wasn't going to make her flustered. She had been in academia for long enough that she wasn't going to be bullied by someone with only one PhD. She took a breath and lined up a ballistic retort, but he got there first.

"Jack assured me when I built that thing - "

"Jack?" She crumpled. Oh, god, he knew Jack. The room spun. She had forgotten there must be a Jack in this world too. How much would he know? Was he dangerous too? Was she never going to get away from him? She had to get out of there. She had to get out of every there. Some place where she and Jack had never met.

But to do that she needed a door. And to do that she needed equipment.

One step at a time, Ali.

Dr Cochrane was watching her curiously. She rearranged her face.

"Jack is not the lead researcher on this paper. I am. And I am known for being a perfectionist so I I don't think this should come as a surprise that I measure twice, cut once."

He pushed his glasses up his nose. "I'm afraid I don't know that phrase, but I get the gist. Just try not to find anything startling, won't you?" He turned back into his room, laughing at his own joke so she joined him heartily, backing away down the corridor. When his door slammed she turned and ran.

Back in her room she started hunting for the cathode ray tube and oscilloscope. She eventually found them in the back of her storage cupboard. What the hell were they doing back there? If they were publishing data, why was all the equipment packed so completely away.

Something she did find that made her day, though, was an old phone. Finally. She switched it on and rebooted it from her backup. Her apps and passwords all repopulated themselves one after another. She was back in business.

Now for equipment. She stopped to think then turned back to look at her desk. There was an object on there that she had glanced at once then discarded in her search for her tools. It was sitting next to her laptop, which she quickly bundled up and stuffed into her bag. But she had never seen this before. It was small electronic device with sensors on the front and a screen which looked like a bastardised iPod screen.

Could it be?

When she picked it up it nestled beautifully in her hand. Underneath it on the desk was a hard copy print out of a paper. The title was "Doorways in space and time; proof of alternate universes". Her and Dr Jones' names were underneath in bold capitals. Bingo.

She speed-read the abstract. At the words "created a device for detecting and registering ionic disturbances which indicate the presence of such doorways" she allowed herself a little "yes" under her breath, stuffed the paper and the device into her bag and left, locking the door behind her. She pocketed the keys. No point in letting anyone see the device was missing just yet.

She had a way home.

Problem two. Finding a map through infinite universes.

It had taken about five minutes over coffee – wonderful coffee! - to work out how the device worked. She switched it on. It asked her if she wanted to detect. She said *yes*. And there was a door. Right on the other side of the coffee shop.

The screen showed a video feed of the world in front of her but superimposed on top was a blue shimmer. Rectangular. Upright. Just like any other door, in any other building.

There was an empty table next to the doorway which the customers in the busy coffee shop were all studiously ignoring. Perhaps some part of them knew the danger. She swapped seats so she was within a few inches of the door. The customers gave her curious glances but quickly went back to their coffees. She became invisible again.

It still amazed her. Less than a foot from her right arm was a doorway to another dimension. Where another universe carried on cheerfully without ever knowing how close they were. Another coffee shop full of all the same patrons. And all these people could go through into that coffee shop at any time. Whenever they wanted to.

So could she.

She stared at the read out. It looked like any other door. She could go through it right now. She could be one step further away from here, from Jack, from this whole nightmare. Completely alone. In a universe where not a single soul shared a history with her.

Man, this was harder than she thought.

All the weeks of travelling to far distant dimensions. It had seemed so easy. A hop skip and a jump and everything was better, everything was fine. Problems whisked away at a moment's notice. Guided by a man with supreme confidence.

One time she and Chris had been driving through Rannoch Moor. There were going on a camping trip, apparently. She hated camping. Rain and bugs did not make a good holiday in her opinion. But he insisted. And then they ran out of fuel. Brilliantly and so urbanely. No phone signal. No other cars on the road. So Chris had walked off down the road to find signal, or a petrol station, or people. And she had waited in the car with the guidebook which gleefully informed her about the many many unprepared humans who got lost or drowned or went missing forever and ever in this desolate spot. And she got cold and it got dark.

263

Rannoch Moor was clearly the inspiration for a thousand fantasy horror films. Petrified, bleached tree trunks scratching their way out of stagnant pools, miles and miles of heather strewn wasteland, distant hills looming across and chance of spotting civilisation. Not a light to be seen. And the car, up until that moment a beacon of progress and man's mastery over nature, had become a cold metal box. And she was a feeble human adrift in a giant landscape with no idea where she was. She had never felt so alone.

Until now.

A barista stopped by her table to take her empty cup. The noise of the coffee shop eased into her cold mind, dispelling the memory of that moor. She and he performed the empty coffee cup routine together and parted with a smile.

She had just sat and waited on that moor. And Chris had come back and got her, on the back of a motorbike, with a can of petrol in one hand. She got lucky that night. Because he had saved her. How pathetic. She should have saved herself. Why hadn't she gone for petrol?

She wasn't going to sit around and wait to be rescued any more.

She put her hand out, watching the tips of her fingers fuzz. There was a pulling sensation. She could go through that door right now, into the great unknown and start her very own search for petrol.

She allowed her fingertips to inch forward. There was a pulling sensation which spread through her hands, up her arms and then, wham. She was sitting in another coffee shop. A couple of deep breaths to ease the nausea. The device showed the doorway fading out of view. It would be back later when the ions recharged. But for now nothing and no

264

one could follow her.

In this world her coffee cup was full.

Chapter Thirty

He was tricky to find.

Social media was her friend. She still had a Facebook account in this reality and her password was the same one it always was. Terrible for security but great for dimensional travel. Searching Jack Shepherd came up with thousands of possibilities, even filtering for country. Maybe LinkedIn would be better, but what was she going to put in the search bar? Dimensional shift expert? That was nonsensical. And he wouldn't have a LinkedIn page.

She had thought this through a lot. Either the Jack in this world was just as crazy as the Jack she knew or there was just one crazy traveller Jack. A non-traveller Jack wouldn't be able to help her in any way. A traveller Jack might try to kill her. Not an easy fix either way but she couldn't think of a single other course of action.

She had to think laterally. The Jack she knew hadn't worked a day in his life. She cursed having not gotten to know him better. How could she be so stupid to spend months alone with this man and not know a thing about him. Every question had been met with a knowing smile and a joke. She had been tempted to walk off into the ether with this man and she didn't know the name of his parents, where he was born, what his interests were. To fall for so much flattery. What kind of person was she?

Anyway, this wasn't helping.

What kind of online profile would a sociopathic narcissist have? The kind where he could lay traps for unsuspecting women so he could sleep with them, take their stuff and then vanish without a trace. Tinder.

It took her all of five minutes to set up a profile. She focused on everything she knew Jack liked. This, at least, she knew very well.

She started with Edinburgh. He had been here to begin with, so it made sense.

An hour later she was feeling a lot less smug. There was no search function, so she just flipped through profile after profile. She didn't even know if he was in Edinburgh. All these pictures of men with puppies, men with sunglasses, men with their shirts off. Was this really what they thought people wanted?

An hour later, unbelievably, she found him. She so nearly swiped past him but thankfully caught herself in time. The picture was full smirk. Not a hint of modesty anywhere. Made sense.

The bar was full of people. It had felt like a good idea. Somewhere public. But it was noisy, and everyone seemed to be in couples. The air was tinged with pheromones.

She waited nervously in the bar sipping a lime and soda. It looked enough like a gin and tonic for him probably not to buy her another drink quite yet.

She had no idea what to expect. He could be a sleaze, a saint, or anything in between. Her stomach felt queasy. What if he recognised her? But he couldn't. In this world they had never met, she had made sure of that when she got here. Dr Cochrane was back to being Simon and Simon had no idea who she was talking about. But Simon was now divorced. This world sucked.

Jack was going to walk in here any minute, ready to size her up as a mate. The thought made her feel sick. She remembered his breath on her neck and her skin crawled.

She couldn't do this, couldn't face him. It was too horrible. Fumbling off her chair, she started struggling into her coat. She could just keep going from world to world until she stumbled onto the right one. It could happen, right? The heavy thump of the device in her pocket against her leg made her stop. She took it out. The screen had activated at the motion and the summary screen glowed.

Door summary
Active doors within one-mile radius: 1438
Battery: 40%
Shit.

She was a physicist for god's sake. The statistical probability of stumbling onto the right world was infinitesimally small. This was it. For now this was her only option.

She took her coat off again and sat down. She wasn't going to be able to do this sober.

She flagged down a passing waiter. "Gin and tonic please."

He took the half empty soda glass with a smile. Probably knew she was being stood up. This was humiliating.

The door went again, and her heart thumped as Jack walked in. He scanned the room and she took advantage of the moment to compose her face into a welcoming smile. He was the same. Cocky. Fascinating. Terrifying.

Her face hurt.

He was wearing a long-sleeved jacket and a shirt underneath. She couldn't see any sign of his tattoo so she couldn't run away just yet. He caught sight of her and walked across the bar. His smile was broad, confident. She swallowed hard.

"Hello." Easy warmth flowed from him. She focused on that. Boyish. Warm. He took her offered hand and, instead of shaking it, leaned in to kiss her lightly on the cheek. The move was practiced and fluid. She forced herself not to react to his lips on her cheek.

"Hi," she managed.

He sat opposite her. His impish grin could have melted steel. All the better to eat you with, my dear.

"So, Alison," he rubbed his hands together dramatically, his peacock eyes twinkling electric green and blue. Mesmerising. "What's it going to take to get you in bed, then?"

All the tension inside came out in a burst of laughter. This was going to be easier than she thought.

This was the Jack she had first met. Defy convention and politeness and get straight to the point. The boy-child that she had distrusted immediately. The one she had almost fallen for. Outrageous. Cheeky. Unacceptable. Irresistible.

Her gin and tonic arrived, and he ordered a whisky.

She couldn't think of a damn thing to say. How was a Tinder date supposed to go anyway?

"So you said you're a physicist. That sounds interesting," he said with no sign of awkwardness at all.

"Yes. I'm studying alternate realities," she said, then almost bit off her tongue. "I mean, the theory of alternate realities.

Far away. In space."

"Interesting."

"Not really. You're in PR?" she said desperately.

"Yes. How did you know that?"

Shit. "You seem like the type."

He laughed. A huge belly laugh that made people turn and stare. "That's amazing. I just assumed you'd googled me."

"Oh, right."

"You've not done this before have you? Tinder, I mean."

"I...no."

"It's ok. It's the weirdest thing in the world. You get the hang of it. Eventually."

"Have you done a lot of this?"

"Some. I was in a long-term relationship, but it ended last year."

"I'm sorry. What was she like?"

"She was lovely. Is lovely. But we just didn't work, you know."

She nodded.

He offered her a peanut. He was still wearing his jacket. Surely he was warm by now. If he would just take it off then she could check for the tattoo and be done with this ridiculous farce. She caught him watching her staring at his chest.

Thankfully, he was still holding out the bag of peanuts - she took one to hold back her blushes.

"How about you?" he said, taking a peanut and crunching it into nothing.

"I'm married."

"I did wonder."

"Huh?" Then she realised what she had said. "No, I mean I was married. Until recently. I'm still getting over it. Looking to get back out there, you know."

He took another peanut and rolled it in his fingers. "Listen, you don't have to do this. If it's too soon. I totally understand."

"No. I want to. I want to be here. With you."

Her sincerity must have convinced him because he smiled his warm smile and she let herself relax into one in return.

He leaned back in the seat and pulled his jacket down over his shoulders. Her eyes went to his arms, the last part of him to become uncovered. As the jacket slid free it revealed long sleeves buttoned at the wrist. Damn it. She looked back up to see him studying her expression. His eyebrow was up.

Fuck it, this was taking too long. She put her hand on his sleeve. "Nice shirt," she purred. His other eyebrow joined in. She took her hand away. Man, she was shit at this. She took a big swig of gin and tried to think. He was going to know she was up to something. How did his type of women do this kind of thing?

She pushed her chair back and gave him her most straight-forward look. "Let's go." She didn't even attempt sexy. Straight to the point without bullshit, that was more her thing anyway. "My place is just around the corner."

He just nodded, downed his drink and went to pay. She pulled her coat on and practically ran to the door, yanking it open and stepping outside. She took a big gulp of the fresh air gratefully.

This was never going to work. He must think she was crazy. Or desperate. Or both.

The door popped open and out he came, shrugging on his jacket. His expression was relaxed, open. No censure or judgement. Of course this kind of thing probably happened to him all the time. This was probably entirely normal.

So it had to be entirely normal to her too. She took his arm and drew him towards her. She was a professional woman, out on the town, needing an itch scratched. It was ok to be nervous, and jumpy and feeling weird. Anyone would be.

She turned him and they walked down the street in the direction she indicated. She'd chosen an Airbnb, so it just looked like an everyday flat. She didn't want him getting spooked thinking she was scamming him or was a prostitute or something. All she had to do was get his shirt off and get him unconscious. It should be easy, right?

She felt cold in her light coat. Were they never going to get there? The end of the road seemed to be a mile away. Each step took an age. It didn't help that her steps were clipped and short and got her nowhere. His were long and easy, half-league boots in comparison.

She glanced up at him. His face was relaxed and easy. This was the man she was deathly afraid of. But this Jack seemed different, kind and thoughtful. She couldn't imagine the Jack she knew offering to call the whole thing off.

It was like Jekyll and Hyde. And Dr Jekyll was kind and charming and smelled so incredibly good. And Mr Hyde was nowhere to be seen. She felt safe. But she would, she wasn't the one about to be drugged unconscious, stripped to his waist and photographed.

Maybe she was the villain here.

As they turned the corner she felt his coat land on her shoulders. She glanced up into his warm smile. His musky smell dropped into her senses like a bomb, making her head spin.

She smiled weakly at him and wished he would stop being so nice. "Thank you."

"You're welcome."

As she let them both in he stood a respectful distance away. Not too crowded, nothing threatening. If she had felt even slightly threatened she would have bottled it and slammed the door in his face. She assumed he knew that too.

She showed him into the living room and offered him a drink. A beer, as predicted. The wine was safe, so she poured herself one and fetched him the pre-opened beer from the fridge. She hoped it hadn't gone flat. But he chugged it happily.

He was draped over the end of the leather sofa looking around the flat. She perched on the other end and did the same. How long would the stuff take to work? He wouldn't keel over immediately. How long did she have to keep this up for?

He looked around the bland and tasteful flat as he took another sip. *That's it, keep drinking.*

"Nice place," he said.

She looked around. Traditional with a modern decor. Artful trinkets. Huge canvas picture of a yellow rose taking up one entire wall. "Yeah. Corporate let. Not really my kind of thing but, you know."

She became acutely aware that she was perching. She kicked off her shoes hastily and tucked her feet under her, resting her right arm of the back of the sofa and sipping from her glass in her left. Slow down, Ali, don't get tipsy. She saw him note her movement and he smiled at her wolfishly.

"Are you here for long?" he said. It didn't even sound calculated, just genuinely interested. She wondered if he was sizing her up for a place to stay or just trying to help her relax.

"A few months."

"Where are you from?"

"London. You?"

"Lincolnshire." His actual origins. She was surprised. He leaned forward, put the bottle down on a coaster, and started to take off his jacket. She watched the muscles move under his shirt.

He was too awake still. What if this didn't work? What if he never went to sleep at all? Would she have to sleep with him?

Her brain stalled at that and she struck out desperately for something to say.

"What's your story, then?" She had tried for flirty, but it sounded accusatory to her ears. He didn't seem to notice.

"Edinburgh is my home. I came here ten years ago and found permanence." He picked at a fold in the bottle label, never breaking eye contact. He had pulled loose a tiny strip of label, severing the top of the gold star. "My parents moved around a lot. I love it. The people, the culture, even the weather. It's where I belong."

"Tough childhood?"

"Tough, but exciting. I travelled more before I was ten than most people do in their lifetimes. I had good parents. That helped. You?"

Damn he was good. The little lost boy who covered up his loneliness with jokes and charm. And who was never going to stop making eye contact apparently. She was feeling hot, but she didn't want to take off anything in front of him in case things started moving too quickly. She had to keep stalling.

"Oh, the normal," she said. "Parents, school, university. Nothing different about me at all."

"Oh I don't know. You invited me back here with barely a second thought. That's pretty unusual." He saluted her with the bottle.

She buried her face in her wine glass. "Oh well, you know. Working away from home," she muttered.

"I think it's pretty great, actually. No bullshit. Just going for what you want, just because you want it. No games."

He took another swig of the bottle and placed it down on the coffee table. The movement bought his knee closer to hers. She looked into those beautiful eyes and saw nothing but sincerity. She felt a familiar pull. The temptation to just fold herself up into a little box and give herself to him to hold.

"I just don't want you to think I'm some kind of predator," she said, without thinking.

His eyebrows went up. "Well, I didn't until now," he laughed.

She laughed with him. The wine had started to do its magic. She was finally relaxing. Was he the same? Was he looking sleepier? She felt herself lean forward.

His eyes were darker, pupils larger. She felt his breath on her face. She was too close. But she couldn't draw back. When had he got so close?

He reached a hand up to her face. She felt herself nod, just a little bit. And then they were kissing.

The smell of him drowned her senses, already submerged in the wine. Her hand reached up to grip his arm and she was pulling him forward. His hands were in her hair. She felt a little knot snap open in her chest and then she couldn't get close enough. She was up on her knees, crawling closer. His arms snaked around her, coiling her in heat, securing her in place. A moment of abandon and then he slumped into her lap.

She stared at the back of his head. What?

Oh, the beer. She had drugged the beer. Right.

What the hell was she doing? How did she fall for this every time? What kind of a masochist was she?

She shoved him off her knee onto the sofa, wriggling out from underneath him. He landed lying on top of his left arm. Of course he did.

She took her glass back into the kitchen then went into the bathroom and splashed some water on her face.

"Stupid. Stupid," she told herself in the mirror. "Pull it together. What the hell were you thinking? Map. Now."

He was right where she left him, snoring slightly. She turned his head to ease his breathing.

Luckily this wasn't Chris. She'd never be able to move him. It was moments before she got his arm free and mere moments longer to undo his shirt cuff and pull it up his arm.

No map.

She let herself out.

Chapter Thirty-One

Her phone bleeped a 1-minute notification. It said "Dad. I Rouge. 2pm."

The notification winked out.

Which Dad was he? The father she never knew, or the man she had met briefly who was warm, and sweet and real? She could have him all to herself.

She checked her phone for clues and found a Facebook page of her life in this world. There was no Dad in any pictures. This Dad was one of the ones who left.

She had things to do. She hadn't been able to find Jack in this world so needed to skip to another one, hunt him down, get a date lined up. The detector thrummed in her hand. She didn't have time for this.

And yet her feet took her to I Rouge and deposited her outside.

She stared at the red doors. What would she even talk to him about?

How's things? What have you been up to? How could you leave your wife and kids destitute and alone? What the hell is wrong with you? Why didn't you want me?

Her breathing was getting laboured. She should go. This was a bad idea.

She should go.

Her hand opened the red door and her feet moved her inside into the hubbub. The tables were full. Couples, families, young men. No one that could be him. Waiters and waitresses danced like mayflies, avoiding her eye. The heat was unbearable.

A hand touched her arm making her jump, but it was just a waitress who apologised. She nodded at her enquiry, are you meeting someone, and gave her father's name. As the waitress led her through the restaurant she kept her eyes fixed on her back. Maybe he wouldn't be here yet. She could get settled and compose her face.

The waitress stopped. There was a table. At the table was a man. He was older, well dressed. It was him. He looked nervous. As he should.

He cleared his throat. His eyes were surrounded by laughter lines. He was lightly tanned. His shirt looked soft and well made. The fingers of his clasped hands were twitching and jumping. The nails were bitten short.

"Hello, Alison. It's really good to see you."

So they weren't best pals. There was certainly no hint of any hugging. She sat down carefully but didn't reply.

Why were they here? Jumping into other people's lives was like opening a book halfway through. All you had to go on were references to things that everyone assumed you understood. But the advantage was that you had nothing to lose.

"Why are you here?" she said, as calmly as she could.

He seemed pleased that she was at least speaking. He looked

relaxed. How dare he? "Because it's been a really long time. Because you asked me to come."

"I did." Probably. "But why did you come?"

"You're my daughter. If there's a chance we can have a relationship it's worth taking."

"And why is it we don't have a relationship?"

"Oh, come on now." He scratched his ear awkwardly. "Must we go over old wounds?"

She found herself leaning forward. "Actually, I really need to hear what you did."

He shifted in his seat. "I left. I ran away from being a father and husband and abandoned you all. Does it help to hear it out loud?"

She stifled a snort. Instead she said, "Are you looking for forgiveness?"

"No. You're still angry. I can see that. I'm looking to give you peace. I assume that's why you called."

"Peace? After everything you did to us. You abandoned us without a backwards glance. You turned you back on your family, your responsibilities, and left us crawling in the mud. You left us. How dare you sit there and tell me you want to bring me peace?"

He nodded then, like she'd confirmed something for him.

She hated him. Every smug laughter line, his stitched collar, his expensive watch. The rage swelled and crashed in her ears.

"I hate you for what you did. For what you made me feel. For the way you made us live. Fuck you."

The storm peaked and washed past her. The rage was still there but it was partially spent. Her ears rang and the back of her head felt hot like it had expelled a huge burst of energy. She let her head drop forward.

As she breathed to cleanse her lungs she felt her father place his hand over hers. She looked up. His expression was neutral.

"I hate you," she said, but there was no venom, it was just a fact.

"I know. That's ok."

They sat for a while in silence. The waitress brought water. The table next to them was filled by a couple and their small child. The little boy was carrying a stuffed dinosaur. They chattered excitedly as they sat, the little boy on his father's lap. They played dinosaurs together while the mum got out a bag of crayons.

Her thoughts were moving slowly but they eventually came to rest. "Why?"

"Why what?"

"Why did you leave?"

He sipped his water before answering. "Your mother and I were deeply in love. She was my everything. We were really happy together." He sipped again. "I never wanted children, but she did, desperately. I tried to talk her out of it but eventually she gave me an ultimatum. She called it a dealbreaker. I couldn't imagine living without her. So we had you.

"I tried to be a father. I failed. It was already too much, but she wanted more children. She had always wanted two. I said no. She got pregnant anyway. I managed a few years and then I left."

"You abandoned us."

"Yes."

"You never wanted us." She knew the answer was coming but her stomach fluttered anyway. Years of assuming was not the same thing as hearing it. Would he say it?

"No, I didn't."

The butterflies mutated into lead and landed in the pit of her stomach. But there was no associated wave of shame, or hatred, or anything. It was a fact now. Like the existence of sand. Or the death of baby rabbits. A fact of life.

"Why did you agree to have me? No one forced you to."

"I thought I could do anything to keep her. Accept anything. I was wrong. So I lost her anyway. But at least I gave her the two daughters she so wanted before I left."

Self-righteous bastard. "You can't justify this."

"No. I promised her forever. But forever is a lot to promise anyone. I'm not the type to be anyone's dad. I just wanted her. But sometimes that's not enough. For her, or for me."

"She says you lied to her."

"I know. She's still angry. And with good reason. But I never lied. I told her I didn't want children, didn't want to be a father. If I had stayed it would have been worse."

She studied his face. He clearly believed this. Was it a deliberate lie he was telling himself, or just something he never questioned, never examined? She should point out the flaws in his argument, force him to recognise his own cowardice, selfishness. He should understand the sheer lie of his point of view.

His expression was untroubled, he should be troubled. She should make him troubled. Troubled like Mum, sitting up every night worrying about money, her skin grey, her mouth surrounded by fine lines testifying to the constant purse of her lips. The light in her eyes dimming, year after year. Or Jess, crying into Alison's arms, because her own father didn't want to come and see her school play, her face contorted with the pain of rejection. Her mother and sister suffering the pain of this man's selfishness.

He should pay for this.

It was hard to speak around the rock in her throat. "You put your own needs above those of your family. You made a promise. To us. And you broke it."

"Yes."

How was he so calm? He must have suffered for his abandonment, his cowardice. Surely his life was worse for abandoning them, for abandoning her.

She was strong, brave. Jess was upright and honest, and wildly successful. Her Mum, now, was bright and joyous. And this man was meant to be cowed and resentful. Of their success, of what he had lost, of the disaster he had created in his own life. Of karma.

"You don't look unhappy," was all she said over the noise.

"I'm not. I'm very happy. I have a career I love, a wife I adore. I travel a lot." He gestured to his tan. She fought a sneer.

"You think I deserve to be punished," he said, noticing the sneer.

"Yes!"

The waitress, coming over and hoping for an order, looked startled and left. Alison fought to keep her voice low. "Yes, you deserve to be punished for what you did to us."

"What did I do, Alison? I stuck to my principles and did what I thought was best. Look at you all now, Miriam is happy, Jess is happy. What would it have been like if I had stayed? A resentful father, a heartbroken mother, anger, recriminations, silence and misery. I've lived in that family and it doesn't do anyone any good. I'm not a strong man, in general. I'm selfish.

But I didn't want that for her, or you two."

Right, because fulfilling his own needs was best for them. She squashed her cake with her fork, liking the screeching sound of metal on china.

He was waiting for her to stop. "Everyone is happy now, Alison. Everyone except you."

Her eyes flicked to his face. He looked concerned. How dare he.

"Are you happy, Alison? It bothered me that you didn't get further in your career, don't have children. You always loved babies."

"It bothered you?" The anger made her shrill. "You have no right to check up on me." He had left them without a backwards glance. "You know, some things are more important that your desire to fulfil your own careless wants. Like family, like promises, like commitments. You follow though. You live with your promises, no matter what they cost you, no matter what is asked of you. That's what grown-ups do." Why was she crying?

He nodded. "I'm sorry that you believe that. And that's partly my fault, I see that."

"Partly your fault?" The waitress, coming to their table to check on them, backed away at the shrill tone. Alison smiled at her reassuringly and then turned back to this ridiculous man. "You did this to me. You made me like this. Taking care of everyone, at any cost." She slammed the fork down on the table. "You are responsible for how my marriage turned out."

He looked sad then.

She felt something else though. Stupid. And selfish. Good god, is that really what she thought? She had never followed the thought through this far before. She was blaming him for her marriage, for her career. The words she had just hissed came back into her head, is that what grown-ups do?

"I have to go soon," he said. My wife, and the children, are waiting."

"The children?" Shock after shock, after shock. "You said you never wanted children."

"They're grown. They don't live at home. And they're not mine. It's better this way."

Her heart crumpled again.

"It was nice to see you Alison. I'm glad to you asked to meet with me. I hope you have a nice life."

He stood to go. She hated him so much she didn't even bother to say goodbye. He sighed and left.

This was pointless. She needed a map, not a visit from ghosts of the past. She needed a drink and went across the street into a bar.

Chapter Thirty-Two

O f all the terrifying, awful luck in the world. Jack. How had he found her?

She couldn't move. Like a rabbit in a field she daren't twitch a muscle in the shadow of the raptor. He hadn't seen her yet. His tattoo curled up his neck, little wisps of black, marking him out.

He was standing at the bar, chatting to a man, his face mobile and animated. His hair was all mussed up. He was drinking a short, golden drink - whisky of course. His fingers curled gently around the glass as he brought it up to his lips. He was nodding at something his companion said, his attention fixed only on her. Making her feel like the only person in the room, in the universe.

The woman was laughing. She had no idea of the kind of danger she was in. The woman glanced around and caught Alison's stare. She should look away, she was drawing too much attention to herself, but her eyes refused to move. Instead she just returned the look, trapped in horror.

Any minute now Jack could turn and see her. He would surely be wondering what that was all about. She should go.

But her feet were unresponsive. Or at least she should stop staring. Why couldn't she stop staring?

The woman was clearly getting confused by Alison's refusal to look away.

She had to move.

A single step back was all it took. Jack's head swung around like a searchlight. Their eyes met across a crowded room. Her blood ran cold.

And then she was running. Finally her feet were obeying. In fact she could hardly keep up with them. She slammed into bodies, clawed her way through the darkness. The back of her neck prickled, and she could almost feel the fingers catching her clothes, snatching her hair.

She pushed her way outside and suddenly it was dark and cold. She gulped down the air. She had to hide. She dashed down the street and crouched behind a bin.

She had to find a door.

Stupid. She should have done that back in the club. What good would running do? She wrenched the device out of her bag and fumbled with the switches.

Come on.

She scanned the street. No sign of him anywhere but still. A single doorway and she was safe, for now.

The device was still booting. She pressed back against the wall. The noise of the smokers outside the club was still audible. She should go further away.

No. It was loaded, finally. There, a door. Across the street. Not far. Safety.

There was no traffic. She checked up and down then stuffed the device back in her bag. Mustn't lose it. She braced herself to run. Three, two -

"Hey, what's going on?"

Jack. He was there. Between her and the door. Blocking her escape.

There was an odd sound that she recognised as a whimper. It was coming from her.

"What's wrong, Alison? What's the matter?"

He stepped forward, arm out. She instinctively shoved him. "Get away from me." It was a croak, but it seemed to have the right effect. He stepped back, looking shocked.

"I'm sorry. What the hell is going on?"

"Leave me alone!"

"Whoa, what the fuck?" He stepped right back. "Ok, ok, I'm going." He walked ten paces or so down the street. The voices from the club were still close by. She could scream. Someone would come. The door was only five steps away, she could run.

But he would catch her. He was still standing there, his face now in shadow. She could imagine that smile playing about his lips.

Her muscles were tensed and ready, but her brain was flipping back and forth. Scream, run, scream, run, the signals unable to fire.

A long moment passed.

"Alison, can I just talk to you?" His voice sounded calm and reassuring, like snake oil on water. "I don't know what I've done, or why you're so scared. But I'm not going to hurt you."

That's what he said the last time. When she had thought he was a gift from fate, rewarding her for her stoicism. When his eyes spoke of love and possibility. When she had folded herself into his arms and dreamed.

"I just wanted to say hi."

Of course he did.

She found her voice. "No."

He didn't reply, waiting over there in the shadows, but the word seemed to give her strength.

"I don't know how you found me, Jack, but I'm not going with you. I never lied to you. I know I said I was falling for you, but I also told you I was going home to Chris no matter what. I never promised you anything. I never said I would stay." She started edging towards the door. If she could just keep him distracted there was a chance she could make it before he caught up with her. But he was moving with her. Now he was closer than she was. There was no way she could make it. She was stuck here. She had to deal with it here. "You can't just take what you want. You're scaring me. I think you should just leave."

Her breath punched the air. In, out, in, out.

No response.

She should run. Back to the club. To people.

His voice penetrated the darkness, "Bloody hell, Ali, what is going on?" He stepped forward and the light fell across his face. He looked genuinely baffled and not a little bit scared. "I'm flattered you think you are falling for me. I'm not asking you to go anywhere with me. I didn't even know you were in Edinburgh so I can't be following you. You sneaked up on me in the club, remember. And who the hell is Chris?"

"What? But your tattoo."

"What about it?"

She edged towards him, not trusting this. "Show me."

He looked like he was going to refuse then reached up and pulled down his collar. The black tendrils revealed themselves as the quiff of woody woodpecker. She stepped

288

forward and wrenched the collar further. Yup, a cheesy cartoon character. This wasn't her Jack at all.

Five minutes later they were sitting in an old man pub down the road. This was not that Jack. But still she shredded the label off her beer bottle as she sat across from him. There was something about this Jack that was a bit too close to home.

"I'm sorry, I thought you were somebody else."

"Someone else called Jack, who looks exactly like me. Somebody who scares the shit out of you."

She sipped her beer, avoiding his eye. How to respond to that one.

"Listen, I know I haven't seen you in a long time," he said. "But we're friends, Ali. Always will be. I just want to help."

"Thank you. It's just a bit complicated."

"Complicated how?"

She stared into her beer. Maybe she could use the situation to her advantage. Maybe he could give her the information she needed. And then she could get out of there.

"How long have you known Alison?"

"'Alison'? I've known *you* for almost 15 years."

"And to your knowledge have I ever been completely insane? Or ever lied to you? Have I ever led you astray?"

He looked up, his eyes dancing, but then he saw the look on her face and the smile died. "No. Never."

She took a deep breath. "I'm going to say something completely insane. And I need you to believe me. This is not a joke." She studied his face. The laughter was gone. He was serious as the grave. "I'm not the Alison you know. I'm from another universe."

He sat back and stared at her. She returned the look, willing him to believe her. He looked down at his hands. She gave him a minute and sipped her beer.

He was looking at her with a strange expression, but he didn't seem as shocked as he should have done. As she had been all those months ago.

"Ok," he said.

Maybe he hadn't understood. She tried again. "I've never met you before tonight. I never even met my Jack until six months ago."

"Ok."

"I'm serious. I'm not joking."

"I know. It makes sense." He seemed calm and completely fine with it.

"How can this possibly make sense to you?"

He put his hands on the table and leaned in. "I'll tell you a little story. About three months ago I was walking home from work. I was cutting through Princes' Street Gardens, just next to the old fountain. And then I felt a tug, like being pulled over - but there was no one there." My god. He had been through a door too? She wasn't the only one. He was out of place too and he would believe her and help her. He was still talking. "And for a strange minute my head went dizzy, like I was becoming completely detached from the world. And I saw the fountain, looking clean and new, with water in it, working just fine. That scared me and I just thought 'no' and refused to let the feeling overwhelm me. And everything snapped back to normal."

He had resisted the doors? No one could resist the doors. She sat back. "Wow."

"I assumed I'd had a nasty turn. But then this bag appeared next to my feet. And that doesn't tend to happen when you have a nasty turn."

"What was in it?"

"A pile of clothes. Really expensive ones. And two notebooks and a laptop."

"Those are my notebooks! That's how they got lost."

"I read one. There was a story inside. First person. Like a diary. But it was clearly fictional because it was about travelling through the multiverse. There was a man called Jack in it, which got my attention. It was highly detailed and had calculations in the margins and descriptions of completely impossible things. I take it they were your diaries."

She nodded.

"You clearly liked this Jack very much."

She looked away and tried to think back about what she had written. It was mostly scientific, notes from a physicist adrift in time and space. But it was also a journal where she had recorded what she had seen. And what she had felt. About travelling to the perfect life. With Jack.

Pages and pages about her resolve for Chris but the temptation of Jack. About his eyes, his smile. Ugh. Her insides crawled with shame.

But when she looked up he didn't look disgusted. He was looking at her with his lopsided smile and a warmth she didn't deserve.

"I thought it was just some story," he said. "And it reminded me so much of you. It never occurred to me that you actually wrote it."

"Yeah, well."

That time felt like so long ago. When she had been so busy running that she hadn't stopped to look around once. Not at who that Jack was, not at the morality of what she was doing, not at herself. How childish it seemed. Like a tantrum by a toddler who can only focus on herself.

She looked across the table at him. He knew and understood. Once again she was sharing a drink with Jack whilst discussing the multiverse. So familiar. She shuddered.

"You're scared," Jay said. It wasn't a question. He leaned forward. "Who are you scared of. Jack?"

She looked into his familiar face. It was clouded with emotion. Concern? Conceit? Conspiring?

"Tell me about yourself, Jay. You know everything about me but i know nothing about you. Fill me in. So I can trust you. Please. Humour me." It was a clumsy attempt to get information, but it seemed to work. But she couldn't tell him everything. What would he think if she told him she was running for her life from a version of him? That's not something anyone wants to hear. It could mess with his mind. And make getting information much harder.

She focused back on what he was saying. He was talking about his life here, his ten-year marriage to Sarah, their two beautiful girls. He showed her pictures. Sarah was a petite mousy blonde. The girls, Ava and Charlotte, were blonde like their mum but both had Jack's peacock eyes. He spoke of them with affection and pride. When they came along he had given up his job in marketing and now ran a website selling children's products. He was settled and happy. Content.

He was brought up in Suffolk. His dad took a high up job in a pharmaceutical company after the oil company he worked for went bust. Jay said his dad always felt wistful about all the travelling they would have done and adventures they would have had. But he was devoted to his family and Jay's childhood was settled and happy.

He had come to Edinburgh for university, perhaps on

reflection in tribute to his dad's desire to try new things and new places. But he had quickly felt at home there. Had met Sarah in their second year and married right after graduation. Family was everything, he said.

This man was so different. So devoted. So grounded. And yet the charm, the irrepressible smile, and those eyes, were the same.

She looked away every time he caught her eye, although she was tempted to hold the look. She looked at his clothes instead, noticed their high-street-ness, the casual way he wore them.

After a while he talked himself out and they sat in one of their comfortable silences.

What a world. What a place to land in. Was it really that easy? Change his father's job and change his future, his whole persona. There was no anger or desperation in him. No lost boy searching for salvation.

She had made herself believe that she was attracted to Jack because he was broken, abandoned. Just like her. It made sense of why she had fallen for someone so twisted. But that was wrong. Jay was whole and kind, and she still felt herself irrepressibly drawn to him. Did you and I ever...?" The question was out before she meant it to be.

He looked up again and smiled his lopsided grin. "Of course we did."

"And?"

"We had a couple of amazing months at uni. A lot of fun. But she didn't want to settle down. Anyway. By the time she was ready I was already settled. Timing, I guess." He shrugged and looked down. "But I always felt there was something special about us." He was fiddling with a napkin.

When he next spoke it was so quietly she could barely hear. "Where is she?"

Her stomach dropped.

She hadn't even thought about it. He was sitting here talking about his life in this world, with Alison. How could she not have even thought about it?

"I've told you what you need to know. I've proved you can trust me. So please. I've read your papers. Her papers. I know the paradox. If you're here, she's not. Where is she?"

She scrambled for an answer. "She's fine."

"That's not what I asked."

"Seriously, she's just fine. She won't have even noticed the change. She's in a universe so close to this one that she won't even know it's happened. Everyone will be there just as normal. Her life will be exactly the same. She's completely fine." She put her hand over his to reassure him. He didn't respond so she ploughed on. "I've travelled through hundreds of universes. That's why I was confused and lost. She's only travelled one. She will fit right in; she won't even notice the change."

It wasn't having the desired effect, he seemed even less reassured than before. "There's millions of universes. Millions and millions. Millions of Alison's and Jack's. In some of them you did end up together. In some of them you were even married."

There was a lot of silence, but it wasn't comfortable. She waited anyway, trying to decipher his face.

"And when you leave, will she come back?"

"Of course."

"The exact same one?"

"Well…"

"That's a no. Why not?"

"Well, that route is closed." Almost true.

"So she's gone." His voice sounded harsh.

"Not really. I'll bring her back. When I leave the Alison from that world will come here. And she'll be from a next-door universe, so she'll be the same as the one who left."

"No, she'll be similar."

"She'll have the same upbringing, the same childhood. She will be the same as you remember."

He stood up, making her jump. "What the hell is wrong with you?" He rasped.

"What?" What was going on?

"You kidnapped her. Shoved her into an alternate universe with no idea of what's happening. No way back. You don't even realise what you've done, do you? What kind of psychopath are you?"

"Me?" He was getting it all wrong. Jack was the psychopath. She was just trying to get home. To survive. "You don't understand."

"I understand just fine. You didn't give a single thought to the people you have pushed out of their lives did you?"

"I -"

He was getting it all wrong. Why wasn't he listening? What possible difference would a single displacement make? She'd be the same. Not like her, so many universes from home, lost.

He stood up and stormed out of the pub. She did nothing to stop him.

The places she had been. The hundreds of worlds. Sitting on that beach in her nirvana, watching the green sunset, walking down the street of her perfect world, back to her perfect house with her perfect Chris inside. All the risks she had taken, all the good she had done. How dare he judge her like this? Even if she needed him.

And now Jay was gone.

He had the notebooks, her calculations, the readings. She could build another statistical model. She could develop a map.

But she stayed sitting there. Across the table, where Jay had been sitting, was a wall with little mirrors set into it. Fragments of Alison looked back at her. They looked horrified. They looked disgusted. She looked away.

She had to fix things with Jay. No more thoughtlessly causing damage to people's lives.

She went up to the bar and paid. As the payment was accepted she felt a little kick in her conscience. That wasn't her money she was paying with. She could hear the voice in her mind, "you can't just steal from people, Jack. That's horrible." She swallowed hard and stepped out into the cold nighttime air. It stung her eyes. That was why they watered as she strode down the hill.

Taxi after taxi passed her but she couldn't raise her hand to flag them down. It wasn't her money to spend.

She walked through the streets, her mind numb.

The conversation in her office played out again.

Jack saying, "It's not an actual person. It's a theoretical adjunct. It's a person in null space."

She remembered her reply, "Every single one of them is precious and important. Every single one is irreplaceable."

There was a cough in the cold air. She looked up. A man was standing three feet away, face half hidden by a scarf. She stepped backwards. Where was she?

The Meadows. At midnight. Alone.

She took a sharp breath. Maybe she could scream. But who would hear her here? That's why the muggers loved this place so much at night.

She didn't scream. She shouldn't be here. This wasn't her world.

"Do you have a light?"

A light? In this day and age? Was it code for something? "I - no, sorry."

"Are you ok?" The voice was kind.

She felt herself relax. Felt tears prickle her eyes. Maybe she wasn't so bad after all.

"You shouldn't be out here."

"I know." Was it that obvious?

"Go home, yeah?"

She bristled. Who was he to tell her what to do? Even if he was right too.

Her brain was full of fog again and she turned left and right until she stopped at her gate. She realised with a shock where she was. Her flat.

Autopilot again. Always. She always came back to her flat. The buzzer said "Stevenson." She placed her cold hands on the black wooden door and rested her head against it.

More than anything she wanted to open that door and walk back into the last place that she had felt truly herself and in control. The last place where everything had made sense.

Her tiny red and white kitchen. The overstuffed armchair and bookcase overflowing with books. The tiny bedroom with the view of the garden and the windows of the flats behind, a converted Victorian school. She would watch the young couple opposite play backgammon as she lay on her tiny double bed studying for finals and drinking tea from a chipped cup, dreaming of her illustrious career.

The cold wood pushed against her forehead. Even in the multiverse some doors remained locked. She turned away and went back to her hotel.

In the morning she woke with the world's biggest headache. Her head felt connected by a single thread. She daren't move.

Had she drunk anything the night before? A single beer.

This was a shame hangover then.

She watched the shadows on the ceiling stretch and drift. If she focused on them hard enough then nothing else could intrude.

Eventually she'd have to face the day. Eventually she'd have to find Jay and somehow convince him to help her. Convince him to help the woman who he perceived as having banished one of his oldest friends to the multiverse, to help her find a map to do the same thing again. It would be easier to just move on. Start again.

The shadows on the ceiling seemed to darken as she slipped back into the void. One of them was in the shape of a finger wagging admonishment. No, a sword. A stop sign.

She sighed. She allowed herself a moment to look at the extent of the task ahead.

There were a million versions of her out there in the multiverse. All connected into a spiderweb of universes. She could picture them, like bridges over a dark void, each only wide enough for a single pair of feet.

She couldn't go forward; she couldn't go back. And they were all turned away from her so she couldn't see the other Alison's faces. She was trapped.

In the distance she could hear someone calling her name. It was Chris. "You have to hurry. It's leaving. You're going to miss it."

She looked down. She couldn't get past without falling. "I'm stuck. Help me."

"It's leaving. Hurry."

"I'm trying." She tapped the Alison in front of her on the shoulder. She would understand. She was her too. But the figure didn't react in any way. Not even when she pulled on her shoulder.

"Hurry." Chris called. "I'm waiting for you, but you have to hurry."

Alison tried to squeeze past, but she stumbled and fell. The woman in front reached out for her hand as she fell. Alison only got an impression of a flurry of clothes and strong hands as the figure pulled her back from the sucking void beneath. She ended up standing exactly where she had begun.

"Wait." She wiped off the hot sting of tears.

"Try. There's no time left."

"I can't."

"Please, don't leave me on my own."

He was her purpose. Her future. Nothing else mattered.

She took a step, then another, pushing past the woman in front. Grasping her clothes, trying to swing her around behind her. There was no room. The woman tipped and fell, her arm snatching out of Alison's horrified grasp. She made no sound as she dropped into the void.

There, it was done.

She ran now, barrelling past woman after woman. They parted like skittles and she ran on and on towards Chris' voice. "Hurry!"

She woke with a start, panting. The shadows had fled leaving a dull glow on the ceiling. Her cheeks were wet.

She had no choice.

A simple internet search had found Jay's office address. It was the castle tower which stood at the edge of the churchyard in the centre of the city. She had passed it a thousand times on the bus and wondered what it was for. Housing a company that sold children's products online apparently.

She knew she was as white as a sheet when she opened the door from the cold graveyard into the warm, modern reception area. Like an apparition from another world.

The receptionist was friendly when she said she didn't have an appointment.

Jay was in a meeting, the girl said, but she was welcome to wait. So she sat on the pleather sofa and tried to rehearse what she was going to say.

Outside the door people were hurrying through the graveyard in hats and scarves. On the corner of Princes Street and Lothian Road, this church was a handy shortcut to the station, so it was permanently busy. All those people hurrying through their lives, rushing past rows of people who had probably done the same. How many people, in how many graves, throughout all the multiverse. So many lives, so many lives gone.

A cough brought her attention back into the room. Jay was standing next to the receptionists' table. He didn't look pleased to see her.

She raised her hand in a half wave and said a tentative *hi*. He nodded. The silence stretched on. The receptionist looked back and forward between then, clearly enjoying the show.

Was he going to ask her to leave?

Finally Jay spoke, suggesting they take a walk. She gratefully accepted.

Outside the door it was bitterly cold. She stuffed her hands inside her sheepskin gloves, bought with his Alison's money.

"I'm sorry," she said.

He grunted.

Jay set off on the path towards Princes Street Gardens. She caught up to him and fell into step beside him. He had his hands deep in his pockets, his head bent against the wind. He wasn't making this easy.

They passed a mausoleum covered in columns. There was a bunch of roses laid on the step, leaves crispy from the cold. The petals glowed a radiant pink in the soft sunlight.

She tried again. "I know I've done something really awful and I know you won't be able to forgive me for it."

He didn't respond, the skin on his cheeks was pink from the cold and she couldn't read his expression in the gap between hat and scarf.

"Look, I know you don't want me here. I'm not the woman you know and love." He abruptly stopped walking, his back to her and she ploughed on, not wanting to lose the thread. "I want to make up for it. I think I have a way to fix it. I can fix this, Jay."

"How?" He turned back and glared at her. His eyes were slightly red, she thought. She looked away. Down the pathway they had been walking was the exit into Princes' Street Gardens, to the fountain that he had been standing next to. If she leaned sideways she might even be able to see it. Where the door had been.

"I need my notebooks. I can't stay here anymore than you

301

want me here. But if I had a map I could make it right. I could put everyone back where they belong."

His eyes bored into her. "You said you couldn't bring her back."

His gaze was uncomfortable on her face. "Not if I were to go on. But if I were to go back the way I came I could give you your Alison back. I could put everyone back. It'll take some time, but I can do it."

His stare lasted a long moment. It was probably the appropriate response, but she had somehow, bizarrely expected more. Maybe a round of applause. But that was a terrible thought, childish and unreasonable.

Eventually he said, "They're your notebooks. You can do what you want with them. I'll leave them at the desk at your hotel."

He didn't want to see her again. That was fair. "Ok. Thank you."

He didn't say goodbye. Just walked back the way they had come.

The next day the notebooks and her old laptop were at the desk as he had promised. She had calculations; she had the ingredients for a proper map.

She opened them out onto the bedspread in her room. They felt like old friends. She opened the red one and read a few sentences on the first page. They were about how she would record this journey for the future of science, about the difference this could make. She closed it back up. She had been so naive.

This was going to be worth it. It had to be. She started putting the calculations together. It was depressing how little time it took to plot the course back from the world with no pollution to her original world. She opened up the screen on the detector. Another simple course to where Jack had asked her to stay with him forever. So easy.

The two routes didn't meet. Like two ribbons, fluttering in the breeze there was a gap. But the notebooks she had written in secret and hidden in Jack's version of a perfect world would seal that gap. All she had to do was go there and get them and she could put everyone back in their rightful place.

Chapter Thirty-Three

She tapped the screen of the detector but, of course, it wasn't broken. The gentle blue glow was constant and unafraid. It was just the memory that was empty.

As empty as the little shelf in the linen chest.

What had she expected? Well, printouts, notebooks and a flash drive. That's what she had expected. But she had been wrong about everything else so why in god's name would she be right about this? She surveyed the scattered towels and sheets, evidence of her frantic searching.

Of course he knew her hiding place. It was his world, his life. Or at least a portion of it. Had a previous Alison also hidden things here? Had she kept secrets? Had they been her undoing? She couldn't stop thinking about these other women. The other versions of herself.

She started putting the towels and linens back in their place. She mustn't leave evidence that she had been here.

Mrs Johnson downstairs had been delighted to give her the spare key. Had joked she should charge a lending fee for the thing. She'd laughed heartily along with the old lady but only because she'd already established Jack wasn't in so she could

304

spare the time.

As she had sneaked into her own flat she had come face to face with the photos on the wall. The first time she had seen them she had been so excited to see the life she could have, the life she had lived. But this time they seemed alien. That woman wasn't her. That life was not hers. How had she ever rejoiced that "she" had been to Singapore. The Alison who lived here, to whom this life belonged, had travelled this world, not her.

She was just a hermit crab, climbing inside the vacated shell. The shell that was a little bigger, a little fancier, a shell she had thought she could grow into. She was a fraud. She slunk down the hall, avoiding Alison's happy, smiling eyes.

But now the papers were gone, and she had no way back. No route or calculations to follow. Finding her way back to her original world was as likely as tying herself to a firework in the hopes of landing on the moon.

The house creaked and tucked around her. It was getting late. Some version of Jack lived here now, probably in this house. She couldn't stay here.

Alison's eyes followed her out. The Alison who had lived here for the last week was back in the world where she belonged but the Alison who belonged here was in the next step home, the step she couldn't take.

But so far her promise to Jack was upheld. Every Alison up until this point was back in her rightful world. For better or for worse they were going to have to make their way alone and unsupported, or unencumbered, by the knowledge that they had temporarily stepped into a different universe. They would also never know that everything they had ever believed was true. It still tasted bittersweet, giving them their lives back, without telling them the grand adventure they had been on.

The Alison on the wall, her of the happy smiles and international travel, she was still out of her place. And unless this Alison could find those notebooks, that's where she was going to stay. There was nothing she could do about it here, no matter how disappointed it would make Jack if he knew.

She let herself out of the flat and popped her key back through Mrs Johnson's front door as requested. It was dark and chilly when she stepped out into the street and turned the wrong way, away from the station. Her hunched shoulders itched, and her breathing didn't level until she was a good few streets away, in a direction that Jack would never go.

What was she going to do?

She walked to the next underground stop, a different line, and made her way to King's Cross. She caught the sleeper train to Edinburgh to give herself time to think. Her universe was accessed up there. In her life she lived there, barely ever left, so the final step would be somewhere in that city. Maybe the car park where she had first left her world.

She sat back in her seat as the train rattled through London. As the houses thinned the streetlights retreated and the only thing left to look at was the reflection of her own face in the darkened glass.

She turned away from her own accusatory stare and looked at the detector instead. The dots on the train were few and far between. One in standard and five, depressingly, in First Class sleeper compartments. Were those Alisons successful or merely unscrupulous, like her? She could have swapped places with one of them in the dining car and enjoyed Lobster Thermidor, or whatever they served on trains to rich people these days. Then swap back afterwards with no one any the wiser.

But Jack's face kept swimming into her mind. The nice one. His horrified reaction when he realised what she had done.

Well, he had his friend back now, didn't he? His precious Alison was back where she belonged.

She didn't belong anywhere. Still.

The dots on the screen rushed past. Out in the darkness versions of herself lived in infinite places. Infinite Alisons were within atoms of where she sat. At any time hundreds were accessible. But she didn't want their lives. She wanted her life, the life she had given up everything for.

She put the detector away. Any of those dots could be her perfect world and she would never know it. Chris could be sitting on this very train, returning home from a visit to friends. Throwing back his blond hair in a laugh of pure joy while she sat opposite him, drinking in his perfect beauty. She could be holding his hand, kissing his cupid's bow mouth. Rich and happy, connected and content.

Damn Jack. Because of him she'd had to let all that go.

She stood up to convert her seat into a bunk. She'd bought both seats to guarantee privacy and tried not to think of what the saintly Jack would say.

He was out there somewhere. Both Jacks were.

The Jack she had first met was probably prowling. She could imagine him, leaping from bright life to bright life, searching for her.

She had misjudged him so badly, believing everything he said to her. What kind of naive idiot was she to fall under the spell of someone so completely out of touch with reality. She had told him so many times that she was going to go back to

Chris. Why hadn't he just let her go?

She sat up so suddenly that her forehead grazed her ceiling.

The sonnets.

She scrambled for her bag. He had been so convinced that he had won her over that he had written her that map. She still had the sonnets in her bag.

She dug inside, rooting through her clothes and books, convinced that they wouldn't be there. Then convinced that the back page would be missing, then convinced that it wouldn't be where he said it would be.

But it was, and it wasn't, and it was.

Her brain ached to focus. The numbers swam and pooled and ran down her face.

The three simple markers for the steps from her perfect world back to Jack in his. All she had to do was reverse them and she could go home to Chris.

The rest of the journey to Edinburgh she slept the sleep of the dead. The blues dots on the detector streamed past unheeded and unwanted. She was going home.

Chapter Thirty-Four

The walk back to her house was so familiar, so welcome. The hedges were a special kind of green. The parked cars sparkled in the brief rays of the sun. A passing seagull left a dollop of pure whiteness, a pool of liquid crystal, on the pavement. It glowed in the hazy light, the sky smothered in pillows of white and grey.

The hill was less steep than she remembered, but gratifyingly longer so she could revel in the feeling for a moment longer.

She was home. This time it felt real - purer. She had fought hard to get there. The first arrival had felt bittersweet, leaving Jack. He had led her through a merry dance. An easy journey hopping through worlds of easy virtue. It had been easily won. This time she had earned it on her wits. Now it felt truly hers.

She reached the house. The tiny front garden was a neat as a pin. The path smooth under her feet. The front door yielded to her key and she stepped into her house.

The house was peaceful. Cool, like a cave in summer. She took off her shoes and coat and ran her hands gratefully down the smooth wood of the coat stand. Not a splinter or dent to mar the mirror-smooth surface. She curled her toes in the soft hall runner and inhaled the pure air of her future.

So, to find her perfect husband.

"Chris?" she called. She waited as the sound echoed through the house. Footsteps, then her beautiful man appeared in the door to the kitchen.

"There you are," he said.

She drank him in. He radiated completeness. His carefully styled hair, his glowing skin, his soft brown eyes, his face lit with a smile when he saw her.

She walked across to him and slipped her arms around his neck, drawing him into a deep passionate kiss. It was perfect. Everything was perfect.

He pulled back and smiled down into her face. "I was getting worried about you. Come on, we're going to be late."

He dropped her hands from his neck and picked up his man bag and keys.

Where were they going? She couldn't ask, but wherever it was it was going to be perfect.

She slipped her feet back into her shoes, shrugged on her coat and walked through the door he was holding open for her, like a real gentleman.

They slid into the luxury seats of his Mercedes. It purred as he started it and she snuggled into the soft embrace of the leather. As he sped up the road, barely noticing the speed bumps, she watched his face. He was frowning slightly as he concentrated on the drive. Perhaps sensing her stare, he looked across and smiled.

He turned right at the end of the road. They were heading out of the city. She watched the shops and cafes slide past.

Everyone packed and noisy, even though her phone told her it was a Wednesday at 3.

A midweek getaway? Maybe it was a special occasion. Maybe an anniversary. She hadn't had time to reboot her phone so the calendar couldn't help her. Was she supposed to know where they were going?

She was well practiced now at extracting information. She thought about where to start. But Chris got in first. "Nervous?"

Nervous? Were they going on a plane?

She hedged her bets. "A bit. You?"

"Of course. But everything is going to be fine."

She'd forgotten he wasn't a fan of flying either. It was not like they had been anywhere abroad for a long long time. In her world at least. She tried for a confirmation. "It's perfectly safe these days."

"Of course it is," he said and reached across to squeeze her hand. "Nothing to worry about."

Good guess. She smiled warmly at him. A lovely long weekend was exactly what she needed to take the tension out of her bones. A long-haul flight was nothing after what she had just been through. Maybe they were going somewhere special. Somewhere luxurious. Somewhere she and Chris could reconnect, bond, enter into their new life together. Like a second honeymoon.

But when they reached the bypass he turned left, away from the airport. Were they flying from Newcastle? But that was a good two hours away. Surely not.

Maybe they weren't flying at all. A countryside break.

She looked for clues in his face. He looked tense. Happy, but tense.

He caught her looking and smiled a big smile, but she saw that it was tight at the corners. What was going on?

"Oh," He said. "I forgot to say, I have the forms. They're in my bag."

Forms?

He reached into the back seat without taking his eyes off the road, fumbled in his bag and brought out a brown envelope. He passed it across to her.

She turned it over and pulled open the already opened slit. A pile of paperwork dropped into her lap. A word caught her eye: appointment. When she opened the folded letter the name at the top of the paper was NHS Lothian. X-ray Department. Pre-natal Scanning Unit.

Pre-natal.

No.

Her eyes dropped to the body of the letter, clawing for words that said anything other than the words that were there. "Pleased to confirm your appointment…. 12-week pregnancy scan…. ultrasound."

God, no.

Her joy liquified and ran, sinking through the seat, down through the car and onto the bypass surface, whisked away by the movement of the car.

This couldn't be happening.

Suddenly the little weirdnesses made sense. No wine at dinner, her high heels pushed to the back of the cupboard, the grand plans of one last frivolous holiday, the way he looked at her like she was made of magic.

The road slid like silicon under their wheels. Nothing slowing them down from arriving at an appointment with an empty scanner screen.

He would think she had lost the baby. He would think his baby was dead. She had killed his baby.

Oh god, what kind of a monster was she?

Jack was right. She had pushed a pregnant woman out of her universe. She was completely insane. She was a complete psychopath, a monster.

"Stop!" She frightened herself with the shriek.

To his credit the car didn't waver, but his expression was horrified. "What?"

"Stop the car."

"Alison, what's wrong?"

"Stop the car. Now. Please."

They weren't far from the hospital, just slowing for the Sheriffhall roundabout that would take them there from the bypass. Chris tuned onto the quieter A road. There was a newly built business park not far from the turning.

"There," she yelled.

He didn't react quickly enough, so she reached across, grabbed the steering wheel and pushed, forcing him to veer across the lanes and off the roundabout, into the business park.

"Alison, what the hell?"

"Stop the car!"

The car park was rammed. He pulled over into the disabled car parking space. He put the car in park and turned to face her. "Ok, we're stopped. Now what the hell -" but she was already pulling at the door handle.

She stumbled out of the car and pushed herself away from its shiny silver surface, catapulting herself towards the grass verge, retching and gasping for breath.

Chris was there in a flash, his hands rubbing her back.

"Let it pass," he said. Her head went blank for a minute and then she realised, he thought she had morning sickness.

"No." That was even worse. She pushed his hands away, sobbing. She swept angrily at her eyes. She didn't have the right to cry.

His concern was quickly turning to alarm and he tried to put his arms around her, pull her into a hug.

"No, no," she mumbled, pushing her hands against his chest, forcing him back. "No, don't please."

"Ali, what is wrong. It's just a bit of sickness. It'll pass in a second."

"You don't understand. How could you understand? I'm sorry. I'm so sorry."

"For what?"

"You don't understand."

"Understand what?"

She felt her strength go and fell to her knees on the grass, her hands over her face. "I didn't know. I didn't know."

"What's wrong? Are you hurting?"

She shook her head, scrunching her eyes shut. She had to make all of this go away.

"Is it the baby?"

"Yes." Yes. She had taken his baby away from him. But his intake of breath made her look up. "No," she said quickly. "The baby is fine. It's fine. And I'm well. I promise." Now she was the one grasping his arms, comforting him.

"Are you sure?"

"I'm sorry I scared you. It's not that. I was just sick, that's all. It's gone now. I'm fine."

He searched her face for a moment clearly not convinced. She let him hug her, but her insides burned with shame.

He released her from the hug and kissed her tenderly on the lips. The softness of his feelings almost broke her again. As he pulled back she avoided his eyes, swiping at hers as if she were still crying. But there were no tears. Her insides had turned to ice.

"Come on," he said, slipping an arm around her waist. "We'll be late."

She went rigid. They couldn't go to that appointment.

He tugged on her arm, but she didn't budge. When he turned to face it, it was with compassion again. "Still sick?"

She nodded. She bent over and breathed deeply. Buying time.

"I'm fine. Go back to the car." Thankfully, he went. Perhaps they had been through a similar scenario before.

She took some deep breaths as if fighting the nausea and looked around. There was the office, the Harvester, a car park, the bus stop and nothing else. Could she run? But he could catch her with no problem and then she would have to explain.

What could she possibly say that would make him agree to cancel? He was already nervous about the baby now. She didn't think morning sickness was going to cut it. A suddenly remembered appointment? But what could be more important than this? Seeing the heartbeat, watching his child on screen for the first time.

As she deliberated a bus appeared on the road. A number 33, heading into town. She could get her bag, find a door, sort this whole mess out. Plan later. For now she had to make her escape.

Chris was back at the car, looking at something on his phone. If she timed it just right...

Now.

She went from her wheezy crouch to full sprint in a heartbeat, racing across the car park just as the bus pulled to a stop. She raced to the bus stop and leapt on, fumbling for change and overpaying hugely to the surprised bus driver.

"I'm late," she panted.

The driver nodded, closed the door and moved off.

She had half expected Chris to be right behind her, or standing in front of the bus, but he was just standing, one foot in and one foot out of the car. His face was blank, but his jaw was hanging open.

She was never going to be able to explain this to him. Maybe that's why this was her first thought. There was no coming back from this. But it was better than the alternative. Watching his face crumple as he saw the empty screen.

He should share that perfect moment with Alison. And she should see her child for the first time with its father. She had to undo the appalling crime of trying to steal Alison's life and the love of her life. The joy of seeing their baby would overshadow the weirdness.

The last view of him was the shiny silver car and his blonde hair glowing bright in the sun.

She had to give Alison her life back. But where to find her?

She came up with a plan as the number 33 wound its way back into town. Only five minutes had passed. It felt like a lifetime. She had spent three of them berating herself, one squirming from the expression on Jack's face, and the final minute making preparations.

She texted Chris, *I'm sorry for scaring you. I forgot something important. Stay in the car park. I'll be back soon.* It was a terrible text but what else could she say?

She got off at Cameron Toll shopping centre and jumped into a taxi. It seemed to take forever to get back to the house. She willed it onwards. Her shoulders felt like rocks. Her fingers tapped an agitated rhythm on the seat next to her.

She made the driver wait and ran inside just long enough to pull her bag out from the eaves where she had stuffed it. She didn't look around. Her sight was fixed on the bag, the carpet, the door; otherwise she might never leave.

As the door closed behind her she debated putting the keys back through the letterbox. That way she couldn't come back, no matter what. But how would the other Alison explain to Chris why she had two sets of keys. She took them with her.

In the taxi the buzzing of her phone became incessant. She turned it off. Not yet, Chris.

The plan that had formed was, in the end, surprisingly simple. Real Alison was only a single jump away. The doors would be recharged, and she could simply swap with her. The map would show which world was the right one. She just needed Alison to be in the same place as her, right next to a door when she was. And where else would Alison be today but the scanning appointment, of course.

Unless in the minutely different world Real Alison was now in the appointment was tomorrow. Or next week. Or... no, this was the best chance of catching her. She had to try and take it.

The taxi fled through town. Out there in the multiverse were a whole gaggle of Alisons who were getting their scan today. Including an Alison who she had placed in the position of being at that scan and no baby to be found. An Alison who had no idea what was going on, who couldn't fix the horror she had been tipped into. What good could a pair of new designer shoes do to her? How had she thought this process had no losers?

As the taxi pulled into the hospital car park she saw with horror the silver Mercedes abandoned on a curb. Shit. Chris was here. Why hadn't he stayed put like she said?

Well, she would have to do it anyway.

As she ran down the corridors she held the detector out in front of her. Nothing yet. She barrelled into a nurse as she rounded a corridor, apologising over her shoulder as she kept running.

Finally she saw the door to the ultrasound suite. Through the window she could see Chris standing at the desk, arguing with the receptionist. Shit.

She looked down at the detector and the map. Yes. There it was on the other side of the room, next to the chairs. A door. The right door. Alison was right there.

She could create a distraction? Maybe a fire alarm. No, not in a hospital.

Could she talk her way though?

Chris was leaning forward and trying to see into the receptionist's computer. The receptionist stood up, turned out to be a big bloke with muscly arms, and carefully unfolded Chris's hands from the monitor.

She took her moment. She flung open the doors and ran across the room. Chris and the receptionist both turned to look at her, open-mouthed but the element of surprise won the day. She flung herself into one of the chairs, passing through the door as she did so.

Her stomach lurched, her skin squeezed tight then released, and for a moment, she saw, or imagined she saw, the other

Alison flash past her.

She landed on the seat with a thump.

Everyone in the room looked up. The room was silent and expectant but nothing to do with her. They looked back down at their paperwork and magazines. To them she was just that strange woman who had randomly lurched in her seat.

Back in the other world it was the Real Alison who would have to deal with the angry receptionist and frantic Chris. She would be confused and lost. But she would be home. And the baby with her. It would blow over once they got the scan. Everything would be fine.

Then the tears came. Pouring out of her eyes, pouring out of her heart. She had found everything she had ever wanted and now it was gone. Rightly so, but it was gone. And she was left with the knowledge that she had acted appallingly. She was not the person she had claimed to be. She was no better than Jack.

A hand on her arm made her jump. She looked up into Chris' warm eyes. Her stomach dropped.

"Ready to go?" he said. No face of anger. Why would there be? In this world everything had been perfectly normal. Until now. "I've got the printouts," he continued. "Come on, hormonal mama."

Another world. Another Chris expecting a baby. Would this never end?

He pushed into her hands three black and white scan prints. There was a baby on it. Heads, hands, the whole shebang. Her baby. Hers and Chris'. A tiny little life they had created together.

The tears fell again.

"Come on," said Chris, taking the photos out of her hands.

"We'll get charged a fortune for parking. You can get all soppy at home."

He took her arm and started to lead her from the room. The nurses and receptionist waved them out with happy smiles.

Just outside the door she remembered the bag with the map and detector on it. She shook off Chris' arm and ran back in. When she emerged again with it slung over her shoulder Chris commented that he hadn't remembered her bringing it.

"Emotional time," she said.

On the drive back into town she sat and thought about her options. Chris wanted to talk but she told him she had nausea, keeping a hazy smile on her face so he would think she was just overwhelmed.

This Chris needed his wife back too. They all did. The sheer scale of her stupidity was hard to fathom. But she had to keep pushing that thought aside: she had to focus on fixing it.

By the time they got back to the house she had a plan. Not only for putting back what she had broken but for stopping Jack from breaking anything else. She had to get back to Jay.

Chapter Thirty-Five

I t was surprising how simple it was to find her way about. All she had to do now was track back the way she had come. A simple matter of isolating the marker and waiting for it to develop into a door. The detector had the functionality built in. A notification simply popped up when the door opened with the location on a map.

It took a few days, but she was soon back in Jay's world.

She reassured herself that it meant her perfect Chris had back his perfect, pregnant wife. All the Alison's from that part of her journey were back how they should have been. She had already fixed some of the harm she had done. Ten down and another few hundred to go.

His house was tasteful, generous and neat. A double-upper villa in the northern side of town. The road was leafy and quiet this chilly autumn morning. Cars dotted the roadside, the gaps signifying driveways.

She stood on the path to the front door for five long minutes, hand hovering occasionally over the bell. He must hate her by now. But this was the only thing she could think of doing.

She felt hot and cold the thought of his expression when she had to say why she was there. Maybe she should just leave him alone. Go away and sort this out by herself.

She would if she could.

Even though the thought of seeing any version of Jack again made her insides scream she reached for the doorbell.

A woman appeared at the door. She was wearing a business dress and fluffy slippers. The woman from his photos. Jay's wife.

"Alison," she said. "What a lovely surprise. Come on in."

"Hi, Sarah. I'm really sorry to bother you."

"No, no, come on in."

Sarah stepped back and allowed her past into the hall. It was cluttered with shoes and bags. Some of them were small.

Oh god, they had kids. This was a mistake. She couldn't ask this of Jack.

"Jay's in the livingroom. Come on through."

No, she had to get out of here. "Look, sorry, this is clearly a bad time. It doesn't matter. It's not important. I can come back."

Sarah was looking at her quizzically. Having ushered Alison through she was now blocking the door.

"Alison?" Jay's voice behind her made her spin around. He was standing in the doorway, looking the same as the last time she had seen him, except for his own incongruously fluffy slippers.

"Jay. Hi. I'm sorry. You guys are busy. This is obviously a bad time. I'll go."

He stepped forward, wiping his hands on a tea-towel.

"You're back," he said. "What happened?"

Surely he couldn't tell. She was speechless.

"Alison," he said into the silence. "This is Sarah, my wife. Sarah, this is the Alison I was telling you about."

Sarah's expression changed. Was it hostile? Judgemental?

"Hi," said Sarah. "It's nice to meet you."

Alison squirmed. "Hi. I'm sorry to come by like this."

"It's ok. Jay told me all about you."

Jay's expression was neutral. He was leaning nonchalantly against the doorpost. Sarah was still blocking the exit. She felt suddenly like a science experiment, standing in the confluence of their gazes. She took a deep breath and re-grouped. This was probably better. No deceit, no playing a role.

"Come through, Jay said and turned back into the room behind him. She followed, peering around the door in case there were children there. It was empty. They headed for a pair of sofas. They took the soft, grey, three-seater, leaving her the smaller one. The clutter from the hall continued into this pleasantly decorated family room, muted greys and polished dark wood. A games console, trailing its cables, books on every flat surface, board-games in a jumbled heap next to the fireplace. But the soft watercolours on the wall gave it an elegant air.

"Tea?" Said Sarah.

She nodded automatically but was dismayed to see Jay get up and head through the archway and into the kitchen. Sarah was studying her thoughtfully. Her grey eyes exposed the lie of her mousy exterior, their gaze direct and unflinching.

"Are you ok?" was her first question. How to answer that one?

"Mostly, yes. I'm unhurt."

"Well, that's a start. Why are you here?"

323

She glanced across at Jay, not twenty feet away, putting milk into a small jug. He glanced back but there was no message in it. He could hear them just fine.

"I need Jay's help."

"For what?" said Jay coming back into the room with a tray. He sat down next to Sarah and poured out three cups. He put milk into hers without asking and handed it across.

"I need to stop Jack from doing what he's doing."

"You've put everyone out of their place again?" asked Jay. Sarah put her cup of tea down and sat back, resting her hand lightly on Jay's shoulder.

"Go on," Sarah said.

As Jay took another swig of tea she felt like she was able to see their thoughts. She had done terrible, selfish things. Inexcusable. They were upset and angry.

She felt something, deep in her stomach. It was an echo of the shame she had known before.

Usually she would be scanning his face, trying to draw out an opinion, a clue, trying to decipher what she could do. And she would follow that advice avidly, hoping to control the shame by being controlled by it.

Instead she felt bad for what she had done but she also felt certain about what she could do to fix it. She didn't need his approval.

"I need you to come with me. I have a plan to stop him, to keep him trapped in one place but I can't do it on my own because he would catch me before I could get there. But with you to hold him off..."

Sarah sat forward again. "That sounds dangerous."

Jay had been looking interested, but he frowned when Sarah spoke.

324

She had one chance to convince them. "Sarah, I've done damage, but that Jack has done so much more. He's out there switching versions of himself and Jack around the place with no concern for what impact he has on them.

"You missed your Alison; you don't like being given a version of her that's similar because you know it's not her. Out there are Sarah's being given the wrong husband, or some other person missing someone who matters. Jacks are being uprooted from their lives every day that he is looking for me."

Sarah's eyes had widened but Jay simply nodded.

"Jay can resist the pull of the doors. I'm sure he's told you."

"Of course." Sarah's hand tightened on Jay's.

"So he can get me to where I need to go. And then I'll bring him back."

Sarah and Jay exchanged a long look.

"Sarah and I need to discuss this," he said, turning back to her and starting to stand up.

"Of course," she said. She put her cup down on the tray. "You have my number. I'll wait to hear from you."

Jay showed her to the door. As they left the room she looked back at Sarah. Her expression wasn't friendly.

Alison stepped out into the cold and the door closed behind her.

Chapter Thirty-Six

Alison led Jay down another street. It was cold in this world, but his forehead was damp with sweat. Again she felt a stab of guilt for what he was having to do for her.

Each doorway seemed to be further away than the last. They took a taxi. They took a train. Each one in focused silence. The hours seemed to last for ever and it wasn't even night-time yet.

The worlds seemed to slide away from them. One almost the same as the last. She had told Jay she had a plan. A route to a place where they could end this. She felt bad lying to him - it was only 20% of a plan. But would he have come with her knowing that this was 60% guesswork and 20% blind hope? If he knew would he go back? She had to make this work.

Jay was getting tired. They had to rest.

As they neared another door, another jump, she spotted a hotel on the street they were trudging down. She stopped abruptly and he ran into the back of her.

"That's not a good idea," he said. "Surely it's not much further?" His face was pale.

She hated having to admit she didn't know. "A fair way, I think. You're not going to be able to do this much longer."

"I know. That's why I was hoping you were going to say, 'nearly there'." The lightness in his voice was clearly forced.

If only she knew.

Everything kept twisting and shifting. This morning they had been ten feet from a door which according to her calculations would take them a long way in the right direction. Ten feet away and it had snapped shut. She had been looking straight at the screen when the little marker had blinked out.

She hoped that the Alison there had simply moved away, changed her mind and gone on about her day. Any other option didn't bear thinking about.

If they were being sabotaged who knew how much longer this could take.

Jay was looking frazzled from all the concentrating. He was leaning against a pillar. This world had an elevated transport system making the street dark and moody, like something from an American movie. Since they had stopped two trains had rumbled overhead. The air tasted of oil and pigeons. She looked across at the hotel nestled under the overpass. The hotel was once a beautiful building, but the sandstone tracery was now crumbled and worn through an onslaught of pollution. It was cheap and uninviting. But more inviting than what would happen if Jay got too tired.

Would she even see the change as this Jay got sucked into another world and she came face to face with Jack? She shivered.

"I have an idea how you can get some sleep," she said. He nodded for her to go on. Then he shook his head and indicated behind her with a stern look. She turned around.

"Alison?" It was Simon. Damn. She glanced at Jay. He was in the process of rearranging his smile to look charming and unconcerned. It was slightly alarming, like watching the old Jack put on the charm. She shook off the feeling and turned to Simon.

"Hey, what are you doing here?" she said.

"And nice to see you too," he laughed.

"Sorry. Sorry. Hi." She gave him a big hug. "Nice to see you. But what are you doing here?"

"I'm getting my license renewed. I left it too late. You?" He smiled at her and then glanced quizzically at Jay. Did he know Jack? Would this Simon have met him? How on earth to phrase that introduction.

Jay saved her from the problem by stepping forward. "Hi, Jack Shepherd."

Simon shook Jay's hand but there was no recognition there. He looked back and forth between her and Jay with a look that meant, I'll ask you later. Probably not friends then. "Nice to meet you."

He looked like he was going to say something else, distracting Jay further, so she grabbed his arm and swung him around. "Great to see you, Simon!"

"Ok." He was clearly not convinced but this was Simon - he shook it off and went back to talking about work. "It's lucky I ran into you actually, I needed to check with you about the 14th."

"The 14th?" She carried on with her bright smile. They didn't have time for this. "Yes of course. Let me look at my diary and get back to you."

"Your diary? What are you talking about? We still need to go over the presentation. Alison, it's the day after tomorrow.

You are ready for this aren't you?"

Over Simon's should Alison saw Jay's charming smile fading, sliding back into an exhausted frown. They had to get him some rest. "Simon, I'm really sorry. I just don't have time today. Can I call you tomorrow?"

"Alison, what's going on. Everything ok?"

"Yes, fine. Sorry, I have to go."

She took Jay's arm and pulled him across the road to the hotel feeling Simon's eyes on her back the whole time. Another world she had screwed up in. Another problem she had to go back and fix later. If there was a later. This was never ending. Every time it happened it added another one to the pile. She felt like she was losing track of all the damage. And if she lost track she couldn't make good on it all. She looked at Jay's face as she guided him inside the hotel. He had come all this way with her on the promise she was going to fix everything. She couldn't let him down.

She stopped at the reception desk and smiled brightly at the clerk. It was called the Palace something. With a few practiced moves she got them a luxury room. Or as luxury as she could.

They ordered sandwiches at the desk, nothing that took too much time to come. And no drinks for her. She couldn't risk needing to pee while Jay was asleep. They clumped upstairs to the room.

Jay sat on the edge of the bed and focused on a spot on the wall. What was the other Jack doing out there that was putting such pressure on him? Was it a constant pull, or was he just concentrating just in case? She couldn't imagine what he was feeling. She didn't dare ask in case it distracted him. A single second would be all it took.

Unless. "Jay, let me tell you my idea." He focused on her. She had to say it quickly so he could go back to concentrating. "Jack wants to swap with you to get to me. But if we were attached together then he couldn't take you without me. And if he took us both then it would just be like going through a revolving door. We'd end up safe on the other side no matter how many times we swapped. And he couldn't do anything dangerous without risking me, and apparently he wants me unharmed."

Jay nodded. "Handcuffs?" he said.

She smirked. "You wish." His wan smile was worth it. "No, that might take an arm off. You sleep and I'll be on watch. If you get taken I'll... go with you."

His expression didn't change. She looked away from his gaze, embarrassed.

His hands were shaking, she noticed. They had to do this.

She cleared her throat. "I mean that I basically have to hold you the whole time you are sleeping. "

"Oh."

She knotted her fingers together. It sounded like such a line. Something his doppelganger would have tried. She didn't dare meet his eye.

"I presume we won't have to be naked?"

Her heart thumped, once. But his eyes were twinkling. He was laughing at her. Clearly she was the only one embarrassed by this idea.

But no wonder. Jay was happily married, with the focus on happily. He probably didn't see this as being risqué at all. She forced herself to join in with the laughter. What fun, nothing to see here.

He was still smiling when he said, "Seriously though, I'm

glad you're doing the right thing. After what you've been through, being that close to any version of us Jacks must be the last thing you want."

Right. Of course. Last thing. Naturally. She shrugged. Mumbled something neutral.

What was important was that he was tired. Even with twinkly peacock eyes his shoulders were slumped. Her stupid embarrassment, her feelings, were not important right now. She had to help him get through this. She couldn't do this without him.

A knock at the door. They exchanged glances but a muffled voice said, "Room service."

She gave Jay his first and sat watching him eat.

What must it be like, she thought as he munched in silence, suddenly being yanked out of your life? Maybe, if you didn't know it was happening, it was just a little twitch. Unnoticed. Like that feeling you get sometimes just before you fall asleep. Or a stumble down an uneven step.

But if you knew. Trying to resist the pull of gravity, the spin of the universe, how did you do that? That dread that a comedian gets when he's dying on stage. One more bad joke and the hook.

The last of her sandwich stuck in her throat. She went into the bathroom and spat it out into the dustbin. She couldn't meet her eye in the mirror, washed her hands thoroughly to cover up her ragged breathing.

When her composure was restored she ventured back into the bedroom. Jay had changed in her absence into pyjamas. He had brought pyjamas. He was lying on the bed, his eyes closed, but his frown said he was not asleep.

The food was only half eaten, the plates piled on top of each other on the tray. She gathered it up and deposited it outside the door.

She could hear Jay muttering to himself as she slipped off her jeans and into leggings. His eyes were still tightly closed, for her modesty she guessed, but she couldn't let him fall asleep yet. She coughed loudly. He opened his eyes and smiled at her.

She switched on the TV and brought the controller with her - she had to stay awake as long as he needed her to. She arranged her pillows in a v - a comfortable position but still very much upright. She placed everything she would need within reach. The door had three locks. She used all of them then scanned the room for anything which might become a problem.

Jay was watching her from the bed. He looked sleepy but still had a half smile on his face.

She nodded at him brusquely and clambered onto the bed. She looped the rucksack containing the detector and her notebooks around one leg and then opened her arms to him.

He blinked at her. "Uh, how do you want to do this?"

"Oh. I figured you could lie here and I'd... wrap my legs around you." She heard her words and snapped her mouth shut. She hoped she wasn't blushing.

"Right." He kept a straight face thankfully and kneeled on the bed. "But I need to hold on to you too. Two grips are safer than one. We don't want you taken by surprise and losing your hold on me. No matter how strong your thighs are."

"Oh god, shut up."

He grinned at her again and climbed into the space between her bent legs. Lying down on his back he wrapped his arms around her knees. But then she couldn't move her legs. She suggested on his side but gripping one thigh with both arms wasn't any better.

"I think I'm going to have to...." He inclined his head towards her middle. She nodded and then tried not to react when he put an arm either side of her waist, his face inches from her own. She held her hands up out of the way and tried not to notice it looked like she was surrendering. He smiled awkwardly at her then lay down between her legs, his movements already getting sluggish, and rested his face on her stomach. His arms slipped around her waist and his hands gripped together, forming a knot behind her lower back. It was incredibly, painfully intimate.

His eyes closed immediately. She quickly wrapped her legs around his waist. They fitted snuggly. She crossed her ankles. Now they were fully entwined they were safe. She focused on her breathing. Keeping it slow and calm while he could still hear her.

The TV blared in the room. The bedside lights glowed brightly.

"What do you think the other Jack is doing?" Jay's voice was soft. She turned down the TV.

"What do you mean?"

"I can feel this tug from time to time. But just every so often. Like he's testing me."

"Makes sense. He's seeing if he can catch you out."

"But I haven't felt anything for the last two hours. Not since we arrived in this world. Do you think he's gone? Do you think we lost him?"

She thought about Jack's furious eyes when she had last seen him. "I don't think so."

"How does he know how to find you?"

"I have no idea. He just keeps turning up. I had to keep running from world to world to get away."

"Not so good for those worlds."

Her stomach squirmed. "No. I know. I'll go back and fix whatever I did."

He squeezed her waist. "Not you. I meant him. It still makes me shudder when I think about him being in the same world as Sarah." His eyes were open and stern.

"Right. Of course."

"You're doing the right thing. Helping to get rid of him."

"So are you."

"I'm protecting my family."

"And doing the right thing."

She felt him smile against her tummy. "And doing the right thing."

"Get some sleep."

He squeezed her again and closed his eyes.

His breathing was light and even to begin with. His head was tucked into her middle and his arms were warm around her back. It was so cosy lying there together. Like a million hotel rooms before, even before she had given in to the temptation of him. He had always made her feel safe. Until he didn't.

The comforting smell of Jay wafted up to her. From this angle she could see his long lashes. And almost flawless skin. As he breathed his lips opened slightly and she felt a puff of breath along her arms which raised a line of goosebumps.

No. Better to focus on the chat show that was playing on the TV.

People she didn't recognise were flogging films and music she didn't know. It wasn't going to hold her interest. The next channel was a news bulletin, but she moved swiftly on. She was tense enough as it was. Next was a film she remembered watching a few years back. Although the lead actor had changed it was still funny. A welcome distraction. She focused on it, willing the time to pass.

The hotel seemed to have been decorated by someone with a flair for beige, there nothing interesting to look at. She should have brought a book. The room was warm. Maybe she had eaten too much because tiredness settled over her like a blanket.

How long had it been now? 20 minutes.

There was probably a bible in the bedside table, or an equivalent for this world. She hadn't been paying attention to which universe they were in. She reached over and slid open the drawer, but it was empty.

Jay moved slightly in her arms, snuggled his head in a little closer. She stroked his head to settle him. He smiled in his sleep. Stupid, she needed to be still and quiet for him.

She wondered if she would start to feel the pull he had told her about. Was it something that would be passed to her now they were basically one person? She searched her body for the feeling, for a tug or maybe a pressure. But all she could feel was Jay's chest rise and fall, his arms around her, his breath on her arm.

Right, so, that film then. She stared hard at the TV. On screen a charming, handsome man was seducing a naive young woman. She changed the channel.

Jay twitched in her arms. It was probably just a dream, like a puppy dreaming of rabbits. She tightened her grip anyway and glanced around the room looking for any sign they were in danger. How would she even know? Jay muttered something and went still.

If something did happen, if Jack got her alone, there was no telling what he would do. If they didn't stick together they were both doomed. But this room was so quiet, so plain. She looked around for any sign of danger, but it stayed beige and unthreatening.

She had a sip of water.

Jay had been asleep for nearly an hour.

On the next channel was a documentary on black holes. Ok, this she could watch, if only to tut at the inaccuracies.

After a few minutes she started to enjoy it. The science wasn't too awful, and the narrator had a pleasing voice. Another hour passed. Maybe this wasn't going to be too bad after all.

Then the channel abruptly changed. She instinctively clamped her legs around Jay's waist. He grunted. Her heart thumped. She scanned the room.

The glass of water on the bedside table was gone. They had jumped.

She quickly examined Jay. No tattoo. She double checked his neck with a wet finger, but it was just skin, no make up.

Her plan had worked. They were both safe. She allowed a little thrill of triumph. Jack couldn't get to them.

But her skin felt clammy. The room smelled of the old Jack's aftershave. It was choking the air from her lungs.

But she had just been jumped into another universe without her permission. It was not a nice feeling. After so many months of going wherever she wanted to go, slipping through doors whenever she chose, she now realised what it was like from the other Alison's perspective. Yanked out of the place she had chosen to be, completely at the whim of someone

336

else. It's made her itchy and tense. And vulnerable.

She could sense Jack's presence. She didn't like it. But then she had Jay clamped between her legs, so that probably wasn't a sign of anything.

Should she wake him? He had a right to know he was in danger too. But the longer he slept the longer they could travel when he woke and the sooner this would all be over and his could go back to his wife.

The practicalities were what were going to keep them safe. Focus on those. She pulled the rucksack closer and checked the contents with one hand. Yes, everything was there. The room was the same. There was nothing to give the change away, except the TV channel and the glass of water. Her throat itched. She looked at the bathroom and saw the water glass, full, next to the sink.

This room had been his room until just a moment ago. He had been right here. She shuddered. He had to have taken another Alison with him for the jump to have worked. Was she ok? He wouldn't do anything to the other version of her. Right? She searched her feelings for some certainty, but it wasn't there. She felt cold at the thought.

She could feel him creeping around the edges of her life.

The mirror on the other side of the room reflected her pale face to her. Her lips were blue.

She reached into the bag and pulled out the detector. She couldn't help herself, she had to know where he was. The screen came to life and she recoiled back. The door was right next to her, on the floor next to the bed. She could reach out and touch it. And on the other side was Jack.

Ok, not helping.

Try science. This was a fascinating way to chart the

progress between worlds. She could gain valuable data from this process. Jack couldn't get to them so long as they stayed like this together. So she may as well get something from this horrible night. She hit record and put the detector back in the bag.

She looked down to check on the sleeping Jay. His face was clouded. Clearly even his sleep wasn't easy now. Was he instinctively resisting or was he out of this fight entirely?

She looked at the clock. It was 2am. Nothing else had happened for over an hour. She shivered as some tension left her shoulders. She was even more cold than before. Surely the shock had worn off by now.

She'd set the thermostat at, what, 22 degrees? The blue glow of the thermostat dial was over the other side of the room. It was set at 16 degrees.

Damn that Jack. If she ever got her hands on him she'd strangle him herself.

In her arms Jay's breath started to speed up. He was getting cold.

There was a blanket on the end of the bed, just past Jay's feet. It looked warm. She tried to reach it with her free arm, but it was miles away. Maybe her feet? She took a moment to plot then rearranged herself. Rucksack over there, around her foot, gently so as not to wake Jay. She slipped her arm out from under his armpit then contorted forward and put both arms on his waist, trying not to squash him. The other leg was now free to reach down the bed. She tried to hook the blanket over it, ruck up the edge, maybe grab the fringe with her toes. She huffed and puffed, quietly, but the blanket was too heavy to move. She was just brushing the fur with her foot.

She stretched, jabbed with her heel. Jay started to stir in her arms. She froze.

He was squirming in her arms, sounding agitated, pushing against her hands. Her grip was less secure in this stupid, contorted position and she struggled to hold on. She mustn't let go, not for a second.

The room began to blur slightly. She couldn't see properly from this hunched position, but the TV stuttered, and she felt a strange sensation in the back of her neck. A tug. Like the pull of chocolate in the fridge. She tightened her grip even harder and then, bam, the TV went silent and the room was warm.

They were back again.

Chapter Thirty-Seven

I t had been a long time since travelling through the doors had made her sick to her stomach. Today the ghost of that feeling was back.

Jay was still sleeping soundly in her lap. The journey didn't seem to have bothered him at all. She scanned the room for anything to give the game away as to what had just happened to them but there was nothing. No change from when she'd been here before.

Which was almost worse.

She took a moment to let the warmth seep back into her skin.

They were safely back, that was the main thing. So far so good. No harm no foul.

Her own words sounded stupidly cheerful in her head. Who was she kidding? She was sitting in a hotel room, at the mercy of a crazy person and the only thing between her and him was a sleeping man and physics. This was entirely mad.

Only another four hours or so to go.

Her throat was rough. She glanced at the water glass. Her body screamed for it. It was exactly the level she remembered but she daren't touch it. God knows what was in it now.

The next hour passed very slowly. The TV was not responding to the remote, she assumed Jack had switched it off at the wall. She didn't want to drain her phone battery. She should have kept it plugged it in but hadn't wanted to in case it ended up getting left behind.

So she sat and thought and tried to stay awake. Her legs were starting to go numb. But sore legs were the least she owed Jay.

She passed the time thinking about the route they were taking. The patterns were starting to give her clues about the right ways to go. More often than not the research totals were climbing now. At some point the science would tip over into public consciousness and then there would be a world where they were safe.

The light snapped off. She jolted upright. Had she been falling asleep?

This room was almost entirely dark. She scanned it for movement. It was as empty as before.

There was a dim light over to her left. She craned her neck and saw that the room door was open. The light from the hallway was spilling across the carpet, a strip of beige in the blackness.

The room was full of shadows. There was nothing in them, but she didn't like the feeling they gave her.

But it was just a quiet, dark room.

Noises from the corridor drifted in. A lift bell. A door closing. She braced herself for someone to come around the doorway. What would they think? Finding her sitting like that on the bed in the dark, her legs wrapped around a sleeping man in his pyjamas. How could she explain it? Or protect herself? But the door didn't move and there were no further noises.

She started to unclench.

Then a creak from the door. It was starting to close.

Was there someone there?

No, it was on a door closer and whatever had been holding it open was being pushed slowly across the carpet.

It was about to get dark.

She fumbled in her bag for her phone. It was half charged, and she had a power bank. How long would that keep the light on? Three hours? Four? One?

She watched the strip of light as it shrank across the carpet.

It was fine. A bit of darkness wasn't going to hurt her. Nothing scary about a bit of darkness.

The door closed with a slam. She took deep breaths and just waited for her eyes to adjust.

That was the curtains - not someone standing there. Just curtains and a chair. And that was the wardrobe. All fine.

Slowly the glow from the thermostat started to fill the room. All the shadows faded back to reveal normal, everyday hotel furniture. All she had to do was stay awake.

She started writing a paper in her head. Alternate Universes and Moral Philosophy. She had a lot of information to use. Hopefully she would remember her changes later. And then this weird and scary night would be of great use to the bank of knowledge of humanity. And she wouldn't always look back on it with abject terror.

The light snapped on. Wincing against the brightness she realised she was back again.

The curtains were pulled down, glass was scattered across the table and carpet, the mirror was smashed. A chair was in bits up against one wall. And Jay's bag of clothes was open, and the clothes lay around the room torn into ribbons.

She scanned quickly but there was no one there. Just chaos and debris everywhere.

As she took in the carnage a glimpse of something red on the wall above her head caught her eye in the remaining shards of the smashed mirror. She couldn't see what it was. She took out her phone and snapped the world's unhappiest selfie. When she opened the photo her blood ran cold. In lipstick on the wall were the words "Where do you think you are going?"

Dear god.

If he was trying to frighten her it was working.

She looked down at sleeping Jay. She so wanted to wake him up. To get moving. She'd had enough of this. But more sleep now meant this would be over with sooner.

Come on Alison. Be strong.

A bang on the door made her jump. Oh Christ, now what?

"Madam?" She didn't recognise the voice. "Madam, we've had reports of a disturbance. Is everything alright?"

He was being too loud. But a glance at Jay told her he was still sleeping soundly.

"Yes, fine," she said, as loudly as she dared.

"Are you sure?"

"Yes, fine. I just tripped. I'm fine though."

"Madam, can you open the door?"

"Um, not right now. Seriously, I'm fine though. Please go away."

Jay stirred on her lap. Bugger.

"If you don't open this door I will be forced to call the police."

No. They'd separate them. That was the last thing they

needed. But she had to call the guy's bluff, or he'd come in now and do the same anyway. "Fine. Go ahead. Just go away!"

Jay muttered and moved around. He was waking up. She closed her eyes and prayed to the gods of hotel workers that the hotel guy would just pass the problem on to his supervisor. There was silence and then she heard footsteps move down the corridor. Finally.

Jay settled again. His hair was sticking up from his forehead, but he was less pale than he had been. But if that man did call the police it was a bit of a moot point. They would have to go.

But where? She pulled the detector out. The first door had gone but there was another one on the opposite side of the room. It was the only one. Who knew how long it would stay there?

She eyed the portal. Jack and whatever Alison he had with him must be on the other side. He was waiting for his chance. If she let go for a second….

Jay would be left facing the police in a trashed hotel room, holding the other Alison in god knows what state.

She felt her insides coil and bunch. This was all taking too long. Too many people were getting hurt. And she was still just reacting. Running.

The portal was still there. She could feel Jack on the other side of it. She gave him the finger.

Another bang on the door. "Police, open up."

Already? Ok then.

She shook Jay. He groaned but didn't wake up. He was so tired.

"Open up." They banged again.

"Jay, wake up."

"Wha-?" He finally opened his eyes.

"Stand up. Come on. Don't let go of my hand."

He blinked at her groggily. *Come on, Jay.*

She yanked at him. "Up."

He shifted his weight and went to stand, moving away from her, tugging out of her grip.

"No, wait!"

Jay looked at her confused, but he stayed entirely still. Scratching at the door suggested they were resorting to the master key.

"Wait, just let me... don't move." She kept one arm around him and dragged her rucksack from around her ankle, jamming it into his arms. She hauled herself up awkwardly, dragging him up with her, her arms wrapped around his waist. They hobbled across the room.

The door slammed open. She had time to see angry faces, blue uniforms. She shoved Jay hard and they landed in a silent bedroom.

They were safe. She could have cried with relief.

She kept her grip on Jay's waist as they struggled up and stumbled into the corridor. Then she let go of his waist, took his hand and ran.

Out on the street, in the cold, Jay finally came back to life. They stopped in a doorway so she could get her bearings. Jay shivered and she noticed he was in bare feet. The pyjamas had seemed so sweet. Now they were a liability. He should have just slept fully clothed.

Next time.

"We need to get you some clothes."

He nodded. "What happened back there? Are you ok?"

"I'm fine." She took a deep shuddering breath. "It worked

though. Jack can't get us if we stick together. He tried. But I dropped him into the trap he set for us. That should slow him down." She suddenly grinned at him. She felt like whooping. Take that, you psycho. Bet it's not so much fun with a squad of angry policemen as a welcoming committee.

But Jay was still looking concerned. He put his hand on her shoulder. And now she wanted to cry. She shook off the feelings.

"Come on."

They walked quickly down the street. She checked him out as they walked. "How's your head?"

"Better. There's no pressure right now." But the frown was already descending. How long would the police hold Jack? How long before he was right back on their tail?

The stories could wait until later. They were out in a cold street, somewhere near the station. There were railway arches and roads, in true Edinburgh style, both beneath their feet and running over bridges overhead.

They walked for a little while. She gave him her jumper and some socks for warmth. It was too early for shopping; walking would keep him warm.

Shame about his bag, his clothes. They would have to be more careful.

But it had worked. The revolving door defence. They were safe so long as they were together. For as long as they needed to be.

346

Chapter Thirty-Eight

The number of published articles in this world jumped from ten to two hundred. They were getting closer. Any time now some government would recognise this wasn't just a theory and would crack down hard. Even here the science media were getting twitchy. Headlines like "a new threat?" Popped up on her search engine.

Just a bit further.

They'd been gone only two days but the constant jumping back and forth testing directions meant she only had a vague idea of how far they had come. Thank god for the detector recording their path. She'd analyse it later. For now they had to keep moving.

She closed off the computer in the business corner of the hotel lobby. When she had rebooted her phone it kept asking for an account and password, and the set up required security checks. She didn't want to throw up a red flag so public computer it was. Interestingly that didn't require anything except a fingerprint.

She was sitting on Jay's lap and he was snoozing against her back. She studiously ignored the smiley looks the other

NOTES FROM A PHYSICIST LOST IN TIME AND SPACE

patrons were giving them. Like she ignored the smiles when he slept on her lap in the trains they took. They even had to eat with arms entwined. From the outside they looked like the perfect married couple, both wearing their wedding rings with pride. But there was no joy in the cozy feeling, only guilt. He was someone else's husband.

She shook him awake and they moved into a small space on the other side of the lobby. This hotel was nicely midrange and had lots of nooks and crannies. It was near the airport, and for once they weren't the only ones looking for a quiet space to snooze. She ordered coffee and cakes to keep the staff happy. Sat in a quiet corner, holding hands, for once neither of them sleepy, they were free to talk. She told him, finally, about how she was planning their route. If he was shocked by how much guesswork she had been doing he didn't say so.

"There's probably not far to go now," she said. "Once the media get a hold of something like this it doesn't take too long for politicians to pay attention."

"What does the response tend to be?" he said, his head resting on her lap, his arm wrapped around her thigh.

"Depends on the world I guess. Back in my world it's usually immediate and paranoid. We had a bird flu outbreak and the whole world went into panic mode."

"Yes, we had the same thing. But it was rats, not birds."

She nodded. Humans were the same everywhere.

"It's probably already happening here. The military is probably aware of us right now. But we need somewhere more overt."

He lifted his head and looked at her. She shrugged, surprised at his surprise. Maybe his world was a bit more trusting than hers. He tightened his arms where they twisted around her leg and put his head back in her lap. She stroked his hair. It was so natural for them to be so close. She had to keep reminding herself that this Jay wasn't for her.

"Not long now," she said.

He sighed, a puff of air which could have meant relief, regret, anything. She blinked back a knot in her throat.

They travelled back into town for the next jump. She was starting to gather the pattern in the route. It was all about timing and location. Now they were getting it right nearly 60% of the time. The likely location was just in front of the main train station, outside a bar she remembered going to with Chris for their anniversary. He'd bought her a rose. She'd bought him cufflinks. It felt like a lifetime ago.

Jay was back to frowning concentration and following her around like a distracted shadow. It was raining and the street was deserted apart from the odd taxi. She wondered what the Alison and Jack on the other side were here to do. What had made them choose to come to this place and stand idly in the street?

As they stepped through the door the rain switched off and the sun burst across the buildings. Poor Jack and Alison, emerging into all that rain. Here, sunlight glinted off the Georgian buildings and crowds of people were hurrying back and forth with a commuter kind of look about them. A train rumbled ponderously by in the station below their feet.

Then the alarms went off.

Everyone in the street froze, their faces showed shock, panic. And then they scattered, running for doorways and alleys.

In minutes the street was empty apart from her and Jay and the sound of the alarms.

NOTES FROM A PHYSICIST LOST IN TIME AND SPACE

Jay was holding her hand. His expression was set. He nodded.

She clenched her jaw. Showtime.

As they waited for some kind of official to arrive a pigeon landed by her feet. With no cars or people in the way it settled down to a feast of sandwiches dropped by the fleeing people. All it's Christmases come at once. She shifted her weight and it stopped and looked up at her. She wondered if she looked the same as everyone else. Was there anything about her to show how alien she was that she was from another corner of the multiverse? That she had travelled further than anyone here could ever dream? Or was she just another pair of feet getting in the way of the crumbs. Perhaps this pigeon was a seasoned traveller through the doors. Maybe here everyone did. Maybe she was nothing special. Just another life. Another story.

But it was her story. It mattered to her. And for once that was enough. She and all her other selves were going to do something a little bit different - they were going to take Jack out of play. Hopefully.

A squeeze on her hand brought her attention back. There were blue lights crossing Waverley bridge. The sirens bounced off the sandstone, challenging the alarms.

The pigeon flew away.

She looked at Jay. What to say? Good luck? Break a leg? Don't get dead?

Everything was on him now. He would have to time this perfectly or he would be trapped here forever. Or for as long as a life sentence was here. Unless they had the death sentence. Oh god, what if they had the death sentence. Why had that never occurred to her? What the hell were they doing here?

This was totally stupid.

They had to go. This was too dangerous. She couldn't let him do this for her.

But his face was set, and she couldn't bring herself to say it. He knew the risks. He wasn't stupid. And he was here anyway. There was nothing left to say. And she might never see him again.

Without thinking she leaned forward and kissed him on the cheek. She put every thank you into that momentary contact. He turned and smiled at her, his eyes flashing peacock blue. Then he let go of her hand and stepped forward.

The police arrived in a flurry of shouting and waving arms. They surrounded him, clamped a heavy shackle on his wrists and hauled him away. Another squad surrounded her. They were all yelling. She held up her hands. They pulled her roughly towards them and another set of shackles went on her wrists. It had flashing lights and a dial set at maximum.

The policeman scowled at her. "That'll keep you grounded," he said, roughly. She smiled at him. It wasn't his fault that this was exactly what she'd been hoping for.

Jay was being led away. He raised his wrists. She nodded. As they bundled her away she saw a flash of his hair as he was pushed into a police car. It drove up the hill and around the corner. He was gone.

The policeman protected her head as she climbed into the car. She slumped into the seat and dropped her head in her hands. A compression on the seat signalled another policeman climbing in next to her. He eyed her hands suspiciously when she lifted her head and pulled them towards him, checking the dials on the shackles. When he saw there was nothing but her tears he let her go and his expression eased. She turned to stare out of the window.

Where was Jay now? Would they go to the same holding centre? A piece of lead settled down for a long wait in her stomach. She didn't really need to be here. There was nothing she could do either way. They had talked about her leaving as soon as they had found the right world, but it seemed so callous. She wanted to be there for him. Even if it did nothing whatsoever to help.

The sun was gone now. The city's stonework had morphed from glowing beige to a slurry grey. The buildings flashed by, one much like the other. Why did they build them all the same? Pointless endless copies of a single idea. Nothing special about any of them.

The police car pulled up outside an ugly brick building. Police station? No, no markings at all. Super secret holding cell, then. Fabulous. Well, at least Jay would probably be here too. How many super secret holding cells could there be, after all?

The policeman bundled her out of the car. The street was deserted. Were they in the West End? It looked completely different. In her Edinburgh this was a park, or was it that building site opposite the hotel?

The disorientation made her hesitate. The policeman's expression was stony, disinterested. As he led her up the stairs she wondered whether this was his first time handling an inter-universe traveller. The presence of a huge building and alarm system suggested not. Was this an everyday thing here?

The doors loomed, then she was in a cold, Lino-lined hallway. There was a window further down and benches either side. People walked back and forward but no one acknowledged them. The hall was painted institutional green and noticeboards lined the walls. As she passed the noticeboards she caught snatches of the headlines:

Be Alert!

Warning!

See it, say it!

Wanted!

The policeman plonked her on a bench opposite another noticeboard and walked off down the corridor to the window opening. She eyed the front door. Maybe she could make a run for it.

And then what? Hang around hoping to see Jay's face on the news?

She checked her watch. They had been in this world for half an hour. The policeman was taking ages. The noticeboard opposite had the same posters as by the door but now she could read the subheadings.

Be Alert! The doors are everywhere. Always use your goggles.

Warning! Travellers are on the increase. Do you know who you are talking to?

Wanted! Have you seen these people?

There were photos of people glaring into the camera. Some from CCTV. All said, Do Not Approach. And there was a photo of Jack.

Her breath caught.

She had been expecting it but still. A piece of a half-thought daydream dropped into reality. Jack was a felon. And it was the Jack, she could see the tattoo.

She leaned forward to read the text underneath. "Unlicensed travel... missing... reward for capture." They were in the right place.

A person walked into her eyeline. "Dr Howden?"

It was an official looking older man. Not a policeman, or at least not uniformed one.

"Yes?"

"Could you come with me, please?"

As she stood up the shackles clinked. The man tutted and indicated to the policeman who was still standing near the window. He came over and unhappily undid the cuffs. Her wrists felt lighter, but she didn't like the feeling. Too unsafe. But unless she asked for them back...

The man led her down the corridor and into a sparse room. A plaque said Interview Suite in official lettering on the door. She thanked him and took one of the hard, plastic seats. He sat down on the other side of the wooden table and put down a blank folder.

"So, Dr Howden. We know you're not from this universe."

Straight to the point then. She didn't reply but he didn't seem to expect her to.

"I'm guessing quite a distance, from your markers."

"You're using isotope markers too?" She couldn't help herself

"Yes. We developed the technology some years ago. It's become quite advanced. We examined your equipment, by the way."

"Already? That was quick."

"It's an uncomplicated machine. Crude, but effective," he continued, in reply to her grimace. "I like the watch interface though. That's something we don't have."

She felt a little better.

"I was wondering if you could tell me why you're here?" he said.

"Am I under arrest?"

"No, this is a processing centre, not a detention centre. Like border control."

"And the handcuffs?"

"Well, you did arrive with Jack Shepherd."

Straight to the point then. Ok, D-Day. The moment when they all assumed she was mad and locked her up forever or the moment they became safe.

"Yes," She said carefully. "But not the Jack that you are looking for."

She had to convince these people that what she was saying was real. That Jack was innocent. She had one chance to be in this with Jay or he was going to have to do it alone. And if they kept the cuffs on there was a chance he would be stuck here forever.

Sarah's face swam into her mind. She didn't fancy having to go back and explain that to her.

But how to convince this nice, official man, that they had the wrong man. And that they needed to trust her, a total nobody, to tell him what to do.

She had her speech rehearsed. Time to begin.

But Peter spoke first. "We know."

"You...What?"

Peter Hill smiled his officious smile. He looked rather smug. "We know who you are. We know who this Jack is. Or at least within a few thousand universes."

Her brain seemed to have stopped working.

She leaned forward. "Then can I speak to him?"

"Not yet. You can understand that we are interested to find out what is going on before we let you run amok."

She opened her mouth to say they wouldn't run amok, but

then reconsidered. She couldn't guarantee that Jack wouldn't once he finally arrived.

"So," the man said. "Why are you here?"

She looked at him across the chilly table. He seemed nice and officious, he looked like the kind of man to have grandchildren and run a local football team. But then she thought Chris was good husband material and Jack was a charming rebel with a heart of gold, so what did she know? He was probably the chief executioner.

The man nodded to himself. He opened the file and spun it around. Jack's face was front and centre, his stare grinding into the camera. Even here she couldn't meet his eye. It seemed to her that something in his face was distinctive now, that she could tell him and her current travelling companion apart. The glint in his eye, the tight smirk in the corner of his mouth. Something cold.

"Dr Howden," said the officious man. "I think we need to work together here. I never introduced myself properly. I'm Peter Hill. I run this processing centre but I'm also responsible for controlling the flow of illegals in and out of this reality. At least for Scotland. For my sins. You won't know this but there has been a fair bit of panic for the last few years since it became clear that these portals were real, and everywhere."

She fought her tongue, which was trying to ask the obvious question. But she knew if she asked she would give something away. So she sat and waited. Luckily he was happy to share.

"We found the first traveller about five years ago," he said. A clueless young lad called Ted whose hair changed colour right in front of his Nan's eyes. It led to a bit of panic. Military involvement. We had a period of tight controls and media hysteria. They invented door goggles for outside spaces and highlighters for inside. Everyone was on edge for a long while. I had a team of two hundred officers at one point locking up people who had travelled, intentionally or otherwise. But six months ago our scientists discovered this ionic tracing and came up with a blocker. Now everyone wears a little badge which stops them slipping. Since then, apart from a few appearances on daytime talk shows of people who want a divorce on the grounds of inter-dimensional swapping, it has been very quiet."

Wow.

"What information do you have on Jack?" she said.

Peter tapped the folder in front of her. "Jack came to visit about seven months ago. He kidnapped a key member of the scientific team working on the blockers. At first we thought it was terrorist activity, an attempt to keep the doors open. But her colleagues said they were involved, romantically. Her husband had no idea, of course. Came home to a post-it note, of all things, saying she was leaving him."

Alison leaned forward and read from the folder. Of course it was her own name in the notes.

"We sent a team out to find her. Her research wasn't quite finished and the version of her we ended up with, her Exchange, didn't have the experience. It took some time, but we found her two worlds from here. She was shaken but unhurt. That's when the funding was released, and the blocker was activated."

Peter pulled the folder back towards him. "So, that's what you needed to know. How about you tell me a few things."

She nodded. Where to begin? So she began back on that day when Jack had walked into her lecture theatre. Of course she understood now why he was there, what he had wanted, what he had got.

As she told the story the policeman jumped in with little unwelcome comments.

"Chris' contract fell through," she was explaining when he interrupted.

"That's right. Dr Howden told us about that. The whole contract was a sham, a plot by Jack, I understand, to get you ready to go."

She couldn't speak for a good ten seconds. Of course it was fake. How had she missed that?

She wondered, as she spoke, how much of that initial journey was carefully planned out. The trips to worlds where she and Chris were driving each other to poverty and ruin. The sad, divorced Alison who wanted nothing more than to go back and leave so much sooner, who had felt like her life was wasted. Had he picked those all out in advance.

The Nirvana world where Chris had arrived unexpectedly. Surely Jack had set that up. The surprise party with her mother and all her friends.

God. She was such a fool.

She didn't say that to Peter Hill of course. All he needed to know was that she had made a stupid mistake and now she wanted to fix it.

He sat in quiet contemplation for a moment after she finished.

"So how shall we do this?" he said.

"Do this?"

"We're not entirely clueless here. Dr Howden left us well prepared."

"Dr...?"

"Howden. She left detailed instructions of what to do when you arrived. In fact a few variations on a theme. We're all ready to go at this end."

"Right."

He was calm and contained, like he was talking about an overturned parking ticket. He pushed an envelope across the desk to her. It was addressed to her in her handwriting.

She stared at it.

Peter Hill nodded at something internal and stood up. "I'll leave you to read this. You can find me out at the front desk." And he left.

When the door closed behind him she reached out and turned over the envelope. The paper was good quality and resisted her attempted to pop it open. In the end she slid her finger under the flap and pried it apart. Inside was a simple notelet with a sunflower on the front.

Hello Alison, it said. *I been tracking your progress for a while. I have made the necessary precautions. Jack has been causing havoc for a while, so I've had help from a few neighbour Alisons to come up with a solution. We have been going back and forth for a couple of years now preparing various obvious landing points. I've been doing my best to limit the damage Jack has done. All that's left is for you to spring the trap.*

Good luck.

Your, Alison

She sat back down on the chair with a thump. She didn't even remember standing up. Of course she wasn't the only Alison dealing with this problem. She had just assumed.

How arrogant. How naive to think they were all just waiting for her to solve the problem all by herself.

Her nose was tickling, and she sniffed away tears. All those

days of abject terror and there was an Alison here planning
and putting what she needed in place.

Chapter Thirty-Nine

She and Jay were the only two left in the chamber. The door clanged ominously shut. There was no pressure, Jay said, no one trying to get through.

Did Jack know it was a trap? Would he stay away?

Jay was sitting in the metal chair, examining his hands.

She wanted to say something reassuring but couldn't think of the words. Instead she shuffled her feet on the pressure pad.

Peter had explained the concept. If Jack tried anything she could simply step backwards and the pressure field would activate, changing a dense particle cloud and making the air solid.

"You ok?" Jay was looking up at her.

"Yeah. Just worried about you."

He smiled warmly at her and her heart did that little flip flop again.

"I'm fine. I get to leave the scene and get escorted home. It's you I'm worried about."

She gestured to the pad. "I'll be ok."

He nodded, looking stern. His peacock eyes smouldered

in the overhead light. "Just don't do anything heroic. I don't want to have to worry about you for the rest of my life."

"Promise." She wasn't sure if she meant that as a statement or a question. His eyes were fixed on hers and she couldn't look away. "Don't forget about me." The words were out before she could stop them.

"Never," he grinned. Her heart swelled. Then she saw he was indicating the scar on his forearm. Ouch. But his eyes twinkled, and she found herself laughing despite the sting. In the end they were both grinning like fools.

She itched to reach out for a final hug, to feel his arms safe around her. But any movement and he, and she, would be clamped tight in the force field. Not how she wanted to be remembered.

Maybe she could say something instead. Something memorable, something profound. Or just something true.

"Jay, I- "

The intercom crackled loudly. "Ok, folks, we're ready this end," said Peter Hill, sounding tinny. "You good to go?"

She closed her mouth with a snap. All she could manage was a nod. Jay gave a thumbs up to the one-way mirror.

"Ok, we're releasing the clamps in 5…"

This was it.

"4…"

The last time she would ever see him.

"3…"

And now it was time to face Jack.

"2…"

She was ready.

"1…"

She clamped her hands into fists. She had a few choice

things she wanted to say.

"Clamps released."

Jay nodded at her and she gave him a wink in return. He grinned.

And nothing happened.

She lined up the words in her head. Waiting. All the pain and frustration. All the fear she had felt. She would tell him all of it. She would explain *you can't treat people this way. It's wrong and unfair and cruel. You are not the victim here.*

Staring straight at Jay she felt like she was already speaking the words out loud. *There is humanity, in you, Jack. There must be. Your childhood, your choices, they have led you here to this person. But you can make other choices. If you stop treating the world like your enemy you can have love and connection and companionship. But you have to choose it. And you won't. Because you don't even see that the choice is there.*

I feel sorry for you. I actually, truly loved you, or a part of you. But I love me more and I won't let you hurt me anymore. Nor anyone else, ever again.

Maybe he would listen. Maybe he would, finally, understand. Maybe he would even take some responsibility for the mess he was making. If she could just get him to understand.

Jay coughed, making her jump. She refocused. It was still just her and him. No Jack.

Perhaps he wasn't coming. Perhaps this was all for nothing. Maybe he had given up and just gone on his way and would be out there forever, always there *in potentia*. Always on the edges of her life where she could never escape.

Jay's expression changed. He tensed. The air blurred and where Jay's warm smile had been sitting Jack's snarl took its place. He leapt to his feet. He was triumphant and angry. He was terrifying.

She stared straight into his eyes and stepped backwards off the pad. The air around him instantly froze.

He was held tightly in place, his snarl fixed on his face. His eyes glared balefully out at her. Now was her chance to say everything she had stored up inside.

She turned around and walked out of the room without a backwards glance. She was done.

Now she just wanted to go home.

Chapter Forty

It took a few hours to fill in the paperwork. She left copious notes for Professor Alison and copies of everything in her notebooks, just in case they hadn't already got them. Anything that might help them in their task.

She had lunch with Alex. He was a lovely guy. He was probably easy to live with. No drama. He had made her a fish pie, white fish only. Exactly how she liked it. Exactly the kind of person she needed to refocus her sights onto.

She packed her bags to go and sat in Alison's living room, waiting. Another cluttered, busy, cosy room. At least some things were constant.

A knock made her look up. She was expecting an escort once they had located the right door, but it was Dad standing in the doorway. Well, not her dad, Alison's dad. She got to her feet, tamping down a wave of wariness.

"Hi," he said. He looked good. Younger somehow. Certainly dressed much better. His eyes had crinkles around them and there was no mahogany tan but otherwise he looked the same as when she had last seen him in that cafe. "Can we talk?"

"Of course, come in."

He walked around the sofa and cautiously sat on the edge. She sat too, not too close.

"All packed for home?"

She nodded. "Once more unto the breach," she said, then winced at the forced jollity.

He smiled. "I don't want to make you uncomfortable. Alison told me a bit about your life, and your dad."

Oh god. "It's fine."

"About how he treated you. About how I treated you."

Oh god. "Honestly, it's fine. It's not your fault. It wasn't you. "

"I know. But it was you. And I'm sorry."

She felt her throat close and hastily stood up. "It's fine," she croaked, waving a hand. "Honestly."

He stood up too. She stepped hurriedly back. He was already too close.

"Honestly, it's all good. It's just life isn't it." She grabbed at her bag. She had to go.

He didn't move but the smell of him did, wafting closer. He smelled of peppermint and musk. He smelled of bedtime and peekaboo. She stumbled.

"I'm sorry," he said through the rush in her ears. "I'll go if that's what you want. I'm not here to hurt you. I just wanted to come here and say I love you. I'm so sorry that you didn't get that from me. I can't erase it or fix it, but you can shout at me, or throw something. Just get it out. Because I poisoned you."

A single drop hit her hand and she felt more tears slide down her cheeks. Then she had sunk onto the sofa and his arms were around her and she was crying for every missed birthday, every absent chair at school plays. And his arms felt familiar and loving and fitted into the empty hole inside.

After she had cried it out she sat back, and he let her go. His jumper was soaked on one shoulder and she blotted it ineffectually with her sleeve. He chuckled and took her hand. This time she didn't feel the need to draw back.

She wiped her face and smiled at him. He wasn't her dad, but he cared enough to try. Somehow it had shifted something in her, and she felt a little more whole.

"Thank you," she said.

"Least I can do," he replied.

Chapter Forty-One

Alison stood in front of her house. There was a notice stuck to the door. It said "eviction" on it. Her key didn't work.

When she looked through the door all the furniture was still in place. Well, that answered that question. Her books, her artwork, the photos, they were all gone.

The house looked expectant. Maybe it was waiting for its next owner. She wouldn't miss it. Not really. She had never bonded with that house.

She turned away and walked her familiar route to the university. It was a normal Edinburgh day, windy clouds playing with the sun. Blown leaves collecting against every solid surface, coating the ground with a rainbow. The wind on her face was refreshing.

She crossed the Meadows and stopped at the missing whalebone arch. She rested her hands on the mottled stone plinths, feeling the rough stone on her palms. In a way that arch felt like it *was* the doors. It's absence a signal that this was her real world, that that part of her life was behind her.

She set off again. As she walked she imagined all the other

Alisons, billions of them. Some walking the same route, some driving in their flying cars, some adjusting the dials on their spacesuits or taking their pet octopus for a swim with their children, or grandchildren, or a dog. She could almost feel them with her. All those possible lives. It seemed ridiculous that she had felt so trapped in this one. All the things she could do.

As she neared the university she ran into Chris.

"Alison! There you are. I was looking everywhere for you. Where did you go?" His face was flushed, his eyes darted back and forth from her eyes to her mouth. Panic radiated off him.

"I went for a walk past the house." she said. She studied his face. There was nothing different about him. He looked concerned, he gazed into her eyes. His expression was open and honest, pure. He fussed over her, telling her how worried he was when he couldn't find her. He tried to tell her again that he was sorry about the house, that he was going to make it up to her, that everything was going to be ok if they just stuck together. He ended with their famous line "you and me against the world."

She studied his face. She couldn't tell if he believed all of this and just didn't understand how the world works, or whether these disasters were just his way of keeping her with him. What better way to foster togetherness than to create an enemy to fight? Or maybe it's a test of her loyalty, her resolve to stick with this marriage no matter what. If she stayed with him through another crisis, through homelessness and bankruptcy, then, and only then, would he be sure she truly loved him. Probably. Maybe just one more test to be sure.

He put his arms around her, pressing his head into her shoulder. He was grasping her like a lifeline. The only thing tethering him to a reasonable approximation of a life.

She let him cling. It's a familiar feeling. She didn't have to do anything. If she just let him cling she could avoid conflict, avoid the fallout. If she just remained as his rock, his ballast, just stayed then he would be ok. He could continue to be the man he was, and she could continue to accept him, flaws and all, no matter what - the true definition of love.

The only one who would get hurt is her. And she was strong enough to take it. Stronger than her mother, stronger than her dad, stronger than Chris. She could take all her pain, her disappointment and fear. She could take all of theirs too. She could hold it safe, push it down into a little ball deep, deep in her stomach where the only thing it would do is chase sleep away, fill her mind with nightmares, leech the strength from her bones, turn her prematurely grey and trap her forever in a life that was lived for them.

"Chris." Her hands pushing on his chest were firm. He couldn't resist.

His moistened eyes seemed to convey the pure depths of their love, the doomed romance of it all, the lengths he would go to, how he would find her, even after death, how they would live together forever in the stars, how songs were sung about love like theirs.

She looked deeply into his eyes. "I don't want to do this anymore. I don't want to be in this relationship anymore."

Tears flowed. There was begging. He told her that their story couldn't end this way. That he loved her more than his own life.

"I'm sorry," she said. "But I want something different for my life."

He left then, marching off into the city. Her mother called

shortly after. Chris had called her. She told her all the reasons why she had made the wrong decision, how disappointed she was, how she was letting the family down.

She walked on to the university and sat down at her desk. On the table she set down the detector and the map. Both were blank, inert. She carefully dropped them both into the bin.

Printed in Great Britain
by Amazon

She does the same thing after each one of Amal's visits. She goes around with some treats and toys for the kids. She asks Amal if she's okay and her friend nods emphatically *yes, yes!* She is always grateful for that *yes, yes* which absolves her, dismisses her and allows her to return home to think about what else remains on her list for the day. And it could continue like this—their arrangement—except he goes too far and Amal never shows up again.

DISCOURSE

Samir was in one of his moods. He was ready to talk. It had been a long night and once his tongue was loosened, Amir knew the night had more hours remaining in it than had been left behind.

He started with 'The King and the Slave', a story they had all heard before.

'Once upon a time long ago, there was a king who had thousands of slaves. The slaves were blue and green, red, pink and white. They were every colour that existed under the sun. The king had slaves to arrange his pillows, slaves to tie his shoes, slaves to polish his mobile phone, slaves to spin silk so that, if the fancy took him, he could order silk socks in every colour while he drank champagne and complained about his weight.

'His slaves conspired in the only way slaves can, turning foolish fantasies, thinking *one day, one day* when men, let us be clear, they had as great a chance at freedom as another man has of spending a night between my wife's legs. They could plot as much as they liked, they could dare to look at the palace's walls but tell me, how did they mean to survive outside when they did not even own the scraps they slept in at night? They had never been outside and they knew zero about the world and some of them believed there was no other world, that the entire world was what was contained within the palace walls. And in a sense they were right because the palace was the world in miniature, with all its suffering and stupidity, its fighting and fantasies, and if they needed to study the world, they need only look around them.

'But there was a slave who dreamed of freedom. Of course there was such a slave or else our story has nowhere to go. We shall call him Zaki and this name suits him more than the one his parents could provide.

'As a young man, he thought about the world outside, he studied the paintings and photographs in the palace for clues by which to understand the world he had never seen in his life. Ah, it is easy for me and you to make our plans but what if your life is reduced like Zaki's, how would you even begin to imagine an escape? Your parents tell stories of slavery as their parents told them—in this fashion all the way back—so that no other life ever existed, and no other future exists except more of the same.

'He looked in books, at the pictures, he was alert to what the messengers brought in their news, he watched the merchants who brought goods to the gates and often he was one of the slaves sent to retrieve the crates but they were never allowed when the gates were open because our king is wise and knew better than to permit the enslaved a glimpse outside. Our king is wise—of course he is—because if he was the stupidest man, he would have been educated till his head was as stuffed as his belly, even then if he showed signs of ineptitude, his advisers would save his royal grace so he'd be counted the wisest of men, the best, the greatest, the grandest and the other words attached to royalty from their birth.

'Let us consider Zaki's options. If he made a run for it, he would be gunned down. He could attempt to sneak out but believe me, there were no holes in the walls he had studied his entire life. He could smuggle himself out like a parcel in a cart of weapons and he supposed that was his best chance. And that is what he did. He lay down in the cart, he did not dare breathe, he had no plans beyond his escape. The cart moved, he had no way of guessing how far he had travelled. He was in so much darkness because of the covering, it may as well have been the darkness of a night.

'The cart stopped and the covering removed and tonight I am in a good mood, I sit with my friends, so our slave jumps up like this'—Samir demonstrates, almost knocking the card table with his feet—'and he gets away and he is free just like you and me till the end of his days.

'But we are realists and despite our good diet of optimism and dreams and God on our side, the chances of Zaki finding his freedom are so tiny they may as well not exist. Say they catch him and they drag him back to the palace by his hair and his feet, his leg is chopped at the knee so he cannot repeat the offence. Say he makes his dash for freedom and he escapes but his only life is begging on the streets. You know, this is the likeliest outcome for Zaki and so while he is a free man he will be forever denied the pittance we use to keep poverty at bay, those morsels we have in our reach. Say he escapes and he finds fortune, maybe he finds a gold coin and that is his start but the elephants will fly and my name would not be Samir and I would chop the ends of my moustache and put on a woman's clothes so that everyone knows how wrong I've been, but I won't be wrong: Zaki probably dies and his chances of surviving—a proper free man—are so miserable he may as well resign himself to his lot in life.'

One of them throws a peanut at Samir. Another tells him to focus on his cards because he had lost another hand, but later I took his story, it kept me up at night, and I imagined Zaki in his bid for freedom, and I dreamed he finally escaped, he sat in the sun, he played cards with his friends, he had kids and a wife, and in the morning I wake in tears, unsure if it was because of my dream or if it was Samir's words that continued to play on my mind.

FACTS

'I am going to see Abu Khalil about some work.'

'There are other ways to sell your soul and they won't cost you so much.'

'The future is on my mind. There is a change I want in my life and I need more money than I currently have.'

'Is this about her?'

'No, not just that,' I lied. He knew the truth anyway.

'Work harder in the job you have.'

'I can only make so much that way.'

'I want to tell you money doesn't matter but of course it does and anyhow, if you're thinking like this, no matter how much money you have it will never be enough.'

'It's not like that. I know the situation. I tell myself that if she was after money, she would go for someone else. I console myself with this but . . .'

'If she's going to leave, no amount of money is going to make her stay.'

'I know that.'

'But do you understand that you are powerless, that this is out of your hands? Have you resigned yourself to the facts?'

'And what are the facts?'

'She will always be richer, she will always belong to another world that is different to the one that is your home. If you can make a life together like this, so be it but if you cannot, you won't be the first to fail.'

I wished he'd add some sweetness to his words.

He looked at me. We were face to face. 'You are my friend and you have always been like a brother to me. The thing you want is the thing I once wished I had. If it weren't for her, we would not be having this conversation in the first place. You would not be telling me you are going to sell your soul to be in the service of the fattest rat there is in this town. I know the lure of money. We want more to fill our eyes but if you do this, you will lose your sleep, you will lose your peace and you will lose any chance at a life with the one you wish to keep at your side. She will not recognise you. You will not be worth looking at twice. As you make your calculations, do not forget to include this in your tally as well. You remain poor, you keep your hands clean or you gather your riches and forever there will be emptiness in your life.'

He offered me a cigarette and I took it and I did the same with the next ten after as he first did when we were twelve. When he said my hands were shaking, I said it was the combination of coffee and cigarettes. He smiled and left it at that.

FIGHTING

Lubna said to her, *It is all right, I will go into the store alone.* With that, she marched in without checking if Jamila was coming in or staying outside.

She trailed after Lubna who was already arguing with the owner of the store. The dress was laid between them, a territorial dispute, and she could hear both their voices rising: Lubna yelling that the dress was not of the quality promised, look here at the stitching, the looseness of the threads . . . and the owner shaking his head and saying you have done this before, trying to return a dress you have already worn.

She stayed where she was, smoking a cigarette in the doorway, trying to blow the smoke outside. She listened to their voices and each time she thought they were reaching an agreement, they gridlocked and the argument continued on.

Lubna had in fact worn the dress. She had worn it last night to the wedding and when she'd been asked how she could afford such a dress (*They can't afford to eat* was whispered), she merely smiled and said she had her ways.

Lubna explained the situation on the way into town. *Really, I have only borrowed the dress. It is as good as when I bought it yesterday. Put it next to a new one and, trust me, you can't tell the difference between the two.*

Hence the trip, hence the argument, hence Jamila wondering if this argument would ever end. She considered walking in and offering quietly to buy it, but later when she'd tell him about her day, about the dress and how she'd bought it, he'd shake his head and say, *This is one more instance when you think your money will solve the problems of the world.*

It wasn't like that. It was a simple solution. Everyone would be happy. Everyone could walk away, assuming that is what Lubna wanted in the first place. *Everyone can walk away if they have money, everyone can make the choices I make if they had the money I have.* She imagines telling him this and to prove her imaginary point, she almost walks in and pays for the dress but instead she walks away because she can. As for Lubna, even if she could walk away, she would not, but that was not Jamila's problem anyway.

LIES

She lied. They all lied. She consoled herself with this.

She was less guilty because other people were guiltier. Guilt was not decided in isolation. Guilt was relative and so she lied and so did they but she lied less than them.

She told him she was on a break. A break from work, a break from life. The break stretched from the expected month and she had been here almost a year and she made no plans yet to leave.

She did not want to leave him. She did not want to bring him with her. She worried that if she returned to her life, she returned to her pain and it would break the both of them, and so she sheltered here on a permanent holiday, keeping her head down so no one would ask after her plans. She had this sense—stupid, she knew—that someone was going to call up and ask her to explain herself. *What are your plans, when do you plan to leave, why aren't you working?*

She would protest, she would defend, she would lie some more, she went through these days expecting always to be exposed. The truth would be laid bare. She stayed because she had nothing else she wanted to do. She stayed and she thought her life could pass like this, and was that such a terrible way to live?

He made no demands of her except to say he wanted her for life. *Do not say that to me.* And he said it again and she was silent, silent, then she pretended to sleep. She did not fool him though because he whispered it again in her ear. She ignored him. She tried out a vision: a future of them together—the regular trappings—the way she tried on a dress.

I want you with me forever.

Who knows about forever when I can barely see the day ahead?

Forever and I mean it.

You don't know that. How does one even plan for the rest of their life?

He sighed then and retreated to his side. He cloaked himself with silence as she had done so many times.

I need time.

He said nothing.

I don't know what I want.

Still he said nothing.

She left it and he fell asleep and she knew she lied to him and that she lied to herself. She knew what she wanted but her fear was greater and she was weighed with guilt and she hid behind a lie, a tired defence that had protected her so many times.

ADDITIONS

This would be her ninth. Lulu of the good figure, Lulu of the laugh, Lulu on whom they all had a crush. Amir once considered asking for her hand in marriage but reasoned she was out of his reach. Considering who Lulu ended up with, his chances were better than he'd thought them at the time.

For her first child, there had been excitement, congratulations, money in an envelope. For the second a gift, for the third something small. No one could remember what it was. For the fourth, the question: *Again?* And the fifth was much the same. Six, seven, eight—*they can't afford anymore*—and now the ninth, the wish there would be complications, that Lulu would need to abort.

In town, they smiled, they shook hands, the words were exact copies of the previous eight, but a curse had befallen them, like rabbits really, and in this day and age.

They discussed inviting her husband and giving him advice over cards: *Chemists, doctors, here is something you could use*, but none of them volunteered to look him in the eye and say the words. And—this was their conclusion every time—what business of theirs was it what Lulu and her husband did in their spare time, and what children were born as a result? He did not have to carry them on his head—and he said this to the rest— and they nodded. It was not their place but judging by their clothes and how rundown their house had become, a little money here and there was nothing major. And publicly weren't they the best of friends?

WARNING

It was their first proper fight. They both lost the battle. They both said, *Yes, this fight is a reference point in our lives.*

He had spent the evening with the boys and Jamila always encouraged him on this point. She knew it was the only time he saw his friends, it was the only free time in which they could talk.

Her first comment had been about Samir's wife. 'Doesn't she mind having you all around every night?'

'We sit outside. We are never in the house so we are not in her way.'

It was a comment—nothing—and he didn't give it another thought.

Later he saw that as the very start but Jamila insisted she never said the words he attributed to her, that if she said them they were innocent and she was making conversation.

A week later: 'Do the others ever bring their wives?'

Amir had been stupid enough to overlook the first comment. This time he looked up. This was not an idle question he could address with a word or two. There was more at stake than he had realised.

'Never. It is always just us. Some days, his wife has her friends over but they sit inside and I've never seen them.'

He wondered about bringing Jamila with him one time and he imagined how his friends would behave: polite, friendly, hospitable, but proper as if hosting the president. He imagined her trying to make conversation with Samir's wife, two women who knew how to talk and could therefore pass the time but without a point of commonality in their lives. It did not matter. It would not happen. He and Jamila would spend their days separate and alone, as long as each night ended in her bed.

He left it. No more needed to be said.

The following evening as she finished her tea, she told him she wanted to go with him to Samir's that night.

'Is it that you want to go out? Is it that you want to spend the evening together?'

'No, it's not that I want to go out but I want to visit Samir with you.'

'But why?'

'Because he's your friend.'

'But I have many other friends and we can visit them together if that is what you want but you know it's not proper unless you are my wife or we're thinking along those lines.'

'It doesn't have to be like that. Can't we visit people without being married? What is it with the people in this place, their stupidity, their fussiness, their gossiping all the time?'

He knew to be careful and he tried out many lines before stepping out cautiously as if to face a snake. 'We can go visit Samir, if you like, but it is not something I'd recommend.' He tried for lightness. 'Why don't you just marry me and we wouldn't be having this argument in the first place? Then we can visit all the people you want.'

She put her cup to one side. She wiped her mouth. She avoided his eyes. She let the silence grow. When he ventured her name, she shrugged and said never mind, and he was relieved by what he took for agreement that they would go to sleep now, that they could return to the peace they knew and liked.

When he woke in the middle of the night, he knew he was alone in bed. He found her on the roof smoking a cigarette. It was the height of winter and she was barely dressed. He kneeled before her and kissed her free hand, which was very cold.

'What is it that you want?' he asked.

'I just want a normal life.'

He laughed and remembered his marriage. All he had wanted was peace and quiet, all he had wanted was a simple love in their home.

A normal life. . . like the sort they lived here or the one she knew from her overseas life? Which one did she want and was it even in his power to provide?

He left it, he walked away, he thought about it for days after, he wondered about the impossibility of language, of being able to ever understand someone else. He saw the end much like a wave. It was rising over them and one day it would collapse on their heads but when he spoke like this, she laughed at him and said, 'It's not so bad.' But he foresaw it and he knew and it did not matter what she said. They could not live their lives here together without a union endorsed by the state.

It was foolish and her dreams belonged to another place and no matter their intentions and their hopes, these were dead fish that had no room in the life they shared in this place.

They were silent the entire way. He drove his car and their few attempts at conversation ended in silence. They had tried, he told himself later. They were both so desperate to keep the peace, to make it work.

Samir paused a second before he smiled and opened the door wide. 'Come in, come in, we're sitting in here,' he pointed to the living room, which Amir had set foot in twice before in his life. He and the others, they always went around the outside. That way, Samir's wife and children were undisturbed inside.

Jamila settled on the big couch and he noticed her eyes studying the contents of the room. She was discreet but he knew her and that this room was not to her taste, and he wondered if she was horrified.

Samir's wife came out and it was obvious she had thrown the robe on quickly and that underneath she was still in clothes for around the house.

The women talked and Samir called for a girl to bring tea and whatever biscuits they had in the house. He tried to remember the girl's name. Zeina or Zeinab or something like that. She was probably under ten and he thought the youngest was somewhere around five.

Samir asked about his day, a formal question they'd never used before in their lives. He answered—no swearing, his voice light—and he wanted a cigarette but Samir once said his wife didn't allow any smoking inside.

Later Samir will tell a story and he will wonder if it was from the time Jamila visited. *There is a camel so great yet it tries to tie its ankles so it is as slow as everyone else.*

He wonders about the camel hobbling about and how a camel in those conditions could ever be satisfied.

TAMING THE WOLF
(A FABLE)

Amir is hopeful.

It is another time, it is another life.

He thinks of the past, he thinks of the future, he thinks how nightly he tells Jamila, *You are the one I love.*

The past, he is sure, was a time he tried to carry a burden not his and pray emptily for life to flourish in a land that was hostile and also dead.

In the early days of his marriage, he loved his wife and badly wanted their union to work. He told himself things could be so much worse. He knew so many stories of men married to difficult women who counted the day they met as a curse. He did not feel like that. Not in the early days.

He remembers telling Samir his worries about his marriage.

Samir listened without replying, without making a single sound. Amir left that evening defeated, empty and alone, and knew it was more peaceful to leave her the bed and sleep on the couch.

Samir, his friend Samir, like a brother Samir, who did not make a sound. He felt foolish for speaking and he told himself from now on he would keep quiet about his burdens and he would not trouble anyone else with his woes.

That night, he slept terribly and many times he thought it should be morning but when he checked outside, it was still dark. He went through the following day as if in a haze and although he was tired, he went to Samir's just to get out of the house.

They had not yet started to play when Samir put down his cards and said, 'There is a story I wish to share with you boys.'

They put down their cards and waited. If only Samir could read and write, he could have shared his stories with the world.

'Once upon a time there was a lamb and there was a wolf, and both of them pretended they could get along.'

Amir avoided Samir's eyes but he listened and wished he had not come tonight so he could avoid hearing what Samir was about to say.

'The wolf had lived long among the sheep and could act like a sheep most days. And the lamb in our story thought the wolf knew enough about sheep that one day the wolf would grow wool and count itself as a lamb but we all know how useless such a hope is and that really such a thing would only happen when the sun rose from the west. Still, the lamb kept trying despite the wolf showing its teeth and threatening to eat the lamb alive. *These threats can't be real,* the lamb told itself. *There is no way the wolf will attack me as though I am any other lamb.* But one day the wolf did attack and I am not sure the lamb managed to escape with its life.'

Samir picked up his cards, lit another cigarette, and signalled they should continue with the round.

Amir did not speak his troubles to Samir again because his friend had heard and this would be his only reply.

Now he thinks about the story again and he wonders if once more he is trying to make the wolf into a lamb. The circumstances are different and if he were to compare Jamila to his wife, he'd struggle to find one way in which they are the same.

Still, perhaps the ground has no life and it is better to walk away. Or perhaps she does not respond to his proposals because she means soon to go away.

He can hope, as he then hoped, but if she leaves, she leaves, and if she stays, she stays and over the thing he desires the most, he knows he has little say.

HAPPINESS

They all called Rana a whore but none had the heart to say it to her face.

The facts: she was widowed at eighteen and had a child at nineteen. She never worked a day in her life and her child was often in trouble at school. *No aptitude* was written on the boy's report and they agreed the verdict was correct. She got engaged in her twenties but alas the relationship didn't work out and within two months they went their separate ways. She once spoke of her fears to a friend—*I worry that I will be lonely for the rest of my life*—but the friend was later found to have a loose tongue.

The friend admitted it herself that she had spread what Rana told her but as is often the case, she lightly changed what she had heard. *She is determined to find someone else. She doesn't want to be lonely. She needs a man in her life.*

These were the exact words of the friend. Someone who heard them made sure to write them down and then took the story back to the original source, saying, *This is what so and so has said.*

Those are the facts.

Here are the words that got around.

The child was not her husband's. He was born a month too late.

She needs to study, she needs to work. I wonder how she finds the money to feed herself.

It's not her family that supports her but a foreigner who is often out of town.

Even at school, she was already sleeping with the boys.

She should keep her nose clean and her knees together. What kind of mother is she to her son?

He heard these words. He could not avoid them. They were whispered behind his sister's back and the only true part was that her son was a royal brat. Twice he wanted to throw him off the roof and each time he had left without a word, shocked at how he could barely contain his rage.

More truths: he gave his sister money and so did his parents. His uncle abroad sent her money every month. The money arrived in envelopes but his uncle was a quiet man who said good deeds should be done in the dark, they should not be advertised with words.

He has two memories of her and they are there when his mind goes her way.

When Samir's sister was going to get married, Samir went personally to Rana's place and, over the fence, he invited her and the boy to attend. The night of the wedding, Rana looked again like a girl of sixteen. She danced the entire time, she clapped till her hands hurt and she later said it was the best night of her life. After everyone left, she made her way on foot through the dark streets of their town even though he said he could take her home. 'It is all right,' she said, smiling. 'I can see in the night-time and I am not afraid of what hides in the dark.'

She went away whistling, though she did not go to her own home but to their parents' place. She let herself in and the next morning, they found her sleeping in her old bed. She breakfasted with their parents and he was surprised to see her there when he dropped by. She rolled a cigarette for their father and one for herself and she said to no one in particular, 'Last night was the best evening of my life.'

That was the first memory and the second one was a happy one as well. In her forties, her son had gone off to his future and Rana met a man who worshipped her, who told her, *You shall be my wife.* They married without telling anyone and she packed up her home and moved into his house. Most days she smoked many cigarettes and her husband indulged her, which he later regretted when she spent the last decade of her life in ill health. Before she died, she wrote her uncle a letter to thank him for his years of support. She thanked her brother, her parents, she told her son to stay out of trouble. Finally, she made a phone call to Samir and said, 'I wanted to tell you directly how much that wedding of your sister's meant to me all those years ago. I know I don't have much time left and I can fairly say it was the happiest night of my life.'

She died—we all do—and while her misery would have been justified, he remembered her as always having a smile on her face.

THE LOVERS

FOR RODRIGO

An uncertain loneliness was his home. *You make a pact with the moon and the dream will come good.*

He wrote:

> *I want her, this companion, be she human or feathered and winged, be she a creature who lives in caves. I have done my penance. I am ready to shed my loneliness this final time, to make for her—this gift you send me—a place in my life.*

The moon was silent. He stared upwards in longing every night. He became a keeper of the moon, a tracer of this pale satellite. He wrote its patterns on pages that he fed to the fire at night because he may as well have etched the words onto his own heart.

The moon was silent for months. The moon did not smile. The moon never frowned. It is the serene face of eternity. None can make it tremble, none can touch its surface by reaching out.

He tried again:

You have become a symbol of my absent love. You are present in my life but you live beyond the reach of my hands. I mean for a possession, one of gentleness, kindness, and you have observed my life and you know these words are not lies.

The moon did not change in any way. The wave can smooth the rocks. The wind wears away at the cliff face so it does not hurt the world with its razor teeth, but the moon, his moon, their moon, was to be remote.

He took to praying and he was not a praying man. He flung his wishes into the face of the world silently, he wore a cloak of solitude, he forgot how he lived before his days were dictated by a futile hope.

One night, the lines began to arrive. They formed themselves like soldiers in his mind.

Isn't hope by its nature futile? It is the desire bared to the world, accompanied by the head that is bowed.

She will arrive. You are learned in patience. I make no promises about her timing or how long she will choose to stay.

You are not forgotten. Your wish is the wish of a billion others. It is the very beat of life.

He heard the words and he wrote them on a paper that he kept safe in his pillow as he spent his nights alone.

He was sleeping one evening, fitfully, his mind roaming through the years of his life, when there was a knock at his door.

Excuse me, is there anyone home? I am in need of some help.

He clothed himself and let her in to warm herself by the fire. He wondered about her. Perhaps she was a woman like all those other women who filled the world, with nothing to distinguish her from them, nothing that made her more his than anyone else's.

He wondered and watched her, careful not to let his gaze became a stare.

They had been together an hour when she shook herself like a creature that had emerged from the sea. 'I wish to tell you a story and I hope you believe what I have to say. A year ago I had a dream about this house of yours and the moon spoke your name to me. Those were the only clues I had: a vision of a home and then a name so I come here after a long search and I mean to ask your name. If it is the name the moon said, I will stay for all time and if not, then we will each go our own way.'

He hesitated. He thought about the moon. He thought about the words he had in his pillow, how he could quote them to her and hope that his visitor would remain. Instead he told her his name. She smiled and took his hand said, 'I think the moon means for me to stay.'

INERTIA

Jamila said she had come here for a month and she had now been here a year. She had needed a holiday, she said. She told people that even when they did not ask but one night, in bed, he asked what had really brought her here.

'I needed a break from my life.'

He nodded, lit a cigarette and she didn't say anymore.

When he left in the morning, she slowly got up and went to sit on the roof, a place she could visualise if she shut her eyes. There was the sea in front and the mountain at her back. She had settled into a routine, and while once the desire to escape had made her seek out this place, now inertia kept her here.

She had no wish to move, she didn't want to go to another place. Her days were repetitions, replicas of each other, and it shocked her to realise that this was what had driven her from the other place. Each day was a copy of the previous one and she went through her days in a fog. There were too many evenings when she came home to a dinner of tinned sardines before collapsing into bed, only to rise in the morning to repeat the pattern across the day ahead. She had fled not because she needed a holiday. Instead it was with the sense that *this is not a life*.

But she did not tell him this. She did not elaborate when she had the chance, and then as time passed it seemed unimportant to mention to him anyway.

Perhaps people make the decisions of their lives from a place of willpower but that has not been her experience so far. She goes some place, she does something without a reason in mind, and then she continues there because she cannot think of anything else she wants. It is a vine creeping through her life but she will not let anyone into the truth of her life. Let them see excitement. Who cares for the dull truth when a lie is shinier?

THE BED AND
THE TABLE

We all knew the story. Still we listen when Samir puts down his cards and lights a fresh cigarette and speaks of the disappeared, those we assume are likely dead.

To begin: we all knew her. Noura had lived in her apartment since we were kids. There had been a husband but he had died and her children were scattered, borne away by dreams and changes in the wind. (These are the words chosen by Samir who has this tendency towards poetry and words that rhyme and ring.)

Noura had fallen on hard times and her family propped her up because no one else would, but by her eightieth year she had outlived most of her relatives and whatever had been left to her by God's will.

We had seen her home emptied of valuables, her fingers stripped of gold over the years, until—as the story goes—she was left in that place with nothing but a table and a bed and her memories. It was enough, the rent hadn't been paid, the owner said, and four strong men were sent in to remove Noura and her possessions and dump them in the street, no matter her protests or the tears she shed.

We watched as the men carried Noura out with her lying on the table as if it were a bed. The table and Noura were placed outside the gate, and then the men went back for the bed and whatever else remained inside. All that time Noura cried and beat her chest.

When it was done, they locked the windows and the door, securing the place so she would have no way back in.

We helped her to her feet, we offered her something to eat. I want to tell you she found another home but the truth is that soon after, Noura disappeared.

The neighbourhood waited a week and when they heard she wasn't coming back, they broke the bed and table for wood, and who could blame them, because that winter was very cold indeed.

CHANCE

Jamila met Amir at a wedding. Really it was the stupidest thing. All those times she went with her family to a wedding and her mother pointed to a young man and said, 'What do you think of him?' And she considered the one that had caught her mother's eye to be the same as the others, also dressed in their best, dancing around him. She had hated how artificial it was, her prospective love singled out in this way as if they were out window-shopping. She wanted fate, destiny, the stars aligning.

So that wedding had been the universe's trick.

She passed him bread. He filled her glass. She considered his face nice enough and there was only one thing that distinguished that night from the hundreds of other weddings she'd been to. At the evening's end he said to her, 'I hope our paths cross again.'

The words were for her and no one else.

She weighed that sentence in her mind for a week, wondering why a sentence stayed with her when other words had completely disappeared.

She asked him later, 'Why did you say that to me?'

'Because it was what I meant,' he said seriously.

It was not the answer she craved, it was not the hand of destiny ordering her life. Instead it was a chance encounter that on another day would have failed to resonate.

Imagine her mother had pointed him out.

She shuddered.

It was the chance of it and her desire to weave it into a larger pattern that drove her to seek the fortune-teller she'd heard Samir speak about. 'She lives in the mountains. Anyone can tell you the way.'

She took her car and drove like a madwoman, wondering about the rationality of the details that make up a life. She found the fortune-teller, an ancient woman who babbled and had the appearance of being blind. *You speak to her and maybe she'll tell you something that speaks to your heart.*

She felt herself a fool for speaking to an incoherent woman who twitched and drooled, who smacked at her thighs to shoo away invisible flies.

The woman said nothing to her, nothing that stood out, except when she paraphrased the line of someone else. *We all find in the world what we seek.*

Jamila drove down the mountain with that line. She clung to it as if to a raft. She whispered it to him when she was sure he was asleep.

I sought you without knowing. I sought you as if in a dream. And now I wait to see what time will reveal.

He stirred and she kissed him. And then she returned again to her sleep.

VISITATIONS

Without telling anyone, his mother went to pay her a visit. Jamila was painting her nails on the roof, still in her bathrobe. She heard the knock and the maid answering the door, and she wondered which of her relatives it was this time.

It wasn't any of her relatives. It was his mum.

She debated meeting her in the living room, taking her sweet time doing her hair and make-up but it was defiance in the face of judgement that made her invite his mother to the roof where the sunshine might disarm her and allow Jamila the time to arrange her cards.

So this was his mother. In the photos Jamila had seen, she always wore a smile but now her face was serious as she politely accepted the chair that was pointed out.

This was his mother, this was the matriarch.

She realised how alone she was here. Her family had returned to the place they now called home, her friends were asleep on the other side of the world. She had no one to help her pick apart the significance of this visit, which broke with tradition and etiquette.

When he talked about marrying her, he insisted it must be done properly: his parents would call her parents, he would correctly ask for her hand. There would be no hiding, no mistaking his intentions, and she would be free of all doubt.

What then to make of his mother—alone—coming to visit her house?

They spoke as they had both been schooled to speak. The weather, the prices in the market, what the week held for each of them. She studied the orange trees below; she wondered what he'd make of this visit, if it would fill him with rage.

For a dove, use the usual traps but for a tiger, you'll need something else.

They went around and around, they joked, they laughed as if they were on stage reciting lines. After an hour, they walked out together and she waited at the gate until his mother drove off.

She went back inside and wondered how she'd break the news to him tonight.

When he came by, she suggested they go up to the roof.

It was close to sunset. They agreed it was quite a sight.

He put his cup down and she cleared her throat. 'Your mother came to visit today.'

He tensed but he held his tongue and clenched his fist. Then he shut his eyes, telling himself to relax.

'We had a good chat.'

'Did you now?'

'Yes. You could say that.' She lit a cigarette, offered him one, but he waved it away.

'What did she want?'

'She said I was welcome to visit anytime, that at a time convenient for us, she wishes to have us for dinner.'

'She said that?'

'That's what she said.'

'And what was your response?'

'I told her let's start with a cup of tea and see where it goes.'

He smiled then. Both possibilities were unconventional but it suited these unusual times.

Suddenly, he saw it had not been ruined, that his mother had not trampled the ground he had laid. Maybe, just maybe, his mother had added the fuel to finally make Jamila his wife.

KICKED IN THE PANTS

One day when she is alone, she will live her life.

It is a line that first occurred to her when she was fourteen and it is still with her at forty-three. She is going to live her life one day ... in a distant future, her pieces will be arranged, she will know where she is going and then she will begin.

What she fears is legitimate. It is the breath at her neck that says, *You will never have your pieces arranged, you will never be alone. Listen, woman, your life is going to waste.*

She wakes sweating, she tosses, she turns and falls back to uncomfortable dreams.

In the morning, she tells him, afraid he will laugh.

Instead he takes her hand and kisses it and says to her, 'You had better begin because one day you will be dying and by then it will be too late.'

Now when she thinks, *One day, when I am alone, I will live my life*, she sees him before her, her hand raised to his mouth. She hears him saying, 'One day you will be dying,' and she rises as if kicked in the pants.

MONEY

When she hears of someone struggling, she wonders: how much?

When she hears they've fallen on hard times, she calculates quickly in her mind.

When it's *he lost his job, they've called their family for help*, she keeps an ear out in case there's no response.

He watches her at this and largely he keeps his thoughts to himself, except once he opens his mouth and says, 'You have to realise your money is not going to save the entire world.'

She is furious. She goes to say it's not like that, that's not what I thought at all, but he is right, so she fixes her hair and in the mirror practises her poker face so she can keep her thoughts to herself.

INERTIA II

One day she will be alone to do the things she wants. One day the stars will align, the sun will be just right, and then she can live her life as she wants. One day, someday, never day, a golden day, an olden day, she will be alone and there she is, living the life she wants.

Here she is, it is today, and she is alone at last.

Instead of freedom, she feels restless.

Instead of possibilities, she feels trapped.

The sea is before her, stretched beyond what she can see, and she cannot figure out if she should stand or sit, if she suffers from hunger or if she is in need of a drink.

She has dragged herself here, to drink at a fountain that has turned out to be a mirage. She contemplates returning home, packing up before an imaginary storm rolls in, but she doesn't.

She stays there, tied by her stubbornness as if an animal to a post, and thinks, I've driven myself here so I may as well enjoy the beach today.

Later when people ask about her achievements, how she rose so high, she looks at them baffled because it was dogged inertia all the way.

LUST

Amir was young, Jamila was young, their bodies not yet wearied with age.

He woke with her name in his mind and he was reminded of the emptiness at his side.

Her scent had long faded from the room and he did not want to be reminded of her with photographs and memories.

There would be no one to touch him, no one to offer the mercy of release.

He sighed and thought of her body again. In the glare of reality, he still had the comfort of her in dreams.

LESSONS

Her father is teaching her brothers. She is seven or eight, she is at her father's side, her hair done in pigtails, in a dress her mother has made for her. It is red and she still has it in a drawer somewhere. She likes the memory of the dress but it is gathering dust with the ghosts she has left behind.

To begin with: a lesson about choosing a wife.

'A woman is chosen for her beauty, her money or her faith.'

Her mother rolls her eyes. Jamila nudges her father. 'What about her mind?'

He smiles and tugs her hair. 'Also her brains.'

'Which is better?' asks Nazim or Ismail.

'Her faith, of course.'

Her mother puts down her cup of tea. 'You may as well continue the lesson. You have a daughter as well.' She fixes him with a stare that is a dare.

'Of course, of course, it is the same for a girl. She chooses a man for his strength or his money or his faith. Sometimes—in my case for example—he is chosen for his faith, but let us be honest, most women go for money because either they are stupid or they don't want to lift a finger.'

She looks up at her parents and tries to understand. 'Wouldn't it be best to choose someone for their brains?'

He puts her into his lap and hugs her. 'Yes, my dear, but to make a good choice takes brains and that is something most people today don't seem to have.'

LONGING

Every time she looks at the map at work, she picks out where he is and she imagines him walking in his part of the world.

He is so far away but his country is simply an area bordered by a line, and within that land he has a defined space.

She has no servants now. That was a luxury she could afford over there but here she does her own dishes, she opens her own gate.

She has mental conversations with him and each sentence begins with a word made of two sounds that represent him, that distinguish him in the emptiness of space.

Amir.

The word is a body that was once a smile but now it causes her pain.

The word is a man full of life and left behind, and she tells herself he belongs to the past.

The word is one she tries to erase from her mind but sometimes she thinks it and always with a sigh.

In her conversations with him, she explains herself, and he nods and tells her he understands. The reality is they agreed that they had no future, their paths converged briefly but it is better they each go their own way.

When she speaks to him, she asks who it was better for and that *more than anything, I wish to see you one more time.*

Only one more time. It is a point she emphasises, and she hopes the universe will grant her this because it has all the power in the world while she is only one being, her wish pitted against the others of the human race.

This is foolishness, she knows. It is time to move on with your life.

HOPE

Days and no word.

No calls, no messages.

It is the end, as they both said.

But there is hope.

One asks deep in the night: hope for what?

Hope for a return, hope for another chance, hope for the sound of his voice.

She waits, he waits. This impasse.

There is a message.

It is small.

It is nothing in the grand scheme of the world.
There is a smile.
Its name is hope.

CLICHÉ

If someone had predicted a future in which she lusted after a man from the village, Jamila would have laughed in their face. Such men were hard-headed, they thought to make a possession of their wife, and she was determined that she would never let herself fall for their sweet-talking ways.

She had friends who had fallen for such men. These men wove webs filled with castles in the skies. They promised the stars with tears in their eyes. They vowed to make the woman a queen, a singular imperial power over their male life.

And these women she knew—educated, intelligent, savvy, worldly women—fell for the lie. She put it down to their biological clocks. What else could explain how these women had lost their minds?

She saw the trajectory of such unions. A month after the honeymoon and already their faces were tired. Their plans were all routine and their choices mirrored those of their parents, only with a contemporary vibe.

She would not do that.

She would go and enjoy herself, she would allow no one to pry apart her thighs.

When she told him this, he laughed till he couldn't breathe, and when she told him to be serious, he lost the laugh but she could see the amusement in his eyes.

When she told him she wanted him forever, he said, Only if you'll be my wife.

When she told him she wanted to have forty children, all of them his (a biological impossibility), he said, We don't need to have children for us to live side by side.

When she told him her fears for the future, he told her to live with strength and to banish the demons from her mind.

When she told him she loved him, she imagined her friends laughing at her and saying, *Look who's fallen for the oldest cliché after resisting all this time.*

She argued with them afterwards in an imaginary debate. It was ridiculous to waste her time like this but it was her only defence against their attacks when she finally announced her little truth before the criticism of their eyes.

To hell with them, she whispered, and he asked her what was troubling her in the middle of the night.

Nothing, she lied, nothing. And it would be nothing, even if it meant staking her heart, mind and life.

THE STORY

This is the memory that is printed on her mind. Life starts in the concrete and then retreats to mental territory.

She resists attending the wedding. She has been resisting these social events. Secretly she thinks these people are backwards. Look at their ideas about politics and the country swamped with refugees. If only they stood on their own feet, the country wouldn't be a mess. If only they weren't so keen on handouts from overseas, this country would not be on its knees for fifty, sixty years.

She tires of the circularity of conversations such as these. She cannot stand the small-mindedness of the women and, yes, it is the lack of education, it is ignorance, but how does that help me when I try to converse with an imbecile who thinks the world is housework and dishes and that is all a person should aspire to in life? And the men who hide their weakness, who pretend they are in control of their little domains?

She is tired and she wants no more of it.

Still, it is her first invitation of this sort and so she attends, her lack of make-up an act of rebellion, her dress lighter, tighter than what the other women would recommend. *Let them talk*, she thinks. They will be done up like dolls while she has barely brushed her hair. Simpletons, and if they were before her, she would strangle them by the neck.

In the car, she lights a cigarette, the ash falling into her lap and making a mess, but she brushes it away and besides, the light will be dim and her lap will be tucked away underneath a tablecloth.

She greets, she kisses, she waves hello. *This is not my place*, but she claps on command, she smiles as a reflex.

When he sits down at her table with the others, he is distracted, his eyes are elsewhere. Her impression is of averageness; he is one of many and there is nothing to set him apart.

He smokes, he rolls up his sleeves, he eats absently, he asks her name, he asks how she's finding the place.

Distracted talk, round in a circle, she does not yet know she is trapped. He offers her a cigarette with his next one, lighting it for her before settling back in his chair. It is then she notices him and her mind goes to the future. She imagines their entire lives in an instant, she shakes her head as she shakes off the ash, and she refuses him as an option because he is not who she has in mind.

A man from her parents' village. That has already been done. And she sees her life then, how she has wanted greatness, how she has refused the common, and how much pain this resistance of hers has caused.

It is not a capitulation that she accepts him. He is nothing of the sort. If he was in a line-up of all the men in the world, he is still the person she would want. Even if she had her pick of other men—the handsome, the rich, the smartest, the fastest—he is the one she wants by her side and between her legs.

Whenever you are near, the world elsewhere ceases to exist. It is only you.

He laughs at this, her declaration of love, and he kisses her head, and later he will say: *Tell me again about the time we met.*

And she can predict his reactions, exactly the lines that will make him laugh, or those will make him so still it's as if he no longer breathes.

It always ends with a kiss: her mouth, her neck, the top of her head. He pulls her to him and he utters her favourite words. *There is no one else.*

FAIRYTALE

He said he loved her. The others said the same. He took her hand and kissed it and said, 'Wait here, I will only be gone a day.'

She waited, faithful like a dog. She kept herself entertained. She made up games about the clouds, she counted the white cars going past. She wondered did he mean a twenty-four-hour period when he said a day or another full day after the one when he'd left her? She should have clarified this and she resolved next time she would ask.

She waited and warmed herself with thoughts of him, she read the letters she carried in her bag, she smiled at this secret she kept that none could ever touch.

She waited and one sun set and then another, and she grew cold. She thought to seek shelter but she worried he would return and not find her and that would be the end.

She waited another day. She moved to a cover of trees from where she could see the spot he had last been seen. She dozed, she dreamed, she conjured up the sound of his voice.

On the fourth day, as she was telling herself that was that, he returned, shiny like crystal, and kissed her all over. *I am sorry, sweet thing, I am sorry I was kept away. I am sorry but it won't happen again.*

She kissed him and told herself the wait was justified. He was here and it was the same as it had ever been.

They spoke of the future and then he hid her in the cupboard. He called to her from the other side of the door, 'Just wait here where you will be safe. There is food and water on the shelf. Dangerous people walk by here so it is best not to call out.'

He left before she could ask if a day was twenty-four hours or another turn of the earth after the day he left. He made no promises this time but she warmed herself on the plans they made for the future. What was a little wait when eternity would be theirs? She waited and they laughed outside her door, she waited as she heard crashing and fighting, she waited as someone put their mouth to her door and whispered for her to come out. She sat still and told herself she was no longer in the world, anything to keep the dragons from eating at her mind.

She thought to read his letters but there was no light. She thought to eat a little more but she worried about her food running out. She thought to stand and stretch her legs but who knew what howled on the other side?

She thought about the passage of time, the universe contained in each minute that passed.

She thought about their future, she thought about when their future would finally begin.

She thought about when they met and wondered if it was the happiest day of her life or if it was the beginning of a curse.

She thought about this and their love and her devotion and her hopes and every single dream and how it was better for them to die than it was for her to lose her life. She said goodbye to him, silently in her mind, and she hoped he heard because she was taught to be kind, and with that she stepped outside. *One world has ended and I am afraid of what lies ahead*. Never mind. She walked out, thinking it better to face what was outside than die in the cupboard forgotten by the world.

ANGUISH

He is alone. Days alone, decades, centuries, each minute is the history of the universe. Alone, his private world. Once there was a skylight but the light has been turned off.

It is dark.

He often forgets to breathe. It would be easy to die if breathing weren't automatic. A reflex prompts him.

Inhale, exhale.

He forgets. He is weighed down by memories.

He thinks: I shall let go.

It is easier to stay alive than to find the strength to die.

Once upon a time there were lights above. Dark. It is dark.

He shuts his eyes. The darkness is resident in his mind. Inside, in his head, the worm in the apple.

Sometimes he sleeps. Other times he tries until he is too tired for wakefulness and then he slides bodily into the dreaming time.

POISON

She never meant to love across the lines.

She would love, of course, but religion was prerequisite number one. If he did not share it, he would not make the cut.

Her father explained it. A woman follows the man, not the other way around. She takes his name, his religion, she moves to the house he provides. She lets him drive the car, she lets him beat her for relief when he is down.

That is how it works so to ease the trouble, it is better to love and marry one of our own but even without love at the start, give it enough time and it will grow.

How long did she carry those words inside? Each time she loved a man, she wanted to parade her love, fling it in her father's face. It was a provocation, a declaration of war. It was revenge for the hurt of the words he had uttered in the past.

Her idea of love was demented. It was a misshapen creature. Give it wings of bamboo but no matter the love and attention and devotion you lavish on it, you cannot make this creature fly.

How many broken birds did she nurse in the dark? Each of the men said, *Thank you, see you later, I had a nice time*, and she was left with her rage and the poison of her father's words as she wondered if he was right.

She had tried the wrong places.

She could not make a dead bird fly.

Jamila, give up, no love is written for you at this particular time.

She should twiddle her thumbs, she should plant some trees. That is how she could find peace once more in her life.

She waited . . . a spider in the dark, biding her time. She waited so long she gave up and forgot what she was waiting for. It was something—a sense perhaps—but her memory was faraway, and she loosened her hold on it until it floated away into the unknown, and with this freedom, she found she could once more live her life.

LOVE

From early on, I sensed your solitude. You were like an island alone. What interested me was that you were yourself and you would only permit people ever so close. I remember this now because I read my notebooks recently. Lately I want to keep you to me. It is something I tell you repeatedly. I sense you carry a lot of sadness inside and I would like to hunt these dark animals you keep and rid you of them but I do not have that power. Even if I knew every little detail about you, even if we spoke endlessly for the rest of time, I would still not have this power, not even if I knew you from the beginning of our lives. There are limits to how much a person can occupy another person's life. There are limits. We are humans. Our days are not endless. Our days are finite. We will die at our appointed time, and when that day comes, I do not want to die wishing I had told you I loved you, wishing I had bared my heart to you when I had the chance. I do not want to die with regrets. I wish to live freely and with courage and to give you all of my love.

I could write more words. I could defend, expand and explain but words such as these need no extra support. They can stand on their own, as we stand in each other's lives, as a presence, as a witness, as a person who loves the other unconditionally, as a person who walks towards someone even when they are afraid.

So many things grow quietly in the silence. They are there with us at this distance when we are apart. There is the silence. Let our love always be great.

You do not need to put on a show for me. I don't need to be entertained like a child. The tricks and charms you wear for others have no home in the place I occupy with you. Each day I shall love you without the antics we perform in the hope of being liked. Put them to one side when you come to me because it is the truth I came for, not the pleasant fantasy of a shining lie.

From the day I met you, I sensed your openness to me. I sensed that you were available, that whatever space you inhabit is a space you would share with me. I arrive here to share it with you, be it lavish like palaces, be it the bareness of your body that nightly occupies my dreams. Your presence is a phantom when you are not around. Your voice is a phantom limb. Some days I string together sentences and it is as if you speak them with your phrases and I receive them on the inside of my ear.

These words I write have a meaning and it is love, though we are separated by the greatest ocean in the world. It is possible for an ocean to separate bodies but not two spirits connected before time even began. You are like eternity to me and I exhaust myself with what I wish to say to you.

I want to draw you close so you are against my heart.

I want to give you so much pleasure because to me, you are passion and desire, and they are intertwined.

I want to imprint myself upon your life till you know you will never again walk alone.

I am here for you, I am here, I am here for whatever time fate has given us in this life.

I am here before you and I say this to you as always with all my love.

THE VEGETARIAN

Jamila woke Amir at three in the morning to tell him about the time she tried to save the world.

Later he thought about her words as he dressed for work. Later he wondered if he had hallucinated their conversation, if Jamila telling him a story while he was half-asleep could be called a conversation.

It started when she was fifteen. She wanted to save the pandas and tigers, she wanted to chain herself to a tree. The older the tree, the better.

I told my parents we had to cut meat from our diet.

I told my family people like them were ruining the world.

So I became a vegetarian. I wanted to shave my head but my dad would have locked me in my room until my hair grew back.

Amir imagines her in a room alone, waiting for her hair to grow back so she can go outside. He imagines the walls are bare, the room illuminated by a small window covered with bars. He imagines her refusing food in the middle of a hunger strike.

When he describes his vision to her, Jamila laughs so hard she begins to cry.

Chances are I had enough books and magazines and CDs to keep myself entertained for months. I wouldn't have lasted an hour on hunger strike. I just don't have the capacity for grand political gestures.

He is puzzled and he asks how long her vegetarianism lasted.

'It was less than a month.'

Amir suspects it was closer to a week but he says nothing because he doesn't want to force her into a lie.

At times, he imagines her as the vegetarian on a hunger strike, and the thought of her without any hair still makes him smile. His smiles lasts a second and then he remembers this is his vision and the reality was not what he has in mind.

They are out on the street and she speaks of the people they know.

It is so nice Khadija has the support of her family, that she can live with her children under her parents' roof.

He does not tell her that Khadija has no means of supporting herself, that her ex-husband is a coward, and that Khadija lives with her children in her parents' house because she has no other choice.

I like that people here have not lost the simple joy of living. They eat in a simple way, they gather together for all their meals.

It does not matter that there is bickering, that people get on each other's nerves, that patience and tolerance with one's family are already stretched so thin.

I like that couples get married and that then they are together for life.

That's because they cannot afford a divorce. It would put too much pressure on their families to separate, so they are resigned to their disagreements and nightly they argue behind closed doors.

I like that . . .

He interrupts her before she can say another word. *Remember you told me you became a vegetarian? And how afterwards you went back to how you ate before? You had a choice, a luxury that people here do not have. I could not be a vegetarian, no matter how much I wanted to because I would not be able to survive. People here stay together because they have no other choice. Khadija lives with her parents because her other option is the streets. If you told her right now,* You can have a place of your own but it's on the other side of the world, *she would leave with her children immediately, even if it meant never seeing her parents again.*

She avoids his eyes. *You misunderstand me. I do not mean to romanticise their lives.*

The truth hurts her so he keeps quiet.

They continue on, talking and walking aimlessly.

There is the love between them, obvious to the casual eye, but some days he wonders about this separation in their lives.

LAMENT

There is the silence that can be filled and there is the silence that cannot.

I think these words with the knowledge I will never say them to you.

I think of our future and I fear that what we have is all there is.

I know that the world prizes the man for his money and I reject this but will we be comfortable on what you earn, will your pride suffer if we spend instead what I have?

I have these ideals and I have carried them all my life, ideals of how I wish to live in defiance of society, and I am afraid that despite my ideals and hopes, time will prove me weak.

I wonder if we should have children, if this isn't one more trap for a woman's ankle to a man's until the inevitable resentment kicks in?

Will we resent each other in time? Will we become first comfortable and then indifferent and then will our hearts become hard and cold?

I pose these unanswerable questions but I do not ask them of you because I do not think they are fair. I do not wish to burden you with the thoughts that cross my mind.

Would I be content with the normal life we'd have together?

Would I be content for us to have coffee in the morning, to kiss you goodbye, and then go about our separate days like couples all over the world?

I want to be content with this.

I want to say it will be enough but I fear my restlessness, that I lack the staying power others have.

I refuse to say this to you because I love you and I tell you this every day. I could not bear your disappointment or, worse, could not bear to discover that you predicted this and in fact you understand.

I don't know, I don't know, I don't know a thousand times.

I write this while sitting across from you and I ask you what it is that makes you smile.

You tell me it's this—us together—the companionship after each of us being alone.

My thoughts are a betrayal. I wish to be cured of them because they make me so afraid.

TOGETHER WE WERE ONCE UPON A TIME

I wish I had known you when you were young.

I wish I had known you when you were five.

I imagine you like this, the child version I have seen in photos. I see you with a backpack on your way to school.

I think of us together in the same class. Perhaps it would not have worked as I imagine in this alternative life. We might have been in different classes or else our schools might not have been the same.

I imagine watching you across a desk, our love beginning so young. We could have been two trees, our lives growing in parallel.

I think of you older. You are ten, twenty, then you are thirty-five. Then we are old together, we have known each other all our lives.

There is a sense when you meet someone. You talk, you discover each other's lives. I have had this sense with you. We have known each other once, we were separated and then we came together later in our lives.

I do not see the time before I met you as a waste. I know that no matter how much time we have together, it will never be enough.

It is an endless well. You are at the end of the tunnel and I am forever swimming to your side.

DESPAIR

The end
we carry it with us
from our start

In the end, she felt despair.

There is a photo of her in her parents' house. She is
aged six. She has a crooked smile for the camera. The
world is a paradise still.

Long ago, there was a summer on the beach. There
were the countless consecutive days when they would
go early and not leave till it was dark. There were the

days of blindness, when one avoided being beneath the sky because the sunlight was too bright. As the summer dwindled, she despaired at the end of the holidays, that soon she would be back at school and it was not enough to have the compensation of her friends.

Her father used to laugh at her tears when they left the beach, at how she cried over the last swim, the last ice cream, the last barbecue in the park nearby. *It is the last one now*, he told her, *but summer always comes again.*

It is not enough. It will never be enough to stare in wonder at the stars unreachable and far away. It is not enough to love and have it die despite your hopes and have someone tell you, *It is all right. Love will come again.*

What if it does not, she whispers to herself, *what if summer only exists as a promise and I never see the sunshine again?*

You're being melodramatic, her father said to her whenever she was tearful. But you grow to adulthood and no one thinks you need comforting again. There is the assumption you will manage by squaring your shoulders and arranging your face before the world.

In the end, there is no comfort. There is no word that will give her peace at all.

It is over. It is time to walk. There is a wall and its name was always despair.

THE LETTERS

1

The things I wish to say to you, the things I wish to do, they multiply. When I shut my eyes, day and night, there you are. Your face I have memorised but I wonder if I will see you in this life again.

Why did we walk from each other? What impelled us to walk away from a love like ours? What craziness, what lunatic possession convinced us that it was better to leave than to turn around and fight? You know that movie I love—the one where the hero is chased until he is cornered in a tunnel and only then does he turn and fight. I feel like that now, that I no longer wish to be away

185

from you, no longer do I accept the premise that we must be apart. No, my love, it is time to hold one's ground, it is time for us to reverse our course and prepare to fight.

What is the alternative? You are all things intelligent and I know that the future weighs ever on your mind. What is the alternative? We both leave, we both continue to walk away, our love becomes disused and empty like the broken cities of the world, and in time our great love will lie down for the final time and at last it will die.

And what happens then? There will be regrets, there will be bitterness, there will be the conclusion that life is unfair, that the world has nothing to offer us—we who wished for passion and a colourful love. The world offers us nothing. We will surrender our other dreams as we did the greatest thing in our lives. What is it to hand over the little that remains when the greatest has already been lost?

I write this, I send it, and it is with a spirit of hope. Countless times we marvelled that despite our differences we two are cut from the same cloth, were born of the same spirit, that never have two people been so united in the outward expression of their lives.

Do you remember we said that? Do you remember we both agreed?

So I write this with the hope you still agree, that we can build a future together, one of harmony and kindness and our love, which has been the best thing in all the days of my life.

I remember always the day I met you. I remember it as a day of music and sunshine and curiosity. I remember you always as a spirit of light.

What do you say? What about we give this another try? Can we return to the day we parted and from there we pick up the thread and see if we can't be companions who care for each other till the end of time?

2

Do you remember how our days used to begin? Do you remember that one would wake the other with a kiss? What lightness to begin the day like this! I feel an absence from how those days used to begin. If there is one thing I miss above all others, it is that kiss.

We are separated and it is no one's fault but our own. Yes, there is an ocean between us now but we chose to put an ocean in our path. We chose this as we once chose to begin the day with a kiss.

When I remember those days, they seem to me to be days of sunshine, days of leisure that collected together too quickly to become a year. I remember keeping track of those days with you: *It's been a week . . . a month . . . three months . . . do you realise we have been together an entire year?*

We never meant for it to be a year. We fumbled like children. I can write this here: that we were like children in our love. There was an innocence and we thought, as all lovers must think, that nothing could interrupt the spell in which we lived. But it was interrupted, and the world is faultless, and instead we are the guilty pair.

I do not want these to be letters of blame. I do not want to fixate on a specific moment when our course was changed. Perhaps you will agree on the moment, perhaps you will not, but that is not the purpose of these letters anyhow.

I shall tell you what I do know, what is a conviction in my entire being.

I loved you and you loved me, and there is no reason that we had to part. We can come up with stories about why we are not together, stories that will convince another person's ears, but there are no reasons, no version that I accept peacefully. There are none and I don't believe there ever will be a set of facts that will persuade me of the soundness of the mutual decision we made.

We were very solemn, we were like businesspeople. We could have shaken hands, and this is where we went wrong. There was a morning that did not begin with a kiss. It was this empty morning that undid the future in which we had begun to implicitly believe. If I were to blame something, I would blame that morning or else it would be our foolishness. We were so innocent in our belief, in our trust, in our openness, in how we took to each other as if alone we could no longer breathe.

Come back to me. Do not hide from me. Do not keep from me to honour a decision we made together, even though it dishonoured us both. Do not hide away because of a sense of pride. Do not keep away because you believe I have lost interest. I have not. If for whatever reason I should find you changed or that your love for me is not what it once was, I would count it the tragedy of my life.

Come back to me. You will find no aspect of my love has changed. The person you met at the beginning is the same person who takes the time to call you back, so that once again our love has every chance to flourish in our lives.

3

Do you remember the first time we fought, how we were shy afterwards like lovers before their first night? I remember being afraid. What if this was the end and you decided to send me away? My terror of abandonment was at the forefront of my mind. And then there was the weariness. How exactly do we recover the ease that existed between us only yesterday?

I made you coffee and presented it to you in the hope you would notice me and smile. A smile would mean that there was a way back from the argument of the night.

You were sad. It was plain on your face. And it occurred to me that I would prefer to hurt myself a thousand times rather than see that sadness again on your face. Even after we spoke of it, your sadness lingered, I think, for days. I am tired, you told me, and I believed you but I should have realised it was your sadness still and it hung over our heads. A similar sadness hangs over my life now that you have left.

When I think of the future, when I think of seeing you again, I wonder if we can return to how we were before, if we can meet each other again with the ease and openness that we both expected when we were face to face. I know things have changed, I know they will not be the same, but I think of seeing you relaxed again, your presence like a smile, a symbol that joy will find its place between us again.

4

Do you remember our former separations? You once said you could only bear a few days. Here we are and now it has been weeks.

The first time it was a day, one whole twenty-four-hour period, and when I saw you at the end of it, I thought, *I hope we never have to do that again.* I told myself, *Come on, you're being silly, these theatrics over being apart a day.* For most people, this is routine, for most people, this is commonplace but why should I judge my love with you by what others are accustomed to? Let them be parted for a day and not blink at the absence. Let them calmly go about their day of emptiness without an ache. Let them be sensible adults while I call on heaven and say, *God, please do not subject to me this again.*

You are the one who told me to drop this urge to compare, to quantify the mystery of intangible things. *Why do you do this when there is no answer, no comparison? Why do you subject the contents of your heart to a running race?* Yes, they are content, they are unaffected if their beloved is distant for a day, but I am not and I refuse to be, and I do not want your absence to be commonplace and expected, something that I should take in my stride. Worse, imagine I begin to welcome it. I mean this in all seriousness but I would prefer to take a gun to myself before I accept your absence as ordinary as putting on my clothes.

5

We are separated by an ocean now as we were separated by it before we met. The difference is our consciousness. I did not know of your existence, your life on the other side of the world. I was not conscious of being cut off from the world. The ocean I knew every day of my life was the horizon. It was the backdrop of my life but now it takes on the character of a barrier. It is the wall between me and the one I love. Once it was an ocean I swam in, its waves known to me as far back as the stretches of my memory. I never saw the ocean before but now it is all I see. I have this vision that if I take a boat out onto the water and row beyond the horizon, I will find you there waiting for me, a creature born of the sea. I will touch you with my hands and mouth, and I will remember that before I met you, before I tried to claim you, you had your life at the end of the ocean, that you are your own world, that before I attempted the futility of possession, you had constructed a tower of yourself and placed it at the world's edge.

How do I call you back, the one who has slipped from my life? You are a figment of my dreams and if it weren't for the few photos I have, I would doubt your existence completely.

Except you are real. You exist. You do not belong solely in the world of memory and dream.

I imagine us again. I imagine a scene like one from a film. We run to each other, you are once again in my arms but I know you, I know myself, and chances are we would be struck shy all over again.

I am not one for faith, I am not one for God, but I find myself bargaining with the One in the middle of the night. *Grant me this, only this, and I promise, I the faithless believer, that I will never ask you for anything again.*

6

I imagine you as a child. I imagine you before the world and its sadness has touched you. I imagine you before you learned of heartbreak and the lessons it teaches. I am not here to glorify pain, not when I wish for your love in my life.

We assume in surveying our lives that when it is asked of us, we will be able to love with the purity of poetry, that we can bare ourselves, when in truth we cannot imagine our existence without the protection of clothes.

I imagine you as a child because it is the part of life still resplendent with possibilities. Life is difficult; it bites at the spirit and it trims the edges of our hope. So I imagine you as a child, full of smiles, your hair lighter before it was darkened by time. I imagine you as this child that you assure me is nothing like the child you were. *I was despondent, I raged against the world.* From a distance, the image is one that makes me smile but close up, I want to soothe your fears and rage.

With you, I recovered the innocence of childhood. I remembered a time when I believed I could love completely. It was you who returned that paradise to me.

7

Do you remember the nights I loved you?

Do you remember you were mine in the night-time hours between dusk and dawn?

Each day for me your body was a continent that I wished to explore with my hands and tongue. I wanted to burn myself upon your skin so that later you would remember and the memories would make you blush.

I wanted knowledge of all the tricks that would please you and I wanted to do them again and again.

I miss your body. I will not lie. I miss that our times in bed were an expression of our love.

When I think of you leaving, I believe I could die. I say that it was our decision to break apart but the truth is you are there and I am still here. One of us has left and the other is too immobilised to do anything but stay.

I write you these letters and I sense I could throw them down a well for all the good they will do. I will not send them because I have my pride and I do not wish to beg.

What saddens me the most is that for all our talk of love and how we would honour it, we fell into the same traps as everyone else, and no matter how great our love, in the end, like those sad stories, it could also die.

LINES FLOAT IN AN OCEAN
IN A LETTER OF LOVE

The tenderness of strangers on the street.

A father pulls his child close and hugs him till the child protests. *My bones begin to hurt.*

Your ankle tied to mine in a dream.

When I cried, there were tears in your eyes. When I laughed, you said I was so alive.

The possibilities of life unfold fruitful when we are side by side.

The smell of you after you have taken me inside.

Every story, every poem, every film ever written about love, no matter how clichéd.

Your hand on my arm as if that is where it belongs.

I cannot lose you. I cannot bear the emptiness of a colourless life.

An old couple pressed together, each thinking: *The other is my life.*

The recognition that Gibran was right. Stand together yet not too close. You are but the witness to the other's life.

There is a memory of you. It is summer. You breakfast in shorts and a shirt. You are the centre. The universe is a stage for my beloved to live out a golden life.

I wish you sunshine and warmth for every day of your life.

Dance, my love. The world is glad you are alive.

8

Do you think the weariness of routine settled in? We had no fights, we had no arguments, it was not even the rot of complacency. Perhaps we knew what to expect here, our passion cooled, and then we each wished for colour elsewhere in our lives. I offer this by way of explanation for why we walked away. There are many factors and I am hitting blindly in the dark, but did we decide love itself was not enough? It reminds me of that film you like where the girl says towards the end: *Can one ever have enough of love?* Can this question ever be asked? Is it a legitimate question at all? At what point does one have enough of love, at what point does one abandon the boat for a future that cannot yet be seen? Did we underestimate what it takes to tend love, to protect it so that it can warm us in the darkness and the light? There was a point when you grew distant and I knew it but would not admit that your mind and heart had already left. You were still present, you made the usual jokes that we both liked but they were words said to fill the time and they lacked the life they once had.

Perhaps I expected too much, placing too great a weight on our love beyond what it could bear. Perhaps my mistake was to make you the centre of my life when to you this was temporary and your future lay elsewhere. It is a question I offer with the awareness that it has no answer, that I will not send these letters I write you, that their end is the grave silence of eternity.

ENDINGS

She imagines it and how it will be.

As he once slipped into her bed, she slips into his city easily.

There may be a spot of awkwardness. It is a cloud that will pass.

They will be reunited. They will laugh. Perhaps they will cry as well.

They will agree: let us never be parted ever again.

LEAVING

She is leaving, she is leaving. She has already left and he watches her exit the room.

He means to call out.

He does nothing.

He does nothing at all.

She leaves and he is left behind.

It is not what he imagined as their end.

It is not meant to end like this.

THE PIANO

There is a park with a bench around the corner from her house. Sometimes she goes there in the middle of the day and it takes her a long time to realise it is because someone plays the piano in an apartment overhead. She had thought her choice of place and time was random.

The music she hears triggers a memory. She is with him again and they are ready to dine. In the restaurant, a piano is played out of sight. She comments on this and he looks around and says, 'How do you know it is live?'

She pauses and considers the question, struggling for evidence to support the sense she has. In the end she can only shrug. And she thinks, *If you knew a thing or two about music, you would know this is live.* Except she does not think this but says it aloud, and she is embarrassed by her blunder which has the power to harm him in the world outside.

He lights a cigarette and says with a directness she does not like, 'Am I not refined enough to tell if a piano is being played live? Am I better suited to card games because that is the destiny of someone in my station of life?'

She hates this directness. It makes her want to hide. She knows she should apologise but if she does, it will give greater weight to the mistake she's made, and it will be lodged forever in his mind.

She considers her options. She can apologise or attack. Is it possible that their entire relationship can be undone by the slip of a tongue?

But was it merely a slip? Is there more at stake than repeated professions of love in the night?

She apologises. Of course she does, and he accepts it as one does the apology of a silly child. It has passed . . . yet it does not, and later, he kisses her goodnight, and he promises her he is not angry, they will speak in the morning. *Forget it, you have apologised enough.*

She realises now he lied to her and she believed him, and once this piano made her miss him but these days it makes her cry.

THE MAGPIE

At the time of his death, Amir took on a magpie's form.

This was a dream she'd had before. He dies and she is in widow's clothes and it does not matter those who tell her that white is the colour of death, that the soul is pure, it is now with God.

Black is my mood, black is the ground in which he has been enclosed, black is the world where once upon a time there was light.

In the dream, he is a magpie and she is another bird. They wheel and dive, they talk in different tongues but one another they understand. It troubles her that she cannot see herself, that she can see him clearly but is unsure of her own form.

When she wakes, she is in tears, and she realises her emptiness is because the truth is reversed. He has disappeared. She cannot see him anywhere, not even if she shuts her eyes. She has her human form and she needs photographs to remind her of his face so she can fill in the fantasies she has of him at night.

She speaks to him but never is there a response.

She is alone in her bed, she is alone at home once more.

The only time she is not alone is when she sees one of his birds. This is a bird that speaks, its deathly blackness and the patches of white. It rolls sounds into a song and she imagines him speaking to her from the lamppost.

Her friends tell her to go out. They tell her to not spend so much time alone.

She considers catching an army of magpies and freeing them within the walls of her home. They can fly in circles, they can beat against the window as they seek to free themselves from her trap.

She could capture it. The magpie she sees today is the same one each time and it has become friendly in recent days.

She imagines holding this bird, stroking its black-and-whiteness, and with a kiss bringing it into the house where it belongs.

The world will not miss this bird. Its mate will not call out its name. Its children will grow into their lives and her loneliness will not hurt so much.

She could have trapped him. She could have begged him to stay. She could have used the tricks women use but then he would have been her magpie in a cage.

She leaves it, this uselessness, this empty dream. She says goodbye to the bird—her companion—and slowly returns to the world.

THE DOG IN THE ROSES

This was Samir's favourite story and any one of us had heard it many times. Had Samir been interrupted, any one of us could have recited it word for word, line by line.

One time there was a dog who lived at the bottom of his world. I am being polite of course because I know, as the dog knows, that what he calls a home is actually a slum, and rather than call it a slum he calls it a home in the hope of making you think it better than it is. I don't want to hurt the dog so I will say this quietly behind his back and hope he never hears. His slum of a home had garbage everywhere, human waste was what the dog walked through, and while one can dress it up with positivity and hope, let me tell you that there is a big difference between the smell of a rose and the smell of shit. So while the dog liked to believe in roses and he saw them in his dreams, his actual days were less than ideal.

So one day, for some reason or other, the dog saw a garden of roses and it became his most pleasant memory. The roses were better than the pictures, the roses were better than the ones he had seen in films, but a day is not a life and the dog found himself again in his slum of human shit.

Once he had imagined it was better than it was but now he could not ignore what he smelled and what he walked in and how he literally lived in a human tip. Once he had seen the sky and he had seen the clouds, and he had done his dog-best to have optimism and hope and to believe in whatever other lies we tell ourselves when it's ourselves we wish to deceive.

He tried to keep his spirits up, he tried to keep his smile, but he knew about the roses now, how they were better than the pictures, better than those famous films, and he decided then that unless he had the roses, he might as well not live.

THE CHILD OF THE SEA

Jamila's belly is large and he thinks, *How could she have hidden her state from me?* Overnight her stomach holds a child and he does not understand how he did not notice sooner. Only last night he had run his hands over her stomach but now he sees her cross the street and there is that funny walk pregnant women have.

Why has she hidden it?

Why didn't she tell him?

It confuses him. He should have known.

She is on the promenade. She talks to a stranger, a habit of hers. He once chided her for this friendliness and she shrugged and said they were different in this respect. *Why must I go through my life aloof from the world?*

She was right but it was not a habit he could fall into any more than she could stop this friendliness of hers. Perhaps it is women and their chattiness and how they see the world. It is an extension of their softness, their bodies, the sweetness that is theirs alone.

He shakes his head. Her state has gone to his head and made his brain soft.

He has heard her tear to pieces someone who has slighted her.

He has heard her argue down men twice her size and refuse to give ground, even when they moved in to intimidate her.

She calls him the sentimental one.

He stares at her.

She is carrying their child. This is the child they were meant to have.

When will their child be born?

He wants to call to her.

Jamila, what shall we name our child?

Jamila, are we going to have a child?

Jamila, you are my love.

Jamila, Jamila . . .

He shakes himself. She has disappeared in the crowd.

On the day their child is born, she kisses Amir and hands him their child.

At some point, our child will need to feed.

Jamila's hair is loose and she wears a dress. She is barefoot and he wishes to tell her to protect her feet, that there may be glass that will cut her as she walks near the sea.

He is trapped with a breathing child. Already their child is two or three years.

She walks out of their house into the glare of the sun, her hair like seaweed, her dress clinging to her body, the one he wishes to possess nightly and which now belongs in the land of dreams.

Jamila, his walker, Jamila, who is free. He calls to her but she is beyond him. She dives into the water. She is there but then she is not, and their child, the one he holds, the one that breathes, calls to her and then dissolves like a wave back into the body of the sea.

THE BIRD

Your bird died today. Your spirit left the room.

I wonder about this omen.

We lived our lives separated and destiny allowed us a return, a turn together, which is denied to others in this world.

I content myself with imagining a reunion. I imagine if there is nothing, there is only darkness at our end, that I shall never see your face again.

How does one make a life bearable if one is denied the hope of lightness, of something better than this valley I find myself in?

People are filled with advice. They mean well, I know, but I wish for this solitude so I can be alone with you.

I will not condemn myself to this loneliness forever. What a waste to squander our happiest moments together!

I am alone. In a few minutes, I may change my mind. I am alone and I have not been alone in so long.

The bird has died. I buried it as I never expected to bury you. Your body is in the ground but your spirit, it leaves, but then again I feel it here.

My mother comforts me with a story. The spirits who are together at their end. It is only a story—symbolic of course—but I feel protected by it. The universe has its promise, it is full of possibilities. Who am I to say what awaits us on the other side?

If there is nothing, I will at least know that with you I was alive.

If there is something, like the story of the lovers, I hope we find each other, my lovebird, once again.

DREAMS

It was a dream. Jamila knew this because she was in a place she had never been before with Amir.

He was walking from her. She called to him but the wind took away her words and he continued to walk as if he had not heard her.

You are my love.

You are everything.

Please don't walk away from me.

But Amir walked and he walked into the wind and he disappeared, and when she tried to think of his name, it was as if he had never existed, as if she had never known him.

He woke in tears. He had been dreaming. Jamila was trying to touch him but her hands passed through his body as if he belonged to air and did not exist.

He could hear her. She was calling but he could not make out her words.

He used to think that he would never erase his wife's craziness but Jamila banished all thoughts of the past. With her, he achieved a state that he believed was pure fantasy. The rest of the world disappeared, it ceased to be, and yet in these dreams, he was the one fading, he saw again her hands pass through him, her mouth spoke but nothing could reach him, not her words, not her hands, he forgot all memory of her kiss.

He would have taken this dream to Samir for interpretation but already he knew what Samir would say. *You had a love and you let her get away and now she fades from your life for good.* Samir needed no cards, no sand, no coffee to make sense of these dreams. Their meaning was obvious but this did not reduce the loneliness Amir felt.

He thought about calling her. It would be late morning her time. He thought about it, dismissed the idea, ordered himself back to sleep.

He may have cried but finally sleep—elusive—came for him.

DROWNING

She never tells Amir about the dream. How can she? No matter how she explains it, no matter how much she reminds him the dream is not real, it is a betrayal. The worm is in her subconscious, and when she is not paying attention, it will make a break for the surface, and she will betray both him and their love.

In the dream, he is drowning. He is in the surf, the waves are rough and she is at a distance watching on.

He is a human being dying. He could be any human, in fact, and she feels no connection to him. She is not tied to him.

If he dies, it is okay, she will move on.

The mind has forgetfulness and ultimately this will protect her from memories of him.

In her mind, she urges him not to cry out, not to call her name, to go ahead and die, relinquishing any hold he has over her.

She watches his struggle. He is any human, he is any beast. We are born, we live and then we die at our time.

This is his time, she says, and like that she is released from anything that binds her to him.

She turns and walks away. She is thankful the waves are loud, that they hide his cries.

She asks the world to wipe him from her memory. This is freedom . . . to be oblivious to someone else's cries.

She walks away and she does not once glance back.

She assumes he drowns and the thought is enough to end the dream. It forces her to wake once again in tears.

TOUGH LOVE

He has lost once before, he has now lost again. The days pass painfully and he's had enough so he goes to Samir.

His friend is seated around the back of the house on the floor. The fire is lit and the wind shakes the weak walls.

He speaks and speaks until he's empty of words and then Samir holds up his hand.

'You say you love her but you let her leave when you should have tied your leg to hers. You come here speaking of love and it is an insult to me and my wife who is the mother to my kids. It is an insult to the love I have for my parents who are thirty years dead. You talk of love but either you're a liar or you're weak, which, in either case, amounts to the same thing. The universe gives you the greatest thing it has and you spit in its face by rejecting it. The two of you agreed to shake hands and go your separate ways. If Rayan said tomorrow she was going to the moon, I would be on the first plane. If I said to her I was going to Mars, I am certain she'd say, *Give me a moment while I prepare the kids and their things.* If love comes into your life, you hold on to it. That is what you do. I can lie to you and say sweet words but they would be an insult to our friendship, to your intelligence and pride. It is easy for your tears to fall on my knee, for you to cry like this before a friend but you cannot pick up your phone to give her a call. I don't have time for lies, I don't have time for games so don't bring your pain to me again. Either you are a man who does what needs to be done or else you come here and we pretend she does not exist. Here is a cigarette. Dry your face. You know I speak like this in the tough love, as they say in English.'

Amir did as he was told and smoked one cigarette after the next, remembering his former wife and how Samir had never spoken like this when his marriage had fallen apart. If he had rolled around on the ground screaming, Samir would have dusted him off and hugged him with both arms.

He is right. He is all right.

Oh this pain, the pain of being alive.

He thanks Samir who waves him away. He leaves with clarity in his mind. Hold this clarity and do not let it escape and perhaps there will be a chance with her again.

STORYLINES

Years later you say to them: *Tell me how you met.*
    They share a smile. It does not include you.

It was actually at a wedding.

                It was my family friend, her relative.

We were sitting at the same table.
He was off to one side.
She points in the general direction.

                Someone introduced us.
        Afterwards, I couldn't get her out of my mind.

You lie.
There were so many beautiful women that night,
everyone dressed up.
You didn't look too bad yourself.

> He laughs.
> *You know it wasn't like that.*
> *I only had eyes for you.*

All those years ago . . .

> *All those years.*

I think it's seventeen and a bit.

> *And two months.*
> *It was July.*

Yes it was.
And who knew where we'd end up?

> *I always thought we would be together,*
> *that it would be for life.*

Did you now?
How exactly did you know?

I just did.

But how?

You sense that long ago they have forgotten about you, that this is a memory, a story that contains only them, and if you're wise and you treasure your time, this is a cue for you to disappear.

SUBJECTS OF NOTE:
A catalogue

A catalogue of subjects that may have played a part and therefore deserve my thanks:

stars—navigation by said stars—history—world history—lots of history—local history—personal, impersonal and beyond personal history—science (botany, chemistry, biology, astronomy)—poets (Arabic, Persian, Russian, Spanish, Federico García Lorca especially)—Bolaño and Borges—sports such as football, rugby, football, tennis, football, actually just football—travels (past, present, futurepast)—differences between a plaza, square and park—behaviours peculiar to the magpie, red fish and alligator—naval systems and the *Titanic*—robot technologies—disputed territories and geopolitics—the word 'book' in various languages—falcons—music (opera and dance)—the colours red black white—poetry by Ibn Benito Almagro perhaps.